ETERNAL

YOUTH

ETERNAL YOUTH

An Eternal Novel

Book 7

K.G. INGLIS

Also by K.G. Inglis

The Eternal Series:

Eternity Begins (Prequel)

Eternal Covenant

Eternal Possession

Waking The Eternal Dragon (short story)

Heart Of Eternity

Eternal Temptation

Eternal Craving

Eternity Is Forever

Eternal Youth

Hunt For Eternity

Eternity Unveiled

Eternity Unbound

Eternally Entangled (novella)

Eternity Bites

Coming Soon:

Glimpse Eternity

Published by: K.G. Inglis
Covers by: Eerilyfair Design.

ACKNOWLEDGEMENTS

Once again, I would like to thank my family for being such good sports in supporting my writing and publishing endeavours. There's been a lot of grumbles and groans to put up with while I worked out the teething problems of publishing this book myself.

And, of course where would I be without the help from Glen Baker, who has spent so many hours editing this book. Thank you Glen, I couldn't do it without you.

I would also like to thank all my support team who have helped guide me through the pitfalls of self-publishing this book. It has taken me awhile to get up the courage to start self-publishing but there's no looking back now.

A huge thank you too, to everyone out there who is continuing to read the Eternal Series, and for all your wonderful supportive feed-back.

1

Dawn had barely breached the night's hold, the pale light giving the neighbourhood an otherworldly, quiet sense of solitude, belied by the buildings standing stoically side by side along the length of the street she was standing on. The streetlights were still lit, but their luminescence only made the early morning scene more eerie as the thick fog which clung so closely, dampened and smothered everything it touched, ghosting trees and buildings alike in its thick shroud.

But this was when Nadia liked to come outside. She was enchanted, almost mesmerised by what she saw.

A gentle early morning breeze caught the loose strands of her glossy, dark brown, shoulder-length hair, wafting them about her chilled face. It wasn't yet winter, although it was easy to suppose it was. Winter always came early here in the Ukraine.

Swinging open the door, Gustav quietly stood in the opening, leaning against the frame. He stared down at Nadia, a sombre, implacable expression with a slight smile as he watched his daughter's fascination with the world around her.

"It's beautiful. I never knew the world looked like this," Nadia said almost reverently, her voice quiet as though afraid to disturb the peace surrounding them.

"What's it like, seeing things on the astral level?" her father asked.

"It's…um. It's…." Nadia thought about it for a moment. "I guess it's a bit like being long-sighted and you can't see things clearly close up without glasses. Imagine you have something on your shoulder, you know it's there but its blurry and you can't make out what it is, but if you stand in front of a mirror and look at it again through your reflection, it becomes clear because you're looking at it from a distance. It's a bit like that. I can't see things directly in a physical sense anymore, but looking indirectly, I seem to see things more clearly than ever before. I don't see things in a flat two-dimensional view like on a television screen, or in a normal 3D view either. Everything has more depth than it did before, I don't just see the outside of something, I can see through it."

"Like X-ray?"

Nadia chewed her bottom lip and her brow scrunched in contemplation for another moment, thinking on how to put it into a perspective her father could understand. If he had asked her the same question just over a week ago she would have told him to go ask her sister, Paige. But then, just over a week ago she was still only a lycan druid, with no special ability other than to read and speak any known language.

Of course, that was how her life came to be changed so dramatically. Thinking she was helping to save her best friend's life, Philippe, or Pan as most people knew him, she read from the evil sorceress Morganna's grimoire, which of course had led to her blindness, death, and then her resurrection. The last part was thanks to her sister Paige, making her an *Ei'Ambriath*, a Spirit Walker, like herself. What that entailed exactly, Nadia was still trying to figure out. One thing she knew for certain though, her normal eyesight was gone forever. Now, she looked at the world through new eyes.

"Sort of," she answered. "Depending on how much I concentrate, I can see the different layers that make up all the natural elements in the world. The more complex something is, the more layers it has, and each layer has its own set of colours and wave forms. Rocks for instance, only have one layer of energy. Plants have two. Animals have four and people have seven. All the colours swirl together, but if I concentrate I can see each layer individually, like peeling away the layers of an onion."

Awe transformed Gustav's face in wonder of his daughter's new view of the world.

"Is this how Paige sees the world too?" he asked.

"I suppose so. But I think it's different for her, she only looks at the astral world if she wants to. I have no other option. This is the world

I live in now," she sighed. As much as this new sight fascinated her, she did miss seeing the world in the way she used to.

Nadia's silvery grey eyes, fringed with long dark lashes narrowed as she studied the changing landscape in more depth.

A dead pigeon on the pavement, a carbon based inanimate object, no longer radiated the beautiful colours of its living aura. Now it appeared to her as dull brown, no more interesting than the pavement it lay upon.

It hadn't taken her long to learn that while some things had become infinitely more defined with her new sight, some things in the physical world were no longer visible to her at all.

She could see the puddle on the road, yet not the reflection of the streetlights in it. Some man-made synthetic objects too, had become invisible to her, like plastic and nylon. And didn't that just suck. She was living in an age where almost everything being made was either completely synthetic or had synthetic components. Looking at a plastic manikin in a shop window for instance, all she saw were floating clothes. Very creepy.

"Come on inside. Cook's almost got breakfast ready," he told her. Wrapping his arm about her shoulders, Gustav guided his daughter back into the warmth. As the door opened, the stinky smell of wet earth and street garbage, gave way to the seductive aroma of frying bacon and freshly brewed coffee inside her father's restaurant, and her stomach gave a loud rumble.

She'd always wondered if scents had colours. Now she knew. They did, and the familiar aroma lit up the air around them like a beacon. It was just another fascination she had come to appreciate.

Despite the chill and the enticement of fresh coffee, Nadia was loath to enter the building she'd called home for most of her life. Standing on the frosty pavement she realised it didn't feel like her home anymore. Too much had happened. Too much had changed. She had changed.

It felt so odd that in such a short space of time everything that was once so familiar to her, now felt so foreign. Memories from her youth, even from last week, they all felt like they were someone else's. She felt so distant and detached from everything.

3

Nadia shivered. The longer she stood there, the more intense the chill seemed to bite at her. First through her jacket, then her clothes and finally her skin. It was comforting in a strange kind of way, it reminded her that she was in fact, still alive, and for that she was grateful.

"Come on," Gustav encouraged gently, holding the door open for her. "I need to talk to you and your sister, and I'd rather do it inside where it's a bit warmer."

"Oh, what about?" she asked.

"Yeah dad, what about?" Elise asked, climbing the last few steps to stand beside him in the doorway.

Gustav looked between his youngest two daughters with pride, a small smile quirking up one side of his thinned lips. His daughters had him wrapped about their little fingers, and he knew it, but he had to at least try to pretend otherwise. Deliberately, he etched a stern line between his brow and motioned with his hand and a quick jerk of his head for the two girls to follow him inside.

The Bunker Restaurant, a.k.a. home, was once an old WWII bunker which had been converted into a restaurant, complete with WWII memorabilia. Everything from a wax figure of a WWII soldier near the restaurant's entrance, a novelty which appealed to guests. There were also gas masks, medals, old guns and even a hand grenade or two. Some artefacts you were allowed to touch, while others were kept under glass. Understandably, the restaurant had become a popular tourist attraction.

The grey stone walls and domed ceiling remained in their original rustic condition. The only part of the restaurant's interior not original was the floor, which had been updated from cobblestones to a flat slate floor for public liability reasons. The authenticity of the restaurant's appeal was capped off with the original light fittings and dodgy flickering lights. That had less to do with the old fixtures and more to do with the Ukrainian power grid being a little fickle at times.

However, in the level below the restaurant, there was no such power problem. A high-tech generator maintained constant power to Gustav's family's residence and to the holding cells and training centre beneath. While the restaurant was a legitimate business, it was also a cover for their primary concern. The Alliance's Baltic and Northern European Regional Headquarters, of which Gustav was the leader.

Nadia and Elise took a seat at a table at the rear of the restaurant, opposite their father. The stronger scent of bacon and fresh coffee making Nadia's stomach rumble loudly.

"I'm heading back to England this afternoon. There's a meeting at the Club tonight," Gustav told them.

"Is it about Nicholas, have they found the son of a bitch?" Elise asked.

Gustav glared at his youngest daughter with a disapproving eye for her choice of language. Although the words he would have used to describe the psychopathic vampire, were much more colourful and would have required him putting a pocket full of dollars into the swear jar, if he chose to express his thoughts verbally, which he didn't. Gustav's gaze quickly shifted from Elise to Nadia, his keen eye watching her intently for her reaction. "Yes. And, no."

Nadia's expression didn't change, she remained impassive to the news. Relief suffused Gustav's features and his expression softened. He'd been worried that after what Nadia had been through because of Nicholas, just bringing up his name might be upsetting for her. He was pleased to see he was wrong.

"We're coming with you," Nadia told him quickly.

"To the manor, sure. But, not to the club," he told her firmly.

"Of course we're coming to the club. It's their big re-opening since Cassie accidentally blew up the dance floor a couple of weeks ago. The place is going to be pumping," Nadia told him, blowing off his concern with her blasé attitude.

"And if there's a meeting about Nicholas, Pan will be there. Sorry, we can't call him that anymore, can we? Philippe will be there, and that's the real reason you want to go, admit it." Elise smirked at her sister.

Nadia didn't bother to answer that question, they all knew it was true. But why wouldn't she want to see him? After all, she was probably the only person who hadn't seen him since his transition. She hadn't even spoken to him yet. Sure, he'd sent her a couple of simple 'hiya' texts, but that wasn't the same as seeing him face to face.

"Do you think that's wise? You're still trying to find your bearings," Gustav said.

"Dad, stop fussing. I'm not a kid anymore, I'll be fine. Besides, if I go to the club it's not like I can escape the family fussing over me and trying to keep me wrapped in cotton wool, now, can I? I'll not only have you and Elise there, but all my other sisters, their husbands, and *all* our friends." She blew out a frustrated sigh and slumped back into her chair. "On second thoughts I might just stay here, it will be more peaceful and I'll be less likely to want to kill any of you for being overprotective."

Gustav and Elise both laughed.

"I might stay here with you," Elise said.

The bell in the kitchen rang, the jovial tinkle notifying them that their breakfast was ready.

"I'll get it," Gustav grouched, looking between his daughters again who looked like they were ready to argue over whose turn it was to fetch the food. Anybody would think they were expected to make the breakfast, not just collect it from the cook.

Gustav slid from his seat with another grumble, the thud of his heavy boots on slate floor in the quiet restaurant giving him a formidable presence. And for most, his presence was just that…formidable. More than one man had cringed at the sight of him. Sadly, his large, heavily muscled and imposing stature had little effect on his daughters, other than to make them roll their eyes at his stern scowls and dangerous growls. And he'd been blessed with five of them, each one as strong willed and independent as the other. It was enough to make an overprotective father want to cry.

A minute later, Gustav returned with plates of bacon and eggs, freshly baked bread and a pot of coffee. Placing them on the table, he was just about to take a seat with the girls when his phone buzzed in his jacket pocket. Pulling it free, his face hardened with a frown.

"I have to take this. You girls decide what you're doing. I'm leaving here at midday. Sharp. Gwynn ap Nudd is meeting us in the Golosiyivsky Forest with a couple of the other Nephilim High Council."

Nadia and Elise both raised their eyebrows at their father who'd obviously told them all he planned to, walking away to answer the call. This meeting tonight really was a big deal. More than just Nicholas was going to be discussed, of that both the girls were sure. Now, Nadia was even more determined to be there. Elise on the other hand still looked undecided.

Elise moved to the other side of the table, taking her father's vacant seat to sit opposite her sister.

"Admit it, your main reason for going to the club is to see Philippe?" she grinned, reiterating her previous rhetorical comment.

"Of course it is, and what's wrong with that? He is my best friend," Nadia retorted haughtily.

"I remember a time when you used to say I was your best friend," Elise teased, but a hollow kind of sadness lingered in her voice.

"We still are. Of all our sisters you're still the one I come to talk to about my problems. But, you and I both know that things changed after Morganna kidnapped you, and I had to read her damned book so Teagan, Paige and Kaitlyn could defeat the bitch and rescue you."

Both girls dropped their gaze uncomfortably to their plates of food, which suddenly neither one had an appetite for. The memory of that time was still so fresh. For both of them.

That had been the first time Nadia had read from Morganna's grimoire. No one could have predicted the repercussions of something so innocent, but the consequences were severe. At least for Nadia. From that day forward she suffered debilitating headaches for days at a time, and slowly her eyesight had deteriorated until she needed to wear glasses all the time. That wasn't the worst of it though. The cursed book called to her night and day, drawing her back toward its pages, tempting her with its evil power. She would have given in to that temptation too, if it hadn't been for Philippe. He was always there for her, acting as her self-appointed EBA (Evil Books Anonymous) sponsor.

So naturally Philippe became her best friend. They shared everything with each other, all their hopes and dreams, and their deepest, darkest secrets and fears. Or, at least she had. It seemed he had kept his darkest secret to himself. She couldn't blame him though, admitting that his brother was a psychopathic serial killer was a tough confession to make.

As for Elise becoming down-graded to her 'favourite' sister, that hadn't entirely been Nadia's fault. After Elise's kidnapping, she'd changed too. Torture had a way of doing that to a person. She was no longer the happy-go-lucky teenager without a care in the world. Elise became reserved and withdrawn. She spent her spare time learning to protect herself both physically and mentally from anything similar happening to her again. And, she cut herself off emotionally from the one person who had meant the most to her since she was twelve years old. Callum.

Unfortunately for Callum, it had taken him until the moment he pulled Elise from that dank cell to realise his own feelings for her.

"I'm jealous of you, you know," Elise said, breaking the silence.

"What? Why?"

"I liked it when we were the same, just two normal lycan druids. Mortal. You're like all our other sisters now. Teagan is the most powerful druid on the planet and a true immortal. Kaitlyn is mated to a wyvern, so she'll live for as long as he does, which will probably be at least another two and a half thousand years. And now you're like Paige. I don't even know if the two of you are still lycans since you became *Ei'Ambriath's*. Does one cancel out the other, or can you be both at the same time…and be druids as well? And then there's me. The plain Jane of the family. I feel so insignificant compared to all of you."

Nadia laughed. Her pale eyes sparkled with tears she laughed so hard. Elise couldn't help quirking a half smile despite her confusion at what Nadia found so amusing about her deficiencies.

"That's funny. That's how I've always felt about all of you. Teagan can stop things in space and time, and she's the most powerful druid in the world. Kaitlyn can make herself invisible. Paige could make her astral form into a separate physical entity and now she can do so much more as an *Ei'Ambriath*. And you, you can literally walk through walls. On top of all that, every one of you is drop dead gorgeous. Then there's me, the ugly duckling of the family who can read and speak in different languages. Woopie-do! Big freaking deal. If anyone's entitled to feel underwhelmed about themselves it's me, don't you think?"

"I'm boring. I keep a journal of how boring I am. You know the kind, the highlights read: 7:15am ate breakfast; 8:30am had shower; 8:45am cleaned teeth; 9:00am had impure thoughts about…someone; 9:30am started training session," Elise countered, trying to outdo her sister in humdrum stodginess.

"Could that *someone* you have impure thoughts about be Callum?" Nadia needled questioningly.

"I'm not telling."

Nadia studied her sister over the rim of her coffee cup. She wasn't going to get an honest answer from her, even though she already knew the truth. Nadia's new sight came in handy for some things. Elise's aura lit up at the mention of Callum's name. She was still as much in love with him today as she had been when she was sixteen.

"Come to the club tonight, it'll be fun," Nadia prompted. "You can't avoid Callum all the time you know."

"Why not, it seems to work for Marcus and Brin."

"No it doesn't, and if you want to make your point more believable, using Brin and Marcus is a bad example. For whatever reason, they've never liked each other, so the animosity between them works well. For them," Nadia pointed out. "Callum has always been like a brother to you, you don't want to ruin that just because you're a screwed up hot mess," Nadia told her, choosing not to antagonise her sister with the truth of her feelings.

Elise laughed too as she stabbed her fork into her egg. "I'm still jealous," she confessed.

"So am I," Nadia chuckled.

They'd come to an impasse. Neither one was willing to forego their low self-esteem to see that they might each be equally impressive in their own way.

"Fine. I'll come."

2

Pan tried to rest longer, God knew he was still tired enough to sleep for a week, but his restlessness wouldn't allow it. From the twitching muscles in his legs and fingers, to his eyes which continued to dart back and forth behind his closed lids, he was about as relaxed as anyone would be if they'd been plugged into a live electrical socket.

For the past week he'd been on a hair trigger of emotional turmoil. Newly developed testosterone hormones, combined with the guilt of his past decisions and a burning hatred for the one who he'd spent so many years protecting. A hatred so palpable it was like a disease in his blood, it consumed his every thought and desire.

The emotional turmoil was nothing new to him, although the hormones were taking a bit of adjustment.

Perfectly understandable, considering he was one hundred and sixty-six years old, and until a week ago he'd spent his entire life in the body of a thirteen year old boy, hence the nickname Pan. Going through puberty overnight was a hell of a shock to the system. Now, the old Pan was gone, and he was just plain old Philippe, a one hundred and sixty-six year old vampire in the body of a twenty-something year old man. And boy did it feel great to finally be an adult inside an adult's body for a change. At least, he assumed it would once he adapted to his new size and shape properly.

Which of course was why he was so exhausted. He'd spent the last week learning how to use his new body, pushing the boundaries of his limitations and his strengths. He trained day and night, with anyone in the house who could spare the time.

How and why was it that he came to upgrade his outer casing after so many years, you might ask? That's not a simple question to answer but the short version is:–

How? That was thanks to his new sire, Narayan. As the Guardian of the Cup, also known as the Holy Grail, he was the only person with the power to make it happen. Sure, it was a gamble, Narayan had never tried to make a vampire mortal again, then turn him back into a vampire before his body aged, shrivelled up and died at an alarmingly accelerated rate. But hey, it worked and here he was, an adult at last. A new and very much improved version of the vampire he used to be, thanks to the combined blood of not only the original vampire, Alaric, who was Narayan's sire, but also the elder angel Ariel, whose blood he inherited through Narayan's vein.

Why? Because of his older brother, Nicholas. His psychopathic, serial killer brother. Many years ago, Philippe had learned of Nicholas' predilection for killing young women. Unfortunately, so had an even more sadistic vampire who called himself, The Master. In recent times they had also come to know the evil son-of-a-bitch by another name, Scorpion. A fitting name, he was silent and very deadly. A formidable foe you never see coming, always hidden in shadow and always ready to strike.

Nicholas, having been made a vampire by Scorpion, left Philippe's options to contain his brother's proclivities drastically reduced. He could kill him, although he didn't know how to kill a vampire, nor did he have the heart to do so. Nicholas was still his brother. So, instead he begged Nicholas to make him a vampire too. Of course, he had refused. Who wanted to go through eternity with their kid brother tagging along? However, Philippe had always been resourceful, and he outsmarted his brother.

Having found his brother's *trophy* collection of jewellery and body parts he had taken from his victims, Philippe blackmailed Nicholas into turning him. Yet, for all his intelligence, Philippe had still been a very young and naïve thirteen year old boy at the time. He had believed that if he stuck close to his brother day and night, he would never get an opportunity to harm another woman again, and over time he would forget about his fondness for sadistic bloodshed.

Decade after long decade, Philippe stuck to his brother like glue. Everywhere Nicholas went, Philippe was there, watching him like a hawk. Not once did he see his brother stray towards his previous obsession. Philippe thought his plan had worked, that Nicholas' killing spree had only been a morbid phase of his youth, and he'd turned over a new leaf. So, he kept his brother's secret past just that, a secret. Considering their current employers, Saladin and Dray had hunted rogue vampires in the not too distant past, Philippe had thought it prudent.

How wrong he was.

As it turned out, Nicholas had only been waiting for an opportunity to re-offend. Almost as soon as Philippe loosened the leash, his brother quickly fell back into his old habits. Only now, reunited with his sadistic sire, Nicholas' taste for the macabre seemed to have magnified...and so had his hatred toward Philippe.

Philippe's biggest mistake however, after he had suspected his brother maybe responsible for the latest spree of killings around London, was not taking sufficient steps to ensure he was blocked from having access to Nadia. Sure, he hadn't known the depth of the rabbit hole Nicholas had tumbled down, but ignorance was no excuse.

Philippe's oversight meant that Nicholas had casually waltzed into Havenswood Manor and coerced Nadia into reading that damned grimoire, knowing all too well that it would harm her in doing so. Believing Nicholas' lie, she trusted him that the potion he had her make was to save Philippe from certain death.

It seemed however, Nicholas' goal wasn't only to dupe Nadia. His black heart had far darker ambitions. Before he left the manor, he drank the potion Nadia made for Philippe, making himself stronger than he ever had been before. Unfortunately, that wasn't the only thing he did. They discovered later that Nicholas had taken one of the sacred artefacts in the storeroom. The Ring of Gyges, an invisibility ring.

Philippe's brother's treachery didn't end there though, he had also passed along the formula for that potion to his sire, Scorpion, who as it turned out was also one of the leaders of their enemy, The Guild of Ascension.

By the time they learned the truth it was too late.

Guilt weighed heavily on Philippe's shoulders. His false belief that he could control his brother by sheer will alone, that he could change

Nicholas' very nature, had not only put the world's fate in peril, and had directly contributed to Nadia suffering intolerable pain for days before her death. The fact that her sister Paige had been able to give her a second chance at life was irrelevant. Nicholas deliberately harmed Nadia, and for that alone his brother had to die.

Since he was the cause of all this anarchy, it was also his responsibility to fix things, Philippe thought sullenly. He longed for the day when he ripped open Nicholas' ribcage and tore his heart from his chest. That day was coming. Soon. And he was going to take pleasure in watching the fucker die.

Giving up on his attempt at sleep, Philippe sat up and swung his legs over the side of the bed, but that was as far as he got.

The idea of going upstairs and facing his *family*, was as appealing as sticking his hand in a blender. Of course no one blamed him for what happened, he assumed that responsibility all on his own. In fact, they all thought the opposite of him. In their eyes he was the proverbial rock. Level-headed, smart, even-tempered and totally reliable.

Inside, he felt about as stable as a hydrogen atom in a nuclear bomb. Unfamiliar emotions and thoughts had recently become his constant companions, bombarding and overriding his usual commonsense. He had to admit though, if only to himself, that he had no wish to alter his current internal dialogue. Nicholas may loathe him, but it wasn't half as much as Philippe despised him, of that he was certain.

If he got his way, Nicholas' death was going to be slow and painful, with the same amount of cold, emotionless control and skill that he'd shown his victims.

Philippe had to concede however, that staying in bed and fantasizing about his brother's demise was a fruitless exercise, it gained nothing except to make him more agitated.

Pushing himself to his feet, the cold slate tiled floor beneath helped to connect him with reality again, albeit marginally. His thoughts were still as scattered as snowflakes in a blizzard.

Wearing only the track pants he'd fallen asleep in, he plodded from his room, along the long corridor toward the staircase, which led directly into Alaric's study through a hidden entry beneath the enormous fireplace. It didn't occur to him to put on a shirt before he left his room, or even run his fingers through the shaggy, short locks of his blonde hair.

13

There were only two thoughts his brain had room for, revenge and coffee.

"The kids call it yelling when I raise my voice, but I prefer to call it motivational speaking. It's the only way to get through that selective deafness they seem to suffer." Cassie told Mrs Philpot. Their ageing housekeeper's infectious laugh took the heat out of Cassie's frustration, who had just finished telling her daughter Grace, for what seemed like the tenth time that week, that donuts did not pass as breakfast food.

"I hear you love." She agreed, as she upended a basket of freshly washed and dried clothes onto the bench in search of a missing *butt plug*, which she suspected Alex had accidentally gotten mixed up with his jocks and socks. Alex was very fond of his sex toys and apparently, particularly his black silicone swirling bum bliss...or something to that effect. He'd been very distressed when he discovered it missing and insisted everyone in the house search for it. Of course no one did, especially since they knew where it had last been *stored*. Ew! Well, no one except for Mrs. P.

"Some days Grace makes me feel so old. It doesn't seem that long ago when I would've been the one trying to sneak junk food for breakfast," Cassie grumbled. "Truth be told, I wouldn't mind a donut for breakfast sometimes too, but what sort of example would I be setting then?"

Mrs Philpot smiled and nodded as she continued to sift through the warm, fluffed-up pile of clothes. Lifting Riley's Thomas the Tank T-shirt up to her face she rubbed it against her cheek reflectively. It hadn't seemed too long ago when her own children were wearing clothes this small. Now even her grandchildren were fully grown.

"Damn. It looks like Paige is going shopping again." Cassie pointed out, looking at the T-shirt Mrs P. was holding up, which had clearly shrunk in the dryer.

"I would love to put myself in that dryer for ten minutes and come out wrinkle free and three times smaller," Mrs P. chuckled. "I'll be a century old on my next birthday, that's a lot of wrinkles to smooth out." She said wistfully, almost as though she was talking to herself.

"Are you serious? But your birthday is only a couple of weeks away."

"You remember my birthday?"

"I always remember the important things." Cassie told her proudly. "Although I didn't know exactly how old you are. Now that I do, don't think we're going to let this one slide by without some sort of celebration."

"Oh no love. I've never had a party in my life and I sure as heck don't plan on starting now. Parties are for the young and energetic, not for the old and withered."

"Rubbish. We're having a party. End of discussion."

Before Mrs P. could argue her case against Cassie's decision, Philippe shuffled into the kitchen looking more like something the cat dragged in, than a living member of the household.

Both Cassie and Mrs Philpot stopped their conversation, turning to greet the owner of the bare feet plodding toward them. However, their friendly smiles slid when they saw the state of the man who entered.

Their eyes skimmed down his body from his blonde, scruffed up hair in the fashion of unkempt *bed-head*, over his bare broad shoulders and hairless, heavily muscled chest, then down further to his washboard abs and his... The two women swallowed in unison.

"Morning Philippe, how are you feeling?" Cassie asked, the humour in her voice slipping Philippe's notice, although induced Mrs P. to purse her lips tightly to contain her untimely smirk.

"Wonderful. Where's the coffee?" he grumbled.

"Where it usually is." Cassie pointed distractedly, her eyes still watching Philippe curiously. "Um, just a tip Philippe. Don't go wandering around the house like that, you'll either scare the kids or they'll start asking questions I *really* don't want to be answering at their age."

"What the hell are you talking about?" he grumped, his brow scrunching together irritably.

Both Cassie and Mrs P. scanned their eyes down his body until they reached his track pants and stopped. Curiously, Philippe looked down the length of his torso until he reached...

"Fuck a duck! I've got an erection?" At first, he just stared down at the bulge in his pants, his hands lifting up and away from himself as though he was afraid to touch it, like he'd suddenly discovered an alien growth on his body. It was indeed something foreign. Having been made a vampire before he went through puberty, he had never experienced an erection. Ever!

"But I wasn't thinking about sex, I swear I wasn't." His voice rose an octave, his eyes widened, but remained glued to the flagpole projecting outward from inside his pants.

Mrs Philpot laughed. "I believe love, that you'd call that your *Morning Glory*. You've been asleep, it happens sometimes." All Philippe could do was nod. He knew all about how the body worked, it had just never worked for him before now.

Tentatively, he reached for the elastic waistband of his track pants and pulled them open and stared in awe. Slowly, his look of shock shifted as a small smile appeared at the corner of his lips, broadening into an elated smile.

"I have an erection!" he laughed.

Philippe's thoughts of coffee evaporated in an instant, so did his fatigue.

The only thought in his mind now was getting back to his room to test out his body's latest piece of upgraded equipment.

"Gotta go," was all he said.

Mrs Philpot tilted her head to one side in thought as she watched Philippe disappear out of the kitchen at a much faster speed than he'd entered.

"You know love, it looks to me like that's a decent sized plunger he's sporting in those pants of his. He's going to make the girls very happy with that piece of plumbing," she casually remarked.

Cassie turned and stared, her jaw hanging open on its hinges, unable to believe what she'd just heard.

"What? I'm old, not dead." She quipped, waggling her eyebrows suggestively, bursting into a hearty laugh. "Ah, found it!" she exclaimed victoriously, pulling the *butt plug* free of the folds of a towel, crackling with static electricity as it clung to the oddly shaped sex toy. With the missing item in hand, Mrs P. turned and headed towards the same doorway which Philippe had just disappeared through only a moment before.

"Ah huh, you've just proven you're still young at heart. You are *sooo* getting a birthday party now." Cassie called out smugly at their housekeeper's retreating back.

Shifting her eyes to the pile of laundry in front of her, she screwed up her nose and let out a nauseated sigh of disgust. Ughh, maybe she should put the entire load through another cycle in the washing machine...considering what was just pulled from its midst.

Philippe almost slammed his bedroom door off its hinges in his haste to relieve his erection of their baggy confines and explore its contours with his hand.

This new development was a welcome distraction from his usual thoughts and feelings. His pulse raced as a mixture of relief and excitement washed through him. For one hundred and fifty years he never believed this day would ever come. He'd had not even a sliver of hope for it. Even when Narayan made him this, an adult, he still reserved his hope to only a quiet whisper in the back of his mind, yet never truly believed it was possible.

And now here he was, his little twig had become a mammoth bone that was fully engorged and begging for relief. A service Philippe was more than happy to administer.

If he could just work out how.

Sure, he'd seen men masturbate many times, so he knew the actions involved. In fact, Nicholas used to delight in doing it in front of him at every opportunity. It was supposed to be a form of torment for Philippe, except what his brother failed to realise, that since he'd never experienced sexual urges, watching the act of sex or masturbation was no different to him than watching a documentary on animals mating habits.

Not today.

Today his body hummed with sexual tension, all the way from his toes to his fangs. Every muscle twitching, every vein pulsing and his skin tingling with the need to relieve the pressure present within the heavy sac beneath his hardened length.

Not wasting time to remove his pants completely, he pushed the waistband below his hips, the thick pole springing free to jut rigidly between his legs. Its colour ripening to a deep red, the head of his cock another shade darker again as the thick veins along its length pulsed, feeding it with more blood. Philippe sucked in a strained breath between clenched teeth at the feel of the fabric brushing over the sensitive head, sending a shock of sensation up his spine.

Philippe had spent so many years imaging what this moment might be like, he couldn't help feeling nervous. What if it wasn't what he expected? What if he can't achieve an orgasm?

Whatever the outcome, he was eager to try.

Settling himself down into the padded cushions of the armchair in the corner of the room, Philippe wrapped his fist around that thick length. It was big, bigger than his brother's. The mental comparison may have been petty, but it sent a rush of satisfaction to bolster Philippe's ego. His long, dextrous fingers fastened around the girth at its base, pressing it firmly into his palm. Despite the size of his hand, more than another hand's width remained above it untouched. A slow, tentative slide up its length had his muscles bunching in his abdomen as he stroked himself. Once. Twice. A low moan dredged up from his throat. Oh, that felt so good, he thought.

Sliding down into the chair further he spread his legs wider, planting his feet far apart as he pumped his shaft in the same steady motion.

With a rough swallow, Philippe increased the pace a little, moving his hand in a twisting motion, testing which movements felt good and which ones sent his senses soaring with waves of increasingly exquisite pleasure. Up and down along his shaft, around the mushroomed head, over and over until he found the perfect rhythm.

His blood rushed through his body pooling in his groin, his breath stalled as the tingling sensations pulsed through him. Sweaty palms made the pumping action easier. Closing his eyes Philippe bit down on his bottom lip. He was too far gone in the experience to notice his fangs had fully descended and had punctured through his bottom lip.

Philippe increased his pace, his head dropping back as he sucked in ragged breaths through clenched teeth, a moan building in his chest. Anxiously he muttered words of encouragement to himself.

His neck corded as the sensation built, his toes curling into the plush rug beneath his feet, and his hips flexing involuntarily as sharper jolts speared through him. He watched with increasing excitement as a drop of moisture beaded the tip of his cock and he felt his testicles swell and retreat up into his groin.

Oh, he was getting close, he could feel it, and that knowledge spurred him on with greater enthusiasm.

His heart raced and his skin seemed to burn with anticipation.

Fisting the thick stalk, he tugged and stroked and massaged every sensitive nerve he discovered, awakening an intoxicating desire he was sure he would never recover from.

Philippe felt lightheaded as he hurtled toward his climax.

"Yes. Yes. Oh, God, please yes!" he cried as he felt the unfamiliar orgasm coiled in his balls, detonate with the explosion of a nuclear bomb. The pulsing waves shook his whole body as spurts of his seed jetted onto his taut belly.

A distant, unfocused grin was followed by a deeply gratifying sigh and an immediate yearning to do it again.

And he did.

Twice.

He would have gone for yet another round, God only knew he had enough Testosterone stored up for the job, but it seemed it would have to wait for another time as he heard a rap on the door.

"Alex, what do you want, I'm kinda busy here." Philippe told him bluntly, self-consciously trying to cover his perpetual erection with his track pants when Alex rudely barged into his room.

Alex grinned but said nothing, amazingly.

"Narayan's looking for you. Something about a driving lesson?"

Philippe looked across at the bedside clock, it's illuminated red numerals showing he'd managed to fill in three hours of time with his self-exploration.

"Shit. Okay, tell him I'll be there in five." Philippe griped. Running his fingers through his scruffy hair in frustration, his minor gripe turning into a cursing groan as he realised he'd just recreated a scene from the movie, 'Something about Mary', varnishing his blonde locks with a glob of semen. "Ahh, crap!"

A quick shower later and a change of clothes, he headed upstairs once again. However, the hard rod of flesh in his pants remained. Philippe was quickly discovering that not all his bodily functions were within his control. His body was strong, his mind equally so, and both responded dutifully upon command. But his hormones were an anomaly which defied his strict discipline. Fortunately, his jeans, together with his loose fitting T-shirt contained the majority of the bulge from obvious notice.

At least he hoped so.

3

"Are you ready?" Narayan asked Philippe.

"I've been ready since the first car rolled off the assembly line," he replied enthusiastically. "Which car are we taking, the Maserati, the Aston Martin? The Hummer. I know, the Pagani Huayra?" Philippe could hear the clinking of metal keys in his mentor's hand. It frustrated him that Narayan was keeping its contents hidden from view, and with it the identity of the car he was to drive. He'd learned over the years that not all surprises were worth looking forward to. Finally getting to drive a car however, was exciting no matter what car he was taking for a spin.

"We're taking the car that most fits your driving skill." Narayan smirked.

There was no shortage of cars to choose from. With nine adults living at Havenswood Manor, the five women each had one car and the four men, except for Narayan, each owned multiple cars. Alex had three, Alaric had four and Sebastian kept three at the manor, rotating them with several others he kept in a warehouse nearby. But, these weren't the only cars stored in the twenty car garage. They also kept a car belonging to Raif and one for Kaitlyn when they visited from Fey.

Since not every car was easily accessible in the crowded garage, they kept all the car keys in a pottery bowl by the front door for those who either needed to move a car or two, or to simply borrow one which belonged to someone else. The latter option was on the agenda today for Philippe's first driving lesson.

Philippe exited the house, down the broad, sweeping stone stairs from the manor's porch, and followed the paved path to the rounded end of the gravel driveway. The rough pebbles crunching beneath his feet as he made his way quickly past the fountain at its centre, coming to a halt beside the enormous garage doors. Nervous energy pumping through his veins.

It seemed this was a day for firsts. It was barely lunchtime and already he'd had his first erection, his first masturbation session and first orgasm. Well, three actually, but who's counting. Now he was about to have his first attempt at driving a car. Could the day get any better?

Well, actually there was one thing that would make it perfect. Sex. He was yet to test out his joystick with another person involved. He enjoyed what his hand had to offer, but he couldn't help wondering what it would feel like to have his hard length buried to the hilt inside a female's body…or surrounded by moist lips and stroked by an eager tongue inside a female's mouth.

Philippe let out a groan as the tight confines of his jeans suddenly became painfully uncomfortable. He had to learn to get a grip on his libido. The last thing he wanted was to go into public for the first time with a perma erection announcing his new status of virility. He'd already had one embarrassing Testosterone fuelled moment this morning, he didn't need another. Maybe if he thought about something disgusting, that would help cool his libido's overzealous jets.

Following that line of thought he pictured a snotty nosed baby, a ripe baby's diaper, a woman giving birth….a man having sex with a woman and making a baby. Shit. Even when he was consciously trying to keep his mind off the throb in his pants, his subconscious was bringing things around full circle. At this rate, he was going to have to make a quick bathroom stop to relieve the pressure in his balls before he even stepped foot inside the garage.

Narayan stepped up beside him and pressed the buzzer on the garage door's remote control. Slowly one of the doors cranked open and the fluorescent lights inside flickered to life.

"Which one are we taking?" Philippe asked excitedly, his eyes skimming over each of the clean and shiny cars lined up just waiting to be driven.

Narayan ignored the question, instead he wove his way through the rows of cars until he reached an old duck egg blue, four door Fiat 131.

Philippe blinked a couple of times in surprise, it took a couple more seconds before he could recover from shock to connect his brain with his mouth. "You can't be serious. This car won't make it to the end of the driveway. It looks like the only thing holding it together is the rust."

"You could be right." Narayan agreed, handing him the keys with a broad grin.

"So where are we going?" Philippe grumbled disappointedly as he opened the driver's door, its unoiled hinges cranking open noisily in protest.

"To the end of the driveway."

"And then?" he asked hopefully.

"Back down the driveway."

"That's it? We're going up and down the driveway?"

"Until you've got a feel for the car, yes."

Why did Philippe get the feeling he was about to relive a scene from the Karate Kid. '*Wax on, wax off*'. Not that he was complaining, but like Daniel whatever-his-name-was in that movie, Philippe was impatient.

Climbing into the driver's seat, he quickly adjusted his seat back, rear mirror, side mirror (there was only one) and...nope, that was it. The rust bucket was too old to have an adjustable steering wheel column. At least it had a decent stereo, he decided as he turned the key and the engine came to life on the first go.

With confidence, he put the car into Drive, took the handbrake off and with great care, eased the car out of the garage. He'd watched it done more times than he could remember, so he was extremely optimistic that he was going to ace this driving lesson and be racing the McLaren around a track by tomorrow.

The revs in the old Fiat's motor increased its tempo to that of a rumbling sewing machine, as Philippe put his foot a little harder on the accelerator and pointed the car up the driveway.

Up and back he went. Six times. That may not sound like he'd covered much distance, but when you consider that Havenswood Manor's driveway was a windy five hundred metres long, it didn't take long to clock up a couple of miles behind the wheel before he'd even left the property. Reaching the end of the driveway once again, he was preparing to turn the car around to continue the *'Wax on, wax off'* routine he'd previously envisaged, but Narayan grabbed the wheel to stop him.

"Turn left."

"Onto the road?" Philippe was a little surprised, regardless, he wasn't about to argue, quickly swinging the car onto the narrow country laneway which led to the main road just outside the little village of Cadley, another couple of miles away. A broad smile plastered on his face.

Reaching the main road he waited for further instruction, checking the road in both directions dutifully like every good driver does.

"Turn left here." Narayan pointed.

"As you wish," Philippe replied, quoting a line from one of his favourite movies, The Princess Bride. He felt a bit like Carey Elwes in the movie, tumbling helplessly down the mountainside, except he was rolling along on four wheels. He had a sudden feeling of being in motion without being in control. Gripping the wheel more tightly he was at risk of leaving permanent finger indentations.

"Okay, you're doing well. Follow this road until we get to the highway."

"Where are we going?"

"Oxford, but we'll take the back roads. I don't think you're ready for the motorway just yet."

Good thinking, he thought. His earlier confidence having taken a backseat to anxiety. It was an hour to Oxford along the motorway, it was likely to be double that following the country roads.

"Philippe, you can drive a bit faster, it's okay." Narayan suggested after they had been travelling for about half an hour.

"This is an old car, I don't want to strain the engine."

Narayan covered up his chuckle with a cough, clearing his throat. "Maybe you want to change lanes then," he advised. Pan looked in his rear vision mirror. Behind them was a cue of frustrated drivers waiting to get past, which of course they did...once Philippe moved over onto the shoulder of the road. That included a car towing a caravan passing them by at a reasonable pace. And didn't that just suck, the driver towing that caravan looked to be ninety, and the guy was still driving faster than him.

24

Little by little, Philippe gained more confidence and sped up to the speed of the traffic around him, and the silence in the car dissipated as he became more confident with multi-tasking. Who knew it took so much effort to drive and talk at the same time.

"This meeting at the club, I'm assuming Nicholas is the hot topic?" he asked.

"One of them, yes. Nicholas, Scorpion and Marek's venture back into the Guild's London headquarters I think will be high on the agenda. I believe that the psychic from India is also arriving today, so there's a chance she might be there too." Narayan told him.

"The one who helped us locate the Cintamani stone at the bottom of the ocean, that psychic? The one Dray's employed to help us find Nicholas' stash of *trophies*?"

"If he actually has one. But yes, hopefully she can help us find it, and him."

"Oh, I can guarantee you he has a new trophy collection. A leopard doesn't change its spots. I'm just sorry it took me so long to realise that," he bit out angrily. Without realising it Philippe's foot pressed down on the accelerator a little harder.

"There's going to be a lot of people there for this meeting today. All the Alliance leaders have been invited." That was a heavy-duty list of powerful leaders. Raif and at least one of his brothers, probably Wade, from the Wyvern city of Avengard. Vaughn from the city of Lemuria, plus both Gwynn ap Nudd, the leader of nephilim from Dun Turidd and his 2IC, Gallan. Not to mention all the local leaders from the Lycan clans and all of their own family members. "With the reopening of the club tonight, I believe Nadia is also coming back from the Ukraine with Gustav and Elise." Narayan told him. The mention of Nadia had the desired effect, shifting Philippe's scowl into a smile, releasing some of the tension Narayan could see building in his clenched muscles.

"I haven't seen her since she first woke up as an *Ei'Ambriath*. Her dad whisked her away so fast I never got the chance."

"She's also never seen you all grown-up."

"No. She hasn't." Philippe's brow began to crease again with renewed anxiety. They'd both gone through some major transitioning recently. What if she didn't like what he'd become? What if those changes affected their relationship on a deeper, more fundamental level?

He didn't want to contemplate things between them. He'd known for a long time that he was in love with her, but he'd also long since reconciled to the reality that a relationship with her could never be. He'd been a man inside a boy's body, no woman could love that. Nadia saw him as nothing more than her good friend and he was fine with that, but the idea of their personal metamorphoses changing the dynamics of their friendship or destroying it altogether, made him want to kill something. Okay, so that was probably an overreaction, deciding instead to chalk that one up to his turbulent Testosterone levels.

Once again, as his mind became distracted with negative thoughts his foot pressed down on the accelerator.

"You might want to slow down around this bend..." Narayan began to say.

Philippe took the corner so sharply the wheels squealed in protest, hitting the breaks a second before the car ploughed into the back of a caravan. The same one which had passed them earlier.

Philippe managed to swerve to the right collecting a post on the other side of the road and came to a sliding stop when Narayan quickly pulled on the hand brake.

The elderly driver had stopped for a rest break. Unfortunately, the concept of making sure both his car and the caravan were off the road was clearly one he hadn't mastered yet.

"Oops, my bad." Philippe's heart raced from the burst of adrenaline pumping through his veins, and he was panting as though he'd just run a marathon. Driving was a stressful business he concluded.

"That wasn't the ideal way to stop, but hey, it's not too bad for your first effort." Narayan praised shakily.

"You think?" Philippe asked sceptically. "I think I owe you a new car."

"What? Why?"

"I broke this one."

Narayan looked at him quizzically, then quickly scanned the dashboard. No lights were flashing a malfunction. He looked over the steering wheel. It wasn't bent out of shape, neither was the front of the car. The post which they'd hit was in far worse shape than the front bumper bar.

"Um, I broke the brake pedal." Philippe confessed sheepishly.

Narayan looked across at the floor of the car beneath Philippe's feet. Sure enough, there was a hole beneath where the pedal used to be. As Philippe pulled his foot back out of the hole, a metal clanking was the only sound to be heard as the pedal fell onto the ground below.

"Sorry."

"There's no need to apologise to me, it's Alex's car." Narayan couldn't hold back a smirk at the horrified expression on Philippe's face.

"Oh, crap!" he squeaked out.

"Don't worry, he hasn't driven it in years. It's been sitting in the garage gathering dust. I'm actually surprised the old bomb is still running." He thought at least the battery would be flat and in need of recharging, or the oil would need changing before they could get the old girl started. But no. It had started first go and even looked like it had been recently serviced when he'd checked the car's engine earlier that morning.

They both got out of the car to take a closer look at the external damage. A minor dent in the front bumper and a punctured tyre.

"Are either of you hurt?" The elderly man called out as he ran to their aid.

"Thank you, we're fine." Narayan told him with a reassuring smile. "It's nothing, really. We'll just change the tyre and be on our way."

Making a show that all was well, Philippe moved to the back of the car and opened the trunk, only to quickly slam it shut again, letting loose a string of hushed curses. Narayan kept his smile in place as he turned toward Philippe who casually leaned on the lid. Despite his casual posture his eyes flared wide in warning to Narayan to hurry the old man along.

"Dead body in the trunk." Philippe muttered as he put his hand to his face and pretended to cough. The comment was made too low for the old man to hear but it came across loud and clear to Narayan, whose responsive spluttering cough was genuine.

"Dear boy, you don't look fine to me at all. You look like you're suffering a wee bit of shock." The old man said worriedly to Narayan.

Unfortunately, however, before they could convince their good Samaritan to move along, their situation became a tad more complicated.

Appearing around the bend was the local police patrol car, slowing and coming to a stop directly behind them.

"Fuck." Philippe cursed again under his breath.

Straightening up, Philippe continued to lean against the trunk, tipping his head in greeting as one of the police officers got out of the car. "Officer." He greeted.

"Looks like you're in a spot of bother," the officer stated as he walked a path around the car, inspecting the dented bumper and kicked his boot into the flat tyre.

"Yes sir, but it's only minor. We'll change the tyre and be on our way." Narayan told him with an easy smile.

"Are you the owner of this vehicle?" he asked.

"No. It's my brother-in-law's car." Narayan answered.

"Did you know the registration on this car has expired?" the officer noted as he inspected the sticker on the front windshield.

"You don't say." Narayan feigned surprise.

"Who was driving this vehicle?" the officer asked in a serious tone.

"That would be me." Philippe told him.

"Could you show me your licence please sir."

"Um. Actually, I don't have one....yet."

"Could I see your learners permit then?" the officer demanded.

"Ah, yes...Yes, no problem." Philippe told him politely and opened the driver's door and leaned into the car. He fumbled about for a moment, opening the glove compartment and the centre console, re-emerging a moment later holding out a four-year old K-Mart catalogue and handed it to the officer. The policeman's face hardened into a scowl as he looked Philippe in the eye. Big mistake by the officer to look a vampire in the eye, not that he knew that though. "This is my permit." Philippe told him smoothly. Instantly the man's glare of annoyance shifted to vague confusion, and then to a congenial smile as the cogs in his brain seized and realigned in accordance with what Philippe had compelled him to believe.

Quickly Philippe put the faux drivers permit back in the car and returned to leaning against the trunk as the second police officer got out of the patrol car and approached.

"Everything okay?" he asked.

"Thanks for your concern officers, but we have things under control here. You can leave now." Narayan told them both, turning the suggestion into an order with a little push of mind compulsion.

Unfortunately, while the first officer complied and turned to leave, the second only looked bored and remained unmoving beside their car.

"Would you like some help with that tyre?" The officer asked instead.

It was just their luck that only one of the officers was susceptible to mind compulsion, he silently cursed.

"No. No. It's okay. We'll manage. Although, I don't think changing that tyre will help us much today I'm afraid." Narayan told him, as he ushered Philippe with a wave of his hand to get under the front of the car. There was no way they were opening up the trunk again to get the spare tyre, not with that body lying on top of it. Not that changing the tyre would make the car any more drivable considering it had no brakes. Nor were they going to try to explain to the policemen how Philippe broke the pedal.

Taking the not-so-subtle hint, Philippe crawled under the car on his back and stared up at the under carriage of the engine and contemplated ripping out a few wires. Then he spotted the solution to their dilemma lying a foot and a half away from him.

Grabbing the post which they had knocked over, he drove it up into the radiator, causing a rush of steam to be evacuated with a hiss through the grill of the car, and a leakage of boiling water spilling out through the newly created hole at its base and onto Philippe's face. His arms and legs twitched in a minor seizure, and he bit down on his lip, resolutely remaining silent as he cursed gravity and waited for his facial burns to quickly heal before he slid back out from under the car. His pasty smile not quite reaching his eyes.

"Damn. Radiators gone too. Looks like we'll be here for a while. There's no point any of you waiting around though, but it was nice of you all to offer your help." Philippe said, shaking hands with each of the officers and the elderly man in the hopes they'd all leave.

"We'll call a tow for you then." The second officer said.

"Thanks, but we don't want to put you to any trouble, we'll handle it." Narayan told them, following Philippe's lead and shaking each of their hands. They were only about ten miles out from Oxford. However, the only phone call they planned on making was to Dray for a cleanup crew, i.e. scrap metal collectors and body disposal experts.

"No need. I've already called one for you, it'll be here in a few minutes. It's the least I can do, I feel like I was partly to blame," the old man told them contritely.

Oh, for fuck's sake. Philippe swore silently as he gripped the car door handle in frustration.

"You didn't need to do that, we've got someone we...can call." Narayan told them distractedly. The sound of the door handle breaking off the car in Philippe's hand, followed by another string of muffled curses had Narayan struggling not to laugh. This was a serious situation after all, but that didn't mean he couldn't see the funny side to it.

"It's an old car. It looks like the door handle was as rusted as the rest of this bucket." Philippe blurted out, trying to look innocent as he waved the shiny metal handle around self-consciously while all eyes stared at him. He threw the handle into the car through the open window and clasped his hands together behind his back to keep them still and avoid causing any more damage. His cheeks flushed a healthy shade of pink, but that probably had more to do with the fact that they were still healing after the scalding from the radiator, than from embarrassment.

Heaving a heavy sigh of resignation, he planted his backside on the trunk of the car, resting his feet on the back bumper and thought, *Fuck it!* The situation couldn't possibly get any worse, might as well enjoy the company while they waited for the tow truck, and struck up a conversation with the elderly man and police officers.

By the time the tow truck arrived, Philippe had a professional driving lesson booked with one of the officers and a date booked for his driver's test a week later.

Narayan was left shaking his head in amazement. Philippe had always been known for his silver tongue, he was pleased to see that hadn't changed. Yet, he couldn't help feeling worried. He wasn't the *Pan* he used to be. His physical and hormonal changes aside, Philippe's attitude had changed. Where once he had been the eternal optimist, always looking for that silver lining in any situation, now his hatred for his brother consumed him. Bitterness and retribution seemed to be the order of the day.

Still, a week wasn't very long to wrap his head around such a major upheaval to his life, with a bit of guidance there was still hope for him yet, Narayan thought optimistically. And, who better to give him some behavioural coaching than a five hundred year old philosophical Buddhist ex-monk.

First on the agenda however, was getting to Oxford and find out whose body was in the damned trunk and why it was there.

4

Mums are better than any CSI agent. They know what you did, how you did it and whom you did it with, and they can hear you trying to hide the evidence.

"Does one of you want to tell me what happened to all the donuts? Hmmm? I know there were half a dozen here this morning and now they're all gone." Paige asked Grace and her son Riley, her gaze spearing each one in turn sternly as she held open the empty box.

Despite being told earlier by Cassie that the donuts were off limits, it seemed the youngest members of the household thought differently.

Not surprisingly the six and three year olds just stared up at her innocently.

"There seems to be two mysterious people living in this house. Somebody and Nobody. *Somebody* did it and *Nobody* knows who. Is that how it is?" Paige asked.

"Yes." They both answered enthusiastically, wrongly thinking they were somehow off the hook. The fact that one of them had chocolate in the corner of her mouth and the other had a smear of sugar on his cheek told another story.

"Maybe it was Uncle Alex?" Grace proposed.

"Hmmm, I don't think so. I'm sure Uncle Alex is guilty of something, but eating all those donuts isn't one of them. Do you really want to get him into trouble if he's innocent?" The tilt of Paige's head and her quizzical brow had them shuffling uncomfortably on the spot.

"We did it." Grace confessed, Riley nodding his agreement as he stared pouting in disgrace at the floor.

"Yes, I know. I just wanted to hear you both say it. Now go and wash the evidence off your faces. You're confined in doors for the rest of the day as punishment." Not that their punishment was terribly harsh, it was raining outside after all. Still, to two energetic children it was still worthy of a few disgruntled groans and miffed sighs as they trudged gloomily away.

Typical of children their age they didn't remain downcast for long. Within thirty minutes they had managed to spread out virtually every toy they owned through the length of the ground floor level of the manor, with several trickling down the staircases.

"I was planning on making more donuts later." Megan told her when the children were gone.

Paige looked around the kitchen at the mountain of food Megan was preparing. "I don't think that's necessary. It looks like you've already made enough to feed an army."

"Aye," she laughed. "But this lot isn't fur us. Cassie told me about the party we're throwing fur Mrs P's centennial birthday in a couple of weeks. That's a butt load of food I have to prepare and not much time to do it in."

"How many people do you think will be coming?" Paige asked.

"Oh, I don't know. A hundred, a hundred and fifty, maybe more."

"Really? I didn't think Mrs P. knew that many people, she's a bit of a recluse here at the manor most of the time."

"Aye, that's true. Although, she's been living here fur more than fifty years. She knows practically every family in Cadley. Then there's her own family, plus all of our extended family."

Paige let the figures tally up in her brain for a second, her brow rising higher as the rounded off figure settled to become a sizeable number of people. "I think you'd better cater for about two hundred adults and about thirty to forty kids."

"Really? In that case I need someone to pick up more supplies."

"No problem. Ring the suppliers and one of us will pick up your order."

"Aye, okay. Just don't let Alex go. Last time he went he took the liqueur chocolate sauce that I needed fur the poached pears. When it turned up in the pantry three days later there was only half a jar left."

"What, did he have a fetish for chocolate sauce?" Paige asked a second before her brain put together the answer. "Oh, I see. He had a fetish for eating chocolate sauce off Abby."

"Aye."

"Did you throw the rest of the jar out?"

"Not exactly. I didn't want it to go to waste, it was good quality chocolate sauce."

"Ew, you didn't use the rest of it in our food, did you?" Paige cringed.

Megan laughed a little bashfully. "No. I was telling Sebastian what Alex did and he insisted I hand it over to him."

"And he threw it away?"

"He threw the jar away when it was empty."

"He ate it?" Paige screwed up her nose in disbelief.

"Aye. Off me." Megan answered cheekily.

"Um, Megan. How many bottles of that sauce did you buy?"

"Two."

"Is the second bottle still in the pantry?"

"Aye. Second shelf at the back. There's also a can of whipped cream in the fridge if you want it."

"Nah, just the chocolate. Narayan's not a big fan of cream," she answered as she pulled the jar from the cupboard and inspected the contents, artfully calculating how many body parts it would cover. "Can you make sure you put a few more jars of this on your next order?"

Megan laughed. "It's already on the top of the list."

The sound of rain falling through the trees was relaxing in its monotony. The light pitter-patter of water droplets onto leaves blending with the deeper sound of dripping water into the puddles beneath. Nadia enjoyed days like this. Normally she could stay out here for hours. But not today. Today she was eager to get to the manor. With any luck Philippe was still there, although she wasn't holding out her hopes on it. He probably had things to do, or he may have already left for the meeting in Oxford. It must be mid-afternoon by now, and she knew how much he hated to be late for anything, she thought.

They'd planned on arriving much earlier, but it seemed Gwynn's 2IC, Gallan kept finding one reason or another to delay their departure.

Nadia stepped to the side of the portal next to Gwynn and waited semi-patiently as her sister, father and finally Gallan, stepped through. With a wave of Gwynn's hand, the portal snapped closed and disappeared as though it had never existed.

Stepping carefully along Savernake Forest's path, Nadia wondered at the beauty of the place. She'd always loved these woodlands, but she'd never really seen them properly until now, thanks to her new sight. This truly was an enchanted forest. With the Elder tree at its centre feeding the whole region with vitality, she doubted there was another place on Earth that looked or felt so alive.

That didn't mean that Havenswood Manor, which sat at the forest's border, felt any more like her home than her other home in the Ukraine did. Sure, she stayed at the manor often enough to warrant having her own bedroom, but somehow she still felt like an outsider. The only time it really felt like her home was when Philippe was also staying there. They'd sit for hours talking, watching movies together and simply enjoying each other's company.

It had only been just over a week since she'd last spoken to him or seen him, and she had to admit, she missed the little guy. Ahh, he wasn't so little anymore, she reprimanded herself.

A pang of anxiety swept through Nadia's thoughts. What if now that he's finally outgrown his pint sized body, he's also outgrown their friendship. It would explain those text messages he'd sent her, they were so impersonal. After all, hadn't they only become such good friends because he felt the need to help her beat her fatal attraction towards Morganna's grimoire? Since that was no longer an issue, what reason did he have to want to hang out with her, she realised. After her body had died, the book's evil grip on her was broken. She no longer felt even the slightest urge to go near that book ever again.

Not that she could even if she wanted to now anyway. Besides the ward on the storeroom which ensured the book could never leave that room, Teagan had sealed the lead lined box it resided in. Not even the strongest man on earth, a nuclear bomb or God himself could open that box without Teagan reversing the spell she cast on it.

A low branch flicked in her direction, spraying her with rainwater and snapping her out of her thoughts. Wiping her face with her sleeve, she picked up her pace. As the shortest in the group, Nadia had to walk quickly to keep up with them. Gwynn ap Nudd topped the group at seven feet tall. Gallan was only a few inches shorter and her father, Gustav was a healthy six foot two inches. Even Elise was taller than Nadia's five foot six stature by a few inches.

Breaking through the forest onto the outskirts of the manor's gardens and lawns, Nadia's anticipation at seeing Philippe again had her increasing her speed with her competitive younger sister. They practically ran through the vegetable and herb garden to get to the kitchen's back door first, the two of them bursting through simultaneously.

"Falbh dàirich fhèin. Tolla-thon!" Megan yelled in Gaelic at the ceiling.

"I gather you're not telling the Angels how much you love them." Elise queried warily, as she pushed the door open further and stepped into the kitchen.

"Oh, shit. Ye gave me a fright." Megan squeaked, a cloud of flour dusting the air as she jumped. Rushing around the kitchen bench, she gave Elise a half-hug, her flour coated hands dangling aimlessly in midair.

Nadia looked about, every bench was covered with trays of pastries, pots and bowls, some dirty and some clean, but all showing evidence of a major bake-off.

"Sorry, didn't mean to scare you." Elise told her. "Can we get a translation of whatever it was you were yelling at the angels? I'm assuming it was the angels you were yelling at and not us."

"Aye it was. And no, I'm not translating that." Megan said flatly, embarrassed that she'd been overheard.

"Would you like a word for word translation or just a general overview?" Nadia asked her sister, ignoring Megan's scowl and not bothering to hold back her chuckle.

"No, don't." Megan begged, her cheeks becoming rosier beneath a smear of flour.

"The full translation, definitely." Elise answered.

"Okay, she said…"

"No! Damn it." Megan cut her off with another string of Gaelic, this time aimed at herself, her shoulders slumping in a huff. "Okay, ye might as well tell them what I said."

"I intended to anyway." Nadia smirked, turning her attention toward Elise. "She said, *Go fuck yourself, arsehole.*"

"Wow, them's fight'n words, Megan. I didn't think you even knew such bad language. Can the angels hear you when you talk to them like that?" Elise laughed.

Megan snorted out an uncomplimentary huff. "I wish. And FYI, I was being polite when I said that, ye know."

"I'm sure you were. Listening to that lot jabbering on 24/7, would be enough to drive anyone to distraction." Nadia told her sympathetically, leaning in to give Megan a hug.

"Aye. Yer such a good, understanding friend." Megan told her, hugging her tight and deliberately leaving a pair of white handprints on her sweater as payback for *sharing* her meltdown moment with everyone.

Gustav cleared his throat to cover his snicker. He considered telling his daughter about the handprints on her back, but decided against it. After all, Nadia had enjoyed embarrassing her friend. Megan was entitled to a little harmless payback.

"Where's Alaric?" Gwynn asked.

"He, Sebastian, Alex and Narayan have already left fur Oxford, but Raif's in Alaric's study waiting for ye."

"Thanks." Without a second glance in their direction, the three men filed out of the kitchen and disappeared down the long corridor.

"What about Philippe?" Nadia asked hopefully.

"Pan…ah, sorry…Philippe. I can't get over how hard it is to get used to calling him by his real name," Megan said, "Philippe left a few hours ago. Narayan was giving him a driving lesson."

"Oh. Okay. No doubt I'll catch up with him soon." Nadia tried to sound unfazed by the news, deliberately putting a nonchalant inflection in her tone, but deep down her disappointment left her feeling a little flat.

"I'm sure you will. If he's going to the meeting this afternoon, there's a good chance he'll hang around at the club fur awhile afterwards. You'll probably catch up with him there." Elise told her in an equally indifferent tone as she shot Megan a covert conspiratorial wink.

"If Raif's here, where's Kaitlyn and Finn. Did they come too?" Nadia asked.

"I think they're down in the lounge room." Megan told her.

In a house the size of Havenswood Manor, the lounge room wasn't exactly pokey. It had originally been built as a ballroom back in the days when no respectable castle sized home would be without one. Of course it was never used. In recent years however, it had become a giant lounge room/games room, and the most popular room in the house.

"I'll go down and say hi." Nadia said.

"I've got something to do upstairs, I'll catch up with you a bit later." Elise told them.

Parting ways at the far end of the hallway, Elise quickly climbed the stairs and Nadia took a sharp turn to follow yet another corridor towards the laughter and squeals of children playing.

Nadia walked along the hallway with confidence. She could have found her way through the house blindfolded, she knew it so well.

On opening the door, the room suddenly went silent. At least it did until the three youngest members of the family realised who it was coming to see them and their high-pitched squeals resumed at a deafening volume as they all ran toward her.

Matching their excitement, Nadia took a couple of steps towards them.

"Watch out for the…." Kaitlyn yelled.

The warning came too late.

Nadia tripped on a plastic toy. The high-pitched squeak of the toy blended with Nadia's own high-pitched shriek as she toppled forward, landing heavily, face first on the polished boards, and let out a string of self-deprecating curses.

"Are you okay?" Kaitlyn asked, rushing to her side.

Nadia reached for Kaitlyn's outstretched hand and pulled herself up. "Yeah." Nadia grumbled, rubbing her sore shoulder, knees and chin. "I think I need to come with a hazard label or something."

"Nahh, you'll be fine. People trip over me all the time when I'm invisible. You get over it," she smiled, trying to lift Nadia's self-loathing mood. "You have to start thinking more positive."

"I am. I'm *positive* I hit the floor hard enough to squash a small child."

"Not even close. You didn't even scare the dog away." Kaitlyn told her sister, pointing to Tilly who sat only a few feet away staring at her curiously along with Grace, Riley and Finn, who all thought it was the greatest entertainment they'd had all day.

"What did I stand on?" She asked.

"It was a Minion doll, from the movie Despicable Me." Grace told her.

"Is there anything else on the floor I'm likely to step on that I can't see?" i.e. anything else plastic.

Kaitlyn and all the kids looked about at the floor strewn with toys.

"What can you see, point them out." Kaitlyn prompted.

Nadia pointed to half a dozen toys nearby.

"Ah, okay. Don't move until we clear the minefield around you."

Just as Nadia was winding up with another negative comment about herself, Raif stuck his head through the doorway.

"We're leaving now. I'll see you later at the club, okay?" he told his wife, giving her a peck on the lips before quickly disappearing again.

"Bye." Kaitlyn said to the empty air in his wake.

"The guys are leaving already? What's the time?" Nadia asked.

"Yes, thank God. It's four o'clock, and you know what that means don't you?"

"That the guys are running late for their meeting?"

Kaitlyn rolled her eyes at her sister. "It means that *we're* running late. We only have three hours to get ready before we have to leave too."

"Three hours? That's heaps of time. We only need to throw on a pair of jeans and a top, slap on some makeup and shoes. That won't take three hours, it'll take ten minutes."

Kaitlyn's grin broadened, a calculating glint backlighting her eyes, causing Nadia's pulse to tick over nervously. Grabbing Nadia by the hand she dragged her out of the room and up the stairs, kicking more *'invisible'* plastic toys aside as they went.

"You kids be good. I'm coming back to check on you in a few minutes. Got it?" Kaitlyn yelled as they reached the staircase.

"Got it!" came the faint reply in triplicate and a gruff bark from Tilly.

"Why are we in Paige's room?" Nadia asked just as the door slammed shut behind them. Nadia's nervousness doubled when she saw that they weren't the only ones in the room. Paige was there...so was Elise, and Cassie...and Abby. "What are you all up to, is this some kind of intervention?"

The way they all laughed at her question wasn't reassuring at all.

"No. But tonight's the night you're getting lucky. Strip."

"What? Lucky how?"

"Strip. We're giving you a makeover." Paige's tone left no room for argument. "We might be off the market, but you definitely aren't. We have to live vicariously through you. At least until you meet your Mr Right."

Paige was quite pleased with herself for coming up with the plan. If she could turn match making into a career, she'd excel at it, she thought to herself. As much as she wanted Nadia to feel she was 'On the Market', she was pretty certain that Philippe might not agree. Sadly, the two of them were blind when it came to matters of the heart. They need a little push.

Grudgingly, Nadia did as she was told, stripping down to her underwear.

"You're not wearing those granny pants. And that bra...tsk tsk tsk!"

"Why not? They're comfortable."

"The colours don't even go together."

"Sorry. I seem to be a bit colour-blind these days. They look fine to me."

"I hate to break it to you sis, but you've always been colour-blind when it comes to fashion. Nope, you're not wearing those. Take them off."

Nadia griped and grumbled, but did as she was told, again, stripping down completely naked. Paige was going to get her way eventually anyway, she figured. It was better just to go along with her.

"Ohmigod!"

"What now?" Nadia huffed.

"That bush. Seriously? When was the last time you mowed your lawn?"

"Not that long ago," she answered defensively, doing her best to cover herself with her hands.

"Well, you can't wear any skimpy undies with a forest hanging out the sides. We're going to have to get drastic."

"What are you going to do?" Nadia asked, not really keen to hear the answer.

"We're going to trim that hedge and wax the sideburns." She looked down lower. "Hmmm, and your legs."

"Anything else?" Nadia demanded haughtily as she shoved her fists on her hips, fully aware she was exposing herself again, however she was too irritated by her sisters' well-meaning interference to care.

"Hey, the way that honey pot looks right now, you're hardly going to be attracting any bees, are you?"

"I have no intention of letting any 'bees' near my honey pot, thank you very much. I'm saving it for Mr Right."

"And what happens if Mr Right is at the club tonight. Hmmm? Did you think of that?"

"I'm not having sex with a guy on the first date." Nadia countered.

"Maybe not. But what if he wants to go to second base? Or maybe he wants to do a little dirty dancing on the dance floor, what then? Are you going to stop him from running his hands up your bare legs, cupping your butt cheeks in his large hands as he pulls you against his hard body and grinds his huge, hard cock into your belly while you're dancing. Even if he doesn't see you naked, you're still going to feel unsexy if you haven't manicured all your *bits*. Trust me." Abby told her.

Nadia huffed out a frustrated breath in surrender. "Fine. Do your worst."

"You didn't really think you had a choice, did you?" Elise asked rhetorically.

"I guess not. I can't believe you're all ganging up on me though," she grumbled.

"It's for your own good." Cassie told her sympathetically.

"What are you going to do to me?"

"You'll see. Go jump in the shower and get squeaky clean and we'll have everything ready when you come out." Paige said excitedly.

Kaitlyn waited until she heard the shower turn on and the shower door close before voicing her thoughts. "Do you think she has any clue what we're doing all this for?"

"I've been keeping tabs on her thoughts, and I can guarantee she has none. She's totally clueless, which is why we decided to do this in the first place, remember." Abby told them.

"What if it doesn't work? You said it yourself Abby, she's clueless." Cassie said.

"It will work. She just needs a little push in the right direction. We all know how Pan...ah, Philippe feels about Nadia. And, she's always talking about him, thinking about him, hanging out with him. I think he's only stayed in the friend zone because of his pint sized stature. Now that he's all grown up, I don't think it'll take much for her to realise that she's actually in love with him too," Paige told them.

"Philippe's never been interested in a woman sexually before. What makes you think that's changed just because he's in an adult body now?" Elise asked.

"Ohh, he's definitely getting the sexual vibe now." Cassie told them, remembering his arrival in the kitchen earlier that morning, his *morning glory* on full display through his track pants.

"But it doesn't mean that just because he's got a hot body now, that Nadia will see him as her potential *mate*." Elise proposed.

"Don't worry. I've got that covered. I spoke to Teagan earlier. She's arranged for a couple of the regular girls at the club to be extra attentive to Philippe tonight. I know Nadia, she won't like sharing Philippe's attention. By the end of the night she's going to be so jealous she'll not want to let him out of her sight." Paige told them.

"And how do you guarantee that Philippe will notice Nadia if he's surrounded by fawning women?" Cassie asked.

"By the time we've finished with her, she'll be the *only* woman in the room who Philippe notices tonight." She chuckled.

"Because she'll have every guy in the club drooling over her?" Cassie asked.

"Exactly." Paige grinned.

Nadia finished her shower and the girls got to work. Paige, with her previous profession as a hairdresser, did her hair and makeup. Kaitlyn, who was a nurse, was allocated the job of waxing. Elise was on mani/pedi duty, while Abby and Cassie put together an outfit that was sure to make every man in the club trip over his tongue and revert to caveman mentality.

Keeping to their three hour time limit, they transformed Nadia into a sex goddess in heels, with just enough time spare to get themselves ready.

Nadia looked in the mirror, she barely recognised herself. The crimson coloured, figure hugging, low backed dress from Abby's wardrobe barely covered her backside, making her legs look far longer than usual, and her breasts look even bigger. And the matching patent leather pumps on her feet gave her calves and thighs a very shapely, muscular appearance. Her hair was pulled back to give her neck a long slender appeal, and her makeup and nails had been applied to maximise the benefits of the nightclub's lighting.

"Wow!" was all Nadia could find the words to say.

"You still think you're not going to find Mr Right tonight?" Kaitlyn asked her with a sly wink.

5

The meeting got started around 5pm. They had a lot to discuss before the club's doors opened at 8pm. Already there was a cue of people lining up for admission. It didn't take a genius to know that their re-opening was going to be a very busy night.

The Phoenix Nightclub was the most popular club outside of London. Many patrons travelling for miles and cuing up for hours for a chance at gaining admission. Not all of them did. The club was popular enough that they could be very selective with whom they let in.

Of course, most of the patrons didn't understand why they were so attracted to this venue in preference to so many others. The club's dual purpose was totally lost on them. Providing nightly entertainment for the humans who frequented the venue was of course a high priority, but so was providing a safe and controlled environment for vampires who went there to feed, i.e. a smorgasbord restaurant for vampires.

It was all very consensual. No coercion was allowed and the rules were strictly enforced. A vampire could only take a willing human to the private area of the club where, depending on *how* consensual the agreement was, the vampire could feed and/or have sex with them. Since sating the need to feed fuelled the need for sex through the hormone produced in their bite, the two often went hand in hand. Sadly for the participating humans, their memories were wiped clean afterwards. What they did retain however, was a subconscious craving for the addictive high that a vampire's bite creates. This in turn seemed to keep their human patrons coming back again and again in the hopes of recreating that sense of euphoria. Those humans were affectionately known as *Fang Bangers*.

One more side effect to the vampire's feeding is the donor's incredible thirst and hunger afterwards. And so, in accordance with the club's policy to look after *all* its patrons, this side effect has been easily rectified with a voucher for a free drink and meal at Bite Me, the all night restaurant next door. Which of course they also own. With so many fang-bangers and newbie's arriving daily on the hearsay of the devotees, and the Phoenix Nightclub's growing reputation amongst the supernatural world, the place was packed from 8pm to 4am seven nights a week. Normally.

That was until Cassie accidentally blew a two-meter crater sized hole in the dance floor a couple weeks ago, effectively shutting down the club for repairs and giving the employees an impromptu holiday.

Not that the club's temporary closure made any difference to the other business handled within the building's walls. As England's Alliance headquarters, the club never really closed. Saladin owned the venue, but his wife Teagan managed both the club and the restaurant next door. That freed him up to concentrate his time on following up pertinent underworld information collected via their many sources, along with Dray, his head of night club security and intelligence expert for the Alliance. Saladin had become somewhat of an intermediary between the various Alliance leaders around the world.

As a result, he had been spending more time at the club with Dray these days than he had at home with his wife. It worried him that he disappointed her so often, making plans only to have them cancelled at the last minute. Although, with the club having closed so unexpectedly, he was happy to say they'd found more quality time together. Despite the obvious complications of his job, he was determined to make it a regular occurrence and not a rare treat as it seemed to have become.

Saladin followed Gustav, Gwynn and Gallan, the last of the Alliance members to arrive, into the restaurant and locked the doors behind them. With so many people attending this meeting, their usual meeting space in his office wasn't nearly big enough.

Clearly, he'd missed some of the discussion, tempers were already flaring.

Off to one side Philippe sat beside Marek. It seemed they were the only two in the room who weren't Alliance leaders, and that fact made their presence amongst them more tangibly awkward. Philippe didn't know all the foreign leaders, yet clearly they all knew him, at least they knew his connection to the recent events. The group watched both Philippe and Marek with a suspicious eye, undecided whether or not they were worthy of their trust. Not that Philippe could blame them.

"Alex, I have a bone to pick with you." Narayan told his brother-in-law in less than congenial terms.

"Don't tell me, you're the one who took my car this morning? When I realised it was gone, I thought about tracking down whoever took it, but then I thought....Fuck it, let whoever has it, deal with the body in the trunk." Alex enlightened his brother-in-law cheerfully.

"Yeah, we discovered that nice surprise *after* we were in an accident. We had to wait for the tow truck while the *police* waited with us. What the hell were you thinking leaving a body in the car?" Narayan growled.

"Well duh, obviously it was there so I could take it somewhere to dispose of it."

"Whose body is it and what were you doing with it in the first place? Did you kill the guy?" Alaric asked.

"Pfft, no." Alex let out a dismissive laugh and waved away the question, then thought on it for a second. "At least I don't remember killing him specifically. I might have, but I killed quite a few so it's possible. Actually, I don't really know, I've lost track of who they all were." His tone was devoid of concern, partnering well with his tactless deliverance of the information.

"Alex, you're testing my patience." Alaric bit out angrily.

"Keep your knickers on bro, the guy was one of the Guild's men we killed back in Alabama last week. I brought his body back so I could run some tests on it. I wanted to learn how that enhancing potion might have affected him. And I wanted to see whether I could make an antidote."

Okay, so that was a legitimate excuse which they couldn't really be angry with him about, except for one thing.

"Was the stick up his arse really necessary?" Narayan asked.

"You stuck a stick up the guy's arse?" Oliver chuckled.

"It wasn't a stick, exactly. It was an old-fashioned bovine thermometer. I was using it to test the body's temperature. I just happened to accidentally leave it in there." Alex stated.

The room burst into laughter. "You stuck a cow's thermometer up the guy's shit hole? Oh, that's classic. You do see the cliché in that, don't you?" One of the foreign leaders roared, wiping his eyes of tears he laughed so hard.

Alex cleared his throat. "Did you happen to retrieve it before you disposed of the body. I wouldn't mind getting it back."

"Hell no. You'll have to buy yourself a new one." Dray told him.

"Damn."

"Did you learn anything useful?" Saladin asked, shifting the topic back to what was important. After all, he was on a schedule, no time for joking around even if it was at Alex's expense.

"Yes and no. I learned that the potion affects them on a cellular level, and they look to be permanent."

"Are you sure? There's no chance that it might wear off over time?" Vaughn asked.

"I guess there's always a chance, in this case though, I highly doubt it. The changes I saw affected the guy's DNA."

"That's not good news. Do you think you can create an antidote for it?" Philippe asked.

"In time, maybe."

"What if we made some of that elixir for our own men, made them stronger and faster too?" Gallan asked.

"No. That's never going to happen." Alaric told him flatly. "We don't know what the long term ramifications are of that brew. It could make a man go insane or make his body eat away at itself like cancer, for all we know. You can't forget that this is one of Morganna's concoctions from her grimoire. I don't recall her creating anything with anyone's long term health in mind."

"I concur," Saladin said, followed by a round of agreement from each of the leaders present.

"Besides, the only one who can read that damned book is Nadia, and we've taken extra precautions to ensure that it's well out of her reach from now on," Alaric told them.

Philippe's heart rate jumped at the mention of Nadia, warming his blood, concurrently sending a shudder of guilt through his body, pooling in the pit of his stomach like a cold, hard and very heavy stone. He should have been there to prevent his brother from coercing her into reading that book. In fact, he should have been there to stop his brother, period. But he wasn't and that fact ate away at him every day.

"What is being done to locate Nicholas?" one of the Asian leaders asked.

"We have a clairvoyant who has agreed to help us track him down. Philippe believes Nicholas will have hidden the *trophies* he's collected from his victims somewhere nearby to wherever he's holed up. If we can find his stash, we should be able to find him." Saladin told them.

"Yes, your brother has a long history of depravity, doesn't he?" the Asian stated, barely containing the sneer in his tone.

All eyes in the room turned toward Philippe. He hated what he saw on their faces, half looking at him with scrutiny and suspicion, the other half with sympathy or pity. He didn't know which was worse.

"Where's this clairvoyant now, I thought she was coming to this meeting?" Gallan asked.

"She's on her way from the airport right now. Her flight from India was delayed due to bad weather," Dray replied in his usual emotionally economised manner. The man's facial expressions were comparable to *Spock*, from Star Trek. He only had one, and he used it for every occasion. Deadpan. Not that it seemed out of place, it matched his sense of humour. He had none. Dray was a straight arrow and politically correct to a fault. Unfortunately, that straight arrow of his was permanently located up his arse. He was controlling and a hard task master, at least as far as…well, everyone who had to deal with him, was concerned.

"Why not get one of the nephilim to open a portal for her?" the South American leader asked.

"She is still adjusting to the supernatural world. She has only recently been made aware of vampires and lycans sharing this world with humans and our dimensional connection to Fey. We felt it was best to ration her exposure, so we put her on a plane." Dray told them.

"But if she's a psychic, isn't she already acquainted with the supernatural?" Gallan asked.

"Not our kind of supernatural. Her gift no doubt would open her mind to accepting concepts and facts beyond what the average human would understand, but without reality to back it up, it remains intangible. Too much exposure to our world too soon could be detrimental to our cause. We want her to feel relaxed and comfortable around us, not overwhelmed. She's not likely to find Nicholas' stash or lead us to Scorpion, if we cause her to have a mental breakdown." Narayan told them.

Point taken. Once again nods of agreement went around the room.

"Okay, does anyone have any other news to share?" Raif asked.

"Yes. We have an update on the Guild's status." Alaric told them, turning his attention toward Marek.

As everyone's attention focused on him, Marek looked about with a mixture of nervous trepidation and guilty contemplation. The tightly controlled world of his double identity which he'd fought so hard to stop from fraying at the edges, had now completely unravelled.

Admittedly he took on the role of duality for both noble and selfish reasons, although it appeared he may not have been the only one to have played that game.

That potion which Nicholas had Nadia create from Morganna's grimoire, he remembered it clearly from a time long ago when Morganna had written it. She had written it for him, or more correctly, she had written it to torment him. A dangling carrot meant to keep his loyalty tethered to her.

Nicholas' choice of potion had been very specific. How could he have known which one to choose from a book he couldn't read? It certainly wasn't from the headings written above. Morganna had always been paranoid, she deliberately labelled all her spells and potions with obscure titles.

Somehow Nicholas had to be in contact with Morganna, either directly or indirectly through Scorpion.

That thought sent icicles through his veins. His greatest enemy was conspiring against him with the one person he'd once called a friend.

Did Nicholas know about the trap the Guild had set at the Jefferson Tower?

Of course he had. He'd helped to set it up.

Hawke had nearly been killed in that battle, so had Nicholas' own brother, Pan, ah...Philippe.

Then the realisation struck. Killing his younger brother had been his intention all along, and he didn't care how many innocent people became collateral damage in the process.

How did this happen?

Marek knew exactly how it had happened. He'd been so busy trying to run subterfuge within the Guild, he didn't stop to consider how Nicholas would be affected by *his* exposure to the evil organisation. Nor had he once stopped to ask himself what his friend was doing with his spare time.

Now he knew.

Nicholas had been honing his skills as a serial killer and developing a very unhealthy relationship with someone on the inside of the Guild. Someone with enough power to go behind Marek's back and make changes to the hierarchy of the evil organisation. The question of who his mentor was had puzzled Marek initially. But now he knew for certain it was Scorpion. A vampire who had managed to infiltrate the Guild and make his way to the very top of the power tree without ever having his identity exposed.

That was another mystery which had puzzled Marek, until he heard about the potion which Nicholas had Nadia make.

All the pieces were falling into place.

And the final clincher that Nicholas, Scorpion and Morganna had teamed up together? At the battle in Alabama, after Scorpion shot Hawke's mate, Anna, he was seen to wrap his hand around an amulet and disappear. Morganna's amulet.

Holy crap on a cracker. They were in serious trouble.

They were all waiting for him to speak, Marek cleared his throat uncomfortably.

"Well, the good news is, I can confirm that the computer virus which Sanders and Hawke uploaded into the Guild's server in Alabama has corrupted their entire system. They've lost critical data on their financial investments, offshore accounts and also information they've accumulated on various Alliance members, which I hadn't been previously aware of. The bad news is, they will most likely recover most of that information over time. They're working hard at finding a paper trail that will help them at least recover their financial holdings. In the meantime, they've suffered a serious dent in their cash flow. None of the larger drug cartels are willing to do business with them after what happened to the cartel in Alabama, and the small-time dealers can't produce a big enough turnover to fund an office party let alone the entire organisation," Marek told them.

"How did you find this out?" One of the foreign leaders asked.

Marek could have just told them, but a visual explanation was far more effective, he was a skinwalker after all. One moment Marek sat before them as himself, the next he was Feinman, the dead Guild leader. "I went into the London headquarters."

Murmurs and the sound of shuffling feet and cracking knuckles could be heard amongst the Alliance members who weren't as familiar with the rephaim's gift.

"How will we know when they've got their operation up and running again? Can you go back in there?" Vaughn asked.

"No. That won't be possible anymore. Unfortunately, when I went in, Scorpion was waiting for me. He made a big show of how *Feinman* had been the one to turn traitor to the Alliance and he made an example of me...ahh, Feinman, in front of at least a dozen witnesses by slitting my throat. Unless I can kill Scorpion and assume his identity, I can't get back inside that building again."

"That's too bad, it would've been handy to have you on the inside."

Marek wanted to point out that he'd already been working on the inside for the past three years on their behalf, but the point seemed moot now.

"But, if Scorpion knows you're not dead, why did he let you leave." Oliver asked.

"He doesn't see me as a threat to him. He's arrogant enough to believe he's above our reach." Marek told them in a flat tone.

What he didn't inform them was the reason why Scorpion felt he was so insignificant. Before he'd had Marek, err...ahh Feinman's body removed from the building, Scorpion showed him a photograph of an old ring containing a very familiar sapphire at its centre. It was Marek's binding stone, the one which tethered his soul.

For years Marek had searched for that stone. It had been his initial reason for infiltrating the Guild, to use their excessive resources to hunt for it. He'd believed it lost forever, but as it turned out, his use of Guild resources had placed it directly into his enemy's hands. That knowledge was equally as horrifying as it was depressing.

If the stone was destroyed his mortality would be restored and Morganna could finally have her greatest wish. She would kill him.

The discussion continued around him in a drone of voices, his attention straying into the abyss of memories and regrets. Beside him, Philippe also appeared to have drifted off into his own thoughts as they sat at the periphery of everyone's scrutiny.

Dray took a step away as a voice came through his earpiece.

"She's here boss." Hawke told him.

"Thanks. Tell her to wait inside, I'll be there in a minute," he replied quietly and excused himself from the meeting, which finally looked like it was about to wrap up. Not a minute too soon either, it was nearly opening time, and if he was correct, and he usually was, and judging by the excited crowd waiting outside which he could hear through Hawke's mic, it wasn't going to be just a busy night, it was going to be a crazy night.

Hawke ushered the two women through the front doors of the club, past the reception desk and between the heavy curtains leading into the club's main room.

Looking about, Shani noted the open space was broken up into several areas. Just inside the entrance was a plush seating area with sofas and coffee tables. Leading off from that were several tall pedestal, round tables with stools dotted about close to the walls. And, at the far wall was one of the longest bars she had ever seen. Not that she had seen many, Shani had lived a very sheltered life. Then her eyes fell to the centre piece of the room. The dance floor. It was set into a pit a metre or so below the rest of the floor, corralled off by an intricate iron railing and accessed by a single staircase, where every occupant could be ogled and admired from a higher vantage. Overall the club wasn't what she'd been expecting. Actually though, she really didn't know what to expect. This was the first nightclub she had ever been inside. Next to her, her cousin and escort, looked far more accustomed to the surroundings, even if the club wasn't yet open.

Almost as though that thought silently triggered the opening of an unseen flood gate, the music suddenly cranked up a couple of decibels and the people waiting on the footpath started flowing in through the doorway she'd just entered.

"Prashani, it's great to finally meet you." Teagan pulled her in for a hug that was as big as her smile. Anyone looking on would have assumed the pair had known each other all their lives.

"Shani. Please, just call me Shani." She said, pulling back a little more shyly. "And this is my cousin, Yasmin. I'm staying with her while I'm here in England."

"Oh, where about in England do you live?" Teagan asked eagerly.

"Just outside London, in Brentwood" She replied politely.

"And you're planning on commuting back and forth every day? No, no, no. You can't do that, it's too far. That's the other side of London. I'm not sure what Dray has told you, but these guys don't keep regular hours. The last thing you want to be doing is travel long distances in the early hours of the morning, or worse, in peak hour traffic." Teagan told her, her brow furrowing as she thought through the options.

"I don't mind, really." Shani answered.

"Why don't you come and stay with Saladin and me. Our house is more than large enough." She suggested energetically.

"No, I couldn't. I'm quite happy to commute." Shani countered politely.

"Nonsense. I insist. Did you come straight from the airport. Are your bags in the car outside?"

"Ah yes, they are."

"Great. I'll have someone come and collect them later. Now, why don't you go and get yourselves a drink at the bar and I'll go and find out what's keeping Dray. I'm sure he's eager to meet you. Now, if I could just work out where Saladin put the bar schedule..." Teagan said distractedly. She thought she'd arranged for extra staff for tonight although they seemed to be a little light on. Unfortunately, with all the madness of getting ready for their re-opening, she'd left some of the arrangements to Saladin. Now she couldn't find the work roster, and she was a little worried he'd forgotten to call the staff.

"I believe you'll find it beneath a large red book on a dark coloured desk with an old-fashioned fountain pen on it." Shani told her, relaying the picture she saw in her mind.

"Wow, thanks." Teagan grinned, she knew exactly where that was. Saladin's desk. "Are you sure you can't stay here permanently, we're always losing things around here."

Shani smiled, but it didn't quite reach her eyes. "I get asked that a lot."

"I'm sure you do. Ah, great timing. Here's Dray."

Shani's gaze followed the direction Teagan had turned. For a moment she forgot to breathe. Like the approach of a violent storm, the air became electric and came to life in the form of a man.

That's Dray?

"I'll leave the two of you to do your introductions. If you'll excuse me, I've got lots to do." Teagan told them in a bubbly tone and disappeared through the doorway which Dray had appeared from.

Dray stopped right in front of her, almost moaning out loud as a startling tingle of sensual awareness lit off a short burst of heat in her core. She was close enough to touch him. He smelled like the incense her mother used to burn. It was a heavy blend of sandalwood, cloves and valerian, intoxicating and very masculine. Every hair on her body stood to attention, but not to be outdone, her nipples also strained against her lacy bra in tight buds of excitement. An immense power radiated off him, like the force of a tornado barely held in check, along with determination, confidence, ruthless intelligence, and something....strangely raw.

Shani giggled, a hysterical edge glinting under the laughter, her stomach fluttering uncontrollably as he extended his hand toward her. Why was she reacting this way? She wasn't sure. Maybe it was because she'd never met a vampire before. Or, it could have been that she'd never expected the man she'd been doing business with, mostly on-line for the past year to be so...so...drop dead gorgeous. Dead straight, raven black hair reached down to his waist, cheekbones that could cut steel, and a double scoop of sculpted butt that even his loose trousers couldn't camouflage. And the sun-kissed colour of his skin, so similar to her own and yet so exotically flawless.

As Shani took his hand in greeting, it felt like she was being struck with a bolt of lightning, leaving her feeling dazed and more physically aware of the man in front of her than anyone she had ever met. Every nerve ending in her body tingled, and she could have sworn that for the briefest of moments, the world had shrunk down to hold only the two of them.

The instant their hands parted, the connection was severed.

For a second Dray stared at her curiously. Had he felt it too, she wondered.

"Did you have a good trip?" he asked, breaking the awkward silence.

"Huh? Oh, yes, thank you. A bit bumpy, but not too bad overall." It seemed to take an embarrassingly long time for her brain to connect with her mouth. She'd spoken with him on the phone numerous times, but the cadence of his voice in person was mesmerising and had her senses spinning out of control. "And this is my cousin Yasmin. I'll be staying with her while I'm here."

"I believe that arrangement has been re-negotiated. I think you'll find that your luggage is being collected and relocated to Saladin and Teagan's home as we speak," he told her matter-of-factly.

"What? No. I can't do that." Shani almost went into a flat panic, spearing her cousin with a desperate look for help. Yasmin's concern showed on her face, yet she opted not to object.

"Yasmin, I can't stay there. I *have* to stay with you."

"Shani, think about it. Think very carefully. If you stay with them you'll be able to do your job without any interruptions or prying eyes, won't she Dray?"

"I can guarantee you'll have whatever you need to do your work." Dray reassured. There was an unspoken meaning beyond Yasmin's words that passed between the two women, catching Dray's vigilant attention, although he put it down to the stress of Shani finding herself in such foreign waters. Not just in the literal sense either. She was a long way from her home, her husband and her family, and Dray assumed that for Shani, entering their supernatural world must feel like stepping inside the twilight zone. Her sense of reality had shifted and as yet she was still unsure of her bearings. Wanting to stay with her cousin would only be natural. Just not practical.

"You really think it's a good idea?" Shani asked her cousin.

"I do."

"But...."

"But nothing." Yasmin speared her with an uncompromising glare.

When Shani visibly relaxed a little, so did Dray. Not that anyone could tell the difference, yet again his expression didn't change.

As the club continued to fill up, a few familiar faces appeared through the doorway, heading in their direction.

"Shani, Yasmin, let me introduce you to Teagan's sisters, Kaitlyn, Paige, Nadia and Elise. And, these other ladies are Cassie and Abby. You'll probably get to know them all quite well while you're here. They like to interfere in everyone's business." He said, letting his gaze linger on each of Nadia's sisters. Nothing escaped his notice, especially when that plotting and scheming was done right under his nose. Poor Philippe and Nadia, he thought shaking his head.

"Nice to meet you both, but I can't stay and chat right now, I have to find Teagan." Paige said, deliberately ignoring Dray's comment.

"I'll come with you." Kaitlyn told her twin.

"And I'm off to the bar." Abby said.

"I'm coming too." Elise piped up.

"And I'm going to..." Cassie began.

"You're going to go nowhere near the dance floor. You're banned. You hear me?" Dray warned.

Cassie rolled her eyes with a huff. "Fine. But I can't guarantee it won't happen again if another female tries to feel up my husband."

"In that case, as soon as the meeting's finished, I'll expect you to stick by Alaric's side like glue."

"Pfft, that's what I intended to do anyway." Cassie told him, rolling her eyes in feigned exasperation. "Great to meet you two girls, but I'm in need of a drink too." With that, Cassie quickly disappeared into the swelling crowd to appear a minute or so later at the bar.

"Looks like they've all deserted you." Shani said to Nadia.

"It seems that way, but that's okay. They don't get to come here as often as I do, it's a bit of a novelty for them."

"For me too. I've never been inside a nightclub." Shani told them shyly.

"Seriously?"

Shani looked down at the floor, annoyed with herself for having made that confession.

"What, don't they have nightclubs in India where you live?" Nadia asked her.

"Yes, they do, but..."

"Our family is very old-fashioned. Shani's parents never let her go to a nightclub and now that she is married, it is considered inappropriate." Yasmin told them, stepping in to cover Shani's awkwardness.

"Oh, I see. Do they know where you are now?"

"Ah, it's complicated." Shani told them, sparing a quick glance up at Dray, whose attention toward her seeming to note her every twitch, and calculating every nuance in her tone as she spoke. Was it a vampire thing to be so intense, or just a Dray thing, she wondered. She was looking forward to finding out. For a moment those heated butterflies in her belly returned at the thought.

"Dray, I know I'm late, but I thought you wanted me to sit in on your meeting?"

"Not this time. I think you have enough to absorb without being overwhelmed by that lot in there too. I'll leave you with Nadia for now. We'll talk later." He told her.

"Um, okay. Well, it's nice to finally meet you in person." Shani told him with a smile, holding out her hand in the hopes she might recreate that zing of electricity she'd felt when he touched her earlier. If, for no other reason than to convince herself it had only been in her imagination. However, Dray pursed his lips tightly together and only nodded before turning away abruptly.

"Does Dray always look so...so..."

"Bored? Serious?" Nadia offered.

"Constipated." Shani said. "He looks like he's in pain the poor fellow."

Nadia laughed. "I like you. You're going to fit in here just fine."

"And, is Teagan always so....um, upbeat?"

"Yeah, well, she's 90% water and 10% caffeine. Just wait until the caffeine in her blood runs low, it's like a Jekyll and Hyde transformation."

Shani laughed. "I'll remember to carry a flask of coffee with me at all times."

"If you do that, she'll be your friend for life."

"That's good to know," Shani said, turning to face Nadia more fully their eyes met. "Please don't take offence at this, but um, are you wearing contacts?"

"No, why?" Nadia asked curiously.

"Under the UV lights your eyes look like they're glowing."

"They are?" Nadia's voice rose an octave in surprise. She pulled her phone from her purse and activated the camera as though to take a selfie. "Ohmigod, they are. Wow!"

"Are you a vampire too?" Shani tried to whisper, but had to almost shout to be heard above the beat of the music.

Nadia laughed. "No. I'm something else." She was an *Ei'Ambriath*, a spirit walker, whatever the hell that meant. Besides her eyesight being tuned to the astral level, she didn't feel any different than she did before. Although, her pale grey eyes glowing under the UV light was new. If the outfit her sisters dressed her up in didn't get her noticed by the opposite sex tonight, she was pretty sure her eyes would. Whether that was a good thing was yet to be decided.

Right now, there was only one person in this place she wanted to meet up with, and that was Philippe. Everyone was raving about how great he looked after his transition, and she was impatient to see for herself.

Nadia made small talk for a few more minutes with Shani and Yasmin, her eyes straying regularly toward the security door which led to the club's offices and the back entrance of the Restaurant. Any minute it would open, she told herself.

Any minute....

The door opened and through it streamed a line of men, most she knew and some she didn't. And then, nearing the end of the procession one man stood out.

Stopping herself from wiping her mouth to check for drool, she watched him scan the room with his eyes.

He was the most incredible man she had ever laid eyes on. Just like a moth drawn to the flame, she couldn't look away. It wasn't a choice to openly stare at him, it was a compulsion.

"Philippe?"

6

The music thumped through his body, everything hitting him at once as he exited the corridor into the nightclub. His eyes scanned the room looking for only one person.

Philippe stopped walking so abruptly, Oliver slammed into the back of him.

"We need to install brake lights on your ass." he complained, side stepping around him. Not that Philippe seemed even remotely interested in Oliver's opinion, his attention was fully engaged on the object of his search.

"Nadia."

Nadia was already halfway across the room toward him before he managed to get his brain back into gear.

"I've missed you." Nadia told him, wrapping her arms about his neck to squeeze him tight, his arms sliding about her waist in response, lifting her off the floor.

"I've missed you too. You look amazing, and your eyes...wow." Philippe couldn't look away, completely mesmerised by her glowing irises.

"It's the UV lights." She told him, her eyes scanning his face curiously.

Philippe slowly released his grip on her and let her slide back to the floor but didn't release her altogether, leaving one arm anchored behind her back.

"I wasn't sure if I'd recognise you all grown up. But you look the same...but different. I mean, you look different on the outside. You look hot. Really hot," she told him with a laugh, waggling her eyebrows and making his cheeks blush a little. His tall, muscular frame certainly radiated a virility he had never possessed before, and she was quite happy to admire it. "But, you're still the same Philippe." *My Philippe*, she felt like saying. But that was crazy, she had no claims on him, and he certainly didn't think of her as anything more than a friend, she mentally reprimanded herself.

"I've been so worried about you. How have you adjusted to being an *Ei'Ambriath*? What about your eyesight, has it improved at all?" he asked.

"I'm getting there. My sight hasn't come back, not the way it used to be. I can still only see things from an astral plane perspective, although I'm getting better at seeing all the different layers at once which makes the picture clearer. I still can't see anything made of plastic though," she screwed up her nose remembering her earlier face plant in the manor's lounge room. "What about you, how have you adjusted?"

Philippe told her about his own minor incidents, i.e. learning to deal with his new size and strength, and the results of his first driving lesson that afternoon. He didn't however, tell her about his other 'first' for the day. His discovery that *all* his newly enhanced body parts were now fully functional.

Conversation between them flowed as easily and naturally as it always had. Philippe leaned down close to her ear, not because he was concerned she couldn't hear him over the noise in the club, but because it gave him an excuse to pull her closer.

His fingers stroked her neck, their lips so close he could taste the lime from her tequila shot she'd had earlier as her breath caressed him, and he shuddered with a foreign desperation pounding through his veins. Arousal. This was what it felt like to be so fucking horny his balls were ready to burst. He never believed it would ever be possible for him to feel sexual arousal, and he never imagined it would feel like this. Here he was developing a major case of blue balls. And God dammit, he wanted better relief than what his hand had to offer.

Philippe groaned and pulled back, dropping his hand from Nadia's waist. He couldn't help it, it was a reflex, as though he'd somehow crossed an unspoken friendship boundary.

"Philippe, is everything okay?" Nadia asked, concerned that she'd upset him somehow.

"No. Everything is hunky dory. Why don't you go and get us a couple of drinks." He suggested through a tight smile.

"Um, okay. What kind of drink do you want?" she frowned.

"Whatever. Surprise me."

Philippe was ready to bolt to the men's room to quickly relieve the pressure in his balls before she could come back. The last thing he wanted was for her to see him tenting his pants with enough pressure to pop the zipper. Or worse, blowing his load inside his pants just from being so close to her.

But as they say…Even the best laid plans, and all that.

Nadia hadn't gone two meters from him before he was surrounded by a crowd of women.

"Hiya big boy, you looking for some company?" one of them asked.

"Thanks for the offer but, no." He answered awkwardly.

"You sure about that? You look like you could use a girl to show you a good time. I'm a great dancer." Another one said as she ran a finger over his bulging biceps.

Seriously? "No, really, I'm fine. I'm waiting for someone."

Philippe wracked his brain for an excuse to get rid of them, but he couldn't think of any. He'd never been in this position before. He was always the insignificant, forgotten one in the corner, watching everyone else's interactions from afar. He had no clue how to handle a group of drunk, horny women who were coming onto him.

Oh fuck! Nadia stood a couple of feet away with drinks in hand and stared wide-eyed at him through the crowd. Before he could tear himself free of his unwelcome entourage, she'd turned her back and disappeared.

Fuck. Fuck. Fuck!

"You'll never want anyone else after you've been with me. I'm like a sexual tornado," a third woman told him seductively.

"What?" Philippe's frustration was beginning to bubble over. Being horny and trapped by a bunch of man eating she-wolves, figuratively speaking, was almost too much for a newly matured man.

"You know that description of yourself isn't as appealing as you think it is. Tornadoes either destroy your home or kill you."

"Well, I have been known to break up a few homes, although I haven't killed anyone, yet," she laughed.

Philippe looked down at the female who'd pressed her body up against his and almost groaned out loud again, this time from revulsion. Of all the woman in this place, it was just his luck he'd be cornered by her. Vanessa.

"Maybe not directly, but I'm pretty sure there's one or two guys out there who've wanted to kill themselves after you've had your way with them."

"Never. Like who?"

"Like those guys whose happy homes you destroyed maybe."

She unbuttoned his top button.

"Give it up Vanessa, I'm not interested." He told her, swatting away her hand.

"Of course you are, you're still a virgin aren't you Pan? I'm very good with first timers."

"The name is Philippe, and what I am is none of your business. My answer is no. N.O. I can't make that any clearer," he bit out between clenched teeth.

"You'd be making a *huge* mistake to pass this up." Vanessa ran her hands down her body, cupping her breasts suggestively and pouting seductively. Her eyes locked onto the bulge in Philippe's pants when she said the word *huge*.

"I doubt it." He considered covering his groin with his hands to hide the evidence of his arousal from her, but that ship had already sailed. Regrettably, Vanessa thought that it was her who had caused his hardened state, when in reality it was the lingering result of someone much more unobtrusive. Nadia.

His gaze drifted across the room to where Nadia glared at him from her seat next to the woman from India. Her arms crossed beneath her full breasts, plumping them up further in her tight-fitting dress. Not to be out done, her legs were crossed, her foot tapping furiously in midair, emphasising the length of her luscious legs and the short length of that outfit she wore, it was enough to drive a sane man crazy.

Instantly he regretted his testosterone induced diversion of thoughts as the throbbing bulge in his pants jerked with a fresh influx of blood.

Even from across the room Nadia was making him hot under the collar. The other women who were crowding him barely even registered on his radar.

"I know you want it. You can't deny it." Vanessa said, winding an arm about his waist and spearing her free hand toward the front of his pants.

Philippe managed not to recoil as he grabbed her hand and held it suspended only an inch from his groin. It was close enough to feel the heat of his body, but far enough away that even when she curled her fingers, all she could manage was to scrape her fingertips over the fabric of his jeans. She considered stamping her foot for dramatic effect when she didn't get the reaction she was hoping for, but changed her mind at the last moment. All it would have accomplished was to make Philippe roll his bored eyes and ignore her for even longer.

Not going to happen.

"I don't deny my desire for sex. Just not with you. I'm not into other men's sloppy seconds."

Vanessa looked at him blankly for a moment, unsure if he was insulting her or not. Regardless of what she thought, her expression didn't change. Philippe suspected that was the result of Botox. She was dumb enough to believe her smooth complexion was due to the nerve killing injections she continued to have in her brow. Of course that wasn't the case. Her perfect complexion was due to the fact that she was a vampire. However, no one cared enough about the fanged-up brunette bimbo to inform her of that fact.

Not surprisingly, Vanessa's IQ still managed to come in a little below her bra size and slightly higher than her fashion sense and her moral scruples. Both of which had a total score of zero. Each night she came into the club wearing a procession of poor taste and ugliness. Her extra short, extra low neckline leopard print dresses, skimpy lycra crop tops and flared mini skirts, left very little to the imagination. Nothing, if she bent over. Underwear seemed to be an optional extra she didn't bother with. What Vanessa did excel in was having a body hot enough to ignite fire retardant and the ability to turn a man into a drooling idiot, whose only conscious thought occurred in his southern brain, below his belt.

Well, not this little black duck, Philippe thought. Although annoyingly, prying himself from Vanessa's determined hands was easier said than done. Philippe had more chance of escaping a viper's bite in a snake pit filled with vipers, than he did escaping this particular vampire's grasp.

Nadia watched broodingly as the group of women crowded and fawned over Philippe. She couldn't help noticing Vanessa was among them, which put her mood into an even deeper funk.

She'd left him alone for two minutes and a flock of vultures had descended. Although to be fair, even vultures didn't stand a chance against Vanessa. She was like the Remora fish, those slippery suckers which attached themselves to the backs of sharks for a free ride and a free meal. And like the scaly scavengers, Vanessa wasn't known for giving up her prey until she'd finished with them.

Vanessa had only been a vampire for a few months. It seemed that one of the out-of-towner vampires who had taken advantage of Vanessa's eager willingness to sate his needs, had unfortunately wrongly assumed that her vagueness and scatterbrained ability to speak in full sentences, was a direct result of her mind having been wiped one too many times. Thinking he was responsible for tipping her fragile mental state over the edge, he turned her in the hope it would 'cure' her. Sadly, he didn't realise that there was no cure for the terminally stupid. She always had been, and always would be, as dumb as a bag of rocks.

In Nadia's opinion killing the skanky excuse for a woman would have been a much kinder option. For everyone else's sake. Vanessa routinely made a play for any man with a dick. It didn't matter to her whether they were already spoken for or not. Not even the *mated* males were off limits to her, regardless of the fact that they would never be tempted by her so-called charms.

And now she was going after Philippe.

"I don't want to be that cat lady knitting tea cozies out of toilet paper and collecting garden gnomes and barbie dolls." Nadia grumbled sulkily. "Do you think if I glare at her hard enough her hair might catch fire?"

"Try it and see." Yasmin suggested, shrugging her shoulder noncommittally.

Nadia's lips spread into a scheming smile.

While Nadia sulkily watched Philippe and his harem of slutty women, Shani found herself staring at the handsome vampire with the beauty of a native American God, who stood aloof watching everything and everyone in the room.

"Dray is definitely not what I expected, he's intense and standoffish, but he seems like a nice, honest guy."

Nadia blinked.

"Dray's definitely honest. But nice? Most people usually get over that opinion once they get to know him," she joked.

"Then most people are fools." He'd always been nice to her. Admittedly she'd only ever dealt with him over the phone and by email, but he'd always been polite and professional.

"What about that guy you were talking to before. He seems nice too." Shani said, posing the statement as a question.

"Philippe? We're just friends." Nadia protested sulkily.

"You think so? He hasn't stopped staring at you since you sat down. And the way he's staring, the only way he's interested in being *just friends* with you is if it's tattooed on your butt." Shani told her.

"Yeah, right." Nadia snorted. "I thought your clairvoyance only let you find lost things."

"And I thought that you had the gift of second sight. Can't you see he has feelings for you?"

"I see he has a harem of women throwing themselves at him, and he's not trying too hard to get away. I also see that he seems to be turned on by their attention, if you get my meaning." Philippe's aura was lit up like a sexual Christmas tree.

"That makes you jealous?" Shani asked Nadia.

"Of course. Not him getting turned on by them of course, he's waited a long time to have his adult body, and I think he's earned the chance to explore all the advantages that it has to offer. But, I am jealous of the attention he's giving *them*. That doesn't make sense, does it? It's just that, well, we've been friends for years. I would have said we were best friends, but it looks like he's outgrown me since he acquired his new body."

"Hey, there's no point waiting around for him to notice you. Go out there and get yourself another man. There's enough of them with their eye on you to choose from. That is unless you have your mind set on Philippe specifically." Yasmin told her.

"What? No. I've never thought of Philippe as anything more than just a friend." That was true. Until tonight. Not that she was going to admit that to anyone though, especially when he looked like he was enjoying the delights other women could offer him. And no doubt they could please him much better than she could. When it came to men, she was the awkward, ugly duckling. She'd rarely managed to get a second date with a man, let alone get to second base with one.

When she thought about it logically, Philippe was better off with that slutty tag team than he ever would be with her.

"Then what are you waiting for, get out there on that dance floor and collect your own harem. What's the worst thing that can happen? You'll have some fun?" Yasmin told her.

"You're right. I will." Nadia stood and straightened her skirt, letting out a nervous breath. "Here goes nothing. Wish me luck."

"Honey, you don't need luck. I think you might need a stick to fight them all off though." Shani laughed. "Damn." Suddenly her relaxed demeanour tensed.

Without a word or even a glance in Nadia or Yasmin's direction, Shani quickly walked toward the exit as her phone buzzed in her hand.

"Is everything alright?" Nadia asked Yasmin, concerned for the sudden change in Shani. If she wasn't mistaken, Nadia was sure she detected a hint of fear in her aura.

"Yeah, I'm pretty sure that's her husband calling her." Yasmin smiled with relaxed ease, even so, concern for her cousin was evident in the sudden change to the flow and colours in her aura.

"And he doesn't know she's in a nightclub, and she's worried about what he'll think?" Nadia pried.

"Something like that. He also doesn't know about her new living arrangements while she's here."

"Is he likely to be upset with her?"

"He's not going to be happy about it, but he'll get over it." *Or maybe not,* Yasmin thought silently to herself, watching Shani hurry out the door. Eager to shift Nadia's attention away from her cousin, she changed the subject. "What are you doing still standing here, go catch yourself a man or six."

Nadia gave a half-hearted chuckle, spearing a look from Philippe and his harem, across to the crowded dance floor and back to Yasmin. Sucking in a deep breath she took a step forward and stopped. "You really think I should?"

"Absolutely. Go out there and have some fun."

"Will you come with me?" Nadia asked nervously.

"I think I should wait here for Shani." *And find out just how angry Saadir is about her change of arrangements.*

"Okay, well wish me luck." Nadia grinned sheepishly as she once again put one foot in front of the other.

Nadia only made it half-way to the dance floor when she felt a hand grab her arm.

"Nadia, hold up. I'm sorry about before."

"Philippe, you really don't want to talk to me right now." She told him, her glowing pale eyes hardening into ice crystals.

"You're right, you look angry, but I really want to explain."

"Whatever, I don't care. Go back to Miss kitty litter over there."

"Nadia, that's not very nice," he chastised.

"What? It fits." She huffed when he narrowed his glare and raised a brow at her. "Fine. Go back to Sheena, Queen of the jungle. Better?"

Philippe ignored her pretentious dig at Vanessa. "Nadia, please let me explain."

"Trust me, you don't need to. I understand you have *needs*." She lowered her gaze to the bulge in his pants that even the club's poor lighting couldn't disguise.

"What? No. I mean, I suppose, but it's not what you think. It's an involuntary hormonal response, that's all. I'm still trying to figure out puberty here."

"Of course, I understand. I can see all those crazy sexy hormones lighting up your aura." She waved her hands up and down as if outlining the invisible neon sign surrounding him.

"You can see that?" Philippe swallowed uncomfortably.

"I can see you're horny as hell, just like three quarters of all the other guys in the club looking to score some pussy tonight," she sniped irritably. "Not that I'm judging you or anything. As you're friend I'm happy for you. You've finally got what you've always wanted. You're a *real* man. So why don't you go back to your trampy alley cat. You're a free agent, why not take advantage of a woman who is quite obviously begging to show you a good time."

Although Nadia was using every slutty feline comparison she could think of to refer to Vanessa, she was the one baring her 'catty claws', Philippe thought. And wasn't that a turn on. Nadia was jealous.

"Yeah, she's got a smoking hot body, but you couldn't find her IQ if you had a search light."

"Ahh huh." Nadia answered slowly, her eyes hardening into twin shards of glacial ice.

Philippe realised his poor choice of words to describe Vanessa the instant they left his mouth. Damn those delinquent male hormones, twisting his brain into little pockets of pornographic Swiss cheese. At this point he doubted there was anything he was going to say that would please her. If anything, he seemed to make things worse every time he opened his mouth.

"Nadia, I'm not interested in Vanessa. What I want is to spend some time with you."

Nadia let out a very unladylike snort. "Yes, well, maybe another time. I'm busy." Pushing past him with her nose high in the air, diverting her destination toward the bar.

A couple of minutes later, with another shot of Dutch courage under her belt, she headed for the dance floor.

"Are you spying on Nadia?" Teagan asked as she approached the group of women huddled together conspiratorially.

"No. We're just being supportive. We wouldn't be doing our sisterly duty if we didn't make sure she's okay." Elise told her.

"I can see why. He's cute."

"Which one? They're all pretty cute if you ask me." Abby grinned.

"Hey sis, what are you doing over here? I thought you were too busy to hang out with us tonight." Kaitlyn asked.

"I am, but you've made being a creepy stalker seem fun, so I had to come and check things out for myself. One tip though, if you're trying to look inconspicuous, you all suck at it. Any minute now Nadia is going to spot you and then the only thing you will have achieved tonight is pissing her off and by the looks of it, Philippe has done a pretty good job of that already."

"Things would be going much better right about now if you hadn't sicked Vanessa onto him." Paige sniped.

"I had nothing to do with Vanessa. I only arranged for the other two girls to pay Philippe some attention. Vanessa singled him out all on her own." Teagan countered equally as curtly.

"Arrgh. Typical." Kaitlyn grumbled. It seemed that Vanessa's reputation extended as far as the residents in Fey.

"Okay, so what do you suggest we do?"

"About Philippe? Nothing. It looks like he's managed to give Vanessa the slip. But Nadia...."

Teagan pointed to the far side of the room where Dray was currently looking even more grumpy than usual, if that was possible. "If you go over there, it's dark and far enough away that she probably won't notice you, and it'll give you a great view of the whole club."

"But it's so far away. We won't be able to see anything properly. None of us are vampires, remember? Oh, except Abby, of course." Elise complained.

"Not without these you won't." Teagan pulled a pair of binoculars from behind her back.

The girls faces lit up with excitement.

"Give me those." Kaitlyn said, taking them from her sister's hand. "Wow, these have night vision. Cool."

"Yep, they're military grade spy equipment."

Elise giggled as she took them from Kaitlyn and scanned the room. "Where did you get these? Dad?"

"As if he'd help us set-up one of his only two single daughters." Teagan snorted out a derisive laugh. "These are Dray's."

"He's helping us?" Elise asked in disbelief.

"Yeah right. He's even less likely to help us than dad. It would go against his *moral code*," Teagan told them, emphasising the statement in air quotes. "I took them from his office. I doubt he'll ever know they're missing."

"I'd say you could get yourself fired for doing something like that, but I guess it pays to be the boss, ha?" Paige chuckled at her oldest sister's gumption.

"Ahh oh, can you see who Nadia is dancing with now?"

"Yep."

"Wow. If I could pick anyone for Nadia to be with, that guy would definitely not even make it onto the short list."

"Looks like a real charmer, I agree. Arrgh."

"What are we going to do about him?" Elise asked.

"Me. Nothing." Teagan said, ushering them away into the darkened corner.

"What? You can't be serious."

"I've done enough interfering. So have you lot."

"There has to be a solution." Paige schemed.

"There is...." Abby began.

"The solution would have been birth control. Clearly his parents had none." Kaitlyn chuckled.

Abby huffed. "Let Nadia work it out for herself. He's not her type. None of them are. Going by her inner dialogue, I think she's just starting to realise who is."

"Thank the angels for that. Ew, and not a minute too soon." Teagan pulled a face of repugnant distaste. "I think he's going to try to kiss her."

Almost as one they joined in the pained facial expression and shudder of horror as they watched the scene unfold.

"Why don't you step a little closer," the guy suggested to Nadia.

Nadia barely heard him over the thundering of her heart. "What? Oh. Sorry." She reached out to take his offered hand, trying to disguise the trembling that seemed to have migrated throughout her entire body.

His strong hand, cupped the back of her neck, drawing her flush against his body. Slowly he leaned in closer, his puckered lips heading toward hers.

Nadia's breath caught in her chest as she stared up into his glassy eyes. This didn't feel right. *He* didn't feel right.

What was his name again? She couldn't remember.

Had she even asked him his name? She couldn't remember.

Despite this guy being the third one she'd danced with, the first two had been seriously hunky, and this one was, well, cute-ish, her mind was still fixated on Philippe.

Dammit.

Even now as this guy, whatever the hell his name was, Mo, Larry, Curly. He could have been Godzilla for all she cared, was about to put his tongue down her throat, all she wanted to do was vomit on him. Really sexy.

Although, that could also be because of the six tequila shots she'd consumed.

Who would she choose? The guy with the fine arse? Maybe shit-for-brains with the big schlong, as he'd heard others refer to the arsehole? Wouldn't that be just dandy, those two bumping fuzzies every day. The loser leaned closer as if moving nearer would somehow make his slurred words clearer, like a Google translator set to stupid, and all Philippe could do was watch on as they did the bump and grind across the dance floor.

Philippe rubbed his temples and closed his eyes, trying to wipe that picture from his mind, a tight knot in his stomach forming. It hurt to watch her with those other guys.

Too many times to keep track of, he had to talk himself down from breaking the neck of every fucker who had a dick in the place, who so much as looked at her.

From the corner of his eye, Philippe saw the approach of a familiar figure and debated whether to ignore him.

"You're a fucking idiot." Alex slapped Philippe in the back of the head.

"What the hell did you do that for?" he demanded irritably. Clearly, ignoring him was not going to be an option.

"Mosquito."

"Inside a nightclub in late Autumn?"

"It's a proverbial mozzie. That's your woman over there dirty dancing with another guy. Just sayin'," Alex told him, smacking him over the head again. It did nothing to help Philippe's already foul mood, but it seemed to make Alex happy.

"She's not *my* woman," he growled, baring one of his extended fangs in a snarl.

"Only because you haven't told her how you feel."

"And now is a good time? While she's lip locked with that guy?"

"Would you prefer to interrupt them when she's locked at the hips with him?" Alex asked, adding a thrusting hip gesture to emphasise his point.

Philippe glared at the guy who had Nadia in his arms. His fists clenched so tight, his whole body began to shake. Someone bumped into him, but he didn't budge an inch. He barely even noticed.

"Watch it arsehole." The drunk turned to glare up at Philippe, who didn't even look at the guy, but he did growl. A deep predatory sound, chilling enough to curdle the blood in the guy's veins. It was the only warning the fucker was going to get. Obviously, he got the message, practically running over the girl who was next to him.

Alex turned his head to watch the couple flee. "Dude, I really like this new you, it's really edgy," he said, slapping him again. This time on the shoulder.

"Fuck off Alex." Philippe snarled.

"Just trying to help bro. Your girl is right there in front of you. If you don't make a move soon, lover boy over there will."

"She's not my girl. We're just friends."

"If that's what you want to believe, I don't know what to tell you, Philippe. If you need a commiserating hug or something, I can probably pay someone to give you one." Alex told him as he turned to walk away.

He hated to admit it, but Alex was right. If he didn't manage to let her know how he felt, he might as well just let her walk right out of his life. *Yeah, no problem.* And while he was at it, he should just barbeque his heart too.

From across the room, Dray watched Shani re-enter the club with her phone in her hand. Everything about her read *nervous and fragile,* but he doubted it had anything to do with the fact that she was in a vampire's nightclub.

Dark circles hemmed her eyes, and she held her arms around her middle as if she was trying to hold herself together, the woman was clearly exhausted. She acted as though she was about to file a restraining order against her own shadow.

Maybe it was because of her long trip from India, or maybe it was because of that conversation she just had with her husband outside. Did she miss him already? Was he angry that they'd altered her living arrangements?

Dray didn't know. Not that he was planning on asking too many questions. The least possible he knew about her personal life the better. That's not to say he wasn't interested. The problem was, he was too interested. How could he not be, she was beautiful, in that earthy, natural, *the only makeup I wear is Chap Stick* kind of way. Her slim frame had luscious curves in all the right places, and her large, almond-shaped dark brown eyes held the softness and compassion of innocence. Just how he imagined his ideal woman to be. She was also smart, funny and thoughtful. Everything he admired.

His mind flipped back to their handshake.

That spark of electricity between them when they'd touched was a warning sign. How could it not be. It was nature's way of telling him that the chemistry between them was potent. Far too potent for him to safely spend more than the shortest amount of time in her presence, unless he planned on complicating both their lives.

That wasn't an option. He had enough on his plate already. Adding a woman into his time consuming mix of responsibilities, any woman, would be a complication, but a married one...? He let that thought linger in his mind.

Nope, he couldn't do that. He wouldn't do that.

Dray watched Shani take a seat beside her cousin on the plush sofa on the far side of the room.

For the first time ever, Dray felt a twinge of self-doubt that his steadfast, implacable will wasn't strong enough to keep his relationship with Shani on a purely business level. Even now, every cell in his body tingled with the need to be nearer to her.

Holy Hell's balls. This was likely to be the longest few weeks of his life.

7

Philippe made a B-line for Nadia the moment she left the dance floor and headed for the plush lounge area.

"Nadia, I'm really sorry. I think we got off on the wrong foot. Can we start again? Hi. I missed you."

"What you're really trying to say is, you're a jerk and you ticked me off." She replied indignantly.

"Yes, and I'm sorry. I didn't do it intentionally, but I'm not sorry to see those stormy eyes of yours," he grinned sheepishly. *Those very sexy stormy eyes,* he wanted to add, but kept that thought to himself. He didn't think she'd appreciate his true feelings very much.

Nadia let out a frustrated huff, those stormy eyes of hers looking conflicted.

"Talk to me Nadia." Cupping her chin with the tips of his fingers, he applied gentle but insistent pressure, forcing her to look up at him. "What's going on in that pretty little head of yours? It's not just me being a jerk, is it?"

She shook her head a little, causing his hand to slide up along her cheek. It felt so much like a lover's caress that her breath caught, and her eyes drifted closed. Instinctively, she leaned closer into him, wanting nothing more than to lose herself in his touch.

"Nadia?" There was no mistaking the desire in his usually unflappable tone.

Her eyes fluttered open as he swept his thumb over her lower lip. She'd never wanted to be kissed so much in her life as she did right at that moment. His heated gaze bored into her, studied her.

She waited for him to close the small gap between them.

But he didn't.

Instead, he pulled his hand away as though it had been burned by a flame.

The slap of rejection had her mind spinning and her cheeks blushing from embarrassment.

"Is this fucker bothering you?" the guy from the dance floor asked, stupidly thinking in his inebriated state that since he'd danced with her, kissed her and bought her a drink, it entitled him to stake a claim on her. Then he made the biggest mistake of all. Sliding a hand about her waist he pulled her close, letting his hand glide down over her hip to grab a handful of her arse.

The world seemed to go into slow motion as the proverbial shit suddenly hit the fan.

Philippe's head snapped toward the guy who backed away quickly, although not quickly enough. Philippe stepped forward and gripped him by the throat, lifting him easily off his feet to dangle inches from the floor.

"Keep your filthy hands off her, you hear me. If I even see you so much as look at Nadia again, I will kill you," he warned, his voice deep and hard.

"Philippe, put him down. Now!" Nadia ordered. What the hell was wrong with him? His mood swings were giving her whiplash. One minute he's begging for her forgiveness and looking at her like she was the only woman in the world. The next he's pulling away like her touch was poisonous. Then, he threatens a guy who is genuinely interested in her?

Philippe ignored Nadia's plea. Likewise, he ignored the gathering crowd around him, his focus was firmly locked on the guy ensnared in his grip.

"As I see it, you can tell the dick splash to fuck off, or you can kill him. Dealers choice." Alex encouraged as he leaned in.

Philippe gave his advice attentive consideration. It was such a tempting option, just a minor flick of his wrist and the fucker would be history.

"You're not helping the situation, Alex." Teagan glared, about a second away from turning Alex into a toad or giving him major case of jock itch.

"This is your one and only warning. The next time I see you anywhere near Nadia I'm going to perform a manoeuvre I like to call the cranio-rectal inversion."

"The what?" the guy gasped, not too sure if he really wanted a translation.

"I'm going to shove your head up your arse. FYI...Your head may not be attached to your body when I do it." Philippe growled menacingly.

As soon as Philippe released his grip on the guy's throat, he scurried away like his pants were on fire, tripping clumsily as he turned back briefly to check if Philippe was following him.

"Bro, that was impressive. Cranio-rectal inversion? I love it. I'm going to use that line next time I face off with an arsehole."

"Alex, you think everyone is an arsehole." Teagan pointed out.

"True."

"And, you'd probably forget to warn the guy what you're planning to do, and just do it," Saladin added with a growl to his brother-in-law, ready to perform his own form of cranio-rectal manoeuvre on the hormonally challenged vampire, a.k.a. Philippe. He really didn't need the drama of another dead body in his club.

"True too. But wouldn't that be more fun than giving someone warning. You know, like hitting someone with a golf ball and then yelling, *Four!*?"

"Not really." Teagan shook her head in exaggerated dismay.

"Philippe. What the hell!?" Nadia yelled, her tone a verbal version of a theatrical emoji.

"Drama queen." Alex snorted out laughing.

Teagan's stink eye levelled on Alex, and he quickly shut up. He'd seen her glare at Saladin like that on more than one occasion. It was usually a moment before she implanted his feet through the floor or magically turned him deaf and blind.

"I've gotta tell you, I'm feeling pretty fucking unappreciated right now. I was just trying to help," Alex grumbled.

"Nobody needs your brand of help Alex." She growled.

"Come on honey, let's make use of some of your other talents, shall we?" Abby winked, leading Alex away.

"Ooh, you know the holding cells downstairs are empty at the moment." He suggested enthusiastically. "It would be a shame not to make use of the chains and handcuffs."

"You read my mind." Abby agreed.

"Come on hero. Let's go outside and get some fresh air." Nadia told Philippe, dragging him in the opposite direction toward the front doors. Philippe wouldn't have budged an inch, except that her hand had gripped the waistband of the front of his pants, shifting the gears in his brain from caveman to lusty caveman in an instant. With her fingers literally only a couple of inches from his rapidly hardening *dumb-handle*, he would have followed her anywhere.

Gustav followed stone faced, his eyes drilling a hole into the back of Philippe's head.

Stepping out into the cold night air had a sobering effect on Nadia. On one hand she was relieved to be rid of the lecherous sleaze bag, but on the other, she was more pissed off with Philippe than ever. After all, she'd only danced with the guy to prove to herself that she was capable of attracting other men, since Philippe didn't seem to want her. Unfortunately, all she really proved was that Philippe was the only one she wanted.

Pulling him aside, away from the crowd on the sidewalk, she mentally arranged a verbal smack down that would wither his balls to the size of peas by the time she'd finished with him, only to find her father standing right behind her.

"Nadia, sweetheart, let me have a word with Philippe….alone."

Nadia looked between the two men. Philippe's hot temper was no match for her father's seasoned ire.

"Nadia, go back inside please, I want to have a word with Philippe." Gustav repeated more firmly.

"Here's a news flash. So do I!"

"Nadia, don't argue with me." Her father told her. His hard tone left no room for compromise.

With an indignant huff, Nadia stamped her foot as she glared between them, turned on her heel and stomped her way back inside, muttering a string of curses under her breath all the way.

"Philippe, the best thing you can do is go home." Gustav told him firmly.

"I'm not leaving here without Nadia," he bit back angrily, standing toe to toe with Gustav.

"Son, you're not leaving here *with* Nadia. Do you understand?"

"I didn't mean it like that. I meant I'm not letting her leave with that guy."

"Let me make this very plain to you Philippe. I am not letting my daughter leave with *anyone* with a barred-up middle wicket." To make his point, Gustav locked his eyes with Philippe's volatile glare, and his strong hand firmly gripped the bulge in Philippe's pants.

Philippe's rage shifted to shock at having his family jewels clutched, then to embarrassment as he realised that the father of the woman he had just been fighting over, understood all too well the current state of arousal she induced in him. Putting his hands up in the air in surrender, he backed away as Gustav's grip released.

"Fine. I'm leaving."

"Don't think I won't kick your arse if I have to, Philippe." Gustav warned.

"Whatever. I'm outta here." Philippe walked to the end of the strip of shops and then disappeared in a flash of speed.

"Do you think he'll go home?" Gustav asked Hawke, who'd left his post at the front doors to stand a little closer…Just in case Philippe lost his shit. Again.

"Hell no. He's just taken up position across the road on top of that building." Hawke covertly pointed to the location with the tilt of his head.

Gustav gave a humourless chuckle. "Shit. I've got five daughters. They're going to be the death of me before they're all married off."

Hawke slapped him on the shoulder in commiseration. "I think you deserve a medal."

Shani watched in fascination at Philippe's testosterone fuelled display of over protectiveness and jealousy toward Nadia. She wondered

how that would feel, having a man care about her so much that he was willing to make a jerk of himself in public. Her eyes flashed toward Dray who stood nearby watching the whole scene, when his eyes met hers.

His intense dark eyes bore into her with a raw savagery she'd never seen before. It should have frightened her, but it didn't. Shani's breath hitched in her chest from the shiver of delight rushing through her. Secretly she wished it was her that had Dray looking so enticingly hot with sexual tension, and wasn't that just sad and a little needy. Her reality was never going to include the kind of passion she saw displayed between all these couples...not when she belonged to Saadir. He didn't have a single romantic bone in his entire body.

"Is it always like this in here?" Yasmin asked Teagan.

"Sometimes." Teagan shrugged before turning to face her, curiosity burning in Yasmin's eyes. "You don't seem fazed by all this drama. Why?"

This time Yasmin shrugged. "I'm a school teacher. To me this feels like an average day in a classroom filled with seven year olds. Organised chaos," she replied.

Hmmm, interesting, Teagan thought.

"I hear you like coffee." Yasmin said.

"Only with my oxygen." Teagan laughed.

"Oh, here comes Nadia." Shani pointed out. "That has to be the shortest argument in history."

"I don't think she got a word in." Teagan replied, noting Nadia's furious expression, and the fact that her father wasn't anywhere to be seen. Nadia wove her way through the throng of people, trying to ignore the multitude of eyes from interested onlookers, which followed her across the room.

"I'm sorry about that. I've never seen Philippe go off like that before, I don't know what got into him." Nadia told them, not sure whether she should be impressed by his outburst of caveman behaviour, or worried by it.

"Are you sure the two of you are *just friends*? Think about it. Would he be so upset by you being with another guy if he wanted to stay in the friend zone?" Shani asked, looking to Teagan for backup. However, Teagan only pursed her lips and raised her eyebrows, not wanting to get drawn into a discussion that could very well end with her having to confess her own part in the events leading up to the outburst.

"I don't know. Maybe not. I'm not sure. I've never had anyone fight over me before, and I'm not sure if Philippe has a grip of his new body and hormones yet." Nadia was more confused than ever after processing his behaviour logically. She wanted to believe Shani was right, but she didn't dare hope it was true. Her luck with men usually ended with only one outcome. Heartbreak. And, she'd seen nothing to suggest that her feelings for Philippe, or his for her, if he actually had any, would end any differently this time.

"Shani, can I ask you a personal question?"

"Sure. What do you want to know?"

"What's it like being married. Is it everything you expected?"

Shani's gaze seemed to cloud over as her thoughts sifted through her memories. "I didn't really have any preconceived idea of what marriage would be like. I was married when I was nineteen."

"Really? Nineteen? And your parents let you?"

Shani's chuckle was as flat as her eyes. "I had no choice. My parents arranged the match. I never met Saadir until our wedding."

"Seriously? I didn't think arranged marriages were practiced anymore."

"Oh, the custom is still practiced quite often in some regions of India, especially amongst the more traditional and influential families like mine. If I'd been offered a choice, I wouldn't have married so young." *Or married Saadir*, she finished the statement silently to herself.

"Wow. I'm sorry. But if you didn't love your husband in the beginning, do you love him now?"

"I am content with my situation. I have learned to live with the hand fate has dealt me." Shani answered with a casual smile.

Dray stood stoically in a nearby corner eavesdropping on their conversation. Even though he told himself to keep his distance from Shani, somehow he still found himself edging closer and closer toward her. Now he was seriously regretting his lack of conviction.

Had he continued to believe her to be happily married, it would have made it much easier to keep his distance. Hearing her confess she was in a loveless marriage....His mind began conjuring thoughts of luring her away, of offering her pleasures unlike anything her husband could ever give her.

God dammit! Unhappily married is still married!

"I'm taking a break." Dray snarled as he passed by Saladin on his way toward the front doors. Dray's idea of 'taking a break' was relieving someone else of their duties, so they could take a break. In this case, it was Hawke and Anna working crowd control of the exceptionally long cue of wannabe patrons on the sidewalk.

As the girls continued to chat, Shani's phone rang once again and her mood plummeted.

"I have to take this. Sorry. I'll be right back."

"Her husband again?" Nadia asked, her brow creasing in concern.

"Probably." Yasmin nodded.

Not wanting to appear like she was prying, Nadia diverted her attention towards her sister. "Teagan, I'm glad you're here, I was going to ask if I could stay at your place for a few days." Nadia quickly outlined her 'face plant' incident in the manor's lounge room.

"Sure. I already figured you'd ask. Cassie called me this afternoon and told me what happened. The girls put your bags in the car and Saladin has already had them moved to the house with Shani's stuff."

"Thanks sis, you're the best." Nadia gave her a hug of appreciation. "I promise I won't stay for long, just until I can figure out how to get around this problem of not seeing synthetics. There are fewer hazards to trip over at your place than there are at the manor."

"I know. Since you're staying, why don't we see if we can find something in the Book of Shadows that might be able to help you," Teagan suggested, referring to their family's druid magical spell book.

"You have no idea how great that would be."

While the sisters talked, Yasmin's attention veered off toward the front doors where Shani had disappeared. Two calls in just over an hour. She wasn't sure whether to interpret that as being a good or a bad sign where Saadir was concerned.

Shani rushed past Dray at the front door as she answered the call.

"What?!" Dray was so surprised that she shouted, he glanced over at her quizzically. Shani managed a harried smile, pointing at the phone and shrugging elaborately. *Great, now he thinks I'm a crazed mime,* she thought.

"Saadir, I'm sorry, I didn't mean to yell at you, it's very loud inside and I've been yelling all night...Yes, I know. I'm sorry....Okay...No...I said I'm sorry."

Dray listened intently to Shani's half of the conversation, not sure if he was grateful that she was just out of eavesdropping distance to hear her husband's end of the conversation. Regardless, what he heard concerned him.

"I explained that before," Shani replied. "Teagan insisted that I stay with her and her husband Saladin while I'm working with them, because of the odd hours I'll probably have to work.....No, I only deal with Teagan, nobody else.....Yes of course, Teagan is the one I've been dealing with for the past year, she's the one who arranged for me to come here and she's the only one I am working with...You've done what? ...No I can't explain why you can't find any record of Saladin, maybe his companies and home are under another name. I don't know, Saadir." *Or, maybe you're just researching documents eight centuries too late,* she thought smugly to herself. "I can't tell you how someone else runs their life....I'm sorry I can't hear you properly, you're breaking up....What? I can't hear..."

Shani pressed disconnect on her phone with a smug smile. It felt really good to be out of reach of her controlling husband. Maybe not entirely, she looked about the crowded street outside the club. It was highly possible that Saadir already had at least one of his 'paid help', watching her. Well, good luck to him once she's staying at Teagan's house, no one can find the place unless specifically invited. It is protected by a concealment spell.

Shani started back toward the entrance of the club feeling a little lighter than she had all night. Saadir was a burden her shoulders were happy to be free of, even if it was only temporary.

"Shani, can I have a word for a moment?" The serious tone in Dray's deep voice cut through her self-congratulatory moment.

"Yes Dray?" she answered with a congenial smile.

Dray studied her face intently. A fine layer of perspiration from stress peppered her forehead. Her walls of self-protection quickly fell back into place he noticed, her exterior appearing calm even though he could hear her heart race beneath her ribs, and could scent a slight hint of fear on her skin.

"Why did you lie to your husband just now?"

"How do you know I was talking to my husband?"

Dray's minimalist use of words didn't mean he didn't answer her question. His pursed lips, lopsided raised brow and condescending look in his eye spoke a thousand words.

"Right, I forgot. The whole *not human* thing is going to take some getting used to," she said whispering the *not human* part behind her hand.

Dray almost smiled at her attempt at being subtle. It was virtually childlike with her wide eyes and blushing cheeks and her *hand caught in the cookie jar* expression on her face…except much sexier. It was the sexier part that kept his own countenance sternly fixed. It took all his will power to keep his fangs from descending. It wouldn't be seen in a very prodigious light for the head of security to *come out* in public as a vampire with a fangy version of a hard-on, now would it.

"I'm sorry. It's complicated. Saadir is a lot like Philippe is with Nadia, over-protective and jealous. I haven't told him about you being my boss because he…he would have insisted I have a chaperone and I didn't think you'd want anyone else knowing about who you all really are, so I made the decision to keep it from him."

What she told Dray was true. She just failed to mention the other reason why she hadn't told Saadir about Dray, and it had nothing to do with the attraction she felt toward him. She'd been dealing with Dray for a year, however it had only been tonight when they'd finally met face to face, that she'd felt that spark of attraction. No, her reason was much more basic. Keeping Dray a secret from Saadir made her feel like she had some control over her own life, something that he couldn't touch, something that was hers alone. How pathetic was that.

The fact that her new boss not only happened to be male but also a vampire, and she is now dealing with a whole community of supernatural beings was a secret she would take to her grave. Right under Saadir's nose she had managed to find herself involved in a whole other life that he could never be a part of. And as far as Shani was concerned, that was a wonderful thing.

For the first time since she was a small girl she felt like she could be herself, amongst these people who also kept their true selves hidden from the world.

"He's upset by your living arrangements. If you'd like I can call him....or I can ask Teagan to call him to smooth things over for you," he offered.

"You'd do that?" she asked. Her astonishment was genuine, which surprised Dray. For a woman from a wealthy family in India, he would have thought that getting others to do things for her was second nature. No doubt her household held several servants. It seemed there was a lot more about this woman he didn't know yet. Scratch the *yet* part, he reprimanded himself. It wasn't wise to delve into her personal life. He probably knew too much already. With every new snippet of information he learned about her, the more his primal instincts drew him closer to her. He couldn't let that happen. He had to keep his distance.

"It's the least I can do. Would I be right in assuming that your clairvoyance works much better when you're stress free?"

"Yes, it certainly helps."

"Well, we'll make every effort to make sure your stay with us is as comfortable and as pleasant as possible. You should go back inside, it's cold out here tonight."

Shani smiled and nodded. "Yes, Yasmin will be wondering where I got to. Thank you."

As Shani walked back inside, Dray's gaze angled toward the roof top of the building across the road. Pulling out his phone he sent Philippe a message.

Bathed in the light of the full moon, Philippe listened to the activities outside the club across from him.

Gargoyle duty he used to call it. Perching upon rooftops to eavesdrop and observe whatever happened beneath him. Once, long ago, he could pass himself off as a chimney sweep or one of the many homeless urchins who scurried about the city over the seemingly endless roadway of rooftops. But times had changed. Buildings had become taller, chimney sweeps were only found in history books, and the homeless kids now frequented the subway systems instead of alleyways.

Philippe sighed. For so many years the only thing that hadn't changed was him. At one hundred and sixty-six years old, he'd spent so many years trapped in the body of a thirteen year old boy, his brain couldn't adjust to the sudden change to adulthood. Gone were the days when his small, unassuming stature could just blend into a crowd and disappear. That ability had made him a good spy. No, correction. It had made him a great spy.

Now, he had the adult body he'd always dreamt of, but he'd lost his identity, his sense of self. He didn't recognise the person staring back at him in the mirror, nor did he understand the gambit of foreign emotions and new social situations he had to face. Philippe had watched everyone else living those experiences he could only wish for, and he'd wondered why, at times, they seemed to struggle over the choices they had to make. Seeing their situations from an observers perspective he thought he had all the answers. However, as he was discovering, watching and experiencing were two very different things.

Philippe glanced around. Aside from the line of old oak trees that towered over him along the sidewalk, his only companions were the roof shingles beneath his feet, the solar panels that reflected the moon like a tranquil pond, and a pair of rats scurrying through the alleyway behind him.

What the hell was he doing here?

Logically he knew he should have gone home like Gustav had told him to. But, his need to see Nadia leave without her horny escort was a much more compelling force in his decision making process, and no amount of debating the matter was going to make him budge so much as an inch from his current position.

Nadia was the one constant in his life, so he'd thought. But he was wrong on even that score. Sure, he was still in love with her, that remained the same. But before his love was pure, innocent. Now, with adulthood came hormonally driven emotions so intense he wasn't sure he'd survive it. Jealousy topped that list.

He'd been so close to kissing her earlier, he'd wanted to so badly. But then he saw that fuckwit she'd been dancing with honing in on her. And when he grabbed her arse...he just lost it. Not his finest moment.

Now he was alone on a rooftop conjuring images in his mind of Nadia getting cosy with another guy. He had to wonder if his foolish behaviour had damaged his chances with her, not just as his friend, but also as his *mate*.

Mate? He let that thought siphon through to the deeper levels of his being. It felt right. Nadia was his one true *mate*.

And he'd behaved like a right git.

Whether he had damaged his chances with her or not, the knowledge of her true importance to him was the best incentive he was ever going to get, if he had any hope of getting a grip on his numerous delinquent issues and prove himself to her.

For the first time that night, Philippe had a positive outlook on his new life.

A moment later his phone buzzed with a message from Dray.

The message read: *"Bringing Shani through your apartment tomorrow to go through Nicholas' things. Be there at 3pm."*

"Shit," he groaned. He really didn't want a reminder of his psychopathic brother. It really put a downer on his positive moment.

He couldn't help wondering what Nicholas was up to at this very moment. Was he holed up somewhere and lying low, or was he scoping out his next victim. Maybe he was plotting some sort of vengeful retaliation?

Time would tell. Of that Philippe was certain.

The sooner they found him the better.

8

"I can't wait to put my new ring and talents to good use." Nicholas stated distractedly, watching the bus pull up out the front of the building they were staying in.

"Not until you've got a proper handle on both."

"Mmmm," was the only response Nicholas could muster, as he leaned toward the window more intently.

Scorpion peered over Nicholas' shoulder and widened the venetian blind slats marginally, peering out at the object capturing Nicholas' attention.

And there she was, the one he'd been waiting for. The one he'd been watching for the past week.

A homely looking young woman with shoulder-length, brunette hair and copper highlights, boarded the bus. She had a pert little nose and high cheek bones to go with her full, rosy red lips and almond shaped eyes. She wasn't the type of female Scorpion found intriguing, regardless, he found himself staring at her all the same. Her pale blue nurses uniform sat at a conservative length above her knee, her opaque stockings and flat white shoes taking nothing away from her shapely legs.

Scorpion watched with Nicholas as the woman shuffled her way down the aisle of the bus to take her seat by the window. Her plump rounded breasts jiggled as she dropped heavily into her seat as the bus jerked forward, coming to an abrupt halt once more to allow a late comer to board.

"I want…" Nicholas began, but was silenced by a wave of Scorpion's hand.

"I know what you want and the answer is no. This is not the time to take chances." His voice held a hard edge to it, which only served to prickle Nicholas' already overtaxed nerves.

He had been practicing becoming invisible using the Ring of Gyges, and honing his control on his upgraded speed and strength with barely a break over the past week, and he was exhausted. What he really needed was a distraction. A very soft, welcoming distraction. At the very least he needed some sort of compensation for being cooped up in this rat hole Scorpion called a 'safe house'.

"Please. I've done everything you've asked of me. I need to blow off some steam."

"I'm sure you can find something else to do." He answered dismissively.

"I could always play that Rammstein CD again." Nicholas suggested smugly.

"Please don't, that noise will make me want to shoot you. Do you feel like having a cranial leak tonight?"

Nicholas quickly pushed the heavy metal CD to the far side of the coffee table beside him. Scorpion only stood five feet, six inches tall, but his disapproving glare and knife-thin smile was still imposing enough to hold even Nicholas in check.

"You know there was a time when I was as impulsive as you." Scorpion's hard faced, bird-like features softened a little, watching the bus close its doors. "I have wizened through many years of experience that the perfect predator picks his prey and his timing very carefully. My own reckless behaviour has nearly gotten me caught many times by Alaric and his progeny Saladin, and others like them who hunt down and kill rogue vampires."

Nicholas wondered just exactly how many years that might be, but Scorpion wasn't big on sharing personal details from his past. The best Nicholas could guess, the elder vampire was at least a thousand years old, maybe more.

"What about wasting a perfect opportunity, or fun? I know the risks and I've been around a few years myself. I know how to cover my tracks and stay under the radar." Nicholas asked.

Scorpion might as well have been trying to communicate to a deaf man in Morse code or a blind man with visual prompt cards, for all the impact he was making on getting through to Nicholas. He was determined to have that woman no matter what.

Not that Scorpion really cared one way or the other whether Nicholas used her for his amusement. But he wasn't willing to let anyone, not even his favourite progeny, compromise their position. Not when they were currently so vulnerable.

The last thing they needed was for the Alliance to find them now while their escape routes were dramatically reduced, since Morganna had temporarily taken back her teleportation amulet in her pursuit of the Thunderstone. A stone so powerful it had created the dimensional barrier between Earth and Fey. It had also created the seal around the Valley of Vardin in Fey, which held the rogue nephilim known as rephaim, imprisoned. The same valley which had also held Morganna captive for almost fifteen centuries.

It was his thought of Morganna which had him rethink his decision on Nicholas' indulgent request. As cold-hearted as the sorceress was at times, much like himself, she had never denied him his opportunity to explore his carnal delights. That was probably why he loved her.

"You know Nicholas, your passion is your greatest strength. So too, will it be your biggest obstacle if you don't learn to control your appetite."

"I have done nothing but control my appetite since you turned me one hundred and fifty years ago. You made me a vampire in the hope I would go out into the world and wreak havoc." His voice was a little louder than he obviously intended. He took a deep, calming breath and dialled back on the decibels. "What's changed?"

Scorpion's mouth tilted up into a contemptuous smile. "Nothing. But right now, with the Guild's resources compromised and the Alliance using every available means to track us down, we can't afford to screw up our cover." His thoughts shifted from Nicholas to the woman on the bus. "I guess though, as long as you're extra careful I can't see why you can't have some fun."

Nicholas watched the woman with calm anticipation as the bus pulled away from the curb, knowing that in a little over eight hours she would return on another bus. A sense of longing intensified inside him from the knowledge that his craving was only hours away from being sated, and his mood lifted at the prospect.

Her destiny was carved out as finally as her heart would soon be.

He loved this part, immersing himself in the hunting and luring of the perfect woman. His prey. It was such a turn on.

Nicholas lingered by the window as the bus disappeared with the woman onboard. Absently he unzipped his pants and palmed his hard length.

Only a few more hours and she would be his.

His mind wandered, gravitating toward his plan. He would lure her away with his relaxed and easy smile to somewhere secluded, feed from her and fill her with his vampire hormone, stripping her of her inhibitions. Before long her need for sex would be as desperate as his own. And he wouldn't disappoint. He would give her as much pleasure with his body as he would *take* from hers.

Only when it was too late would she realise her error in judgement. That his charming smile and charismatic manner veiled his true violent nature and burning compulsion for depraved defilement and death.

To feel her tremble in his arms, first from the rapture of sex and then from fear. The ecstasy of filling her with his body's seed as he sank his cock as deeply inside her as he did his blade, had him stroking his hardened length a little harder in anticipation. There was nothing like the feeling of an impending orgasm, he thought, except maybe the screams and futile struggles of his prey.

The harder she struggled, the more glorious his triumph.

It was a familiar routine, and he was unapologetic about his need to fulfil his hedonistic desires.

Listening to his victim's sobs and whines for mercy as they turned to wails of unbearable pain. It was music to his ears. As was the death rattle of gurgling sounds in their blood filled lungs as it faded out to silence.

It was almost as good as watching the light in their eyes go out, leaving an eternal mask of fear etched into their face. It was his ultimate high.

Sadly, he couldn't make the process last forever, but keeping trophies from each of his victims certainly helped keep the moment alive. Merely viewing and handling his souvenirs brought a rush of remembered pleasure. However, it was a double-edged sword, the rapture of remembrance also brought with it a renewal to find a new victim, to turn fantasy into reality once again as his insatiable hunger grew and intensified.

For many years he had needed to suppress his cravings because of his interfering younger brother who'd watched his every move. For one hundred and fifty years Philippe chaperoned his every sexual encounter out of fear that he would lose control of the tight leash he held on his inner sociopath, returning to filleting the females he fed on. Well, not anymore, he thought with resentment. And soon, Philippe would become just another stain on his memory.

Killing his brother could very well go down as his greatest triumph. Sadly, since Philippe was a vampire and would turn to dust at his death, Nicholas would not be able to collect his ears or fingers to keep in his trophy tin. It was a disappointment, but one he could live with.

Nicholas pumped his fist around his cock faster, giving it a little twist over the head as he went until he reached maximal tension. His butt cheeks sucked together as his balls drew up tight and his abdominal muscles bunched and rippled under his skin. A growl rumbled through his chest as he stroked himself feverishly, erupting into a roar of carnal delight as his seed jetted from its tip.

Oh yeah, eight more hours and it was going to be party time.

The beat of the music remained constant, but her dance partners did not. One minute she was dancing with one guy, the next it was someone else and then another. They all seemed to blend together into a collage of wandering hands and gyrating hips with that eager look of sex gleaming in their eyes.

Then once again her dance partners changed. She couldn't see his face as he came up behind her, pressing the length of his body hard up against hers as he wrapped an arm about her waist. A thick thigh pressed between her legs swaying her body with his to the beat of the music.

The strength and confidence in his movements so deliciously seductive, Nadia melted into him almost immediately.

As they danced the world around them vanished. It was just the two of them moving to the beat of the music, their bodies swaying in effortless unison. While she couldn't see who it was she was dancing with, who it was that was making every nerve ending and cell in her body feel so alive, she was more than happy to stay there wrapped in his arms.

Spinning her in his arms to face him, he kept his face tucked into the crook of her neck, buried in the flowing folds of her hair. Who was he, she wondered absently. That question might have bothered her more if she didn't feel so much at ease with him, and if this new dance position didn't give her more scope to explore the contours of her latest dance partner.

The strong thick muscles of his long arms flexed, moving beneath her fingers as she gripped his biceps. Her hands explored the contours of his broad chest and the flat of his stomach to where it tapered at the waistband of his jeans.

His hands traced every vertebra of her spine with his fingertips, sending a shiver of delight throughout her whole body while his lips caressed the crook of her neck, tracing a path along the pulse at her neck to nibble her earlobe. His teeth nipped at her jaw as he kissed a path toward her lips.

All the while they danced.

He pulled her close against his body, crushing his mouth against hers, and she instantly responded, threading her fingers through the silky mass of blonde hair.

Kissing her harder, the urgency of his need leaving her gasping for breath. Kissing her again, increasing his efforts, nipping and tasting the length of her neck until he reached the dip where her neck and shoulder met. With his hands gripping her backside, he pressed her hard against his groin and their bodies continued to sway and undulate with the music.

Nadia blew out a shaky breath as his hips rolled into her, the hard outline of his erection grinding against her belly through his jeans and a pleasant rush of warmth flooded her core.

Pulling back their eyes met.

For a moment her heart stopped. Disbelief and relief scrambling for supremacy as she stared up at the man who held her so intimately in his arms.

"It's you."

"It will always be me." Philippe told her.

Nadia moaned as his lips slid over her jaw, kissing a path to her mouth once again, their hips locked cohesively in synergistic movement.

Pleasure coursed through her like a drug. His tongue stroked over hers, tangled with it as they fought for dominance of the kiss. The resulting pleasure sent a wave of pure unadulterated heat flowing through her veins.

Her need became a wildfire out of control.

Philippe's strong hand gripped her thigh, lifting and hooking it over his hip. With purposeful movement he slid her intimately along the ridge of his lethal arousal as they danced.

"Oh, yeah," he whispered against her lips, nipping at them as she began to ride the length of his erection.

Nadia threw her head back, a fevered gasp escaping her control.

It was exhilarating. It was heaven. It was....

"Ouch!"

Nadia's bedroom door burst open as Teagan rushed in.

"Nadia, are you alright?"

"Um, yeah," she groaned as she rubbed the lump on the back of her head. "I guess I was dreaming."

Teagan gave Nadia a quick once over and chuckled. Her head and shoulders were on the floor, one leg was on the bed still caught in the sheets, while the other dangled in midair at an awkward angle, giving her the appearance of a marionette doll with bed head. "That was either a really good dream or a really bad dream."

"I haven't decided yet." Nadia grumbled miserably. And why did her mouth feel like it had a garden growing in it? Hmmm, could be because of all the tequila she'd devoured she thought, as the events of the night before started to slowly filter through her memory. Fortunately, most of it was a little blurry, certainly nowhere near as vivid as her dream had been. Nadia groaned again.

"Must have been some dream if you thrashed around enough to throw yourself out of bed. Sure you're okay?"

"Never better," Nadia smiled tightly, lifting her head up to examine her surroundings. Her stomach still fluttering uncontrollably as the last of her dream faded to become a foggy memory too. "Damn, it was *only* a dream, wasn't it?" she groaned, letting her head fall back with a loud thud on the floor and covered her face with her forearm. Whether she was trying to block out the sunlight or will herself back into her dream, she wasn't sure.

Nadia groaned again.

"You need an Aspirin?" Teagan asked as she untangled her leg from the sheets and helped her sit up.

"I don't think Aspirin will cure the kind of headache I've got."

"Ah, I see. So, I can assume this dream of yours involved someone of the opposite sex?"

"Maybe." Nadia mumbled.

"Is it someone I know?"

"Maybe," her tone filled with despondent gloom.

"I'm going to go out on a limb here, would I be right in assuming it involved Philippe?"

"How did you know?"

"Seriously? The sexual tension between the two of you last night was so obvious even a blind man could see it."

"You're wrong there. I'm blind, kinda, and I didn't see any sexual vibes coming my way from Philippe." Nadia countered.

"Bullshit. You're just afraid to believe it's true. Am I right?"

"No." Nadia answered sulkily.

"I am and you know it. And you're going to trip over that bottom lip if you pout any harder."

"I'm not sure I'm actually awake yet. I think I need an alcoholic buffer before I try to figure out what you're saying."

"You understand perfectly well what I'm saying, you just don't want to believe me. For some bizarre reason you have this false belief that you don't deserve to be loved. Every guy who you've ever gone out with, with the exception of Bryce, he was just an arsehole, you've managed to sabotage the date so you wouldn't have to see them again."

"That's not true."

"It is true. What's more I think I know why you did it."

Now Nadia was curious. She had pondered this question for the last few years, never coming up with a plausible explanation, maybe her sister saw something in her that she herself did not. "Okay, I'm listening."

"Look, you may or may not be ready to hear this, but Philippe has been in love with you for a long time. I think somewhere deep inside you've always known it, and I think that you're in love with him too. It just hasn't been possible for the two of you to get together until now. And because of your bond with Philippe, you subconsciously sabotaged any possibility that another man might fall for you just in case a miracle might happen and you could be with Philippe. Well guess what sis, that miracle has happened and now the two of you have your chance. If you want my advice, get over these false insecurities you've been holding onto and go after your man."

"What?" Nadia was flabbergasted. When she'd asked for Teagan's opinion, she expected her to tell her that she needed to buy a puppy or something. Wow, she hadn't expected any of that. To say she was in shock was an understatement. "Are you certain?"

"As certain as I am that Saladin is my *mate*. I'm willing to bet that Philippe is yours."

"Um, I don't know what to say....but I think you might be right," Nadia replied, a little surprised to hear the words come out of her own mouth.

"I know I am, and I'm sorry to say that the two of you may have actually gotten together last night if it wasn't for us."

"Us who? What are you talking about?"

"All of us, your sisters, Cassie, Abby, Megan and me. We kinda, sorta tried to help push things along, but it backfired on us. We thought you needed some help to realise you had feelings for Philippe, so we arranged for those girls to flirt with him to make you jealous."

Nadia glared at her oldest sister. "You arranged for Vanessa to flirt with him?"

"No way. Vanessa saw him as fresh meat and went in for the kill. But to his credit he managed to fob her off. He only had eyes for you all night." Teagan told her a little sheepishly.

"That's why the girls insisted on dressing me up last night, to make sure that Philippe noticed me?" Teagan nodded. "Well, I guess your plan wasn't a total disaster. I did get jealous and so did Philippe, if him nearly strangling that guy I'd been dancing with is considered jealousy."

"Yeah, I think that qualifies."

"So now what? If Philippe really is in love with me…"

"Oh, he definitely is."

Nadia let out a semi-frustrated huff. "If he's in love with me, do I wait for him to make the first move or should I?"

"I can't answer that question for you. Maybe give him a little time to adjust to being in his new skin and if you feel he's taking too much time, you make a move on him."

That was a plan she could live with. Maybe.

Teagan got to her feet and turned to leave, but before she did a wicked grin tipped her lips. "Yep, you're a goner. I give him a week before you're jumping his bones," she winked, shaking her head at Nadia's doe eyed stare.

"Shut up," she snapped tersely.

9

Philippe heard the footsteps heading towards his door long before he heard the knock, even above the sound of the battle scene from Star Wars IV blaring from his surround sound system.

After watching Nadia leave the nightclub with an entourage of her family at almost five o'clock that morning, Philippe finally relinquished his lookout post on the building opposite and returned home. His thoughts and feelings churned inside him leaving him feeling pissed off and anxious. So, he resorted to something that felt as familiar to him as breathing. A Star Wars movie marathon and a shit load of popcorn, potato chips and a gallon of soft drink to wash down all that sodium.

For the first time since his transformation, he felt like himself.

And then came that knock on the door and his return to reality.

Philippe checked the time on is phone. "Shit, three o'clock already," he groaned as he pried himself off the nest of cushions he had been lazing against on his lounge room floor.

His bare feet made no sound as he crossed the timber floor to open the door.

"Philippe, would you put some clothes on, there are ladies here." Dray growled.

Philippe looked down at himself and then over Dray's shoulder at the group of stern faced arrivals lined up behind him at his door. The only ladies he saw were Anna and Shani. Both were already spoken for, and he doubted neither would be offended by his appearance.

"What's the problem? I'm wearing pants." The same jeans he was wearing the night before.

"There are ladies present. Put on a shirt." Dray repeated, emphasising each word crisply.

"Can't do that. I don't have one."

"Where are your clothes?"

"The only clothes I own that fit me are at the manor and I haven't had a chance to do any shopping yet."

Dray snarled and leaned almost nose to nose with Philippe. "Then put the shirt on you wore last night."

"Can't do that either. It got caught in the garbage disposal." The shirt might have had some help getting *caught*. When Philippe got home, he realised the shirt was covered in Vanessa's cheap perfume, and it really pissed him off that it was the skanky vampire's scent covering him and not Nadia's. So, he shoved the shirt down the garbage disposal. He would have shredded it with his bare hands if he could reliably tear it into as many tiny pieces as the disposal did. "And I'm not putting on any of Nicholas' clothes either." Philippe growled back.

"Dray, buddy. Take a deep breath. It's not the end of the world." Saladin told him, firmly gripping Dray's shoulder to force him to back down. This aggressive, moody behaviour was out of character even for Dray, and it was beginning to worry him.

"Fine," griping testily, he pushed past Philippe through the doorway, effectively relocating him behind the door and out of sight. He was overreacting and he knew it, but he couldn't seem to stop himself. Normally he wouldn't give a flying fat rat's arse if there was a half-naked man walking around. But knowing that Shani was going to see Philippe's buff naked torso had tripped his irrational switch.

Despite his unreasonable behaviour, or maybe because of it, he recognised his poor conduct for what it was. Jealousy. Which only served to piss him off all the more.

It was absurd and illogical. He had no chance of making a claim on her, considering she was already married. Regardless, it was also the plain and simple truth. He had been struck with the jealousy stick, bitten by the green-eyed monster, and he was powerless to fight the tide of unexpected emotion that swamped him.

And right now he was about two seconds away from wanting to kill someone.

One by one everyone stepped inside Philippe's apartment.

"Gustav, glad you could come." Philippe greeted hesitantly from behind the door.

"Philippe," he replied.

Just in case Philippe didn't realise by the frosty tone of his voice that Gustav was still a little pissed off at him, his scowling glare certainly got the message across.

Philippe swallowed and tried to smile, but the combination made it seem more like a grimace.

"I didn't know what I expected a vampire bachelor pad would look like, but I didn't imagine this." Shani muttered to herself forgetting that everyone in the room could hear her as clearly as if she'd shouted.

"Shit. Sorry." Philippe quickly barged past the stragglers entering and threw the mess of cushions back onto the couch and picked up the multiple empty packets of salty comfort food littered about the floor.

"Bro, the lady's not commenting on your lack of housekeeping skills." Sebastian said, pointing a finger towards the items that covered the shelves and walls.

If Philippe's head exploded, then this room would be what came out. It was nerdvana Mecca, filled with superhero collectable dolls, comics, DVD's and various merchandise, worthy of making any respectable geek drool.

It was however, enough to cause brain seizures, a panic attack and a complete mental breakdown for any respectable woman. It was the female equivalent of a guy walking into a girl's room where everything was pink and floral and decked out with a thousand and one frilly cushions.

Seb began to laugh. "Is all this yours or did Nicholas have a fetish for sci-fi toys too?"

"They're not toys, they're collectables and they're very valuable. And no, none of this belongs to Nicholas. Since he was spending less and less time here over the last couple of years, I started to move a few of my things out into the living room."

"You mean you've got more of this stuff?" Hawke asked, not even trying to hold back his amusement.

"A bit." Philippe answered defensively. He couldn't help feeling that they wouldn't be giving him a hard time about his hobby if he was still in the body of a thirteen year old. Nor could he help feeling a little violated by the way they all thoroughly explored and *ridiculed* everything he owned. It was the last time he was inviting any of them over, he thought sulkily.

"Don't worry about them, they're just picking on you to make themselves feel better." Narayan told Philippe as he handed him a sweatshirt.

"What are you talking about?"

"It's easier for them to have a dig at you for still being in touch with your inner child, than it is for them to admit they've lost touch with their own. Ignore them."

"Easier said than done," he grumbled as he pulled on the shirt, letting out a heavy sigh. "It would be easier to do if they weren't so openly and *loudly* mocking me."

"Time, as they say, heals all wounds." Narayan told him with a smirk, giving Philippe a sideways shove with his shoulder.

"Wouldn't it be great if that were true. Some wounds run too deep though. Some indiscretions too heinous to be forgiven, they're like ink on parchment, indelible."

"I see the conversation has moved on from your dented pride to your all-consuming hatred of your brother. Be careful you don't become a slave to your need for vengeance. Remember, *an evil man may wish to injure the virtuous one and, raising his head, spit toward heaven, but the spit far from reaching heaven, will return and descend upon himself.*" He said, quoting one of his infamous Buddhist teachings. "Virtue cannot be destroyed whereas evil will inevitably destroy itself. Nicholas is driven by his pride and self-assurance that he is too fast and strong for us to stop him, but that pride will cause him to slip up, and when he does we'll be ready and waiting to take him down."

"I know you mean well with your advice, but I don't have time to wait for Nicholas to self-destruct. He's responsible for too many lives lost already, I can't let him take any more."

"I fully understand, which as you know, is why Shani has come all the way from India. To use her psychic abilities to locate him. It's also why we've all been training so hard over the last week. But if you let yourself become blinded by your need for revenge, you'll set yourself up for failure before you can get anywhere near him. Success and failure lies within your mind, not your heart. *Quiet minds cannot be perplexed or frightened, but go on in fortune and misfortune at their own private pace, like a clock during a thunderstorm.* You need to find that quiet space within yourself that is untouched by emotion. Only then can you defeat your brother. Now, explain to me what the hell this is." Narayan said, abruptly changing the subject by picking up a fidget spinner, and watched as Philippe's shoulders slumped in acceptance of his little pep talk.

Philippe watched as each person picked through everything in the apartment looking for clues as to Nicholas' whereabouts. It really did feel like a personal violation, watching them go through every drawer and cupboard, every book and DVD case. Everything was upended, opened or pulled apart. Although they did try to limit their search to Nicholas' things, his own possessions which were in the common areas like the bathroom, living room and kitchen were thoroughly scrutinised too. It really sucked to have to sit back and watch, but if they found anything at all that could help them track his brother, it was worth it.

All the while his eyes followed Shani as she slowly made her way from room to room, her eyes slightly unfocused as her hands touched everything. Most things her hands barely glided over, although the more personal possessions like Nicholas' toothbrush, hairbrush and even his underwear, she lingered much longer with, clutching them to her body in the hopes of getting a reading on him.

Dray followed behind Shani as silently as a ghost. That was of course, until she lingered with Nicholas' underwear held to her breast.

This wasn't even close to being the strangest job Shani had been asked to do, that title went to the owner of a jewellery store in Kanpur who accused an employee of stealing a very expensive jade bracelet. Shani told them a cow had taken it. They all laughed but when the cow pooped out the bracelet two days later a very happy employee got his job back. Fortunately for the cow it was considered a sacred animal in India, or it might have become the family's Sunday dinner. However, the cow was no longer allowed to wander through the shop.

This on the other hand, was the most stressful job she'd taken. It was much harder to locate a missing person than it was a lost possession, and the effort took more out of her than usual. However, that wasn't what was stressing her out. The man standing so closely behind her was the cause of her agitation.

Dray was enigmatic, dangerously handsome and completely off-limits. What was a girl to do when the only thing on her mind was not the job she had been employed to do, but the desire to lick the Adam's apple of the man who had hired her, especially when that same man regularly distracted her with a growling sound, vibrating from his throat at semi regular intervals.

"Would you please stop that, I can't concentrate," she chastised, clenching her thighs together to halt the flow of slick heat of arousal which his confounding growl set off, deep in her abdomen. The grunt she got in response was acknowledgement of her request but sadly not compliance. When she traded a pair of Nicholas' underpants for his pillow, Dray let another growl slip free. Not an openly aggressive grumble, but a dominant purr. What was worse she wondered, the deep rumble that vibrated directly to her core, or the light purr that sent a shiver up her spine. Either way she was getting nowhere fast with Dray hovering so close.

"You're really messing with my mojo here, could you maybe wait outside the room, or out on the street or something?" Out on the street would definitely be better.

"No."

Shani's head dropped forward in defeat. "Fine, but if you make one more sound, I'm going to shove these socks in your mouth. Got it?" she told him. Once again Dray grunted his response.

"Fine," she repeated, more to herself than to Dray, as she shook the tension from her arms and legs. She swivelled her head on her neck a couple of times and took a deep breath, clearing her mind to get in tune with the items she was touching.

One by one, Shani touched everything in the apartment. Anytime she touched something which belonged to Philippe she got a clear and instant reading on him. But nothing on Nicholas. Not even a vague hint of a mental picture of him. It was confounding and infuriating, and no matter how hard she concentrated she still came up blank.

Philippe wandered about his apartment like a stranger in his own home. Watching. Listening to all the conversations going on around him, stopping to chat briefly to each person... except Gustav. He made a point of giving the grumpy lycan a wide berth.

Marek stepped up beside Alaric and waited a moment before speaking, silently assessing his mood. "Alaric, I don't know how helpful this might be, but I've drawn a sketch of Scorpion. I know my art skills aren't going to win me the Archibald prize, but I think it's a close enough representation that hopefully you might remember him from somewhere."

Scorpion had proven to be quite masterful in avoiding being captured on camera in the past, and search as they may there didn't seem to be any photos of him in existence anywhere. He was like a ghost, you knew he was there, but you just couldn't see him. Although, just as any ghost had once been a physical being walking and talking in the physical world, so too Scorpion had once been a regular man before he'd become a Vampire.

"Why do you think I might remember him?" Alaric asked.

"He's already proven he has the ability to tolerate sunlight better than most vampires. He also has a great deal of strength and speed. Everything about him leads me to believe he's not just old, but that his blood comes from someone very close to the original vampire. You."

Alaric looked at the drawing. Scorpion did look vaguely familiar, he just couldn't determine why.

"If you think I have another progeny living besides Saladin, Narayan and Abby, you're wrong. There were others, many others in the early years, but they were killed either by their own stupidity or I killed them myself...for various reasons."

"Is it possible that maybe one of your early progeny turned Scorpion?"

"Clearly my progeny had no scruples when it came to making more of our kind, otherwise we wouldn't have so many vampires today."

"Obviously. But I was wondering if you might remember him as being someone hanging around with one of your previous progenies."

"It's possible. That was so long ago though. In the first two hundred years I must have made dozens of vampires, although, after that

I stopped. It was close to a thousand years before I met anyone else who I believed was truly worthy of the gift."

"Saladin."

"Yes."

"If that's the case, if one of your early progeny is responsible for Scorpion, he'd have to be almost as old as you."

"Maybe. Thanks for this, I'll go back through my records and see if there's anything in my notebooks that might jog my memory."

"You have records from way back then?" Marek's surprise was poorly concealed, tipping Alaric's mouth up into a lopsided grin.

"Of course. I was charged by the Elders to protect the Cup and the Spear…and to watch over my descendants. That took careful record keeping to monitor my family tree, and keep an eye on any likely threats from would-be thieves who wanted to get their hands on the powerful relics. As you well know." Alaric reminded the rephaim who had once been Morganna's second in command, and had been directly involved in one of her attempts at seizing the Cup.

Marek cleared his throat uncomfortably. "Yes, well. I hope there's something in your records that can help identify Scorpion."

"Hopefully. One thing I know for sure, he can't hide from us forever. Especially now that we know what he looks like." Alaric looked down at the sketch and gripped Marek's upper arm as he walked away, giving it a squeeze of reassurance that he didn't hold any grudges against Marek for his dubious past.

"Do you really trust the rephaim?" Donovan Eckhaus, the leader of the South African branch of the Alliance asked, bailing up Alaric as he passed by. The lycan clan leader had remained in Oxford after their meeting the night before. Whether out of personal curiosity or a desire to compare methods of operation to his own branch in South Africa, Alaric didn't know, and when he asked to tag along to Philippe's, he had agreed. Howbeit, the man was beginning to get on his nerves.

"I might not have once, but I do now," Alaric replied.

"I'm not sure that I can, given his history and all." Don said.

"If you don't trust Marek's virtue, then trust his self-preservation. He has no need to double-cross us on this." That, it appeared, was all that Alaric had to say on the matter as he stepped aside and continued on his way, leaving the man in his wake. However, it didn't appear that

Donovan Eckhaus was content doubting the integrity of only one of their members, turning his distrustful gaze toward Philippe.

Yet again, made to feel uncomfortable in his own home, Philippe moved about the apartment, keeping to himself.

"What's up with Gustav and Philippe, they've barely made eye contact or spoken a word to each other since we got here." Sebastian asked Hawke.

"I think Philippe is embarrassed and Gustav is pissed off."

"What for?"

"Because last night at the club there was an….incident."

"What kind of *incident*?" Seb asked.

"Put it this way. What would be the worst thing that could happen to a guy in front of the father of the girl you're in love with."

"You crack a stiffy?" Seb answered on a guess.

"Bingo." Hawke grinned.

"Oh fuck!" Seb's spluttering snort of surprise broke free of his control and became a belly aching roar of laughter, "Sorry. I tried to sound sincere but I ruined it, didn't I?"

"Kinda." Hawke snickered.

"You guys are arseholes, you know that?" Philippe grumbled as he walked by, his cheeks showing a little more colour than usual.

"Yeah, we know. But you'll have to forgive us if we're enjoying your puberty. It's the most fun we've had in ages." Seb laughed.

"Right, puberty is a barrel of laughs. I'm so glad I amuse you. Arseholes." Philippe grumbled.

Turning his back on them he marched into the kitchen, determined to put as much distance between himself and everyone else. Not an easy task when his apartment was the size of a shoe box. He managed to achieve a whole six feet of personal space for approximately thirty seconds before that too was invaded. Shani entered with Dray following close behind looking even more irritable than earlier, if that was possible. Although to be fair, right now Philippe felt like he could go toe to toe with the spy master despite the fact that he suffered a major case of petulant irascibility.

Not that it seemed he needed to confront the guy directly to piss him off, it seemed he'd achieved that just by having his phone ring in his presence.

Philippe checked the caller ID. It was Nadia. His thumb hovered over the screen, debating whether or not to answer. Dray's growl however, prompted him to let it go to his message bank. Philippe knew he had to talk to her soon about what had happened at the club the night before. No doubt she had a few choice words to say to him, but now was not the time. He neither had the privacy, nor he doubted he had the ability to talk to her in a calm and rational manner.

It seemed Narayan was right, *dammit!* He really needed to get a handle on his emotions.

Frustrated with himself and feeling extremely claustrophobic, Philippe left his apartment to sit on the top step of his porch, watching the traffic drive idly by.

Dray's eyes never left Shani for a second, not even when Philippe practically ran from the kitchen. How could he when the sight of her curvy legs and perfectly rounded backside in her tight-fitting leggings, swaying so seductively as she walked, had the pressure in inside his jeans reaching uncomfortable levels.

A gentle breeze blew through the open window, inflating the light lacy curtain over the sink as it advanced and swirled its way through the room, sending a fresh rush of Shani's fragrant scent directly into Dray's lungs. Oh, how it teased him. His mouth watered as his eyes drank in every lush curve of her petite form. Those pouting breasts with their rosebud tips, standing pertly to attention under his gaze beneath her figure hugging top. The soft, smooth contour of her slender neck....

It was a good thing thoughts weren't the same thing as actions, otherwise he would be tempted to do much more than just imagine her naked beneath him.

Dray bent closer, his breath teasing her ear, sending tendrils of delight snaking through her body, as he spoke quietly, "Did you get anything that might help us locate Nicholas?" he asked.

Shani shivered at his nearness and quickly moved away, planting her butt on the old vinyl stool by the kitchen bench, which she noted had about as much padding as a plank of wood.

"No. I'm sorry, I don't know what's wrong. This has never happened before." Shani told him despondently.

"Never?"

"No. I've always been able to get some sort of reading on a person or their lost possession, even if I can't locate them right away. But I've got nothing on Nicholas at all. I can't even picture him in my mind."

Dray's sharp mind sifted through the logical reasons. "I don't think it's your ability that's on the fritz, I think there's something else going on here. Don't worry about it right now though, we'll figure something out." Dray laid a hand on her shoulder, his fingers tangling in the long strands of her raven hair. Without any conscious input from his brain, he found himself stroking his fingers through the length of her hair. He couldn't help himself. Nor could he stop his fangs from descending when she moaned in response.

"What was the hardest thing for you to adjust to when you became a vampire?" she asked him dreamily, lost in the sensation of his strong hands gliding through her hair, but quickly backtracked to retract the question. "I'm sorry, I didn't mean to be so personal," she told him.

Shani had interpreted Dray's look of shock as being due to her impertinent question. That of course was an error, however, it wasn't one he was willing to correct. The last thing he wanted to do was confess his impersonation of a stunned mullet was a result of his realisation of just how little control he seemed to have on his body's response when he was around her.

"It's okay. I don't mind," he smiled. Strangely, he really didn't mind. In fact, he had a sudden urge to tell her every personal and intimate detail about himself.

This is bad, very, very bad. Run away as fast as you can, the tiny voice of logic whispered in the back of his mind.

Not that he was listening.

"There was nothing harrowing about my transition." He told her. *Except being staked out on the ground by his Sire for the sun to kill him.* "Life was pretty simple back then."

"What about when technology began to develop, you know, cars and computers. Was it hard to adapt?"

"No. Cars and planes made getting around a whole lot easier. Trains were already invented when I was human. And computers? I love computers," he grinned. "Although I did have some trouble getting used to the loud volume of stereos and the heavy metal modern music."

"And now you work in a nightclub," she pointed out, amused by the irony.

Dray laughed. A subtle chuckle that could have easily been mistaken for a purring growl. "Yeah. What about you, when did you realise you had the ability to find things?"

"I don't really know. I was probably about four or five. My mum was always losing things, she'd get flustered rushing around trying to find her purse, jewellery or her sunglasses and I'd always just *'know'* where they were. When my parents realised I was able to find *anything*, they made use of my ability. A few times they even tried to hire me out to people in exchange for business deals or invites to social functions where only the 'in-crowd' would be invited. That went on for a few years until I was about sixteen. I hated the way they used me to climb the social ladder. I wanted to be like all the other girls my age. I really am just a simple kind of girl at heart."

"You're definitely not simple." Dray told her.

Strangely, if anyone else had made that statement she probably would have been offended. But the way he said it, and the kind of man he was, smart, well-dressed, drop-dead gorgeous, it made her feel like she'd just been made Miss Universe, won the lottery and been offered a lifetime supply of cheesecake, all at the same time. Her chest puffed out, and she couldn't keep the smile off her face.

"Thank you. But other than my ability to find things, there's really nothing special about me. My parents limited my education so my prospects in life would also be limited. That meant they could control me for longer. At least, that's what they hoped."

"What happened?"

"I developed an attitude they didn't like. At first I became sulky, then when that didn't work, I became defiant. You have to understand that my family is very traditional. A woman obeys her husband or father, end of story. When they decided I was becoming too much of a handful to deal with, my father made another business deal. He arranged my marriage to Saadir who was ten years older than me and well-established in his own business. He also came from an influential family with the kind of connections that could make my father very rich."

"So, they sold you off?"

"Pretty much, yes."

At first Shani was happy with the arrangement. She couldn't wait to get away from her father's control. Unfortunately, it didn't take her long to realise she'd swapped one manipulative controller for another.

"Are you happy?" Dray asked, his intense gaze boring into her, assessing every nuance and twitch of her response for the truth.

"I am happy with who I am," she answered.

What he really wanted to know was whether she was happy in her marriage, but she'd expertly deflected away from the heart of his enquiry. He already knew she wasn't, that much was obvious, but he wanted to hear her say the words, openly and honestly. Why? Because he was a dumbass who wanted to torture himself with the hope that he could lure her away from her husband? Christ! He didn't just need his head read, he needed a fucking lobotomy.

Their conversation slipped into an awkward silence as Dray's mood took another downward spiral.

A few minutes later another phone rang. This time it was Shani's, but the low, guttural growl that rumbled from Dray's chest prompted her to let it go to voice mail.

"Um, I think I need to get some air for a few minutes."

Despite Dray's growl being unintentional, he couldn't deny he was pleased she hadn't taken that call. It had been her husband, Saadir. Again. The little snot rag was starting to piss him off.

Anna had been standing at the kitchen door and it didn't escape her notice how *not* taking that call seemed to cause Shani a great deal of agitation.

Anna followed her out to the porch. Shani's heart beat loud inside its cage, her breathing remaining even, if a little faster than usual, and her hands shook ever so slightly.

"Do you want to talk about it?"

"About what?" Shani asked innocently, twisting her hair into ringlets around her finger nervously.

"Whatever it is about those phone calls that make you scared."

"I don't know what you're talking about." Shani brushed aside the remark with a light chuckle, regardless, the well practiced response wasn't fooling Anna. Not one bit.

"You know, you should talk about it. Maybe not to me, but you need to confide in someone. I had a cat once, it licked the same spot endlessly until it licked away all the fur and the patch of skin beneath became raw. He kept up that behaviour until a vet diagnosed him with depression."

"You had a cat?"

Anna chuckled. "That's what you got out of my story?"

"I'm not depressed if that's what you want to know." Shani told her.

"Maybe not. But you're clearly dealing with something that's got you on edge. I'm not trying to pry into your life, but if you need someone to talk to, don't be afraid to reach out to someone."

"Thanks for the concern, but everything is fine."

"If you say so." Anna's understanding smile was almost enough to make Shani cry. She badly wanted to tell someone, even though she knew she shouldn't.

Besides, she did have someone to confide in, she had her cousin, Yasmin.

With the approach of footsteps, Shani quickly blinked away the building tears from her eyes, sucking in a deep breath before once again putting on her smiling mask.

"Shani, were you able to get a read off any of Nicholas' things?" Saladin asked, coming to stand in the doorway before her.

"The deceptive little parasite seems to have masked himself from us," Dray answered for her, stepping past his boss to stand beside her.

"Morganna?" Saladin asked. Dray nodded. "The bitch seems to weave her way into every evil situation, doesn't she?"

"How are we going to find them if they're cloaked?" Philippe protested, his impatience at finding his brother making his tone terser than he intended.

"I have a plan, but we'll need Alex's help." Dray told them.

"You know things don't usually go well when Alex is involved. So, what's the back-up plan?" Saladin smirked.

Dray's face became serious, his gaze watching Shani carefully.

"We need to follow Philippe's initial suggestion. I think we'll find Nicholas if we find where he's hiding his victim's trophies."

Shani's face paled as the implication of Dray's words sank in.

10

"Did you forget your keys again?" Teagan asked in the bored tone of admonishment, opening the door for Saladin....and a rather large group of Alliance members. "Oh, I didn't realise you were bringing back extra company."

Before she could protest, Saladin covered her mouth with his. The kiss was hot and demanding, leaving her no option but to cling to him as he stole her ability to breathe or think straight. Suddenly she couldn't remember what it was he was trying not to get her angry at him for.

Saladin knew he was making half the people on his front patio feel uncomfortable, but he didn't care because that's the kind of guy he was. He made people fucking uncomfortable. And, he enjoyed it.

"Yusuf Saladin, if I wasn't so light-headed right now, I'd be annoyed with you for not giving me a heads-up." Teagan rebuked when he pulled back from the panty melting kiss.

"I know," he grinned cheekily.

"Is everyone staying for dinner?" she asked. Behind Saladin was a muffled chorus of apprehensive mumbles and shuffling feet.

"Probably. Maybe. I guess that depends on what's for dinner," came the various replies.

"I'm making hamburgers."

There was a sigh of relief mixed with a few doubtful groans coming from the group. Teagan would have rolled her eyes in disgust, except they probably had valid reason to feel relieved she hadn't planned to cook anything more complicated. She wasn't the best cook in the world. She tried to hard-boil some eggs once which didn't end well. She forgot about them bubbling away on the stove until she heard a loud bang. The water had boiled dry and the hard boiled eggs exploded. There were lumps of egg stuck to every surface in her kitchen. It wasn't pretty. It seemed though that the majority of people were as confident as she was that she couldn't stuff up hamburgers. After all she only needed to cook a few meat patties and put some salad on the buns, right?

"Is there enough for everyone?" Saladin asked.

Teagan did a quick head count. "There will be." *With a bit of magical help.*

"Well, I for one am not afraid to eat your cooking." Gustav said as he separated Teagan from her husband's embrace, taking his place to give her a big hug and plant a kiss on her forehead.

"Thanks dad. I think." Teagan stated happily, her grin sliding into a half-hearted smile when she realised her father's remark was less of an endorsement for her culinary skills, as it was a statement of courage.

Whatever. If this lot wants to come into her house, they were going to eat whatever she served them. And love it!

"It could be worse, Cassie could be cooking for you." Alaric declared with a lamenting groan.

Alaric's declaration of his own wife's cooking seemed to be the only encouragement the group needed to upgrade Teagan's culinary skills to passable.

"Burgers. Sounds great to me." Narayan seconded.

"Mmm mmm. Love me a homemade burger." Oliver added, leaning close to Saladin's ear as he walked by. "Do you have anything for heartburn?"

"A cupboard full." Saladin affirmed with a sly, if slightly contrite grin under Teagan's glaring eye and disapproving scowl.

"Where's Philippe?" Teagan asked after another quick head check of people now filling her living room.

"He's back at his apartment with Hawke, Anna and Sebastian, cleaning up the mess." Saladin told her.

"How much mess did you make?"

"A bit." A bit more than a lot. What could he say, their search had been thorough. They managed to uncover a couple of hidden spiders, discovered a dead mouse and located a disturbing number of superhero odd socks, but nothing that would lead them to Nicholas.

"Ahh. Nadia will be disappointed he's not here. She's been trying to contact him all afternoon. We had a little chat earlier, and she's had an epiphany of sorts."

"You mean she's finally realised he's in love with her?"

Teagan nodded. "And she couldn't be happier about it," she winked.

"Really! This should be fun to watch." Saladin pulled his phone from his pocket, ready to order Philippe to drop everything and come over.

"No you don't. We've done enough interfering with those two." Teagan reprimanded.

"You might have, but I'm just getting started."

"No. Let them work things out themselves. Besides, I don't think we'll be seeing much of Nadia today, she's feeling a little under the weather from all the tequila last night."

"I'm not planning on ruining things between them, just make Philippe's journey through adolescence more interesting."

"What would be interesting would be seeing you go through puberty for a second time. If you want to interfere in my sister's love life, you might find yourself being the only eight hundred year old vampire with zits," she warned.

"You ruin all my fun."

"Not all, I'll let you have all the fun you want with me later."

"Is that a promise?"

"Yep." Teagan's sultry smile melted Saladin's heart, all that heated blood quickly pooling in his groin in anticipation.

Pulling his wife into his arms again, his extended fangs grazed along the length of her neck. Nipping and sucking on her earlobe, he deliberately nicked the soft flesh, sending a shudder of erotic delight through her body, his healing hormone infusing her veins to close the small wound almost instantly.

"You are in so much trouble later," she gasped.

"I love it when you get nasty," he purred. "But what's wrong with now, I don't want to wait until later."

"We have a house full of guests, honey."

"No problem. I asked them to come, I can tell them all to fuck off."

116

"What, after you promised them all some of my wonderful home cooking? Never! You'll just have to wait."

"This is payback for not warning you I was bringing a few extras home, isn't it?"

"You betcha."

"You're a cruel woman," he complained faux sulkily.

"I do try," she laughed. "What happened at Philippe's apartment, did Shani find anything that can help locate Nicholas?"

Saladin's low growl was all the answer she needed, regardless, he let out a string of choice curses about Nicholas anyway.

"Damn. That's disappointing. So, what do we do now?" Teagan asked.

"Dray has a plan." Teagan looked at her husband expecting an extension to that answer, but he only shrugged. In unison their eyes drifted across the room, Saladin's gaze landed on his head of security and his brow began to furrow with concern at what he spied. Teagan on the other hand, surveyed Shani. The petite woman looked weary, she thought.

"I'll get started on the burgers," she told Saladin. Not waiting for a derogatory reply, she turned her attention toward their female guest, looking out of place and very uncomfortable amongst all the powerful and overbearing men in the room. "Shani, I'm going to whip up some burgers, how are you at cooking?"

Shani grinned and made a B-line for Teagan. "Terrible, but I'm willing to give it a try," she replied.

Teagan's kitchen was ultra-modern. White cupboards, white benches, shiny stainless steel cook top and range hood and all the mod-con appliances you would wish for. Although, none of the expensive gadgets looked like they had ever been used, except of course the coffee machine.

Teagan quickly emptied packets of buns onto the bench and pulled salad, cheese and bacon from the fridge. Shani looked at the pile laid out. There was enough there of everything, except for the meat. She doubted six meat patties would feed more than two of the men in the next room.

"Do you have more burger meat?" Shani asked.

"I will have in a minute. I'll just whip some up."

Ha?

Shani was still contemplating what Teagan meant by that comment when she began reciting odd sounding words. To Shani, they sounded like a mix of Latin and an old form of English, although it could have been Bitalonian for all she knew.

When Teagan said she was going to *whip up* some more burgers, Shani thought she was speaking metaphorically, you know, pull some more meat patties from the freezer and defrost them in the microwave. She never imagined she meant she would magically conjure them out of thin air.

"Wow. Did you really do that, or have I eaten some funny mushrooms recently and I'm actually tripping?"

"You're as sane and as lucid as you were five minutes ago." Teagan said, pulling her purse from her handbag on the kitchen counter and pulled out some cash. With a few more unintelligible words, the money vanished. "You'd better close your mouth soon or you're going to start catching flies."

"What....Where did the money go?" Shani stammered.

"My sisters and I are druids. We use our magic within the laws of nature and karma. We don't use our magic for personal gain, so I took the pre-made meat patties from the butchers shop and exchanged them for the valued cost. Simple."

"Karma, I understand. My whole Indian culture is built on it." Shani chuckled. *It's a shame Saadir isn't a firm believer too,* Shani thought to herself. "I don't think what you did was simple at all, in fact I think it was pretty amazing. I wish I could do magic like that."

"I wish I had a psychic power like yours. I'm always losing things."

"But can't you just use your magic to find things, you know click your fingers or wiggle your nose or something and make things appear, like you did the meat? What about people, can you magically relocate them too?"

"People like Nicholas?" Teagan asked. Shani nodded. "I wish. I can only relocate inanimate objects, non-living things," she clarified. "And finding lost things would be considered personal gain and druid magic doesn't work that way. There are restrictions."

"What kind of restrictions?" Shani asked curiously.

"I can manipulate the natural elements, but I can't conjure things from nothing. To do that would be tapping into the dark side of magic which is very dangerous. And no one can teleport, that's just something you see in movies and television shows."

"I heard that Morganna and Scorpion can."

"Morganna has a device, an amulet that lets her teleport. Where she got it from, we don't know, but we think she's now sharing it with Scorpion. Even if she didn't have it, I wouldn't put it past the bitch to find a way to teleport anyway. She's pure evil and very powerful. She uses the darkest of dark magic, but one day...one day it will destroy her, and I hope I can be there to watch." Teagan told her. Her anger may have been tempered, nevertheless the venom in her tone was still indisputably evident.

Okay, that's a touchy subject. Shani made a mental note to avoid the topic of Morganna from now on. The sound of Teagan's teeth grinding was like nails down a chalk board, putting her own teeth on edge.

"So, what else can *you* do?" Shani asked, eager to change the subject.

"I can do this." Teagan took a deep, calming breath before laying all the meat patties on a tray and spoke another string of oddly sounding words. As Shani watched on in awe, the burgers began to darken and sizzle and the mouth-watering smell of cooked meat filled the air.

"Ohmigod! That was awesome. But wasn't that personal gain, not cooking them yourself?"

"There's a grey zone. I like to think that I performed a public service by not actually cooking them by hand. There's a good chance if I did, everyone would go home with food poisoning or a serious case of indigestion." Teagan laughed.

Shani and Teagan quickly assembled all the burgers. "How long are you going to be staying here in England. Are you going home as soon as we've found Nicholas?" Teagan asked.

"I'm not sure yet." *Not until Saadir tells me I'm allowed to go home.* "I'm planning on staying for a few weeks. It's been a while since I've had a chance to spend any time with my cousin Yasmin."

"That's great. We're throwing a big birthday party in a couple of weeks for Alaric's housekeeper, Mrs Philpot. She's turning one hundred. It would be great if you and Yasmin could come."

Shani's smile beamed. "I can speak for Yasmin, we'd love to come."

Their conversation continued on in easy fashion as they finished assembling the burgers, almost as though they'd been friends forever. Shani had only been there for not quite a day and already she was dreading the time when she had to go back to India. Back to Saadir.

Teagan and Shani each carried a tray loaded with burgers and set them on the dining room table. Next to which, they also deposited a pile of napkins and plates.

The moment Shani returned to the living room, Dray's eyes followed her intently. Her easy and open manner quickly receded, becoming guarded once more under the inquisitive gaze of the men filling the room.

She waited until everyone had taken their burgers before approaching the table herself. It didn't escape Dray's noticed that her hands shook ever so slightly under the group's scrutiny, fumbling with her napkin and dropping it on the floor.

Shani bent over to pick up her napkin, inadvertently giving him a tantalising view of her arse, gift wrapped in those perfect fitting black legging pants. A deep growl rumbled from his chest.

When every eye turned to stare at him, he quickly seated himself in the nearest cushioned arse palace and stared into his tumbler of whisky in his hand. Shani too, stared at him with a mix of curiosity and wistful delight. He tried to ignore her scent which bloomed in response to his caveman behaviour, making him as hard as a fucking rock behind the zipper of his jeans.

Teagan watched Shani take a huge bite of her burger.

"What do you think, is it okay? Did I over cook it?" Teagan asked anxiously.

"It's like little shards of heaven on my taste buds. Cows are sacred animals in India, so normally the only time I get to eat one is when I come to England, which I rarely get a chance to do." Shani confessed.

"I love it that you're not the kind of woman who only eats salad to stay slim and impress a guy." Dray almost swallowed his tongue. He hadn't meant to say that, somehow it just slipped out.

Shani quirked an eyebrow, not sure if that was supposed to be a compliment or an insult.

"As opposed to eating half a cow with all the trimmings and getting fat?" she asked.

"No. That's not what I meant at all. I just meant that you're comfortable in your own skin and you don't care what anyone else thinks of you. It's a credit to you." He needed to stop talking. He didn't want to offend her, but every word that left his mouth seemed to dig him into a bigger and deeper hole. He fucking sucked at giving compliments.

"For the record, I eat like this because I'm happily miserable with my life and I don't care if I get fat."

"What about your husband, don't you like to look good for him?" Saladin asked.

Shani sniggered humourlessly. "You realise you're showing your age. That kind of thinking went out with the Stepford wives. I'm sorry, I didn't mean to be rude. I kinda like that you're all a little old-fashioned."

"I'm more than eight centuries older than you. You don't get more old-fashioned than that." Saladin told her.

"You don't look a day over fifty." Shani said with a deadpan expression, inducing a snort of laughter from Teagan.

"Fifty?!" Saladin griped.

"Just kidding. Forty five."

"You're a terrible liar, you know that?"

Saladin didn't look a day over mid to late twenthies-*ish*, and he knew it, despite the fact that he'd been in his sixties when he was made a vampire. The reversal of age to your prime of life was one of the many perks of being a vampire. Fortunately. But then, a vampire's flawless complexion would make any age look good.

Dray listened to the relaxed conversations and jesting interaction. It had been a while since he'd heard them all laugh and joke like this. As Shani relaxed around them, her easy going nature and comfortable acceptance of the group seemed to be at the heart of the good cheer. He was really enjoying watching Shani laugh and smile.

It sucked that he was going to have to put a dampener on everyone's mood and discuss business.

Then again, when he told Shani what it was that he needed her to do, it would likely change her opinion of him. And that, when he gave the notion closer thought, was probably for the best.

"Can we get on with the business of Shani locating Nicholas' trophies?" Dray's dry tone cut through the group's jovial banter like a blizzard on a sunny day.

Shani almost choked on a mouthful of burger as she tried to swallow, an almost impossible task as her mouth had suddenly gone dry. Lifting her glass to her lips she took a sip of water to help swallow down her food, only to discover that her hand had developed a tremor. Whether it was the result of her nervousness at the sudden turn of conversation toward her direction, or from the way Dray's eyes studied her so intently, she didn't know. The result was the same though. Shani dribbled her water down her chin while she coughed and spluttered up her burger in a very refined and ladylike manner. Not!

"Damn, are you okay?" Oliver asked, patting her on the back.

"Fine." She rasped out between gasping breaths.

"You sure you're okay, can I get you another drink?" Dray asked, coming to her aid.

"No, thank you. I'm fine, really." Shani replied as the last of her coughing fit subsided. No doubt she looked a treat with her face turned a bright shade of scarlet, and tears streaming down her cheeks from coughing so hard. Dray handed her a napkin. Looking down at herself, one wasn't going to be enough. After dabbing her eyes and blowing her nose, she scrunched up the napkin and neatly placed it on her plate and held out her hand silently for another one. Dray handed her a wad of napkins, which she used to clean up the spillage of food and drink from the front of her top.

How embarrassing. If ever there was a time she wished she had Teagan's powers, this was it. Personal gain or not, she'd make the floor open up and swallow her. "I'm sorry. You were saying Dray?"

Hesitantly, Dray began to talk, although his eyes never left Shani, his concern as mildly unnerving as it was, was also very endearing. It was proof that contrary to popular belief, his heart was not made out of stone after all.

"Shani, as you know, was unable to get any kind of read on Nicholas. We can only assume that he's being cloaked somehow, probably by Morganna." There were deep rumblings and guttural curses murmured amongst the group which Dray duly ignored. "We have another option we can try though. We know from news reports that Nicholas has been actively practicing his slice and dice techniques on females recently. According to Philippe, he used to collect trophies from his victims and I'm willing to bet that he's continued this habit. What we need to do is locate his souvenir collection and wait for him to return. With an obsession of this kind, he's not going to be far away from the things he covets the most, his victims and his trophies." Dray concluded.

"You mentioned you needed Alex's help." Saladin prompted.

Dray nodded. "I can hack the police database and create a new identity for one of us to impersonate a police officer, but I need Alex to make the fake ID."

"Thank Christ for that. I thought you were going to say you needed him to interact with people."

"We want to keep this as low key as possible. Alex having any direct input is likely to end up on the six o'clock news." Dray replied in a serious tone.

"So, what is it we're stealing from the Police station?" Oliver asked.

Dray's gaze once again landing on Shani. "Nicholas' last victim, Tracey Niven was found a couple of weeks ago. The police have her clothes and jewellery impounded as evidence."

"You want me to get a read on her things and locate the trophies Nicholas took from her?" Shani asked.

Again, Dray nodded. "I have to warn you though it might be distressing. Her clothes are likely to be covered with her blood, and the trophies he took from her were an ear and a finger."

"I can do it." Shani promised, pushing the corners of her lips up into a forced smile.

"Okay, well if that's all the business there is to discuss and you've finished eating, I'll clear the dishes." Teagan stood and began collecting plates and glasses and leftovers. "Unless you'd like me to make some dessert?" she asked.

"No. We're good. Don't go to any trouble for us." Each of the men quickly answered, talking over top of one another.

"So, that's a no?" she clarified.

"Yes, that's a no. Definitely a no. But, the burgers were great, thanks," her father answered, to which everyone else eagerly nodded their agreement.

Teagan's culinary skills may need some work, but she was an expert at getting people to change the subject of discussion. In this case, drawing people's attention away from Shani, who was looking decidedly uncomfortable under their renewed scrutiny.

"Here, let me take those. The least I can do is wash the dishes since you cooked." Shani told Teagan.

"Oh, okay, thanks." Teagan replied cheerfully, loading her up with plates and cutlery.

Shani walked slowly into the kitchen, careful not to tilt the delicately balanced stack of dishes in any one direction. When she reached the sink, she realised she had two problems. One, she didn't have a spare hand to unload the dishes onto the bench without dropping the lot onto the floor. And two, she had an itch in the centre of her back that was about to send her mad.

"Here, let me help you with those." Dray offered, coming up behind her.

"Thanks, but what I really need….and I can't believe I'm about to ask this…."

"What? If you need something, you only need to ask."

"Oh God. Scratch my back, please. Hurry, please," she begged.

Dray never hesitated, reaching out he scratched her beneath her left shoulder blade.

"No, in the middle…higher…higher. Oh, right there…Oh, God, right there…harder. Oh yeah." Shani cried out with relief. She didn't mean to make her appreciation sound pornographic, in fact, she didn't realise she had. She was just so grateful to be rid of the tormenting itch.

Dray almost lost it right then and there. Her appreciative moan so highly erotic he didn't know what to do. Did he make a comment, ignore it or keep going until he was making the same noises? Strip her naked and take her right there on the kitchen bench?

Shani looked up at Dray. Thick, long satin-black hair, the kind a woman could tangle her fingers in while he kissed her with those full lips. He was so handsome, and his touch warmed her in a way she never knew possible. Her skin tingled with awareness everywhere his fingers had grazed over her, like a lingering phantom's caress.

She didn't want to like that flare of raw hunger she saw in his eyes. Didn't want to ache with want to feel his mouth crush down on hers.

Who was she kidding, she'd give anything to feel his arms around her, just once. Too bad it was never going to happen.

"Thanks. I really needed that."

"Are you okay…about tracking Nicholas' trophies?" Dray asked, doing his best to keep some space between them.

"I knew what you were going to ask me to do when you mentioned it at Philippe's apartment. And yes, I'm fine. I can't say I won't need some therapy after this is all over but hey, there's plenty of people who think I need therapy already." She joked, but Dray wasn't laughing. "Really, I'm fine with it."

Shani looked up into his perfectly chiselled and incredibly attractive, ageless face. The anguish she saw in his eyes nearly broke her heart.

She looked down at the dishes in her arms wondering how to offload them safely in a hurry. She had an overwhelming urge to give him a hug and reassure him everything was fine.

Shani only looked away for a second, yet when she turned around again, he was gone. Simply vanished.

What had she done to offend him? Was it something she said? And why did the thought of upsetting him leave such a heaviness in her heart?

Shani heaved a heavy sigh, her shoulders slumping on the exhale, nearly tipping her delicately balanced pile of dishes onto the floor.

"Here let me get those." Nadia said as she entered the kitchen in her fluffy blue slippers and a shabby terry towelling dressing gown. She may not have looked so hot on the outside, but on the inside she felt fantastic. Realising how she truly felt about Philippe was a revelation that made her giddy with excitement. Not even a hangover from hell could dampen her mood.

Grabbing the top few plates, Nadia placed them in the dishwasher.

"Where did Dray go? He was standing there one second, and he was gone the next." Shani asked confused.

"To safer waters I'd imagine." Nadia answered. Shani scrunched up her nose in confusion. "I don't think Dray trusts himself around you," she elaborated.

"Oh?" He wasn't the only one, she thought to herself. "Thanks, I'd hate to drop this lot. I think I've made enough of a spectacle of myself today already," she said, as Nadia took another pile of dishes off her hands.

"Never. You've got a long way to go before you even come close to some of the things I've done." Nadia laughed.

"Maybe, but I'm pretty sure I can do something to embarrass myself at least once or twice more before the day is over." Shani smirked.

All Dray wanted to do was find Nicholas and Scorpion so Shani could go home. The longer she stayed, the more chance there was that he would need to deal with the feelings he had for her, and that was something he really didn't want to do. He wasn't made for love and all that complicated shit. It seemed though, the longer she was around, the more divided he felt. Right now, he didn't know his arse from a hole in the ground, and it pissed him off.

Dray marched from the room, going directly toward Saladin's well stocked bar, with Saladin only a step behind.

"Alright, who are you and what have you done with the real Dray?"

"What the fuck are you on about?"

"Don't play dumb with me. Something's going on between you and the psychic." Saladin accused, coming to stand at Dray's side. It was like cozying up to dry ice. Dray's mood made the air around him seem sub-arctic. If he could compare the experience, it was right up there with getting gutted alive. And he was speaking from experience with that.

"There's nothing going on."

"You can't bullshit me. You're being polite and thoughtful. It's unnatural. It makes me wonder if the world has suddenly tilted off its axis, and frankly, you're scaring me. You're normally gruff and rude. That's why I like you. You're like me."

"You calling me an arsehole?" Dray asked.

"Yeah, I am. Hey, wait a second. Is that you're backhanded way of calling *me* an arsehole?"

"You said we're the same, who am I to argue."

"I'm not an arsehole anymore, I'm reformed."

A single eyebrow lifted on Dray's expressionless face as he stared at Saladin.

"I'm not. I'm a mated male, Teagan has changed me."

Dray's brow lifted a little higher. "Are you trying to convince me or yourself? What about last week at the club, you cut off the hand of that guy who slapped Teagan's arse."

"That fucknut deserved it. Besides, he got off lightly and he knows it. I could have cut off his genitals but I didn't, because I'm nice, not an arsehole. Anyway, it's no big tragedy he's a vampire, his hand will grow back."

Dray's other brow lifted to make a matching pair. "What about when you made the bartender cry just yesterday?"

"Hmmm, forgot about that. But he did forget to put an umbrella in my drink….Okay, so I'm still an arsehole, just not with Teagan."

"And that's only because you're afraid of your own wife." Dray chuckled, although his smile quickly slid from his face when Saladin replied.

"Aren't you?"

"Shit yeah."

"So, what's up with you and Shani?"

"Nothing. She's new to our world, I'm just trying to soften the blow of constant shocks and surprises with a little kindness."

"Commendable. But it's the way you follow her with your eyes that worries me. You can't have her you know. She's married."

"And very traditional, I know."

"I don't think you do. Her *family* are traditional. If it's discovered she's had an affair, she'll be labelled an outcast by her husband and her family, and they'd no doubt go out of their way to make her life very difficult."

"I haven't laid a finger on her and I never would. I'm well aware of the consequences if I do." Dray growled.

"Make sure you keep it that way." Saladin thought for a minute. "Although, you could always fuck her and then wipe her memory. It wouldn't be a bad thing to cure that sexual tension you're raging at the moment. It might help you get your head back in the game."

"I would never disrespect her like that. And my head is always in the game."

"Really? Right now, your head is so far up your arse you could see daylight. The only head you're thinking with is currently pounding out a staccato beat in the front of your jeans. I dare you to deny it."

"Fuck off." Dray retorted with a gruff growl. He couldn't deny it, and that annoyed him more than his raging hard-on. He wanted that female more than he should. Wasn't that always the way though? You always want the things you can't have.

Ignoring Saladin's drilling stare, Dray stormed from the house letting fly a string of curses.

"It's good to have the real Dray back." Saladin yelled after him.

11

Nadia lay in her bed hour after hour as the night slipped away. Her anxious mind playing over every possible scenario like a stuck record, slowing only long enough to allow for short bursts of fitful sleep. Then came that dreaded moment. Her alarm went off. Only now the anvils holding her eyelids closed were too heavy to pry them apart. Her mind too worn out to care that she was now running late for the very thing she had worried about all night.

It had taken Alex only a day to produce the ID which Anna used to get into the police station where the evidence was kept. She was in and out with a blood stained hair tie and necklace in under half an hour. For Anna, an expert in undercover operations and an ex-DEA officer, the crafty theft was a walk in the park.

So, now they had the items necessary for Shani to scry with, which was the good news. Unfortunately, that also meant Dray would be arriving first thing this morning.

You would assume that maybe Nadia's anxiety related to Shani's ability to locate Nicholas's stash of trophies from his victim's and in turn, hopefully find Nicholas. After all, Nadia had been one of his victims too. Indirectly. Except she had been lucky enough to be revived from death. The others hadn't been so fortunate. However, that wasn't her current issue. In fact, she had barely given a thought to Nicholas throughout her restless night of tossing and turning.

It was Philippe's arrival with Dray that had her so worked up.

Nadia cracked open an eye as her bedroom door squeaked open.

"Come on lazy bones get out of bed, they're on their way. Oh, good Lord, look at you." Teagan t'sked.

"Go away." Nadia grumbled, burying herself beneath her doona.

"One of these days I'm going to come in here and *not* find you looking like something the cat dragged in."

"One of these days you're *not* going to barge into my room unannounced." Nadia bit back.

"This is my house, so technically this is my room, and I can come in here anytime I like. Now come on, get up. They'll be here in a few minutes."

"Why should I care, Philippe obviously doesn't."

"You're wrong about that." Teagan wasn't going to take no for an answer. Despite Nadia's death grip on the doona, Teagan gave it a hard yank, not just pulling it free of Nadia's hands but relocating it to the floor.

"You're a cruel woman." Nadia griped. Regardless, she still had no intention of getting out of bed. Instead, she pulled her knees up to her chest and curled into a ball.

"You think that was cruel? This...is cruel." Teagan told her. With a barely audible incantation and a flick of her finger, Nadia's mattress became a flannel sheet covered ice block.

Nadia shrieked and dived out of bed.

"I hate you."

"I love you too. Now, get in the shower."

Nadia really didn't have a choice now. The side of her body which had been contacting the bed felt like it had been exposed to a blizzard and was in desperate need of thawing. At least she was awake. Grumpier, but *very* awake.

Ten minutes later, after a shower hot enough to blister skin, she was dressed. She hadn't bothered to dry her hair or put on any makeup, and if Philippe didn't like the grungy old track pants and faded sweater she was wearing, too bad.

She'd barely put on her shoes when the doorbell rang, and her heart skipped a beat. He's here, she thought. Mentally reprimanding herself, tamping down her excitement. Philippe didn't deserve her enthusiasm or her attention in general. He was an ass, just like every other guy she'd met.

Still, when she heard the excited squeal of her nephew Finn, her enthusiasm returned and she hurried toward the entrance hall.

"Not so loud, use your *inside* voice, Finn." Kaitlyn reprimanded her son.

"Hey little man, how are you?" Nadia asked her nephew, deliberately ignoring Philippe who walked in behind him. Finn wrapped his arms tightly around her neck and gave her a wet, sloppy kiss on the cheek. With a sigh Nadia hugged him back. At least there was someone of the opposite sex who cared about her.

"Finn honey, why don't you go outside and play." Kaitlyn told him.

"Are you coming too?"

"In a minute, I promise." She told him, scruffing up his hair and offering him a cheesy grin.

"What are you doing here?" Nadia asked her sister.

"Alex insisted on coming to watch Shani do her mojo thing, so I asked to come along too. I need to do some shopping. Finn's growing so fast he hasn't got any clothes he can wear to Mrs P's party."

"I'm surprised Paige isn't here with Riley too. I would've thought the two boys would want to go in matching outfits. They're so alike, aren't they?"

"Yes, they are, but since Paige and I are twins, and Finn and Riley were both born on the same day, it makes sense that they'd be alike too. And yes, they do want to go dressed the same. I'm picking up a second outfit for Riley when I get Finn's." Kaitlyn laughed.

"Hi Nadia." Philippe greeted, quickly filling the gap in conversation between the sisters.

Nadia looked across at him. She opened her mouth to reply, promptly closing it again and looking away. It didn't matter that he looked hot in his muscle loving T-shirt, or that he filled out his jeans so magnificently. He was an ass, she reminded herself with a mental bitch slap.

"Nadia?" he asked a little more warily.

The sudden tension in the room was like an etheric stink bomb going off. Everyone vacated the vicinity instantly, leaving Nadia and Philippe alone.

"Nadia, talk to me."

"I don't want to." Nadia's nose rose higher in the air and her chest puffed out with indignant ire. Crossing her arms in front of her she levelled him with a withering glare.

"Is there something wrong?" Philippe asked.

"Should there be? I'm tired and I'm grumpy. And just in case you're not familiar with tired and grumpy, this is what it looks like," she yelled at him, her face turning a pretty shade of crimson.

"I can see you're grumpy. What's wrong?" he asked perplexed.

Nadia marched to the kitchen with thumping, angry steps, plonking her hands on her hips. Philippe followed only a stride behind. Why wouldn't he be confused about why she was angry with him. Even if he did have feelings for her like Teagan believed, he was a guy and no guy had ever seen her as relationship material. What was it about her that men found so off-putting?

Things were going about as right for her in the man department as if she had spent all of her days breaking mirrors, crossing black cats paths and walking under ladders.

"I've been trying to call you for two days and you haven't called me back." Nadia turned to face him, her pale eyes dark with anger.

"I know. Sorry." He took a step closer and she took one backward.

"Sorry? I called you six times, and you didn't call me back. Did you forget my number? Well, I've got a new number for you, it's five-five-five-bite me."

"Nadia, I'm sorry. I really am, but I've had a lot on my mind lately. I promise I'm not trying to ignore you." He knew he should have called her back, but he assumed she'd understand his need for solitude. Then again, how could she understand if she had no idea what was going on inside his head. And why was that? Because he hadn't talked to her.

Regret didn't begin to cover how he was feeling right now. He had so many emotions battling for dominance.

"Bullshit." Nadia retorted, emboldened by her righteous anger.

Nadia looked at Philippe hoping for some sort of reaction. But his face was inscrutable. Stupid handsome vampires, capable of suppressing their facial emotions.

Nadia pushed past him and left without letting him see her face. Tears didn't serve any purpose at this point.

"Philippe, when it comes to women you're completely clueless, you know that?" Teagan slapped Philippe on the back of the head. "If a woman tries that many times to contact you, you can be pretty sure she wants you for more than your sparkling conversation."

"Nadia isn't interested in me. Not like that. We're just friends."

"Like I said. Clueless. You're a turkey." Philippe looked at Teagan, even more confused and annoyed than before. Teagan huffed and continued her explanation. "She's totally crushing on you. From where I stand, you're the Thanks Giving turkey, walking around clueless that you're on the menu."

"What do I do?" Philippe looked like he was about to hyperventilate from a sudden panic attack.

Teagan smacked him on the back of the head again. "Isn't it obvious. Get out there and fix things between the two of you."

"How?"

"You'll figure it out."

Nadia's tears started to flow as soon as she reached the gardens.

"Hey little sis, do you want to talk about it?" Kaitlyn asked, coming up beside her. In the background she could hear Finn running around slaying make believe demons. While she suspected the imaginary demons would live to be slain another day, she doubted Teagan's prize azalea bushes he was using as their proxy, would.

"I don't know what to do. I'm so confused. Sometimes Philippe drives me crazy, you know?"

"I totally understand. We've got a club, and I think you qualify for a membership card. Do you want one?" Kaitlyn asked.

Nadia tilted her head and scowled at her sister. "What kind of club?"

"We call it the *'Mates of the douchebag males'* club." She smirked.

Nadia wiped away the tears from her cheeks and sniffed back a heavy sigh. "When does puberty end for men?"

"Let me see…." Kaitlyn tapped her chin thoughtfully. "About six months after death."

"What about if the guy is a vampire?"

"Umm…then never." Kaitlyn laughed.

"Hmm, thought so."

"Nadia, don't let yourself get too worked up over this. Philippe may be new to the whole adult scene, but he's a fast learner. He'll catch up quickly. Just give him some time to figure things out. Yeah?"

Nadia nodded as she spied the man in question walking toward them.

"Ooh, I think that's my cue to make myself scarce. I think I should go find Finn and hopefully rescue some of the vegetation in Teagan's garden."

Nadia barely heard a word Kaitlyn said, her attention was focused on Philippe. His long strides ate up the distance between them, yet no matter how close he came, she couldn't shake the feeling of being alone.

"Sunrises are quite lovely, aren't they?" Philippe said as he watched the first rays of sunlight break through Autumn's bare branches at the top of the trees.

"It's well past sunrise." Nadia told him flatly.

"I know, but I couldn't think of anything else to open with."

Nadia looked at him curiously. "You've never been stuck for words around me before. Why now?"

"I'm flirting, but if you didn't get that then I'm doing it wrong."

Flirting? He was *flirting* with her?

She shrugged, wishing she'd developed superhuman speed in her transformation so he wouldn't be able to catch up to her when she decided to run. That's what she felt like doing. Run far, far away, because being around him made her feel…raw.

"Nadia, talk to me, please," Philippe begged.

"I don't want to talk."

"I know the general rule is to leave a woman alone when she's pretending she's not upset when she clearly is, but I don't follow rules."

"Yes, you do. You always follow the rules, Philippe," she grumbled.

"Not when it comes to you, Nadia. So, tell me what's bothering you?"

"I told you it's nothing."

He closed the distance between them. "Please, tell me."

"You tell me something, Philippe. All the stuff you're dealing with, it's not all about your brother, is it?" she probed.

Philippe struggled to keep his eyes off her lips, but at her question he lifted his gaze to hers, he honestly didn't know how to answer.

When he didn't respond, only stared at her, she sighed and tried to turn away, but he stopped her with one word. "No," he told her softly.

Nadia turned back around to face him.

"I've been struggling with my feelings for you," he said. The dusky timbre of his voice sent a thrill of sensation racing along her spine. Philippe heard a heavy sigh.

"Damn it. Why, if you're supposed to be attracted to me, do you keep avoiding me?"

"I...I..." he stammered self-consciously.

"Just answer the question Philippe."

"Because I'm afraid."

"Afraid? Of what, me?"

"No. Yes. I'm afraid you don't feel the same, and I don't know if I could take the rejection. I would rather love you from afar, than tell you how I feel and risk losing your friendship."

"You're such a fool. Do you know how many pieces I am in on the inside without you? You're the only man who has made me feel whole."

Philippe's heart stopped, then restarted, thudding wildly against his rib cage. *Man? She'd called me a man.*

The scent of her wrapped around him, sinking deep inside him until he swore he could taste her on his tongue. So sweet, it made him dizzy.

Philippe's eyes raked up and down over her body as though she was naked, his eyes went straight to her breasts, and his sexy half-grin curved his lips before he sniffed the air.

Mine!

He moaned, softly placing his hands on her waist. Nadia threaded her fingers through his hair, pushing it back from his face as she stared into his eyes.

With a growl, he closed the distance between them, but instead of grabbing her in his arms as she expected, he buried the fingers of one hand into the wavy sable locks of her hair and lifted it to his nose and inhaled.

Okay, she hadn't expected that, although she wasn't complaining either. There was something so primal in the way he touched her, so possessive, it made her shiver with delight.

Nadia allowed her hand to move over his chest. Even fully clothed she could feel the hardness of his body, and she wanted nothing more than to feel his bare skin beneath her fingers, press her body against his. Skin on skin. She wanted to touch him so badly she couldn't hold back a soft moan. She could barely breathe from the need pulsing through every cell of her body. Yeah, wanting him didn't even come close to explaining the depth of what she was feeling right now.

Pulling back a little, she drew his eyes back to hers. "You're mine."

Not giving him a chance to refute her claim, Nadia closed the distance between them and kissed him.

Hesitantly she leaned forward, letting her lips slide along his in a sort of glancing blow, barely making contact, a tease with a promise of more. Before she could pull back to assess his reaction, Philippe returned the kiss with much more force, consuming her mouth with a dominant growl.

Philippe had no idea how he was still standing. Her revelation flawed him. Then she kissed him and his knees nearly buckled beneath him.

When her tongue licked over his lips and their gaze met, he couldn't resist another taste of those lips. A deeply drugging, pleasure filled taste, sending his senses reeling as layer upon layer of intoxicating sensations tore through him. Philippe pulled her bottom lip between his teeth, nibbling gently before nudging her lips apart and deepening the kiss.

Nadia gasped , and he took the opportunity to slide his tongue along the rim of her upper teeth.

Her tongue stroked over his, tangling with it as they fought for supremacy of the kiss. The resulting pleasure sent a wave of pure unadulterated heat flowing through his veins. That little taste wasn't nearly enough.

Her hand against his chest felt right as it explored his hard contours. And when her hand slid beneath the barrier of his shirt...he stopped breathing. Her touch against his skin transporting him to a whole new world, as if it had the power to break his barriers and wipe away his past. It was liberating, and mesmerising.

Nadia's fingers splayed against the bottom of his ribcage, indulging in the silky, softness of his smooth skin. Her nails lightly scraping against the hard ridges of his abdomen sending a shudder of heady delight which shook him to the core.

The blood pounding in his ears and against his temples making it difficult to concentrate on anything except the overpowering feeling of Nadia's hot, eager lips devouring his and the touch of her soft, dextrous hands. A guttural sound boiled up from his chest. Philippe had never been kissed on the lips before, and having his first real kiss with his *mate*, was the equivalent of trying to light his first cigarette with a blowtorch. It consumed him entirely with heat.

Lust hit him like a thunderbolt, right between the thighs.

Nadia too, was only distantly aware of her surroundings. All that mattered to her was Philippe. She didn't have to hold herself back. She was finally free to touch him, taste him, kiss him.

She wanted that kiss. The kiss she had dreamed of. A kiss she was certain she would never have.

His touch was both tender and savage, claiming her, possessing her...branding her with every caress and sensual kiss.

"Look mum, Uncle Philippe is kissing Aunty Nadia." Finn said loudly in his *outdoor* voice.

"Shh. Leave them be and go inside. Now." Kaitlyn ordered, shooing him in the opposite direction. Not that she was planning on taking her own advice.

Kaitlyn waited until Finn was out of sight and then made herself *out of sight* too, at least to the naked eye. Making herself invisible, Kaitlyn crept a little closer. It wasn't that she really wanted to spy on them, she was doing it because she knew the rest of the gang of female co-conspirators were going to demand a blow-by-blow recount of the pair's first kiss. At least, that's what she told herself to justify her creepy stalking behaviour in the bushes.

Regrettably, it seemed Finn's outburst had ruined the moment, and Philippe and Nadia pulled back from their kiss.

"Did you enjoy the show, Kaitlyn?" Nadia asked as they walked hand in hand past the bush where her sister was hiding.

"What? How did you know I was here?" Baffled, Kaitlyn made herself visible once again, shoving her hands on her hips with a huff. When she was invisible, no one could detect her presence unless of course she wanted them too, even her scent was masked. Normally. It was reassuring to see that she had fooled one of them. At least Philippe looked mildly surprised to see her.

"Sis, you forget that I'm not seeing you on the physical level anymore. Until you can learn to hide your aura too, I'll always be able to see you." Nadia told her with a satisfied smirk.

"Damn. That sucks. I'll have to work on that." Kaitlyn grumbled.

Shani stood staring out at Finn playing in the garden, but she must have sensed him standing behind her because she turned her head to look at him over her shoulder. Her smile was enough to drop him to his knees.

"Dray, it's nice to see you again. You left without saying goodbye the other night. Was everything alright?" Shani asked.

"Everything's fine. Are you ready to get to work?" he asked, a little more coldly than he'd intended.

"Right now?"

"Yes, will that be a problem?" Dray asked, his look daring her to object.

"No." Shani answered, keeping her voice low and even.

Shani had no objections to completing the job he was paying her for, but she did object to his sudden frosty attitude toward her. It distressed her in ways she didn't fully understand.

Not that being given the cold shoulder was a new experience for her, far from it. Saadir showered her with affection in public, but privately he never spared her so much as a single kind word...unless he wanted her to find something he'd lost.

Dray was different. He wasn't a two faced chameleon like Saadir. She didn't know Dray very well, but in the year she had been dealing with him, and in the few days she'd known him more intimately, she knew his temperament to be stable. Unshakeable. He didn't put on airs and graces for the benefit of others. He didn't fake an emotion he didn't feel.

So, what had happened to make him look at her so differently and change his manner toward her?

A chill ran through Shani's veins. Had Saadir found out it was actually Dray who was employing her and not Teagan? Had Saadir threatened Dray, she wondered with dread.

Maybe it was her. Maybe she had done something to offend him?

Shani thought back to the last time they had spoken. It hadn't been in the last couple of days, all Dray's messages had been relayed to her through Saladin. The last time she'd spoken to him was when they were in the kitchen together.

When he'd run out on her so abruptly.

Shani's heart dropped into the cold pit of her stomach.

Had he sensed just how attracted she was to him? Was that what he found so offensive?

"I need a few minutes to get my thoughts focused, if that's okay." Shani told him, keeping her eyes down cast. She couldn't meet his gaze, afraid that she might see the truth of her fears in his eyes.

"We'll be waiting in the living room when you're ready," he answered unceremoniously. She'd go as far as describe his tone as being sharply blunt, which of course was an oxymoron, but then so was Dray. He was a walking contradiction. Somehow his behaviour seemed both hot and cold at the same time, gruff and sweet, which made him endcaringly annoying.

"Ignore Dray, he's a cantankerous fart nozzle without a filter for his brain, but he grows on you after a while." Alex offered matter-of-factly as way of explanation on Dray's behalf as he joined them at the window.

Shani made an undignified noise that sounded suspiciously like a laugh. "I'm told that you do too," she answered shyly.

"Which part, the cantankerous fart nozzle part, the filterless brain or how my unique charm grows on you?" Alex asked.

Shani chuckled softly. "All of it."

"When you put it like that, Dray and I are a lot alike, aren't we?" Alex surmised.

"We are nothing alike." Dray growled.

"You can't deny it, we do have a number of things in common. We're both exceptionally smart," Dray reluctantly nodded. "We can both manipulate the fuck out of technology," Dray grunted. "We both have charming personalities," Dray raised an eyebrow. "And, we both know how to make the ladies happy. I'm sure I'm not the only one whose made use of the chains and handcuffs in the holding cell beneath the club for a bit of carnal fornication. Ha? Am I right?" Alex jibed. This time Dray's scowl made Teagan's stink eye glare look pleasant. "Dude, you really should get that eye twitch seen to. Every time I see you it's twitching." Alex told Dray with a consolatory pat on the shoulder.

"Alex!" Teagan growled, joining the group.

"If I was you, I'd shut up Alex. I know that look and Teagan is a microsecond away from making your already tight jeans extra, extra small and squishing your man tackle to the size of peas and a baby carrot." Saladin told him, wrapping his arms around his wife's waist. He loved it when it was someone else in the line of fire for her wrath.

Alex gripped his family jewels protectively. "I'm quite attached to my nads just the way they are, fuck you very much."

"Don't want to burst your bubble there buddy, but what's in your pants isn't really yours. They belong to your wife."

Alex's pleased grin beamed. "Yeah, they do. Although...I wouldn't mind if you could call Abby and get her here before you shrink my twizzle stick and all day suckers. That way Abby can rub them for me until they recover."

"Ew. Haven't you been listening to me Alex?" Teagan accused.

"I was trying not to, but some of it still got through."

"Good, then shut up and let's ignore your over sharing and just get on with this shall we?" Teagan told him using air quotes to emphasise his aforementioned faux pas, in case he didn't quite get her meaning.

"Are you okay to do this?" Saladin asked Shani.

"Yes," Shani swallowed the bile that rose in her throat as Dray produced the blood stained items from a small bag in his pocket.

"Let the shit show begin." Alex crowed more excitedly than the occasion called for.

"I warned you." Teagan said as she flicked her hand in his direction.

"Ahhh!" Alex screamed…about six octaves higher than his usual baritone voice.

12

Teagan should have thought it through more carefully before she shrank Alex's pants on him. She didn't take into account that he, out of everyone she knew, had no reservations about shredding those shrink-wrapped pants and letting his junk hang free in the breeze. While the girls present couldn't help taking a peek, the men weren't so happy about their own junk suddenly being compared to Alex's.

The stabbing Alex received from Saladin may have been a little excessive but hey, it was Alex, i.e. inevitable.

"Teagan told me to come here and make amends with you." Saladin sneered in complete contradiction to his statement.

His wife glared at him until he forced a fake smile on his face.

"So, are we good?" Saladin continued.

"I accept your apology for stabbing me." Alex grinned as though it was the highlight of his day.

"I don't recall apologising for that, it's *you* who should apologise for upsetting the girls with your pecker." Saladin told him, his eyebrow cocked high on one side.

"What the fuck for? They didn't look the least bit upset by my huge shlong."

Saladin growled, taking a deep breath to calm himself down before the urge to repeat the knife incident got the better of him.

"What did we miss?" Philippe asked as he walked in, hand in hand with Nadia. "Why is Alex wearing a towel around his waist, and where are his pants?"

"Long story. Don't ask." Dray growled.

"Does it have anything to do with the knife on the floor?" Nadia asked in a droll tone.

"Maybe." Saladin replied tersely. Both Teagan and Shani nodded vigorously in the background, barely able to contain their smirks. Although Nadia couldn't tell if they were amused by the situation with Alex, or seeing her walk in with her hand attached to Philippe's. Did she care? No. Nothing and no one was going to upset her today. She was too happy.

"Alex can't wear a towel all day. I'll lend him a pair of mine." Saladin grudgingly announced.

"I don't think your pants will fit Alex." Teagan told him.

"Are you implying his weed whacker is too large to fit into my pants?" he growled.

Teagan snickered. "No honey. Alex is a few inches taller than you, your pants would be like ankle freezers on him."

Oh. Right.

Saladin cleared his throat self-consciously. "Good point."

"If it makes you feel better honey, I think the front of your pants would be a bit too roomy for Alex." Teagan told him in her best convincing voice.

"Damn straight." Saladin replied proudly, adjusting the front of his pants as though *his* package was in fact too large for them.

"Really?" Nadia mouthed silently to her sister.

Discretely Teagan shook her head and pouted in disappointment.

"My jeans would fit him." Philippe offered.

"You planning on taking off your pants and giving them to him?" Nadia asked, a hopeful lilt to her voice. The moment the words left her mouth her cheeks began to burn. She hadn't actually meant to say that out loud.

Philippe looked down into Nadia's eyes, his heated gaze made her cheeks burn even hotter. "The thought may have crossed my mind, but no. I went shopping yesterday and bought some new clothes. I can run home and be back in ten minutes."

"What? You went shopping without me?" Nadia asked, surprised and a little disappointed.

"Ah, yeah. I needed some clothes. My wardrobe was filled with kids clothes."

"But, you didn't ask me to come with you to help choose them." Now she sounded deeply offended and didn't that make Philippe feel like an ass. Again.

"Sweetheart, honeybun, sweatpea....Um, I'm not sure how to tell you this, but I don't really like the clothes you pick out for me," he grimaced.

"What? No. You love the clothes I pick for you." Philippe raised an eyebrow as he stared down at her. "Okay, maybe not the ones I buy at two o'clock in the morning from those infomercials on television, but I promise I won't do that anymore," she told him emphatically.

Damn right she won't. If he gets his way Nadia will be otherwise preoccupied at two o'clock every morning in his bed. Philippe barely stifled a groan as the empty space in the front of his own jeans suddenly became cramped again.

"If you're done with the chit chat, Philippe go and get those pants before Alex starts parading his tackle around my house again." Saladin bit out testily.

"Back in ten." Philippe said. Turning to leave, he stopped and turned around again. The sparkle of iridescence in his eyes and the shy smile was the only warning Nadia got before he pulled her against him for a brief, but hungry kiss, leaving her panting for breath and speechless for a full minute after he left.

In fifteen minutes, Philippe was back with the pants and Alex was once again decently dressed. Nadia thought about the jeans Philippe was wearing and couldn't help wondering what he looked like beneath them. One thing she knew for sure, she wasn't going to find out today. Even if the opportunity arose, it didn't feel right to want to get naked with Philippe on the same day they were going looking for the missing body parts of girls Philippe's brother had murdered. It was a serious mood killer.

"Can we get on with this now, please?" Dray's tersely clipped words and foul mood was a carbon copy of Saladin's. The two of them could have been Xeroxed from the same printer.

"I'm ready." Shani answered in a softer, much more subdued tone. Picking up the blood stained hair band which had been placed on a nearby table before the Alex *incident* had erupted, she held it thoughtfully, enclosing it in her cupped hands.

Dray met Shani's eyes. The guarded concern and disappointment he saw there unsettled him. If he could reach around and kick his own arse, he would. Hard. He knew his sudden change in behaviour toward her upset her, but what could he do? It wasn't her fault that he was attracted to her, nor was it her fault that he struggled to remain in control of himself when he was around her. As much as it grated on his nerves, it was better for both of them if she remained wary of him and keep her distance.

Shani broke eye contact with Dray. Drawing in a long, deep breath she closed her eyes and slowly let it out again.

Everyone stood silently around her, watching anxiously, holding their own breaths, waiting for her to speak. The tension in the room mounted with each passing second.

Shani's brow furrowed as an impression formed in her mind. Hazy at first, shifting from one scene to the next before solidifying into a tangible picture.

"I see it," she said, her voice barely above a whisper.

"Where?" Philippe asked, an uneasy frustration tensing every muscle in his body.

"I see a sign, it says *Shadyvale*. I'm not sure where it is, but there's a symbol on the sign like a coat of arms or something," she said. Before she even finished describing what she saw, Alex had Googled *'Shadyvale'*.

"Is this what you saw?"

"Yes. That's it."

"What kind of place is it?" Philippe asked.

"It's a retirement home about a hundred miles north of London." Alex informed them.

"You're certain Nicholas' trophies are there?" Dray asked Shani.

"Yes. I'm positive. They're hidden in one of the resident's rooms."

"Can you narrow it down a bit? There are ninety residents in that home." Alex said.

"Sorry, I can't. I'll know the room when I get there though."

"You're not coming with us." Dray told her firmly. "We don't know if Nicholas has set some kind of trap for us, it's too dangerous. Describe exactly what you see and we'll go."

"I can't. That's not how my gift works, I can't turn it on and off like a switch. Sometimes the information I get is abstract and incomplete. I'll know exactly where to look once I get there."

Dray's intense stare and rumbling growl had Shani swallowing nervously. Not because she felt intimidated by his domineering attitude, but because she didn't think he'd appreciate seeing her blush and go weak at the knees from the arousal that sound caused in her.

After Dray's curt greeting to her earlier, Shani had carefully considered the facts. Initially she thought that maybe Saadir had been informed about Dray being her employer and not Teagan, and that maybe Saadir had threatened Dray. She tossed that idea out the window almost immediately. There wasn't much that Saadir could do or say that would intimidate a powerful vampire like Dray. That left only one possibility. Dray was aware of her attraction to him, and he wasn't happy about it. She wasn't happy about it either, but what could she do, it wasn't as though she could control her feelings, was it.

Shani wasn't a fool. She had no intentions on acting on her feelings, but it didn't stop her fantasizing about something she could never have.

"Shani's right, she'll have to come with us." Saladin surmised, clasping Dray on the shoulder with a little more force than was probably necessary. Although he got his message across. Dray stiffened momentarily before letting out a tense sigh. "We'll leave in five minutes."

The house cleared out quickly. Kaitlyn took Finn shopping and everyone except Teagan and Nadia left for the Shadyvale Retirement Home, a leisurely three hour trip by car.

"Alright they're gone, now dish. What happened before Philippe and I came in?" Nadia demanded.

Teagan's expression became a little sheepish as she rolled her eyes and huffed. "It was my fault I'm afraid." Teagan outlined the conversation that led up to the *incident*.

"Damn, I'm sorry I missed it," Nadia laughed. "Poor Shani, she probably thinks she's gotten mixed up with a bunch of crazy people."

"No doubt. I have to say though, she's certainly taking all our madness quite well. She barely even flinched when Saladin stabbed Alex."

"That's a good sign. I guess she's adjusting to our crazy supernatural world."

"She wasn't too bothered by seeing Alex naked either, but then neither was I. Of course that's why Saladin stabbed him," Teagan laughed.

"Jealous? Does Alex have something that he doesn't?" Nadia enquired.

"No, not really. In fact, they were quite similar in size."

"Oh? They're both well-endowed?" Nadia probed a little more.

Teagan grinned. "Not exactly, but not everyone can be hung like a racehorse, like Philippe. That doesn't mean that Saladin can't perform like a stallion. I'm not saying he's under-developed either, because he's definitely got more than enough to please me, and he knows how to use it *very* well," Teagan told her with a wink.

"Hang on a minute, Philippe has a big...um...you know...?" Nadia struggled to say the word, so she pointed down south.

Teagan's eyebrows rose high as she nodded.

"And you know this how?" Nadia enquired a little haughtily.

"Cassie and Mrs P...." Teagan began but was cut off.

"Cassie and Mrs P. have seen Philippe naked?"

"No. Not exactly. He was in the kitchen at the manor the other day when he discovered he had his very first erection. Cassie told me that what was tenting his track pants was more than enough to please *any* woman." Teagan chuckled at Nadia's flash of jealousy.

"What happened then?"

"Nothing. Philippe ran out of the kitchen, back to his room. Abby told me though, that a couple of hours later Alex went down to his room and he was still giving his, um...you know...a good wank."

"So not fair. I miss all the good stuff," Nadia huffed.

"Little sis, I don't think you have anything to worry about. The way the two of you were cozying up before, I think I'm going to be jealous of you pretty soon. You'll be getting a lot more action than I've been seeing lately," Teagan told her.

"Things between you and Saladin aren't too good?"

"Everything's great between us. It's just that with everything that's been going on, we don't seem to get a lot of time alone together these days."

"Why do you think I'm going to see any more action than you? Philippe is so focused on catching his brother, I've barely registered on his radar lately."

"Philippe might have pretended not to notice you, but that was before he knew how you felt about him. I can guarantee you that no matter what's happening, his focus will be on you, above anything else. The whole world could be crumbling around him and he'll still find time to smother you with kisses, or drag you into an empty office and bang you stupid on a desk, or…"

"Okay, I get it." Nadia chuckled. "Do you really think so?" Nadia asked, still a little doubtful.

"I'm positive. Young love is always like that," Teagan sighed wistfully. "Now, if you want to stand here and dwell on it, fine. Otherwise, we can make use of the time they're gone and see if we can't find something in the Book of Shadows that will help you to see the modern day scourge on the world, plastic."

"Can't I do both?"

"You're far too trusting of me." Dray deliberately avoided eye contact with Shani.

"Are you telling me you can't protect me, or that you being a vampire makes you a danger to me?" Shani asked incredulously. She'd been around Dray and the other vampires long enough now to realise neither was true.

"No." *And Yes. Very dangerous,* but not for the reasons she imagined. He would protect her with his life, but who he wondered, would protect her from him?

"Then there's no problem," she told him. "You can't locate Nicholas' stash of macabre trophies without me. Like it or not, you need me."

If she only knew how right she was. Dray couldn't fault her logic even though her nearness was almost unbearable.

"Fine, but you need to stay close, don't wander off," he replied, a heavy dose of starch stiffening his words.

Dray finally looked at her. Her eyes were watchful, wary, but still trusting. And didn't that just make him feel even more like an arsehole.

"You're overreacting, Dray. It's an old folks home. I'm sure the most traumatic experience we'll have," *besides finding dead girls body parts,* "will be seeing a few old people staring into space and drooling down their chins. It'll be fine, you'll see." Shani assured him.

Dray, Shani, Alex, Saladin and Philippe walked through the Shadyvale foyer, through the coded security doors, and into the main common room. The smell was what Shani noticed first, the heavy scent of disinfectant with an undertone of incontinence. Contrary to its name however, the Shadyvale nursing home was quite bright and welcoming. Large full length windows let in a stream of afternoon sun, warming the already thermal room a little more. It seemed the old folks had an aversion to the cold, so much so that Shani found she had to remove a layer of clothes to avoid sweltering in the clammy heat. Shani looked between her companions and for a moment wished she was a vampire too. None of them even seemed to notice the balmy change in temperature.

Even with her coat removed, her figure hugging, knitted sweater didn't give her much relief from the tropical room temperature, and she began fanning herself with the base of her top. Needless to say, Dray's disapproving growl only made her predicament more intense, adding internal heat to the external heat, and she fanned herself more vigorously.

"Would you please stop doing that, it's very off-putting," Shani berated with a disgruntled huff.

"Do what?" Dray asked gruffly.

"Growl. You're always growling at me. I'm sorry if my presence offends you, but please stop it."

Dray's jaw flapped open to speak and quickly shut it again as she walked right by him. What could he say? He certainly wasn't going to tell her the truth. He couldn't lie, because lies only got you into trouble eventually. It was better not to say anything at all.

A thin, elderly lady approached Shani with shuffling steps. "Can you take me home?" she asked.

"I'm sorry, but I think you live here." Shani answered sympathetically.

"No, I don't. I want to go home." She answered emphatically, becoming a little distressed. "I don't live here."

"Yes, you do, Libby. You've been an inmate here for five years," a balding, older man called out from across the room in a surprisingly robust voice.

"I have?" By her surprise it would be easy to believe that this was the first time the woman had been informed of her current living arrangements.

Shani looked toward the older man, passing his time away at a table with a group of other residents, playing what looked like poker.

The man made the international kookoo sign, swirling a pointed finger at his temple and mouthed the word *dementia,* then pointed at the woman.

Saladin passed by the card table, noting the subtle difference to a regular card game. They weren't playing with cash. They were playing with pills.

"What are the stakes?" Saladin asked.

"The white ones are worth one pound, the yellow are worth five, the pink are worth ten and the blue are worth fifty," the man told them. "Bill's winning."

Saladin looked over at the man pointed to as being Bill, who appeared particularly pleased with himself. "Really?" Saladin did the math in his head, adding up the value of all the tablets in front of him and scratched his head. "Shouldn't he have more pills if he's winning?"

Bill gave a cheeky grin. "That's because I've swallowed half of them."

"Interesting game," Alex chuckled.

Dray looked at Shani, his questioning gaze probing her for directions.

Shani stopped and centred herself for a moment as she touched the girl's hair band in her pocket. A subtle tug in her mind pulled her towards a doorway at the far end of the room, and down the left side corridor.

Shani followed her instincts, walking quickly toward the door and around the corner, almost knocking over another elderly lady.

"Oh dear. I'm so sorry," Shani apologised profusely.

"It's alright love. I've had more falls recently than I think I ever had when I was a little girl. Sadly, I don't bounce as well as I used to," she chuckled sadly.

Shani didn't know what to say, but clearly her face showed a mixture of remorse and pity for the older woman.

"Don't worry about it love. I'm Betty, by the way," she said.

"I'm Shani. Nice to meet you."

"Don't let my age fool you, I don't see old age as a time of inevitable decline, but as a time when childhood fantasies and passion can be reborn." Betty stated firmly, dismissing Shani's concern with a wink.

"How do you figure that?" Shani asked the older lady curiously.

"Well dear, there's a reason why there's not as many men in nursing homes as there are women. Half the women have been sexually repressed for quite some time before they come here, usually because their husbands are dead and they think their love life is over forever. But, then they come here and discover a smorgasbord of men just as eager to play Casanova in their seventies as they were when they were in their twenties."

"Really?" Shani wasn't sure whether the older woman was serious or whether she was trying to spin a story that would traumatise her for the foreseeable future.

"Oh yes. We have special codes. If someone says to you *'I'm in the mood for crumpet'*, you know they want sex. If a woman wants to give a man a head job, she flicks her false teeth out a couple of times with her tongue and the guys almost pass out from excitement. The men swear that a gummy head job is the best they've ever had," she chuckled, her eyes sparkling with cheeky amusement.

Ew. I am never getting that picture out of my head. Shani thought, discretely swallowing against her gag reflex.

But it seemed Betty wasn't finished with her geriatric life lesson. "It used to be really hard for the guys, there being three women to every man in here, but fortunately Viagra has changed that. They pop one of those little blue pills and half an hour later we've got an orgy waiting to happen," the woman told Shani enthusiastically. "Sadly, sometimes the pressure is too much for the men's old tickers and they pop their clogs. But, what a way to go, buried balls deep. The brochures they hand you about retirement homes don't tell you about all the sex that goes on here, but everyone likes a good surprise, right? The best part is, all the women have been through menopause, no one can get pregnant." The woman laughed so hard, Shani was sure she would be the next one to suffer a cardiac arrest or burst an aneurysm when her laughing turned into a coughing fit.

"Are you okay?"

"Oh yes dear. I can't dally though, I'm late for a game of cards," she said as she hurried away slowly with her wheelie frame.

A card game? Would that be the one where you get to eat your opponent's medication or strip poker, she wondered. At least now she knew why the blue pills were worth fifty quid. Shani shook her head with a smile. And she thought life in a retirement home would be dull.

Lost in thought over the whole idea of geriatric sex-capades, she didn't notice she was now flanked by all the brooding vampires she'd arrived there with.

"Which way?" Saladin asked her.

Shani pointed down the hallway. "It's in the last room on the right."

One by one the men passed her in the corridor. It didn't occur to any of them to knock on the door before barging in.

Hurrying to catch up, she put extra speed in her step when she heard them all muttering a string of curses.

"Fuck me dead!" Alex griped.

"Christ almighty, I think I've just gone blind." Saladin blurted.

"Ahhh, shit. Put that thing away." Dray growled.

Shani tried to push her way into the room to see what all the commotion was about, but a wall of vampires blocked her way. By the time they let her through she was glad she had missed the show. A grey haired man with a potbelly, lay on top of his bed and was just finishing tying the string on his pyjama pants, beneath which was a distinctive bulge.

"The name's Jack. Jack Price," the man said with a toothy grin.

"Pleased to meet you Jack, I'm Dray," he replied, offering his hand out, but quickly changed his mind and pulled it back again. Shaking hands with a guy who had just had his mitt wrapped around his ugly stick, was not on his to-do list today.

"And that, was Led Zeppelin," Jack said, pointing to his penis, which was fortunately now tucked away out of sight...mostly, his pyjama pants had a flap in the front which gaped ever so slightly. "But don't worry, he only likes the ladies," he finished with a smug chuckle, tilting his head to get a better look at Shani standing behind Dray.

"You call your man rod, Led Zeppelin?" Shani asked, stepping around Dray's dominant frame.

"Well, yeah. LZ for short, but I figured it made sense, Led Zeppelin was one of the coolest rockers of all time."

"And you think you're cool?" Dray challenged, his incredulous snort earning him a reprimanding glare from Shani.

"I am. And I've still got some serious *lead* in my pencil, so you can see how the name suits me. And now you know, I bet you want to become one of my groupies, don't you?" Jack said, waggling his eyebrows at Shani, and tempting his luck that Dray wouldn't knock his remaining teeth out of that shit-eating grin he was sporting.

Shani had to bite back her laughter. As corny as she found the name he'd given his pecker, she couldn't help thinking he must know how to use it or risk twice as much ridicule from *all* the ladies.

"Keep dreaming stud, I've been educated on how the sex-capades work around here. I'm sure you're responsible for putting the smiles on a few of the ladies faces, but mine isn't going to be one of them," she laughed, giving him a consolatory pat on the shoulder. Shani couldn't help a sideways glance at Dray. His expressionless face gave away nothing, but he held himself stiffly, giving her a sense of tension building inside him, like a powder keg just waiting to blow.

Jack heaved a disappointed sigh. "I had to try."

"I understand, but it's not your ah...Led Zeppelin, we came in here looking for," Saladin told him.

"Ahhh..." Jack rubbed his chin thoughtfully. "I think what you're looking for is in...."

"The Arnott's biscuit tin on the top shelf of the wardrobe," Shani and Jack answered at the same time.

"How did you know that?" he asked in surprise.

"It's a gift," Shani shrugged.

Opening the cupboard, Dray reached behind the pile of extra blankets and pillows on the top shelf. In the far corner was a silver biscuit tin. An innocuous looking box, it barely had any weight to it, but by the slight rattle inside, it definitely wasn't empty.

Philippe stood anxiously at Dray's shoulder as he cracked the lid of the tin open.

"This is it. We've found it." Dray said.

Philippe couldn't speak, couldn't move. He was riveted to the spot, his eyes glued to the contents of the tin. Despite everything his brother had done, deep down he'd still held some distant hope that he was wrong about Nicholas taking up his old habits. That hope died when the tin was opened. Inside was a finger, an ear and a piece of jewellery from each of the girls he'd killed, each neatly sealed in separate snap-lock bags. They had expected to find the remains of two, maybe three victims at the most. Instead, they found five.

Oh lord. How could I have not seen this coming?, Philippe thought.

"You alright there, bro?" Alex asked him.

"Yeah." *Not even close.*

"For an immortal you're not looking too good." Jack commented, looking at the slightly grey shade of Philippe's face.

"You know we're not human?"

"She is, but you lot aren't," Jack said, pointing to each one of them in turn. "You're all like the one who put that tin in my cupboard. Glittery eyes, unnaturally smooth body movements."

"Do you know what's in the tin?" Saladin asked.

"No. Nicholas never let me see inside it and I can no longer reach that top shelf to have a look for myself. I'm assuming it's something pretty important for all of you to come here looking for it. What is it?"

"You really don't want to know." Alex told him.

"Oh contraire. I've been curious since the day Nicholas put it up there."

"How do you know my brother?" Philippe asked.

"Brother? Hmm, yes, I can see the resemblance," Jack mused. "Nicholas just turned up here one day a couple of years ago pretending to be my nephew. I wasn't in a position to stop him from putting that tin in my cupboard, I was suffering severe Alzheimer's at the time. I couldn't remember my own name most days. Anyway, Nicholas was pretty keen to make sure no one would find it, so he gave me a gift."

"What kind of gift?" Saladin asked suspiciously.

"Blood. He gave me his blood. He restored my mental faculties so I could make sure no one went near his tin."

"That makes sense." Saladin grumbled.

"You never thought that was odd?" Dray asked.

"Of course, but what could I do? I'm old and frail. I assumed he was hiding some documents or something. Besides, I was grateful to him. I had my mind back...I just don't let anyone here know," he whispered with a cheeky grin.

"That you're no longer senile, why the pretence?" Alex asked.

"I like my privacy. Sometimes it's easier to let people believe I've still lost my marbles, that way they leave me alone. Plus, the nurses don't get nearly as upset with you when you feel them up if they think you're not in your right mind."

"That's wrong on so many levels," Shani said, scrunching her nose up in distaste.

"If you like your privacy so much and you're no longer senile, why are you still here?" Philippe asked him.

"I get three meals a day, a warm bed and the nurses aren't too hard on the eye. Well, most of them," he chuckled. "I just prefer my own company to anyone else's. I have the television to watch the sports, my books and radio if I get bored. What else do I need? Besides, how do I explain to everyone how I came to be cured of Alzheimer's overnight?"

He had a good point.

"So, you gonna tell me what's in there?" Jack asked.

Saladin looked him in the eye as he spoke. "These are trophies Nicholas has collected from his victims. He's a serial killer with a fetish for collecting body parts."

Jack's jaw went slack, his eyes blinking furiously as he processed the information. If he needed more proof, he had it. Saladin opened the tin and showed him.

"Blimey, I didn't expect that."

"We're trying to find Nicholas before he collects more trophies. Do you know where we might find him?" Dray asked.

"No. He never told me anything about himself. He just came, put stuff in that tin and left again."

"Jack, you can't stay here anymore, I'll arrange for you to be moved to somewhere safe. When Nicholas comes back and finds his trophies missing, he's not going to be in a good mood. He might even kill you," Saladin told him.

Jack chuckled. A soft, sad noise that held no fear.

"No, you won't. Look at me. Look where I am. This is the last stop on the way to the pearly gates. There's only one way a resident leaves a retirement home, and that's in a box. I'm not afraid of Nicholas or what he might do to me. I've had a long and happy life. As evil as he is, he gave me the gift of my sanity back, and that's more than I could've ever hoped for. I just wish I had a few more years left to enjoy my sport the way I used to. But we can't have everything we want, now can we?" he chuckled.

Dray watched Shani from the corner of his eye. She looked as uncomfortable at the old man's statement as he felt. Sometimes life was cruel, even more so for a vampire with an eternity to suffer with his misery, he thought.

"You take care of yourself, Jack." Shani told him. Squeezing his hand, she bent down and kissed his cheek.

"You're a sweet girl aren't you. You can come back and brighten my day any time you like," Jack said. Shani smiled and kissed his other cheek.

Dray's fists clenched with jealousy. It didn't matter that Jack was old and feeble, he was still male and it really yanked his chain to see Shani lavishing him with affection. As much as he wanted to, he didn't pull her away, that would be rude.

"We're done here. Let's go." Dray growled. Turning on his heel, he strode from the room without a second thought to anyone left in his wake.

Silently, Shani followed.

Slowing his pace, Dray came to a stop further down the corridor and waited for Shani to catch up. "You did very well today. I'm really proud of you," he told her. He felt bad for his constant irascible behaviour toward her but felt helpless to stop himself. The least he could do was let her see he wasn't a total arsehole. He could be nice too, sometimes. In fact, he was a fucking peach. A real considerate mother fucker.

"Thank you," she smiled softly. The sense of pride she felt at his compliment was absurd and so deliberately avoided mentally processing that gem. Any minute he was going to ruin the moment by growling his disapproval again of something. His mood swings were giving her whiplash.

As they neared the front entrance of Shadyvale, Libby stopped Shani once again.

"Can you take me home?" she asked.

"I'm sorry Libby, I can't. You live here." Shani told her sympathetically. I hope I never end up like her when I'm old, she thought to herself, sidestepping the woman and accidentally backing into Dray.

Shani stepped aside so unexpectedly, Dray nearly ploughed through her, tipping her off balance in his haste to leave. Gripping her about the waist, he held her against his body to steady her, and....Holy Mary, mother of...Jesus fucking Christ, with a swish of her hair her scent caught in his lungs. Dray's whole body stiffened with awareness of her. Her soft curves pressed against him, the warmth of her skin,... It was overwhelming and devastating.

The hell if he was going to stand there and endure one more moment of this torture. Pining over a woman he could never have held as much relevance in his life as knitting.

She belonged to another man.

You want some balloons for this pity party? Dray silently berated himself.

One by one they left, stepping through the home's front doors and made their way silently back towards their awaiting car. The sun was getting low in the sky, casting long shadows through the overhanging trees which lined the path to Shadyvale. Shani was grateful for the evening shadows. Sometimes when Dray looked at her, she got the unnerving impression he saw far more in her than she wanted him to.

Shani heaved a heavy sigh. Dray's good mood had lasted all of about a minute, as she'd expected, which meant the drive back to Oxford was going to be long and very uncomfortable, she thought.

13

It had been the longest day of his life. The three hour trip back from the retirement home had been the worst, especially after having had Shani's soft and supple body pressed up against his so intimately. The synapses in his brain were firing messages to every nerve, in every muscle of his body, telling him to take her hard and fast. Bury his hard cock deep within her body, share his blood with her and claim her as his own.

Lost in his maddening thoughts, a deep growl rumbled free from between snarling lips, nearly scaring the club's receptionist half to death as he marched through the foyer. Somewhere, far behind him he knew Shani and the rest of the group followed, but he was in no mood to wait for anyone.

The music thumped through his body, people talked and laughed, the scent of sweat and perfume and alcohol, everything hit him at once. Not that he noticed. The sound of his own heart beating drowned out any other sound, and the throb of his arousal had progressively intensified over the long drive back to the point where now, his stiff erection had become painful.

Amongst the crowd, Dray moved through the room slowly but with purpose. All except the drunkest of patrons sensed the presence of danger and moved quickly away to create a clear path wherever he walked.

Reaching the security door leading to the private offices, he punched in the code and strode through the doorway at a faster pace. It was only then that he noticed he was carrying Shani's coat and without any conscious thought, he brought it up to his nose, inhaling a deep breath. His body shuddered from her heady scent, infused into the soft, woollen fibres of the thick, grey coat. It was torture. Complete and utter torture.

She belongs to another man!

Dray should probably return the coat to her, there was a serious chill in the early winter air tonight, but he couldn't bring himself to do it. He didn't trust himself to be within twenty feet of her. Instead, he threw the coat over the back of a sofa by his office door and collapsed into the chair behind his desk. Leaning on his elbows, he scrubbed his hands over his face and then drove his fingers roughly through his hair.

"There you are." Saladin's face in the doorway was both an annoyance and a blessing. At least now he had something else to focus on.

"What?"

"Get everyone together, I want a meeting in my office in half an hour. We need to discuss what we're going to do to catch Nicholas and Scorpion."

"Sure."

Saladin looked at his friend with a critical eye but said nothing. What was the point, he knew exactly what the man was going through, he'd been through it himself before he'd claimed Teagan as his *mate*. Saladin's eye also caught sight of Shani's coat and made a mental note to tell her where she could find it. A second later he was gone, leaving Dray alone in his office again.

Dray buried his face in his hands once again, wishing he could be anywhere else, just for a few hours. He wished he was back on the South Dakota plains, where the breeze was mild and sun was warm, and his responsibilities were limited.

"Scratch that last order," Saladin called out.

Dray grumbled and cursed under his breath, pushing himself up out of his chair.

"Do you want to explain?" he demanded testily, marching down the hallway to stand in Saladin's office doorway.

Saladin turned around with a broad grin on his face. He was holding a pair of Teagan's panties and a note. "Make the meeting a bit later tonight, I believe I have an invitation to be preoccupied for a while," he boasted cockily, ignoring Dray's irritated growl. Pushing past him, Saladin made his way back out to the main area of the club in search of his wife, Dray following closely behind.

"How much later?"

"I don't know, two…three hours maybe." Saladin couldn't keep the smile off his face and didn't that shit-eating grin make Dray want to kill something…or fuck something. Adding a few calluses to his palm came to mind, but it wouldn't be nearly as satisfying as burying himself balls deep in a female's body. Shani's body. *God dammit!*

Dray went back to his office and made all the necessary calls, dealt with all the club related business, followed up on what was likely going to turn out to be a few false leads on Nicholas and Scorpion, and tried his best to ignore the unrelenting pressure in his pants.

What he needed, he decided, was alcohol. Lots of alcohol. Even if he couldn't get drunk enough to forget his problems, it might numb him enough to dull them for a short while.

Reaching the bar, Dray ordered a drink, turning his sharp hearing to the various conversations in the room.

"Hello Dray." A beautiful brunette leaned against the bar and looked at him. "I haven't seen you for a while. Have you been hiding from me?"

Dray only glanced her way before turning his attention back to his bourbon and what was going on around him.

"You're looking particularly tense tonight, Dray. I'd be happy to help you work out some of that tension from your muscles."

Dray's annoyance erupted as a low growl. It was meant to deter her from further conversation, instead it seemed to encourage this female to pursue him further.

Her fingers stroked up the length of his arm to his shoulder, where she paid particular attention to the vein in his neck. The one erotic spot on a vampire which was almost guaranteed to stimulate an aroused response, not just in his balls, but also in his fangs.

Dray growled again, this time however, it came out as a whimper of need. He looked over at Shani, standing talking to Philippe and Nadia, and then back at the brunette. What would it hurt. It was only sex, he'd done it countless times. It wasn't like he was cheating on Shani. *She belongs to another man!* Dray reminded himself.

Staring down at the brunette, he opened his mouth to speak but nothing came out. He was caught in a moment of indecision. "You're...." He was going to say *"You're making it very tempting,"* but she jumped in before he could finish his sentence.

"Vanessa, you haven't forgotten me already, have you?" she said with a sultry lilt to her voice, her hand sliding down his chest, over his abdomen, lightly gripping his groin. Of course, Dray knew her name, who didn't. But for a split-second he almost corrected her to use her nickname, *slut bunny*. However, since he was actually considering using her to gain some much needed relief from his incessant hard-on, he didn't think she'd appreciate it. Then again, she might also see it as a compliment.

"This is what you want." Vanessa stated, though there seemed to be a question in her voice.

"Yes. I mean no. Fuck, I mean yes." Damn, if he was any smoother, he might be confused with razor wire. "What I want, and need are two different things." He breathed out roughly. There wasn't a chance in hell he was going to enjoy this, but he needed to do something to try to wipe away his maddening desire for Shani.

"Let's go then." Vanessa unlatched her grip on Dray's balls and grabbed his hand instead, leading him back towards his office. She knew the way well enough, she'd been there on more than one occasion in the past. "I have to admit though, I'm a little surprised that you chose me, I thought you'd want to stick with your own kind," she said.

"What the hell are you talking about? You're my kind. We're both vampires." Dray growled.

"I meant that girl, Shani. You're both Indians. I thought you'd choose her."

"We're not the same kind of Indian." Dray corrected her.

"Well duh, obviously. You're male and she's female."

"No. We're from different countries. I'm a native American. Shani is a native Indian."

"Really? There are Indians in two countries? That's fascinating," she said with a sing-song sigh, as though the effort to figure out how that came to be was taxing her brain. It no doubt was. Thinking definitely wasn't her strong suit.

"Vanessa, shut up." Dray punched in the code once again to the security door and let her continue leading him toward his office. If he pretended he was going against his will, maybe he wouldn't feel so guilty, he thought to himself.

Shani stood beside Philippe and Nadia feeling like a third wheel. The two love birds couldn't keep their eyes or hands off one another, and who could blame them. It would be wonderful to have that kind of bond with someone. To feel so wanted. Her mind drifted momentarily to Dray. Why did her life have to be so complicated?

She wasn't the only one with issues, she knew, but she felt like she was the only one whose love life sucked. Shani had watched all the couples she'd met since she had arrived in England. They were all so different, but the one thing they all had in common was a deep sense of loyalty and devotion to their *mates*. Now even Nadia and Philippe had found that kind of love too.

If only she had been that lucky.

"I'm going back to the house, it's been a long day." Shani told them with a forced smile.

"Do you need a lift, I can see if Hawke or Anna are free?" Philippe asked. He'd offer to drive her himself but his last attempt at driving didn't end so well.

"No thanks, I'm just going to get my coat from Dray's office and catch a taxi. I'll see you both tomorrow." Not waiting for them to answer, she gave them each a brief hug and left.

Shani knocked on Dray's closed door but didn't wait for an invitation, her only thought was to collect her coat and get out again, preferably unseen and without any fuss.

Twisting the door handle and pushing it open, she just barged through the doorway and stopped dead in her tracks. Shani could almost hear her own jaw drop.

There was Dray, tall, dark and pant-less, standing not two metres in front of her up against his desk...and Vanessa's legs wrapped around his hips.

Dray's head turned in her direction, shock registering on his face as he stepped abruptly back from Vanessa. He didn't turn to face her fully, but he didn't have to for Shani to see how far things had gone between them. A slight glean of moisture coating the length of his heavily engorged manly pole, which stood proud of his body. It's dark red head, beaded at the tip with what she silently hoped was only pre-cum, but it could very well have been the final ooze of his climax.

A choking lump of emotion lodged in her throat. Unable to speak she grabbed her coat and hurried back toward the door. She ran from his office. She ran from the club and kept on running.

The sound of his office door opening brought Dray's head around, and he swallowed a curse.

Fuck, fuck, fuck!

What was he thinking? He never regretted anything he did in his life, but he was definitely doing the I-fucked-up-shuffle now. Sex with someone he didn't give a shit about seemed like a perfectly good idea when he'd been lust blind. But getting caught with his pants down by the one woman whose opinion actually mattered to him....?

The sight of Shani cooled Dray's jets instantly. If having her see him balls deep in another woman wasn't a cock blocker, nothing was. *Shitballs on fire!*

"Get out Vanessa." Dray's hard growl left no room for bargaining.

With a pouting sigh, Vanessa put her panties back on and straightened her dress.

"Until next time then?" she asked, putting a sultry lilt into her question and puffing out her partly covered, voluptuous chest.

Dray really wished he could say no, but it wasn't like he had a life away from his work, so working out his frustrations with semi-regular sex had to be done there at the club. And, since Dray wasn't a big conversationalist, wasting time on chatting up the female patrons rarely made it onto his to-do list. That left slut bunnies like Vanessa. He only had to proposition her with a beckoning finger and she was his for the asking. Convenient and stress free. At least, it used to be. There was an alternative, he could become celibate. It worked for both Narayan and

Alaric for a few centuries each. He was confident he could do it too…maybe.

Dray put his pants back on and tucked in his shirt as he waited for Vanessa to leave. He knew he should go after Shani, but what did he say? He hadn't actually done anything wrong, it just felt like he had.

"Dray, thought I'd find you still in here. When is everyone arriving for the meeting?" Saladin asked, his words trailing off as he took in Dray's distressed look. "What did I miss?"

In his minimalist style, Dray outlined what had happened with Shani and Vanessa.

"You have got to be kidding." Saladin ran his fingers through his hair as he paced back and forth across the floor.

"Do I look like I would make an effort to try to amuse you?" Dray bit back angrily.

"Ahhh Hell's hairy balls. Okay, it's official. Your fucked. Royally, totally fucked. Balls in a meat grinder, butt fucked…." Saladin cursed.

"You think? How the fuck did I let this happen?" Dray growled at himself.

"Damn, if Teagan isn't going to be pissed when she finds out about this. The next time you take a nap, you're likely to wake up with your head 'magically' super glued to your pillow, or worse." Both men knew that Teagan and Shani had become good friends, and if you upset Shani, you upset Teagan too.

"When Teagan finds out about what?" Teagan asked, walking up behind them.

Damn, they should have closed the door, Saladin realised. Too late now.

Briefly Saladin outlined what had happened.

For a moment Teagan was too stunned to do more than blink. "I'm sorry, you did what? I'm sure I misheard you, either that or I think I just had an aneurysm burst in my brain."

"Don't worry, I'll find her and talk to her, smooth things over. It'll be business as usual." Dray told her.

"Don't worry, it'll be business as usual?" Teagan mimicked caustically. "You're a self-serving bastard. Your next brilliant idea will probably be perforated condoms. And, what do you mean, *find her*. You don't know where she is? Seriously? I don't believe this."

"She can't have gone far, I'll find her." Dray said.

"No, you won't. We'll find her. I can guarantee you're the last person on the planet Shani wants to see right now. If you even try to talk to her, I will personally put your nuts in a vice and crush them."

It was an uncomfortable moment to say the least. Dray managed to look a little guilty for a second, or scared, maybe both. Either way, he came across as looking slightly constipated.

"Teagan, I think you should calm down." Dray told her.

"Have you ever noticed that those who tell you to *calm down*, are the ones who pissed you off in the first place?" she said to Saladin, pretending to ignore Dray. At the same time, she did one better than super gluing his face to a pillow, she magically super glued his hand to the front of his pants and left the office. She doubted Dray would have the gall to rip off his pants like Alex had and would serve as reminder to keep his man parts to himself, at least for, oh…about the next six hours, which was when the spell would wear off.

Dray was blowing smoke out his arse if he thought he would run from this shit storm he'd created, Teagan thought angrily as she left the office.

What a clusterfuck.

At that moment Saladin's phone buzzed with a message.

Shani kept running, stopping only when she finally ran out of breath, several blocks away.

Turning a corner into a dim alleyway, Shani leaned against the wall and sank to the ground. Tears gathered in her eyes as emptiness swept over her like a cold wind, spreading numbness through her extremities. She wanted to run further. Run as far away as her legs would carry her. Hugging her middle, she looked around with bleary eyes. She wasn't going anywhere. She had nowhere to go. She didn't belong here, she knew that. But she had no idea where it was that she did belong.

With a shaking hand she pulled her phone from her pocket and attempted to script a text message to her cousin Yasmin, but she couldn't stop her hands from shaking. With a huff she gave up the effort. Besides, the last thing she felt like doing was explaining everything that had happened using only her thumbs, it took too long and there weren't enough supernatural emojis to adequately explain her current predicament.

"Hey there." A deep male voice called from nearby, down the alley.

Shani jumped to her feet in fright. Getting mugged was just what she needed to top off her night, she thought. Although, she had to admit there was a small part of her that didn't care if she was. In fact, she almost hoped it was a mugger. At least it would mean there was a man out there who considered her as more than merely an inconvenience. How sad was that?

"It's okay. I won't hurt ye. I'm Sid."

Out of the shadows of the alley stepped an older man. Short wisps of hair protruded beneath the rim of his knitted beanie and his friendly smile radiated through his thick, white beard. Like Shani, he wore a long woollen coat, although unlike hers, his was old and worn, with small holes near the hem and on the sleeves. On his hands he wore fingerless gloves, in the grip of which was a bottle which he lifted up in greeting to Shani.

There was nothing threatening about the old guy, she decided and returned his jovial smile with her own half-hearted one, casually wiping away the residue of her tears. Sliding back down the wall she sat once again. Shani was surprised to see Sid taking a seat next to her and holding out his bottle.

"Oh, it's a 2017, red something" Shani examined the bottle in his hands. "I bet it's very oaky and corky and full of fruity notes," she said.

"Ye like?"

"It has a very pretty label."

"Have some."

"Sure?" she asked. Sid nodded.

Shani took the bottle from Sid's hands and took a large gulp, then another and another, and kept on drinking until the bottle was almost empty.

"I'm Shani," she told him when she was finished, wiping an errant drop which slipped down her chin.

"I know. There's not much that goes on around these parts that the street folk don't hear about. When yer homeless, people rarely notice yer even there, they don't care what they do or say around ye. It makes us very efficient at collecting information."

"You're homeless?" Shani asked sympathetically, yet not at all surprised going by his appearance.

"It's not so bad, I'm one of the lucky ones." he chuckled, although refrained from elaborating. "Ye look like yer having a bad night."

"You could say that," she grumbled and had to sniff back a new flood of tears that threatened to break free. A more difficult endeavour than normal she realised, as the excessive amount of wine on her empty stomach ran riot through her veins.

"By the power invested in me by the State of Inebriation, I now pronounce me screwed, and not in a good way." Shani grumbled.

"Ye know, a strong person isn't the one who doesn't cry, it's the one who does cry fur a moment, then gets up and keeps on going." Sid told her.

His eyes were warm and filled with something she was afraid to name.

Pity. It was pity. There she'd named it. And didn't that just suck. A homeless man felt pity for her.

"Ye want to talk about what's got ye so down in the dumps?" Sid asked.

"Not really," she answered, but in the next breath she continued anyway. "Men."

"Would that be men in general or one specific man?"

"A couple of specific men actually, but I'm starting to wonder if they're not all alike. Except you," she quickly added, so as not to offend him.

"Of course, not me." Sid chuckled. "Well, ye can't stay out here all night love, ye'll catch yer death."

Shani's jaw dropped in surprise as she watched Sid pull a cell phone from his coat pocket and start texting.

"I'm only semi-homeless these days, I have a place to stay if I want to, but most of the time I prefer the outdoors," he chuckled as way of explanation.

"What? How? Who are you calling?" Shani asked as her surprise turned to suspicion.

"Dray. He'll want to know where ye are."

"Of course he would, because I'm *soooo* important to him," she answered haughtily.

"Don't be so quick to judge him. Dray is one of the best people I know. He's honest to a fault, and......."

"And has a heart of stone." Shani quickly jumped in. "He does everything possible to avoid me and when he can't, he treats me like I'm a burden sent to annoy him. He's an arsehole."

Sid laughed. "I've known Dray fur a few years now, and I agree he can be a bit abrupt at times, but that's because he's so focused on his work. He doesn't like distractions or emotional attachments."

"Ha! He didn't seem to have any problems being *attached* to someone earlier when I saw him," Shani griped, anger tinging her voice.

"Dray doesn't think like most men. To him, women satisfy his male urges and need to feed. Nothing more. He only chooses the females he knows he could never form an attachment with, like Vanessa."

"You know Vanessa?"

"I know *about* her." Sid said firmly, as though her name put a sour taste in his mouth. Shani couldn't agree more.

"That doesn't explain why he goes out of his way to be an arsehole to me though."

"Doesn't it? Think about it. I think what's happened is Dray cares fur ye far more than he wants to and it scares the crap out of him. Yer a married lady, and he's a man with the highest morals," he said, pointing to Shani's wedding ring. "For all the years he's lived and all his smarts," Sid tapped a finger to his skull, "I don't think he knows how to handle the situation."

"You really think that's the problem?"

Sid nodded sympathetically.

"How did you get so wise?"

"Believe it or not, once upon a time I used to be a psychologist."

Shani's eyes nearly popped out of their sockets in surprise, making Sid laugh again, a hearty bellow that reverberated off the alley walls.

"Um, Sid, can you *not* let Dray know that I'm here, please?"

"Sure." With that, Sid redirected his text.

A few minutes later, Saladin appeared around at the entrance of the alley, a sympathetic look on his face. It was a familiar expression she was really beginning to hate.

"I guess you know what happened…how I walked in on Dray, with that woman?" Shani asked.

"I do," Saladin replied.

"I don't feel comfortable seeing Dray again. I think I should go and stay with my cousin," Shani told him.

"You don't have to do that. I can make sure Dray doesn't come to the house while you're staying with us, if you don't want him to. You don't need to come back to the club either, unless you want to," Saladin told her.

"Thanks. Maybe I'll think about it. Right now, I'd really like to get out of here, if that's okay with you."

"Sure. I'll get someone to take you home."

Shani leaned across to Sid and gave him a peck on the cheek, just as she'd done for another older man earlier that day, Jack. She couldn't help feeling a little anxious for them both considering they were both living on the edge. Sid was at the mercy of the elements, and Jack was likely to be at the mercy of a murderous vampire sometime in the not too distant future. Strangely, they both seemed at peace with their fate.

Maybe she could learn to be at peace with hers too. She used to think that she was resigned to the hand life had dealt her. Now, she wasn't so sure. She wanted more out of her life. Probably much more than she was entitled to have.

Opening her purse, Shani handed Sid a wad of notes.

"That wine tastes like dish water, you should buy yourself something decent," she told him with a smile.

"Thanks love, just might do that. Caw blimey," he exclaimed as he examined the amount she handed him. "Maybe I'll buy a whole case."

Shani chuckled at the look of surprise and excitement on his face. "Thanks for the chat, Sid."

"Anytime love. Anytime."

14

It had been a long, tense wait for Philippe to return from the retirement home. Nadia wasn't sure what his mood would be like after finding his brother's latest stash. He'd called her when they were leaving, which surprised her a little, but it also put a huge smile on her face. It seemed their little talk earlier had made a big difference to his attitude when it came to improving the line of communication between them. Not that she could decipher his mood from their brief conversation. *"We're heading back now. I'll meet you at the club,"* was all he'd said before he hung up. The subdued tone in his voice gave nothing away. Sometimes she really hated the way vampires could mask their emotions so easily, whilst contrarily, she wore hers on her sleeve for everyone to see.

Nadia sat on one of the plush sofas facing the club's front entrance, her foot tapping anxiously as she sipped on her glass of Dutch courage, a.k.a. white wine. No tequila for her tonight. She didn't want to risk a repeat of her 'dance-off' performance from the other night. She preferred to limit her embarrassing moments to one a week, if possible.

Then he arrived, along with the rest of the group who'd made the trek to Shadyvale, all of whom walked right past her, their expressions stern from unsettling thoughts, all except Shani, whose relief to be free of the group was equally as palpable.

"Hey Shani, how was it?" Nadia asked.

"It wasn't what I expected, that's for sure."

Shani kept talking, but Nadia's focus had shifted back toward the door, watching as Philippe's eyes searched the room when he entered, when they reached hers and he smiled, it felt like every one of her concerns had suddenly melted away.

"Hey you," she greeted, standing up to plant a kiss on his cheek.

"You miss me?" Philippe asked apprehensively.

"What, did you think I wouldn't?"

"Maybe," he shrugged, his eyes watched her intently for any sign of hesitancy.

"We kissed," Nadia said, as though that statement said it all.

"I remember, and I understand if you want to forget it ever happened."

"I don't want to forget it. It was a great kiss."

"It was?"

"It was. If one of us was a frog, there would have been some seriously impressive consequences."

"You're comparing me to a fairytale?" he chuckled.

Nadia nodded, doing her best to contain a cheeky grin. "Then kiss me again and let's see if we can find you a prince." Heat shimmered in the depths of his blue eyes. Leaning forward, he brushed his lips against hers. Pulling back, Philippe looked himself over. "Nope, didn't work. No prince here."

"Try again. This time kiss me like you really mean it," Nadia said, rolling her eyes at him.

"You'll have to show me how," he smirked.

So, she did. Reaching out she gripped the waist band of his jeans and pulled him hard against her. There was no tentative sampling in this kiss, no getting-to-know-you pecks. He tangled his tongue with hers like they'd been going at it forever. Heat pooled between her thighs and as if sensing her knees were becoming weak, Philippe wrapped his arms about her waist to take her weight more fully against him. Nadia slid her hands up to his neck and buried her fingers in the short silky strands of his blonde hair.

Lost in the sweet aching sensation, she moaned aloud when he pressed his thigh between her legs. His strong, toned body made her want to sigh in anticipation and joy.

"Ahh hmmm. I'm sorry to interrupt, I'm going back to the house, it's been a long day," Shani told them with a forced smile.

Oh shit, they were so caught up in each other they'd forgotten that Shani was even there with them.

"Do you need a lift, I can see if Hawke or Anna are free?" Philippe asked. He'd offer to drive her himself but his last attempt at driving didn't end very well.

"No thanks, I'm just going to get my coat from Dray's office and catch a taxi. I'll see you both tomorrow." Shani gave them each a brief hug and left.

"You're such a gentleman, that's why I love you," Nadia blurted out before her brain could check the words leaving her lips.

Philippe pulled back, his eyes wide with…with…dammit, she couldn't tell what he was thinking. Surprise? Relief? Horror?

Nadia's cheeks suddenly felt way too hot and she wanted the floor to open up and swallow her. She hadn't meant to say that. It was one thing to stake a claim on him, girls did that all the time when they found a guy they liked. But dropping the 'L' bomb on him when all they'd done so far was kiss? Nadia bit her lip as she held her breath, waiting for his delayed reaction, desperately willing herself not to have a panic attack.

"Um, sorry. I didn't mean to blurt that out. I think I need to get another drink. You want one? I'll get you one," she said. Not waiting for an answer and not looking him in the eyes for fear of the rejection she was almost certain she would see there, Nadia turned away and disappeared into the crowd, heading directly for the bar.

Vanessa watched Nadia walk away, leaving Philippe all alone in the crowded room. He looked hot in his muscle hugging shirt, and his jeans bulged in *all* the right places. She couldn't help noticing that the bulge beneath the zipper was particularly large. Just how she liked it. She also liked that he was single and a virgin. Oh, the things she could teach him.

Besides that, she was horny as hell. She was a millisecond from orgasming when Shani burst in on her and Dray, only a minute earlier. Her clit was still pulsing like a bitch, even walking sent small shockwaves through her body. She'd been so close, she just needed someone to finish the job Dray started. It wouldn't take much, even an inexperienced guy like Philippe could do it, she thought as she straightened her dress.

"Philippe, how about a dance?" she asked, giving him her best sexy smile.

"Ah, Vanessa. Thanks, but no. You got me into enough trouble the other night. So, the answer is definitely no."

Okay, so the word *no,* was not in Vanessa's vocabulary, Philippe realised when instead of moving away as she was supposed to, she stepped closer. Invading his personal space Vanessa ran a finger over his jaw and down over that erotic spot on his neck.

He couldn't help the involuntary shudder at her touch. He wasn't turned on, not in the least, it was a shudder of revulsion. He couldn't bare her touch, it actually made him feel physically ill. That realisation made him smile. A male only reacted so negatively to a female's touch if he was already attuned to the touch of his *mate.*

Unfortunately, Vanessa interpreted his shudder and smile as a sign to pursue him all the more.

Oh crap. He couldn't do this again. Nadia would never forgive him, even if he was innocent. Pushing her hands off him, Philippe stepped away but Vanessa moved in unison with him.

"Take your hands off my man, bitch!" Nadia shoved the two drinks she was carrying into the hands of the nearest person walking by, her furious gaze never leaving Vanessa for a moment.

"Yours? You're dreaming Nadia. You haven't got what it takes to please a man like Philippe."

Nadia snorted out a laugh. "You think you do? You'll never be able to satisfy Philippe."

"That's not what he was telling me when he was feeling me up just now."

Nadia shot Philippe a questioning look, but his look of disgust was all the answer she needed.

"Liar, liar, slutty dress on fire." Nadia replied confidently.

"I think...." Vanessa began.

"Don't think Vanessa. You'll hurt yourself." Nadia cut in.

Vanessa's laugh was harsh, her eyes raking Nadia up and down in an ocular version of a bitch slap and snarl of contempt. "Look at you, with your freaky white eyes and your marshmallow figure. Ten years from now he'll look at you and see a frumpy woman with cankles on the end of your cellulite pitted legs. No man wants someone like you, except to experiment with," Vanessa said spitefully.

OMG! Vanessa didn't just go there, did she? Nadia had always been self-conscious of her figure. Unlike three of her four sisters who were tall and slim, she had inherited her mother's fuller figure, just as Teagan had. Although, in Nadia's eyes Teagan wore her extra weight much better than she did.

Nadia gave her best *'bitch, please'* smile, drawing out the loaded pause in silence for as long as possible before replying.

"This, coming from a vampire who still gets Botox injections to stop wrinkles from developing. How dumb are you? No, wait, I can answer that. If you were any dumber, they would have to find a whole new classification for intellectually disabled."

Vanessa gasped in shock. Maybe her brow would have risen in surprise too, except all the Botox in her forehead made the effort to form any sort of facial expression, mute. What was evident however, was the glittering hatred that filled her eyes.

"You're just jealous that I can get any man I want while you throw yourself at them time after time and get rejected. You're pathetic!" Vanessa scoffed. "And an embarrassment. A pathetic embarrassment," she tacked on at the end as her grey matter searched for words to add to her vocabulary. "You wouldn't know what to do with a man. You're a virgin, everyone knows that," she sneered like it was a curse. "Men don't want inexperienced women, they want a woman like me who can suck their cock with expertise, deep throat them and swallow their cum when they blow their load in my mouth. Have you even seen a man's cock?" Vanessa bit out with mock sympathy.

"In case you haven't noticed Vanessa, I'm the one with the man and you're the one whose been rejected, not just by Philippe tonight, but also Dray. Yeah, I know all about it, everyone does, word travels fast in here," Nadia pointed out, running her hands deliberately over Philippe's chest and abdomen in front of her. She'd gotten a text message from Teagan about the whole Dray/Vanessa/Shani debacle before she'd even left the bar with their drinks.

"Slut!" Vanessa growled angrily.

"You know, you're actually supposed to have moral standards before you can morally judge someone else, but I guess a skanky whore like you with the brains of a dead jelly fish wouldn't know that. I wouldn't worry about it though, it's only a matter of time before dementia kicks in and you'll forget all about what a *pathetic embarrassment* you are," Nadia replied, quoting her own statement back to her.

"I'm a vampire, I won't get dementia." Vanessa said.

"I guess you're screwed then, because you're not going to get any smarter either."

"Bitch!" Vanessa trilled. Nadia wasn't sure if Vanessa hit that particular birdlike pitch because she was angry, or frustrated that her pea sized brain couldn't come up with a verbal retaliation. It seemed though that when the mentally challenged vampire couldn't fight with words, she resorted to fists.

And it was on.

Nadia was hit with a body tackle as a fist came flying at her face, and the shrill screams on both sides escalated into a full-blown cat fight.

Within seconds Hawke was there pulling Vanessa off Nadia, while Philippe did his best to contain Nadia with a firm grip around her waist. Thinking she had calmed down, Philippe let her go. Big mistake.

Nadia dove forward as Hawke dragged Vanessa toward the door, kicking and yelling. Philippe reached Nadia just as she stretched out her hand in an attempt to grab a handful of her hair. She missed, but when her hand closed only inches from Vanessa's head, the slutty vampire let out the most blood-curdling scream and began to convulse.

Shocked, Nadia released her clenched fist and immediately Vanessa's convulsions stopped, her dazed eyes looked over to Nadia. It wasn't simple fear she saw in the vampire's eyes, it was terror. Now, instead of fighting Hawke's hold to get back to Nadia for a second round in their boxing match, she was fighting to get out of the club faster.

Nadia stared in astonishment, firstly at Vanessa whose fake tanned complexion turned a sudden shade of grey, and then at her open hand. Her eyes lifted then to Philippe who stared at her in awe. Nadia's gaze shifted to note that nearly every person in the club was also staring at her.

Okay, so limiting her public displays of embarrassment to one a week was asking a bit too much.

Her eyes once again shifted to Philippe nervously as he turned her to face him fully. She was a freak, she knew it. A frumpy freak and after this ugly display he would never want anything more to do with her.

This is it, she thought. *He's going to tell me I'm not the kind of girl he's looking for.* She'd heard those words from every guy she'd ever gone out with. Sucking in a deep breath, Nadia braced herself.

"Did you mean what you said before?" Philippe asked.

"What?" she asked, confused.

"When you said you loved me, did you mean it?"

Nadia nodded nervously, waiting for him to follow through with: *That's too bad, because I don't think we should see each other anymore.*

"Nadia." His voice was barely above a whisper. He looked down, unshed tears glistened along the rims of his eyes. "I never thought anyone could ever love me."

The magnitude of his statement could have been measured on the Richter scale since it rocked her foundations to her core. Nadia wrapped her arms around his waist and pulled him closer, pressing a tentative kiss against his lips. "I do."

Returning her embrace he held her tight, his shallow breaths brushing through her hair as he finally whispered, "I love you too. I always have."

His mouth came down on hers, stifling any possible protest. His lips and tongue worked in tandem with hers, stoking a fire burning between them. Suddenly, without breaking their kiss, he scooped her up in his arms, forcing her to loop her arms around his neck and carried her toward the back of the club, to the privacy of the VIP room.

Pushing past the heavy curtain, he marched to the far corner where the shadows dominated.

Setting her gently on her feet, Philippe smoothed his hands over her face, searching for bruises and scratches. "Are you okay? Did she hurt you?"

"No, but I think I hurt her."

"What did you do to her?" Philippe asked curiously as he rubbed her shoulders, soothing the knots from her tense muscles.

"I don't know. I went to grab her hair, but I missed. I grabbed something though, I could feel it in my fingers. I'm pretty sure it was her astral body. I could see it pulling away from her physical body."

"Are you sure?"

"Pretty. I just don't know how I did it. I was just so angry, I didn't care what part of her I ripped to shreds. She wasn't getting her hands on my man again."

Philippe chuckled, but didn't say anything, he just kept massaging her tight muscles until he felt her begin to relax. It didn't take long before his hands began to move down her back, massaging lower and lower until he'd almost reached her backside.

Turning to face him, Nadia tipped her chin up to claim another kiss, the heat between them building with every swipe of their tongues against one another. Philippe could feel her heart racing inside her chest, beating faster. Sensual, erotic need rose through her senses and left her breathless.

Once again, Philippe lifted Nadia from her feet. Gripping her thighs, he placed them at his hips as he took a seat on the plush sofa behind him, leaving her legs straddling him. The heavy length of his erection, bulging at the front of his jeans, pressed against her core.

Philippe's hands gripped her backside as he shifted his weight beneath her. His hands skimmed over her arse cheeks and thighs exploring the contours, scorching a path to the spot she needed him to touch the most, and drawing a wet, aching response from her body with a rippling coil of sensation as she rolled her hips against him. Damp heat and a storm of sensation erupted in her clit as the pressure on the sensitive bundle of nerves from their position, rippled through her, ricocheting into her womb.

It felt so good.

Addictive.

A pleasure so intense, she knew she would beg for it again later.

Grinding himself against her, his lips took hers once again. There was no escaping the low moan that erupted.

Nadia tangled her fingers in his hair, arching her hips to slowly ride that hard ridge more firmly, wishing more than anything there were no clothes between them.

As though he could read her mind, Philippe slipped his hands beneath her top to cup her breasts, sending bolts of pleasure straight to her clit.

"Ohh, I've dreamt of this," she whimpered in a breathy voice.

"You've dreamt of *me* doing this, or someone else?" he asked, a husky growl rumbling from his chest. It was the most sexy thing she had ever heard.

"You. Only you," she chuckled, sliding her own hands beneath his shirt to rake her nails down over his chest and abdomen, daring him to doubt it.

"Fuck!" Philippe sucked in a tense breath as every part of his body stiffened in immediate response. He'd never known this kind of heat, like a fire curled within his gut, stretching out to encompass every molecule of his being. He'd never burned for a woman's touch the way he burned for Nadia.

Philippe's phone buzzed in his pocket. He didn't need to answer the call to know what it was about. No doubt the meeting was about to start.

"Ignore it," Nadia told him as she nipped his ear. Dragging her lips back to his, he did just that.

Her breathing grew ragged as Philippe's hands and mouth worked in tandem, sending small electric shocks straight to her core. Nadia dragged air into her lungs and tried to think, but her mind was a blur of pleasure and need.

Philippe's phone began to buzz again. Saladin had tremendously bad timing, he thought, but the meeting could start without him.

Nadia's hips rocked against him and his lusty growl sent a rush of heat through every cell in her body. "We need to slow down. At this rate you're going to kill me," he said, half-jokingly.

"She won't. But I will!"

Philippe looked up to see Nadia's father standing behind them, glaring down at them as he put his phone back in his jeans pocket. Oh crap, that had been Gustav calling him, not Saladin.

"Um, hi dad," Nadia said, her cheeks turning a pale shade of crimson as she quickly stood up and straightened her top.

"If you want to keep what's in your pants in one piece, follow me. In case I'm not making myself clear, I'm not talking about your phone," Gustav growled. "If you're having trouble controlling that flagpole of yours, I'd be happy to chop it off for you."

Philippe swallowed uncomfortably and tried to smile, but it came out as a constipated grimace, his hand instinctively covering his groin protectively. He may have only been able to achieve an erection for barely a week of his very long life, but already he'd become very fond of it and had no intention of losing it before he had a chance to use it in the manner nature had intended.

Leaning down, Philippe gave Nadia a quick peck on the lips before reluctantly letting go of her hand, grudgingly following Gustav to the meeting.

"In my next life I want to come back as his jock strap." Nadia sighed dreamily as Teagan came to stand beside her, ignoring their father's scowling expression as he marched Philippe away.

"If you ask nicely, I'm pretty sure he'll let you hold his family jewels anytime you like," Teagan laughed.

"What makes you think he's ready for sex? He's only just started to develop adult *urges*," Nadia said, emphasising the last word with air quotes.

"Oh please...He's so hot for you, I thought he was going to self-combust just now. The bigger question is, are you ready to give up *your* virginity?"

"I've been ready for years. I just haven't had the opportunity. I'm more concerned that someone else like Vanessa will try to steal him away from me."

"It's not going to happen, he only has eyes for you. Trust me."

"Maybe. Maybe not. Look at him, he's a hot, sexy guy these days. Just because he doesn't show any interest toward them, isn't a deterrent to the girls who want to snatch him up."

Teagan had to agree, Nadia was right. Philippe was like a blazing inferno to an ovulating moth. "You stress about stress before there's even anything to stress about. Then you stress over stressing about the stress that doesn't need to be stressed about. It's stressful."

"Is it wrong that I'm stressing about being confused?"

Teagan's smirk was the only response Nadia was going to get.

"I don't like it." Nadia grumbled, not willing to let go of her anxiety just yet.

"You don't like the fact that he's attractive to other women, or that he might find other women attractive?"

"Both."

"Okay, why don't we focus on what's important."

"Right. How do I make sure no other woman gets his attention?"

"I actually meant that we focus on what you did to Vanessa that made her run out of here screaming. But we can start with that."

"I'm glad you agree. No more cotton granny pants for me, only skimpy little silk numbers with matching lacy bras for me. Um, Teagan, I might need to do some shopping."

"Don't worry, I don't think Philippe will be interested in what you're wearing, it's what's underneath that matters to him," she told her with a sly grin. "But, if you need someone to go shopping with you, I'm your girl."

"You wouldn't tell dad if I don't come back to your place tonight, would you?"

"Me, tell dad you want to have sex with your boyfriend? Please," she rolled her eyes with exaggerated disbelief. "Of course not...so long as you tell me every sordid detail tomorrow."

"What?"

"I'm kidding. I really don't want to know."

"Good, because I don't plan on telling you."

"Okay, we done with your love life issues?" Nadia nodded. "Good. So, what did you do to Vanessa?"

"Beats me."

"Seriously, what did you do? She's scared shitless of you, and I mean that literally. I'm pretty sure she crapped herself."

"I have no clue. I was just really angry with that skanky whore bitch, and I grabbed what I thought was her hair. I missed."

Teagan laughed. "Guess you did. And...?"

"I got her astral body instead. Somehow, I managed to separate her soul from her physical form."

"That's really cool, and a bit freaky. I'm really proud of you little sis," Teagan grinned.

"Do you suppose that's one of the abilities of an *Ei'Ambriath*, a spirit walker? If so, I think I might have a new trick I can teach Paige." That felt good to say. For as long as she had known her sisters, it had always been them teaching her, now she might finally have something to teach one of them.

"There's a good chance you're right. I wonder if the club's cameras picked anything up?" Teagan wondered. "You want to have a look?"

"I didn't think Dray liked anyone messing with his equipment, not even you or Saladin."

"What he doesn't know won't hurt him, he's at that meeting with everyone else?"

"In that case, hell yeah."

"Alright then, follow me."

Teagan opened Dray's office door just a crack to look inside. "Coast is clear, he's not here."

"Thank goodness for that," Nadia mumbled to herself with a deep sigh of relief.

"That's because I'm right behind you." Dray's disgruntled voice thundered behind them.

"Oh, crap. You nearly made me pee my pants. Don't sneak up on a girl like that. You scared me." Teagan growled back, silently cursing. Payback was a bitch. He was probably quite proud of himself catching her off guard like she'd done to him only a short time ago.

"Then don't sneak around. What is it you want from my office? You here to steal my binoculars again?" Dray was clearly still in a pissy mood about his hand being magically super glued to his crotch.

"No. What are you doing here anyway, aren't you supposed to be in the meeting with everyone else?"

"I'm going there now. Why are you in my office?" he growled. Intending to shoo them out of the doorway, his brain sent his immobile hand a signal to move, but it just wasn't budging. He let out another frustrated growl.

"Well, we certainly didn't come here to accidentally see you in a compromised position like Shani did." Teagan bit back haughtily.

Nadia cringed when his top lip curled back and his fangs began to descend with a guttural snarl, but Teagan stood her ground without flinching.

"Why are you in here?" he asked again, his words clipped short as his anger continued to rise.

Teagan crossed her arms in front of her and glared at him defiantly. "We wanted to see if the club's cameras picked up the incident between Nadia and Vanessa?"

"Explain." Dray said gruffly.

Nadia told him what happened as thoroughly as possible while Dray listened. Of course, the fight between the two women wasn't news to him, everyone in the club knew, he'd managed to catch the tail end of it himself. However, hearing from Nadia what had actually happened, the anomalies he'd noted in their scuffle, now made sense. Fingers caressed a glass of amber liquid in his one free hand, his hip propped against his desk. His intense, golden brown eyes drilled into her, his head cocked to one side. Nadia hugged herself and held her breath nervously and waited for his assessment.

"But vampires souls are fixed to their bodies like an exoskeleton. That's what makes us immortal. And you just separated her soul from her body?" Dray said in amazement. It was the way he looked at her though that made Nadia feel like a circus monkey who had just learned to juggle knives.

"Yay me?" she answered a little bewildered.

"Well, whatever you did, let's keep this between us for now, okay?" Dray said. Nadia nodded. "Only a small group of people know what happened to you after you made that potion for Nicholas."

Nadia's shoulders slumped, her eyes locking onto the dull beige carpet beneath her feet. Dray lifted her chin to meet his eyes and spoke to her more gently than she thought him capable of. "What's happened isn't your fault, Nadia. But as I was saying, very few people know what happened to you, and we need to keep it that way."

"Why?"

"You wouldn't know this, but before I sent Philippe to Alabama to help Hawke, we had a meeting. Afterwards, Philippe and Nicholas had a fight that destroyed Saladin's office."

"I noticed all the new furniture," Nadia interjected.

"Yes, well, Nicholas came off second best. He was really pissed off and threatened to destroy the one thing that Philippe cared most about. You."

"Me? So Nicholas planned on hurting me to get back at his brother?"

"Yes. And I think that if word got around to the wrong people that you've gone through a transition and have new talents, it won't just be Nicholas who will try to hurt you again, but possibly Scorpion too."

"But, what about my eyes? Doesn't the fact that they're now only a couple shades darker than pure white, give away that I've changed?"

"It does. But as far as anyone is aware, you were sick and you recovered. You're changed pupils are perceived to be a kind of scarring effect."

"Did you start that rumour?" Nadia asked Dray curiously.

"No. I didn't need to. People have come to their own conclusions."

"Am I in danger from Nicholas now?" she asked.

"No. We have enough security around you that he won't get within a hundred metres of you, even if he was stupid enough to try." Nadia should have felt uncomfortable by that revelation, but truth be told, she was used to it. She'd grown up living in the Alliance's Baltic and Northern European headquarters with her father, Gustav. Since he was the leader of that division, she'd been watched like a bug under a microscope all her life. Well, except for the past three or four years when she'd house hopped between her sister's homes. She was still watched, just not nearly as closely.

"Haven't you just confiscated his trophies, don't you think he's going to be really pissed about that?"

"You think he'll come after Philippe?" Teagan asked.

"We're counting on it."

Nadia looked between Dray and Teagan, she couldn't read minds, but it didn't take a genius to know what they were both thinking. It wasn't safe for her to be around Philippe at the moment.

"Don't say it." Nadia growled, pointing a warning finger at her sister.

"Maybe it's best if you stay at my place again tonight. And maybe tomorrow you should go back to the manor until all this is resolved."

Nadia shook her head defiantly. She didn't care that Teagan's house and the manor had protection wards on them. She wasn't going to be separated from Philippe again.

"Nope. Not going to happen. Where Philippe goes, I go." Nadia's chin rose higher until she was practically looking down her nose at her sister, crossing her arms in front of her in a silent challenge.

"And if being with him puts him in even more danger because he's preoccupied with trying to protect you, that he leaves himself wide open for an attack?" Dray asked.

Nadia's rebellious bravado dimmed at the truth of Dray's words. Her heart sank.

"Okay, but not tonight. I'll go to the manor tomorrow, but I'm staying with Philippe tonight."

"Of course he's welcome to stay at my place with you, you know that," Teagan told her.

"No. I meant, I'm staying with him at his apartment."

"That's not wise." Dray said.

Nadia looked to her sister with pleading eyes. "What are the chances that Nicholas will discover his trophies missing before tomorrow?" she asked, directing her question to Dray.

"Probably slim, but we shouldn't take any chances."

"I just want one night with him. Alone."

Teagan's expression was as conflicted as Dray's was harsh.

"Fine. But tomorrow you're going to the manor, no excuses," Dray said, drilling her with a stare she wondered if he'd learned from her father. It was just as effective.

"Fine," she agreed reluctantly.

"Teagan didn't reverse the spell?" Saladin chuckled.

Dray's frustrated growl was the only answer the rhetorical question deserved.

"Where did Vanessa disappear to?" Saladin asked, keeping his voice at a whisper.

"Don't know. Don't care."

"She took off like hellhounds were after her."

Dray grunted but didn't reply.

"Are you disappointed? Were you planning on going for round two with her now that Shani's left?" Saladin probed. The best thing about being the owner of the club was that he could have people thrown out. And tasered. Even cavity searched. Fortunately, he would have to do none of the above with Vanessa. Whatever Nadia did to her, scared her so much she ran terrified from the club. Hopefully, never to return, Saladin thought.

"Not even if my dick was on fire and Vanessa was the only one with a fire extinguisher. I'd rather have my hand stuck to my groin permanently. I've made a decision, I'm going celibate," he growled, giving his magically super-glued hand another fruitless tug.

Saladin laughed so hard he thought his sides might split. His outburst momentarily silenced the speaker in the meeting, drawing every eye in their direction. But Dray wasn't laughing, not even a little. "Oh, fuck, you're serious." Saladin said, lowering his voice to a whisper.

"Never been more serious. Women are too much trouble."

"You haven't accidentally or on purpose, happened to taste any of Shani's blood at any time, have you?" Saladin asked, concerned about the repercussions if he had. There would be no worse torture for Dray if he had. Shani was his one true *mate*, that was a certainty. If he'd tasted her blood his bond to her would be sealed. Celibacy would no longer be an issue, he would be physically incapable of having sex with any other woman. Unfortunately, feeding too would also become an issue for him. Saladin remembered all too well what that was like. He'd survived two years in agony, believing his suffering was the lesser of two evils before he and Teagan had found a solution to their *mating* issues.

"No."

"Good. Keep it that way."

"What have I missed?" Dray asked.

"Not much. We've just been discussing likely scenarios and how we can locate Nicholas and Scorpion."

"I don't think we need to worry about that. He's going to come looking for us and he'll start with Philippe." Dray told him, refocussing his attention on the man speaking, the lycan alpha from South Africa.

"…more importantly is how do you contain a vampire with an unknown amount of strength and who carries an invisibility ring?" the man blustered, his tone harsh.

"How well do you know this dick?" Saladin whispered to Dray, pointing to the man speaking.

"Not well. Their previous alpha died suddenly a year ago. The contenders for succession fought it out, Donovan Eckhaus won."

"I know that, but what do you *know* about him?"

"Truthfully? About as much as you. He's a cynical arsehole with a bad attitude, but his clan seems to respect him."

"So, he's just like you. No wonder I like him," Saladin grinned, inducing a single raised eyebrow on Dray's otherwise expressionless face.

Philippe watched the meeting from the back of the room where he had once again been relegated with Marek, feeling as uncomfortable as the rephaim looked. It wasn't that he was uninterested in the topic of discussion. Quite the opposite. Any discussion involving catching his fucked up, homicidal brother had his attention. On this occasion however, just not all of it. It seemed that the necessary amount of blood flow required to maintain concentration and industrious thought was still being re-directed below the waistband of his jeans. He was trying to keep his mind focused on the meeting, he really was. But he couldn't stop thinking about how Nadia's soft curves felt beneath his hands, or how his body responded when she scraped her nails over his abdomen beneath his shirt...Philippe shifted uncomfortably in his seat, trying unsuccessfully to relieve the pressure inside his pants.

"You okay?" Marek asked.

"Yep," Philippe answered from between clenched teeth as he tugged on the leg of his pants and sucked in his gut until his hardened erection shifted. He almost sighed in relief. "And you? You seem a bit tense."

"Fine. Never better," Marek answered with a well rehearsed, casual smile. What was he going to say, the truth? Hardly. He doubted there was anyone in this room who would care about his problems.

He had hoped that he could speak to Shani tonight discretely, ask her for her help. However, that didn't seem like it was going to be an option anytime soon. Not since she'd decided to stay away from the club for the remainder of her visit to Oxford. He could ask Teagan or Saladin for their permission to visit her at their home he supposed, but he couldn't do that without explaining his reason, and without their permission, he would never get past the protection ward around the property.

That left him with a dilemma.

Considering Shani had been the key to finding Nicholas' trophy collection, which he had no doubt would set off Nicholas' rage. So too, Shani may be able to help him locate his binding stone. The sapphire which was set into a ring and tethering his soul to the physical world, making him immortal. And, since Scorpion has shared with him a photo proving the evil son-of-a-bitch has it, Shani could also be the key to finding Scorpion.

However, Marek knew enough about Scorpion's intelligence to know he'd realise how they tracked him. Marek also knew that Scorpion wouldn't hesitate to destroy his binding stone in retaliation. If that happened, Marek would be mortal again.

Was he ready to become mortal again?

Was he ready to die?

No. He wasn't.

"......and if we only manage to draw Nicholas out of hiding, how then do we track down Scorpion?" Marek heard Donovan ask the group.

"We track him through my binding stone. I have proof that he has it," he heard himself reply as he stood to face the leaders of the Alliance.

15

The room went silent as all eyes turned to Marek. For a moment he actually wondered why they were all staring at him. He heard the words leave his lips but it had been an involuntary action, as though his voice had somehow become detached from his brain, or maybe he'd suddenly developed a case of Tourette syndrome. It seemed that despite his fears for his own well-being, his subconscious was in control and he was being forced to comply.

With a smooth transition from surprise to confidence, Marek pulled his phone from his jacket pocket, searching for the proof. Alaric cursed as he stared at the photo, yet when his eyes lifted to meet his, Marek saw a new level of respect he had never seen before.

They had come a long way, the pair of them. Fifteen hundred years ago they had been enemies. Alaric had been among the nephilim and druids who had captured and banished the rogue nephilim to the Valley of Vardin in Fey. Marek may not have lost his title of rephaim, traitor, but it seemed he was slowly regaining some of his honour. At least in Alaric's eyes. And that meant more to him than he was willing to admit. It wasn't as though Marek wanted praise or even recognition for his sacrifice, and both Alaric and he knew that's what this declaration amounted to. It was the simple relief to know that deep down, the goodness inside him was stronger than the darkness which he had believed dominated him for so long.

"Can you come by my house tomorrow?" Saladin asked Marek.

"Yes." His answer, though short, was spoken with clarity and determination.

"Great. I'll have to check with Shani of course, but if you can come by around two'ish we'll see what we can discover."

Marek nodded his agreement, his eyes scanning the sea of faces still staring at him. Some continued to watch him suspiciously, while others regarded him with varying degrees of concern. Regardless of what they thought, they all talked over the top of one another, passing Marek's phone around to view the photo.

"Are you sure about this?" Philippe asked quietly beside him. Again, Marek nodded.

As Marek's phone came back to Saladin, he walked over to the fallen nephilim to return it to him, clasping his shoulder in an unspoken, thank you. Heading back to his place in the room, stopping beside Dray.

"In case you get any bright ideas about coming by tomorrow, don't. You're not invited," Saladin told him dryly, sparing a pointed look at Dray's hand which was still magically super-glued to his groin.

"I have no intention," Dray growled.

"Good to see some of the blood has finally returned to the brain inside your cranium, instead of the one below your belt," Saladin smirked.

"Fuck off. You can be a real arsehole sometimes, you know that?"

"I try." Saladin laughed.

The meeting wrapped up pretty quickly after that, although not before Dray baled up Philippe to inform him of the discussion he'd had earlier with Teagan and Nadia.

"Are you certain Nadia said she wanted to spend the night at my place?" Although Gustav had already left the room, Philippe couldn't help whispering. Interpreting Dray's snarling growl as a yes, Philippe broke into a broad grin which slid into a worried frown almost as quickly. "Nadia wants to have sex with me. I've never done *it* before, what if I don't know what to do? I mean, I've watched others having sex, countless times, but watching isn't the same as actually *doing* it. Now I sound like a pervert," he flustered.

"I'm not your fucking sex therapist. You'll figure it out."

Dray's sarcastic vote of confidence wasn't helping relieve Philippe's anxiety, which was climbing at a steady pace.

"Fuck. I don't know what to do?"

Dray glared at Philippe with a mild hint of resentment in his eye. Playing matchmaker had never been on his to-do list. Ever. Especially when his own love life was in the shitter and rapidly heading around the S-bend into the eternal cesspool of never-ending loneliness and torment. But, here he was contemplating giving a pep talk on relationships and sex to a vampire who was half a century older than him. How fucked up was that.

"Do you love her?"

"More than anything."

"Do you know how to kiss her?"

Philippe's lopsided smirk preceded a tentative, "Yes."

"Then kiss her and show her how much she means to you. The rest will happen naturally."

"You think so?"

"I know so." If only it could be that simple in his own situation, Dray thought.

"Thanks Dray."

"You're welcome. Do me a favour though, don't tell anyone about this conversation, I have a reputation as a heartless, surly bastard to maintain."

Philippe nodded and tried his best to contain his grin.

"And, just to be safe, don't forget to turn the security on around your apartment. The last thing we need is for Nicholas to pay you a visit when you're *distracted*," Dray told him, adding the last part without any hint of humour.

Nor did Philippe want to have to face Gustav if anything should happen to Nadia while she was with him. As much as he hated the idea of being apart from her again, he had to agree that sending her to the manor tomorrow for an extended stay was for the best. At least until he eliminated his sociopathic brother as a threat to her, and the world in general.

If he was only able to have this one night alone with Nadia, Philippe intended to make it count.

"Keep your phone handy and call me if anything seems even a little bit *'off'*." Dray commanded, leaving Philippe alone to contemplate the next few hours.

"Philippe, is everything alright?" Nadia asked, coming to stand beside him, her hand reaching out to take his.

"Everything's good now," he smiled, leaning down to kiss her lightly on the lips, his blue eyes glittering with the concoction of emotions he was holding back from sharing with her in public.

"You want to go home?" she asked. Her question held some nervousness but was asked with determination and hope.

Did he? Was the Pope Catholic?

In that moment he would have loved to scoop her up in his arms and race her back to his apartment at preternatural speed, but he didn't want to seem over eager. Instead, he kissed her again, a brief press of lips which left the promise of so much more. "Let's grab a taxi."

Ten long minutes later, they were climbing the stairs to the landing at his apartment door.

"Are you sure about this Nadia, because I can't promise I'll have the strength to stop if you change your mind," his voice was a husky whisper. Nadia inhaled sharply as he threaded his hands through her hair, pulling her closer. If he let her inside, she was going to end up in his bed. She knew it and he knew it. There would be no going back.

"Yes. More sure than I've ever been about anything in my life," she replied determinedly.

There were too many words in there for Philippe to process at the moment, his mental capacity having suddenly dipped to caveman level after the word, *'Yes'*.

He couldn't get the door open fast enough.

Philippe burst through the doorway, dragging Nadia with him...and stilled to take in the moment. Dipping his head, he took her lips in a gentle caress which was magnified in intensity by emotion and anticipation.

Nervousness faded away as Philippe's world shrank down to the nerve endings in his lips and his fingers as Nadia settled her weight against him more fully. He held her there with an iron grip about her waist as he hungrily pursued their kiss, locking lips and tangling tongues, all combining to stoke a fire inside him he had no will to dowse.

Nadia's fingers trailed down his abdomen, sliding them beneath his shirt until she brushed bare skin. He hissed at the icy contact against his skin, bucking his hips against her.

"Are *you* sure Philippe? This is your first time too." She leaned into the caress of his lips, angling her head until he was kissing her cheek. Turning her face toward him a little more, as if searching his face for a quirk of his lip, a flicker or sign that he was only trying to pacify her, but what she saw stole the breath from her lungs. His eyes glittered with a need so intense and so primitive, she felt branded under his gaze, and her heartbeat kicked into a higher gear.

"Very."

"Then touch me." Hunger radiated from her pale grey eyes, flushing her cheeks, and her breasts rose and fell in quick succession as she fought to breathe.

"Nadia, can I ask you something?" She nodded. "Why did you never have sex with any of the guys you went on dates with?"

If anyone else had asked her that question she would probably have been offended, especially at a time like this. But this was Philippe. He had seen her at her worst and never once judged her harshly. He may have frowned once or twice, and probably regretted the times when he had held her head up out of the toilet bowl after a big night out. But he was always supportive of her, no matter what.

"Because..." she hesitated, not because she was embarrassed, but because she knew he would be annoyed with her. "I'm not beautiful like my sisters..." And there it was, that disapproving scowl she was expecting. But hey, he wanted the truth, she was going to give it to him. And this was *her* truth. Ignoring his accompanying growl she continued her explanation. "But, I've always wanted what they have. Someone who will love me for who I am regardless of my full hips and my plain looks. Maybe I'm a little old-fashioned, but I wanted to save myself for a man who wants me forever, not for five minutes." Nadia may have considered following the general rule of dating which allowed sex on the third date as being acceptable, however, considering she never got past the second date with anyone, she didn't get the opportunity to test her resolve and see whether she would actually go through with it.

"So, you're telling me that if we have sex right now, that I have to keep you? Forever?" He tried to joke although the effort came out as a strangled exclamation.

"Yes." Nadia looked up at him shyly, expecting his rejection. Once again he surprised her. His heated stare had become downright covetous, making her head giddy and her stomach flutter.

"Well then, if having sex with you is the price I have to pay to call you my own, you've got ten seconds to strip before I do it for you. *Mate!*"

Nadia blinked once, then twice. Had she heard him right?

Not waiting for him to change his mind, Nadia reached a hand behind her and unzipped her dress. Letting the straps fall from her shoulders to reveal the bare flesh beneath.

As Nadia's breasts became exposed, Philippe froze, his eyes glued to those voluptuous mounds with their tight rosebud tips, looking over her bare skin with reverence and awe.

"Oh, sweet Jesus." He sputtered.

It was then that Nadia realised that feeling beautiful had nothing to do with actual looks. It was a state of mind. And the way Philippe was looking at her, she felt like the most beautiful woman in the world.

Philippe growled. The scent of Nadia's arousal triggered the very male part of him, the part that was pure instinct. In a second, his own shirt was gone. Not as smoothly and erotically as Nadia's, instead he'd shredded his into pieces in his effort to be free of it.

Nadia glided her fingertips over his chest and across his stomach to the waistband of his pants. "Now these," she grinned with burgeoning boldness, as she unfastened the top button. Leaning forward she sucked his hard male nipple into her mouth. His sharp intake of breath told her he liked it, so she bit down lightly. Its effect on Philippe was instant. Her dress which had pooled about her waist, now pooled about her feet when he pushed it over her hips, leaving her standing in nothing but her panties.

He couldn't stop his hips from flexing into the warmth of her hand as she slowly pulled down his zipper. Covering her hand with his own, he halted her fingers enthusiastic exploration a moment before she could slide them inside his jeans. He didn't trust himself, he was sure he would come about a millisecond after she touched his bare shaft. Instead, grinding himself against her hand with the barrier of his jeans between them, his lips took hers once again. There was no escaping the low moan that erupted. Both his and hers.

Breaking their kiss, Philippe took a step back to carefully remove his jeans, his eyes locked onto Nadia's, wary of her reaction.

Fully naked, Nadia took in the sight of him. It took her breath away. His chest was broad, diamond-cut flat abs dominated his torso, with his perfect navel and the fine hair adorning his lower belly trailing down to his groin. Long powerful legs rippled with muscle as he flexed them nervously.

And, oh lord…between his thighs jutted an awe-inspiring erection, thick and heavy. The size and thickness was something women dreamed of, artists attempted to immortalise in sculpture and paint, and porn stars envied. A vein pulsed along its length, feeding the dark head as it jerked from the lust surging through him.

Nadia swallowed as her eyes widened.

"Does that thing come with training wheels?" she almost squeaked.

"We don't have to do this tonight. We can wait," he told her, even though the strain in his voice contradicted his statement.

"Not on your life. If we don't, one or both of us is likely to spontaneously combust from sexual frustration," she emphatically told him.

"We'll take it slow then, shall we?" Philippe stepped closer, pulling her into his arms, his lips covering hers in an explosion of pure hunger, yet another contradiction to the statement he'd just made. Not that Nadia was complaining. She really liked this primal side to Philippe.

"I've never been this close to a man's penis before." It was an internal thought spoken aloud in whispered awe as she gripped his shaft with her fingertips, running them lightly along its length to the swollen tip.

Philippe's hips jerked involuntarily and his whole body tightened up, a hiss of pleasure/pain escaping through his gritted teeth as she gently explored him. His eyes watched her intently, his knees nearly buckling beneath him when she licked her lips.

"How does it feel?" His voice was so rough with desire, she couldn't help smiling. However, looking up into his face, her smile quickly slid away. No one had ever looked at her the way Philippe was doing now. His eyes burning with unveiled desire, his fangs fully descended. She'd never seen anything so panty-melting hot in her life. "How do I feel?" he asked again through labouring breaths.

Nadia ran her fingers along his shaft once more, a little more firmly this time, dredging a tortured moan from his throat. "It feels soft, but hard…like velvet over steel," she told him.

He sucked in another hiss of breath. "I'm not going to last long if you keep touching me like that. I'm only hanging back by the sheerest margin of will power here."

"I don't want you to hold back," she told him innocently.

"I *need* to. I don't want to lose control. I don't want to hurt you."

"You won't."

"I don't want to take that chance." What he needed was a diversion, something that would satisfy her while he got his own urges under control.

Reaching down Philippe gripped the back of her thighs, lifting her up against him and forcing her to wrap her legs about him. He was extremely thankful that he hadn't removed her panties when he removed her dress. He could feel the leakage of pre-cum beading at the tip of his cock as it rubbed against the soft satiny fabric, and another groan escaped his lips. In long even strides, he carried her into his bedroom.

Philippe laid Nadia onto the bed, lowering his lips to her collarbone to trace a path lower.

Her back arched in invitation as he pulled her nipple into his mouth. The strong suction of his lips went straight to her toes and the moan that escaped begged him for more. His tongue tormented the hard bud, and the sharp nip of his teeth sent shards of sharp pleasure to clench her womb. Philippe teased and pushed her into a storm of sensation where the world disintegrated into the background of escalating pleasure.

Nadia felt feverish, desperate for more of his touch. She had never known anything like it before. As though her body had been waiting for his touch, anticipating it, and now every cell and nerve ending was coming alive for it.

However, there was still one barrier standing in the way. Her panties. Hooking her fingers under the waistband, she pushed them down, growling in frustration a moment later when she'd only managed to relocate them as far as her knees, seemingly stuck.

"Do you want some help?" he asked with an impish grin.

"Please," she begged.

Shifting his weight above her, he ripped them off in one fast, sharp, determined yank, dropping them haphazardly on the floor, his eyes never leaving Nadia's flushed face, completely entranced by the sensual anticipation backlighting her eyes. Holding his position, Philippe's hand slid down her body slowly, touching, exploring every inch of exposed flesh between her plump breasts to the soft, dark curls covering her mound, now exposed for all his ogling glory.

Shuddering in delight as his strong fingers slid through her slick heat, gliding over her clit with just enough pressure to make her cry out.

"Oh God, Philippe. Are you sure you've never done this before?"

"I'm positive. Why, am I doing it wrong?"

"Not that I can tell. Just don't stop," she begged.

Philippe touched her with care. She was so wet with need that his own need to ram himself inside her almost cancelled out all rational thought, all except his need to make sure she was completely ready for him. He was determined she would feel no pain when they finally came together. He would cut his own throat before he'd let her suffer even a moment of unnecessary discomfort.

His thumb found a rhythm, raking over the sensitive bundle of nerves, caressing them with devastating results, leaving her teetering on the edge of coming undone as the pressure and heat coiled between her legs. Nadia's desperate cries only encouraged him to continue his ministrations, sending her speeding toward exquisite bliss as blistering waves rolled through her.

Tiny quakes of pleasure erupted between her legs and the most delicious spasms rocketed through her. Nadia's toes curled and her fingers gripped the sheets, wanting the sensation to wash over her again.

Satisfied that he'd brought her to one climax using only his fingers, Philippe couldn't wait any longer. The need to feel her climax beneath him with her tight walls clutching his hard shaft, was all consuming.

Lifting his weight above her to take his weight on his arms, he wedged himself between her thighs. His hard arousal rubbed through the moist slit of her sex, over her sensitised clit once, twice, drawing a moan from her plump rosy lips as the rippling sensations began to build once more.

Philippe gritted his teeth as the burning centre of her body called to him, promising a haven unlike anything he had ever known.

"Now. Please. Now," she begged.

Nadia gasped, her hands gripping his shoulders, her fingernails biting into his skin, but he welcomed the stinging pain, it kept him focused. It would have been easy to lose himself in the moment since it wasn't just her first time, it was also his. However, he couldn't restrain the groan that tore past his lips as he breached her entrance. The swollen folds of her sex, silky soft and slick with moisture, opened like the most delicate flower as he pushed the blunt tip of his heavy length between them to reach her weeping centre.

Slowly, very slowly, he moved his hips, working the head of his cock inside the snug depths between her inner walls. He let each sensation, each wave of pleasure, wash over his senses until he reached her hymen barrier.

"Are you ready?"

"Yes," she nodded quickly. Her answer was almost a plea.

"Count to three." he told her.

"Okay. One...two..."

Nadia gasped at the sudden pain. Philippe thrust forward on the count of two, breaking the barrier and then stilled completely, letting her adjust to the width of his erection which he could feel stretching her tight channel to its limits. His eyes watching Nadia intently, terrified he had caused her serious pain. A second passed, then two as she held her breath to contain the cry locked in her throat. Then her expression eased.

Pinpricks of pleasure/pain struck as he breached her tight entrance. A muffled, whimpering cry left her lips as his first thrust was followed by a second, going deeper, stretching her further. Philippe pulled back, then pushed inside her a third time, breaking the barrier of her innocence, and his hard length kept on sinking deeper.

A rasping groan rumbled from Philippe's chest as the exquisite pleasure wrapped around him, equally as forcefully as her narrow walls gripping him. Sensations built and collided, coalescing into a maelstrom of need for more. So very much more.

Drawing back, his heavy length stroked slowly against sensitive nerve endings, inflaming them with the stretching pleasure/pain. She could feel him pushing tender muscles apart, stroking delicate tissue, and sending almost unbearable pleasure whipping through her body as his hips once again began to move, plunging himself deeper inside her with every thrust.

Philippe kissed her, swallowing her cries.

"Philippe," she whimpered against his lips. He answered by sliding inside her even deeper, filling her further, until he found just the right rhythm. She would have been embarrassed how easily he affected her, if he were anyone else. But with Philippe she felt completely at ease to be herself. She loved the way his eyes lit up when he elicited a moan or a gasp from her lips.

Pumping his hard length inside her, pushing through the clenching depths of her inner walls, the pleasure was almost painful in its intensity. He wasn't going to last long, he knew it from the moment he dropped his pants, but he was determined to give her a *first time*, she would remember.

Nadia could feel her response to him spiralling out of control, as though her body recognised the touch of the one she was destined to crave for eternity. There was no pulling away, no denying what she felt. Instead, she wrapped her legs around his hips tighter, lifting into his thrusts, taking him deeper, driving them both to the point of insanity.

"Bite me," she pleaded, knowing full well that the vampiric hormone in his bite would intensify the experience tenfold. It would also seal their bond as *mates*.

Philippe didn't hesitate. *Mine!*

Need consumed him like he'd never known before as he rocked into her harder, faster, until he came undone. A deep possessive growl erupted from him only a second before his fangs breached the soft flesh of her neck, plunging them into the throbbing vein.

The dominant growls coming from deep within his chest were hotter than Hell, setting off electric trails of sensation throughout her body when his fangs pierced her skin. Damp heat coated her slick folds, sensitising her further from the tight buds at the tips of her breasts to the swollen knot of nerves in her clit, detonating her orgasm like a nuclear bomb. Ecstasy was a vortex of swirling, vivid sensation, like a dozen tornadoes whirling out of control, threatening to converge inside her with a final climactic explosion.

And it did.

Emotions overtook her, wreaking havoc on her senses and sending her soul flying into the stratosphere in a blinding burst of pure rapture.

Nadia knew she would never be the same again, there would be no returning to the woman she once was as they came together, in body, mind and soul.

The past was re-written, the future became an open book of blank pages, but it was the present which forged the binding between them.

The moment Nadia's inner muscles clamped down on his stroking shaft, tightening on him, Philippe went rigid as his own climax came at him full throttle like an unstoppable bullet. His seed boiling in his balls exploded from him, the rush ripping all sense of reality from his mind in a dizzying force.

Breathing hard, Philippe collapsed on the bed beside her. Pulling Nadia close, he tucked her head under his chin. Gently rubbing his hands along her back, soothing tense muscles and stroking his fingers through her hair. Then he caught her scent as it wafted up to fill his nose and his lungs. Inhaling deeply, he smiled.

"I'm carrying your scent now, aren't I?" she asked matter-of-factly.

"Yes. Do you regret it?"

"You're my *mate*. I'll never regret it."

There it was again, that declaration of ownership, Philippe thought happily. It may take some getting used to, being told he was worthy of being loved, but he'd never felt so content, so…whole. Philippe pressed his lips to her temple.

"You know, there's another bonus to being *mated* now," Nadia said, twisting her head to give him a wry smile.

"And what's that?" he asked intrigued.

"My dad can't threaten to chop off your flagpole anymore," she laughed.

Yep, that was a huge bonus in his books. Maybe Philippe was faster and maybe even stronger than the lycan leader, but Gustav was damn scary.

"Get some sleep," he told her when he saw her yawn.

When he went to move off the bed, Nadia's arm wrapped about his waist tighter, scissoring her leg between his, and held on tight.

"Okay, how about I stay here with you while you sleep?" he chuckled, content to do just that. There was nowhere he'd rather be than wrapped up in the arms of the woman he loved.

And that is exactly what he did. He lay there for the rest of the night, watching her, wondering how he got so lucky.

Nicholas watched his brother with contempt from the shadows just beyond the periphery of the security cameras surrounding the property. Dark hatred filling his corrupt heart. Loathing for the happiness he had never felt himself.

Contemplating the events of that day, it wasn't hard to conclude that he'd underestimated the Alliance's ability and determination to find him. However, while the psychic's gift may have led them to his souvenirs, they would never be able to find *him*. He was already two steps ahead of them.

If they hadn't been so preoccupied with the contents of his biscuit tin, they might have considered that Nicholas had someone in the nursing home keeping him informed of *'unusual'* visitors to Jack's room. That person was a very naughty nurse who'd been more than willing to notify him the moment the group had left the retirement home. The cost of her loyalty? It was giving her the best sex of her life. Which amounted to about ten minutes of near boredom for him in the supply room, but hey, it was an easy payment.

The debt he'd settled with old Jack was much more enjoyable.

After slipping on his invisibility ring, he casually walked past the Alliance's sentries posted around the neighbourhood. Everything about him was hidden including his scent. It was as easy as taking candy from a baby.

He'd walked through the foyer, into the common room and down the hallway, directly to Jack's room. Although the old man had jumped when he suddenly became visible only a few feet in front of him, he hadn't been surprised by the visit.

"Nicholas, I only have one thing to say. Fuck you!" Jack spat the words out defiantly and gave him the middle finger. Two minutes later the old man was knocking on the pearly gates. A pillow over a man's face had a way of cutting his life short.

And now he was here, outside the apartment he'd shared with his brother until recently.

He'd endured over a century and a half of Philippe trying to control him, judging him and chaperoning him everywhere he went. In the end though, what had Philippe accomplished? Nothing. A big fat nada. If anything, Nicholas' appetite for the macabre had only increased because of the years he had been forced to suppress his base instincts. All he'd had were memories of past conquests, and fantasies about future ones. Now he had the freedom to act on them.

This was the second time Philippe had taken his souvenirs from him, which really pissed him off. Losing them was like losing a favourite pet. Holding them in his hands brought a rush of excitement flowing through his veins as vivid memories of those kills filled his senses. Holding a finger, he remembered the feel of the female's skin against his as he first made love to her and then pared her flesh away with his knife. Holding an ear, he could recall the female's voice, her groans of pleasure and her screams as she later begged for mercy. And holding a piece of her jewellery brought back the memory of who she was, a prostitute, a teacher, a bank clerk.

Now it was time to take something from his brother.

Only weeks ago, he'd promised Philippe he'd take Nadia from him. He'd hoped that he'd already succeeded after she read Morganna's grimoire. Disappointingly, that hadn't panned out as he'd anticipated, although from the reports he'd been hearing, she had suffered a great deal before her recovery. Not that he actually cared one way or another if Nadia lived or died, she meant nothing to him personally. She was just the means to an end in torturing his brother. No doubt Philippe suffered a great deal too when Nadia was so gravely ill. However, if she had died then, Philippe would have only been saddened and possibly pined for her, for a hundred years or so, since she had only been merely an unrequited love.

Nicholas grinned. Finally, this cat and mouse game with his brother was drawing to a close. That's not to say he didn't plan on drawing it out just a little longer, now that the game had just become good.

While Philippe had grown a pair of balls in recent weeks, literally, although how that was possible still stumped him, it definitely worked in Nicholas' favour. Now, Philippe had more to lose than ever before. His *mate* being top of that list. If he lost Nadia now, he would never recover from her loss.

Which is why she would make the perfect bait to lure him to his death.

Hope grew inside Nicholas' black heart as a plan took form in his mind.

As the first rays of the morning sun broke over the horizon, Nicholas once again casually walked past the Alliance's security, cloaked in invisibility, and placed a small box at the front door.

Let the games begin.

16

Nadia rolled over and searched for her pillow but couldn't find it. Drowsily she lifted her head to check the bedside clock and groaned. Had she really only had three hours sleep? Then she remembered why there was no pillow, and smiled. At some point during the five hours before her three hours of sleep, the pillows had been relocated to places unknown during the most incredible sex she'd ever had in her life. Okay, so it was the only sex she'd ever had, but they'd done it so many times, she'd lost count.

No wonder she was exhausted. Deliciously, marvellously, contentedly exhausted. But, where was he?

"Philippe?"

"Coming," he called back. In the time it took Nadia to find a pillow and put it back in its rightful place under her head, Philippe was standing in the doorway looking exactly how she remembered him. Gloriously naked. "I thought you might want some water," he told her, holding up a filled glass.

He was right, although that wasn't the only thing she had a sudden taste for. Nadia's eyes skimmed down Philippe's muscle hardened body and practically purred with satisfaction. He looked even better in daylight. Pushing back the blankets she parted her legs. Lifting her knees out to the sides she slid a hand down over her belly, through the short, dark curls at the apex of her thighs, spearing a single finger between the moist, plump folds. "I have something for you too."

The possessive growl rumbling from his chest was instantaneous. Nadia smiled and licked her lips, her gaze blithely watching him grip his limp cock with his free hand. Under her lustful gaze and the slow pumps of his fist, it swelled. And swelled. It thickened until it jutted rigidly from his body.

Her legs were braced far apart, as if she'd put herself on display for men a hundred times, although he knew better. "You're beautiful."

For the first time in her life, Nadia didn't feel the need to correct him.

Putting the glass of water on the nearby dresser, Philippe approached. The mattress dipped beneath his weight as he knelt between her legs on the bed.

Philippe leaned back to look at her more fully. "You really are perfect," his voice rough with raw emotion, and eyes burning brightly with dazzling iridescent flecks.

How did he do that? Sharpen her arousal with just a look. Nadia stilled in anticipation, while her heart beat harder within her chest from the smouldering adoration in his eyes.

Philippe moaned, a soft breathy sound which seemed to go straight to her core. Wrapping an arm about Nadia's waist he dipped his head to her breast. Her breath caught as his lips surrounded the hard pink bud and sucked it into the wet warmth of his mouth, stroking it with his tongue and massaging it with his lips.

Her body became liquid beneath him as he sucked and laved her nipple, stopping only long enough to swap to the other. The ache within her rapidly grew until it was almost unbearable. She wanted him lower, any part of him, every part of him. She wanted to feel that delicious heat sucking, stroking and filling her core. She wanted his weight pressing down on her as he plunged deep inside.

"So perfect," he told her again, lifting himself higher against her.

She scooted closer, smoothing a hand over the sleek bulge of his shoulder, down the steely rise and fall of his pectorals, across his ridged abdomen.

Groaning, he lowered his head to claim her lips in a long, deep, pulse-spiking kiss. Heat seared her as his tongue slid inside to dance with her own. Every tantalising stroke making her body burn.

Stretching against him, reaching for him, a moan whispered past her lips as her hips tilted upward. Philippe responded, pulling her into the thick ridge of his iron-hard pole pressing firmly against her belly.

The passion between them was beginning to intensify. Then....Nadia's empty stomach growled.

And just like that the moment was gone.

Philippe pulled back. There was no male alive who could withstand his *mate's* suffering, whether it was from the pain of an injury, or the discomfort of hunger. It was hardwired into their DNA to rectify the situation using whatever means at their disposal. Nadia understood all too well and flopped back against the pillow, letting out a heavy sigh of defeat. She'd thought it funny when her *mated* sisters told her about their experiences in similar situations. She wasn't laughing now.

"Breakfast. Any thoughts?" Philippe asked.

"We should get some," Nadia huffed.

"Some thoughts, or some breakfast?" he asked cheerily, which only made her grumpier.

Nadia wasn't a big fan of smallgoods. You know, ham, bacon, bratwurst. But damn, looking at Philippe's hard length, it really irked that she was going to have to postpone nibbling on his salami, or playing hide-the-salami, or...Arghh, why was she torturing herself. *Bad, lusty hormones!*

"Got any cereal?"

"Any particular kind?"

"What do you have?"

"Um, I don't know, I'll have a look." In a blur of motion, Philippe was gone. Nadia listened to cupboards open and close. "Bad news. No cereal," he called from the kitchen.

"What about toast?"

Philippe checked the freezer. "Nope. Sorry," he called again. A second later he was standing in the bedroom door again holding a stick of butter and a half-empty jar of strawberry jam...and still naked. "I have an idea. Why don't you have a shower while I nick down to the corner shop and pick up some supplies."

"Sure, why not. I could use a cold shower," Nadia grumbled.

"I may not have any food, but I do have hot water," he reassured.

Nadia climbed from the bed and shot him a sideways glare that needed no verbal interpretation.

"I'll make it up to you later sweetheart, I promise."

"Will that be before or after you take me to the manor?"

Philippe had to concede, she was right. Their private time together was limited to a few short hours. After that, they would have a dozen interfering busybodies hovering about them twenty-four hours a day. Too bad. It can't be helped though, Nadia needs food, he sighed.

Choosing not to answer her question, Philippe segued back to his original topic. "There's shampoo in the shower stall but if you want conditioner, I think there's some in the cupboard."

"Thanks. Would you mind if next time I stay over, I bring some of my own toiletries?" When Philippe didn't answer, Nadia quickly backtracked. "Sorry, I didn't mean to be pushy. It's cool if you don't want me to leave any of my stuff here."

"No. I mean, of course you can. Move everything in. My home is your home. It just caught me by surprise, that's all. Until this moment I've never considered the possibility that anyone would want to share a home with me. Except my brother, and he only tolerated our living arrangements because I gave him no choice."

"I'm not your brother."

"No love, you're not," he chuckled, looking her up and down covetously. "You'd better get in that shower before my dick develops a painful case of priapism."

"I have a cure for that you know," Nadia chuckled, motioning for him to join her in the shower.

"Oh, I'm counting on it. Just not until you've had some breakfast. The sooner you get in the shower…by yourself," he quickly added, "The sooner I can get to the shops, feed you and then shag again until we both need another shower."

"When you put it like that…" Nadia marched from the room, quickening her pace to a jog when he paddled her bare backside as she passed him in the doorway.

Philippe waited to hear the shower door close and the water turn on. Grabbing a pair of jeans and a T-shirt, he dressed and grabbed his wallet.

Opening the front door, something caught his eye on the mat directly beneath where his foot was about to land. It was a small package about the size of a small box of chocolates, neatly wrapped with bright red paper and a bow. Side-stepping the parcel, Philippe's senses shifted into high gear. His pulse picked up its pace as his eyes quickly scanned the surrounding neighbourhood, his nose sniffed the breeze for anything out of the ordinary, so too his ears listened intently, but he found nothing unusual except for this gift left on his doorstep.

Carefully, he lifted the box. It was light and rattled ever so slightly when he shook it. Philippe didn't know what was inside, but he knew it probably wasn't anything good.

Stepping back inside his apartment he closed and locked the door, his eyes glued to the package in his hand. Did he dare open it? Did he dare not to? There was no label or card with it. However, since it had been left at his door, he had to assume it was meant for him. Who put it there though, and how did they manage to leave it without setting off his security. Maybe he'd forgotten to turn it on last night, he was a *bit* distracted, he thought. Nope, a quick check of the security system revealed it was all switched on and working fine.

A cold block of ice began to form in the pit of Philippe's stomach as he stared down at the box in his hand. With nimble fingers, he removed the bow, placing it on the coffee table. Next, he peeled the tape from one end of the wrapping, then the other. Holding his breath, he peeled the last piece of tape away to reveal the box it concealed. Philippe's hand hovered over the lid, caught somewhere between curiosity and foreboding. Curiosity won. Gripping the rim, he pulled the lid back….and froze.

"Mother fucker!"

Fuck. Fuck. Fuck. Fuck. Fuck!

"I hope you've got that breakfast ready, although I can't promise I'm going to eat more than a mouthful before I start snacking on you," Nadia yelled out as she left the bathroom and entered the lounge room, not realising they had company. "Oh shit. Dray. Hi, what are you doing here?" she stuttered. Thank God she decided to put some clothes on.

"Philippe called me."

Nadia's moment of embarrassment shifted to concern, shooting Philippe a questioning glance.

"Nicholas paid us a visit and left a present." Philippe pointed toward the small box on the coffee table. When Nadia moved toward it to have a look at its contents, he blocked her path. "You really don't want to see what's in there," he told her quietly, but firmly.

"Are you sure it's from Nicholas?" she asked.

"Very."

"Philippe, you want to try that number," Dray urged, handing back the card which had been placed inside the box with the present. The card would have been completely blank, except for a number written in red pen, matching the brightly coloured wrapping and ribbon. No doubt the shade was chosen to compliment the contents of the box. A blood splattered ear, finger and a silver necklace. A perfect example of Nicholas' demented sense of humour.

Philippe dialled the number on the card. It rang once and connected.

"I see you got my present. When you stole my collection, you forgot my latest acquisition. It came from a lovely young nurse I picked up a few days ago." Nicholas' words dripped with sadistic pleasure.

"You're a sick fuck, you know that?"

Nicholas T'sked at his brother's use of foul language. *"I am what I am. Too bad you won't be around to take my NEW collection. I plan on making my next one extra special."*

"You want to threaten me, go right ahead. I promise you though, you won't like the outcome," Philippe grated out in a low, threatening tone. "You've crossed the line and I'll make sure you pay for what you've done."

"You can try, but you'll fail."

"Don't be so sure. I know you. I know how you think," Philippe snarled.

"You think you know me, but you're wrong. I know everything about you though. You maybe taller now bro, but you're still the same snot-nosed shit you were before. You've taken enough from me. Now it's my turn. I plan on starting with your Mate."

The line went dead.

For a whole second Philippe just stared at the phone in his hand before crushing it in his palm, sending the pieces flying across the room, a rhetoric of curses blistering the air around them. Pushing past Dray, he stormed into his brother's bedroom and began destroying everything in sight. Nothing was exempt. In under a minute there wasn't a thing left intact. Every piece of clothing in his wardrobe and drawers was shredded, and every piece of furniture, smashed, all now littering the room as splinters and colourful confetti of varying sizes.

"I plan on starting with your Mate." Listening to his brother say those words tipped him over the edge, and he just completely lost it.

"You feel better now?" Dray asked dryly as he watched from the doorway.

"No. Maybe a little. No," he corrected again.

Dray's attention switched at the sound of the front door closing. Was that someone coming in or going out? Leaving Philippe to finish shredding anything that still looked remotely recognisable, he pulled his gun from its holster and headed toward the front door.

Where was Nadia?

She definitely wasn't inside the apartment, he could neither hear her, nor scent her. Oh, this wasn't good. Had Nicholas somehow snuck back and taken her while they were distracted?

Dray opened the front door, weapon drawn and his finger hovering over the trigger, not knowing what to expect. Fortunately, he had a spare hand to fight with if necessary...now that Teagan's spell had worn off.

Not that he needed it. What he needed was patience and a new word to describe the druid sisters. They were exasperating and infuriating, and at times a little scary. But Nadia was like the baby bird of the bunch. She hadn't quite learned the tricks of the trade like her sisters, and that made her more vulnerable. Especially now, while she was still trying to understand how to navigate the world as an *Ei'Ambriath*. If anything happened to her on his watch, her sisters would do far more than magically superglue his hand to his groin.

"Where do you think you're going?" Dray demanded gruffly, coming to stand behind her.

"Shit, you shouldn't sneak up on a girl. I could have shot you."

Dray looked down at the weapon in her hands. Unimpressed, he raised a single eyebrow. "Inside with you, now!" Not waiting for her to reply, he threw her over his shoulder and marched back up the stairs.

"Dray, put me down. I can find Nicholas. Put. Me. Down!"

Philippe appeared at the top of the landing, his expression one Nadia hadn't seen before. Fear, anger, disbelief, all rolled into one.

Dray carried her inside, placing her carefully back on her feet, but her eyes never left Philippe.

Philippe held out his hand in front of her silently and waited for her to relinquish the weapon. Narrowing her eyes on him in displeasure, she handed him the gun with an exaggerated huff. "Where did you find that?" he asked.

"Kitchen drawer," she answered.

"What the Hell do you think you were doing? Did you think you could kill Nicholas with a bullet? Do you even know how to use that gun?" Dray demanded.

"Oh, please. Have you forgotten who my dad is? I was handling weapons when I was ten." *Against his wishes, but that's beside the point. No point splitting hairs now, sometimes the truth just gets in the way,* she silently added.

"Don't you ever do something like that again. What if Nicholas was waiting out there for you?" Philippe berated. He waited for a response, but Nadia's pursed lips and crossed arms should have given him a clue that she wasn't in the mood. Her frosty gaze spearing between Philippe and Dray, and back again. "Nadia, are you listening to me?"

"I heard you." She growled. "What makes you think you have any control over anything I do?"

"I don't. I'm not that stupid, but it seems you are. You might not be able to die as easily as you could before, but you're not invincible."

"Oh, and you are?" She asked, her anger rising with every syllable that left her lips.

"No, but I'm still faster and stronger than you. If Nicholas was out there, how were you planning on killing him?" Nadia didn't answer, just continued to glare at him. "I don't know if *I'm* strong enough or fast enough to kill him these days," he told her, almost pleading for her to understand and back down. It was wishful thinking, Nadia was born with the same stubborn streak as all her sisters.

"I can see things you can't," she told him. "I can see Kaitlyn when she's invisible. I'm certain I'll be able to see Nicholas too when he's wearing the invisibility ring. I can also see the things that people try to hide from others. Their thoughts and emotions are projected in their aura like a colourful neon sign. Like you right now, you're trying to make me think you're angry with me…"

"I am angry with you. Very angry." Philippe growled, leaning forward, his presence towering over her. She would have felt intimidated if she didn't know what it was that he was trying to mask with his anger.

"Okay, you're a bit angry…but you're turned-on by my defiance just as much as you are angry," Nadia announced haughtily. Okay, a *bit* angry, might be a minor understatement. If it was possible to have steam come out of his ears, Philippe's apartment would be doubling as a sauna right about now.

But the statement shut him up. Philippe straightened, his jaw dropping open on its hinges and began flapping silently as he decided whether it was worth trying to deny the accusation.

"Of course I'm turned-on. I've recently gone through puberty. I'm always turned-on," he told her defensively. Overhead lights cast harsh lines of his features as his glittering eyes narrowed on her impatiently.

"You're such a *man*," Nadia muttered testily under her breath as she turned away.

"I'm glad you noticed. I'm actually quite proud of that fact."

"It wasn't a compliment."

Philippe didn't care. Whether Nadia was angry with him or not, he was a *man*. It had always been his greatest hope, and fantasy, to one day have an adult body to go with his adult mind. However, having the body he had always wanted barely registered as significant on the scale of importance, when it was compared to having his *mate* by his side.

"Nadia, please. I can't risk losing you, it would destroy me."

"I'm sorry, but he threatened you," she blurted out an offhanded apology. "I heard you acknowledge it on the phone. It just made my blood boil, and I had to do something." And didn't that make him love her all the more. There wasn't anything or anyone she wouldn't take on to protect him, including his psychopathic brother. That was also a little terrifying.

"Sweetheart, you only heard half the conversation. Yes, Nicholas threatened me, but he also promised to start a new souvenir collection....starting with you."

Oh. Now it was Nadia's turn to fall silent. Swallowing hard, she sat down on the sofa equally as hard when her knees began to lose their rigid stability.

"I'm sorry," she told him again, this time she really meant it. "You want to send me back to the manor this morning, don't you?" Philippe and Dray both nodded their agreement. "And you're going to stay here and use yourself as bait to draw out your brother." It wasn't a question but a statement of fact. Philippe shrugged. "Well, I have news for you. I can't bear the thought of losing you either. You're my *mate*. Where you go, I go, so you better get used to it," she told him, shoving her hands on her hips defiantly once again.

Philippe sucked in a deep breath to calm the anger rising inside him. "You're going, and there'll be no discussion. I need to know you're safe."

"I don't need your protection. I'm an adult, an *Ei'Ambriath*. Nicholas will learn I'm not as easy to kill as I was before, and my funky sight could come in handy."

"We've already been over this. You're going. End of story."

For days Dray had wallowed in self-pity that he would never be able to claim Shani as his own. Now, as he watched Philippe and Nadia's lovers tiff he felt grateful he didn't have a defiant *mate* to have to deal with. It kinda put things back into perspective.

"You're both going to the manor. Unlike Nadia, I overheard the whole conversation. Nicholas made his intentions very clear. He's after you and Nadia, and right now you're both sitting targets. Clearly, he's mastered how to use the invisibility ring. I've checked all the security recordings from around your apartment and somehow he managed to get right up to the front door without being detected, not even by the motion sensors. Until we have some way of tracking him down, it's best that you both stay somewhere safe."

"I'm of more use if I stay here," Philippe told him.

"No. Right now, Nicholas has too big an advantage. I received word from the men we left to watch the Shadyvale Retirement Home. He slipped past them last night too. Jack's dead."

"I'm sorry to hear that."

Philippe's lack of surprise at the news was no shock to Dray. Despite Nicholas' declaration to the contrary, Philippe did know his brother well. How well, he wondered. How much useful information did Philippe have stored in his memories about his brother? If there was one thing Dray had learned from tracking down rogue vampires over the last hundred and something years, even the cleverest psychopaths follow a pattern they learned from early in their lives. The question is, what happened early in Nicholas' life that set him on this path?

"Nicholas is my responsibility to deal with. I have to stay," Philippe told him.

"It's not your call to make, it's mine." Pulling his phone from his pocket, Dray dialled Hawke and Anna. "Yeah, make yourselves decent and get over to Philippe's place. They need an escort to the manor…Yes, right now." Putting the phone back where it came from, Dray turned his attention back to Philippe. "I need to know everything about Nicholas, from the day he pooped his first diaper to the day he made you a vampire."

"That's a long story."

"We've got time."

It had been a long time since Philippe had thought about his childhood. There were some good memories mixed in with a few very bad ones, most of which he'd tried hard to forget.

"Okay, if you think it will help."

Philippe began with a general overview of his family life in the South of France back in the 1840's.

Nicholas was the oldest of four children, Philippe the youngest, with two sisters in between. Their mother was a kind woman with a good heart, who doted on all her children. Their father was devoted to his business. As a merchant he travelled a lot, leaving his family for weeks at a time.

"From the age of twelve, Nicholas was being groomed to take over the family business. Our father took him on a few business trips with him. It was on those trips that he discovered our father enjoyed the company of other women. Our mother knew, but she said nothing. For a middle class man, keeping one or more mistresses was considered acceptable, and visiting a brothel was almost expected. For many young men in those days, it was their first introduction to sex. Only, our father's sexual appetite was a bit rougher than most. Back then, they didn't have a label for his style of sex, today they'd put it in the category of BDSM."

"At first, our father made Nicholas watch as he had sex with one and sometimes two women together. By the time Nicholas was sixteen, he too was enjoying the company of those women on their trips away. Sometimes they'd share the women. The two of them with one, two or even up to four women at once. By the time Nicholas was about eighteen, he had become a favourite with the women. They liked that he was young and good looking. Our father became jealous. He'd noticed that Nicholas had become quite fond of one particular woman. I don't remember her name, but she was head strong and outspoken, with large breasts and hips. Our father made a point of requesting her for himself just to annoy Nicholas. However, she didn't like our father. She'd give him her middle finger every time he requested her services. One day she was found dead in an alley. Her throat had been cut, an ear was missing with a diamond earring attached, along with her middle finger."

"Nicholas? Was she his first victim?" Nadia asked.

"No. But I believe that's where he got his idea for keeping souvenirs."

"Did your father do it?" Nadia probed further.

"I don't know, maybe."

"How did Nicholas take it?" Dray asked.

"Not very well, he was very upset, and to make matters worse, my father taunted him about it at every opportunity. After that, something inside Nicholas changed. I didn't notice it at the time but on many years of reflection, I think that's when it must have happened. We all knew Nicholas hated our father, but it wasn't until much later that I learned exactly how he'd been treated by him. In those days you kept your family business, in the family. Our father needed Nicholas, but he also resented him."

"You believe his story about your father and the women? How do you know he didn't make it up as part of his warped fantasy land?" Nadia asked.

"I saw it for myself. Nicholas had just turned twenty and my father was about to take another business trip, but Nicholas begged him to stay behind. He'd formed an attachment to Colette, my elder sister Marguerite's friend, who frequently visited our home. He'd planned on paying her a visit to propose. So, our father took me instead. I was almost thirteen, I thought I knew what to expect since Nicholas had told me a few things about what went on, on their business trips. But, I discovered the stories Nicholas had told me were watered down for a young boy's ears. My father made me watch. The things he was doing with those women made me want to vomit. Afterwards, he told me that when I was old enough, he'd let me join in, like it was some sort of rite of passage. I'd never felt so repulsed in my life. It was then that I knew I had to do something to help Nicholas get away from him. I didn't give a damn if we lost the family business, Nicholas and I were both young and strong, we'd find a way to support our mother and sisters if we had to."

"What happened with Nicholas. I've researched all the records from that time, and I've never found any mention that Nicholas ever married," Dray queried.

Philippe chuckled. Dray's methodical research of the brothers had been thorough, he knew, but there were some things that never made it to public record.

"No. He never married Colette. She rejected him. In fact, she laughed in his face. Nicholas didn't take it well. He couldn't understand her rejection when every other woman he'd ever met threw themselves at him. A few weeks later she was found dead. Mutilated. She had a missing finger and an ear."

"Any jewellery missing?" Dray asked.

"Yes, but they didn't know that at the time. I only discovered her locket when I found Nicholas' first souvenir collection. It turns out she had rejected Nicholas because she was secretly in love with another man. Our Father."

"Fuck me. He was screwing your sister's friend?" Dray exclaimed.

"It seems that way, yes."

"So, Nicholas did to her what was done to the prostitute he'd become fond of. Was there anything else similar about the two murders?" Dray queried.

"What happened after that?" Nadia prompted more gently, taking Philippe's hand in hers to ease the agitation she could see building inside him.

Philippe cleared his throat before answering. "I never met the prostitute, but I'm told Colette had a close resemblance to her. So did the next woman who turned up dead a couple of months later, and the one after that. They were all in different towns, in different parts of France, so no one tied them together as being the same person doing the murders. But they were all in towns my father and brother were visiting on their business trips. In under a year, four women were dead."

"What about your father, did he suspect anything do you think?" Nadia asked.

"Nicholas once told me that he did. He taunted Nicholas about it. As each new body turned up, he'd say things to him like: *Another one who rejected you? Can't please a woman, so you kill her?* The rivalry between them had reached boiling point. Then one day a messenger arrived at our door to inform us that our father was dead. He'd met with some sort of accident on the road, and Nicholas was assumed dead too, although they hadn't found his body."

"Holy crap on a cracker. Did Nicholas kill him?" Nadia gasped.

"No. Scorpion did…about five minutes before he made Nicholas a vampire."

"It seems that Scorpion in his own warped way, actually did the world a favour killing your father. No offence intended to you personally." Dray quipped.

Philippe snorted out a contemptuous laugh. "None taken."

"So, Nicholas then returned home as a vampire," Dray surmised.

"No. Although I did some digging through his things and came across his souvenirs. It was very confronting to see the evidence of my suspicions, but I ignorantly blamed my father for Nicholas' new hobby. Then, about a month later, I heard a report that a woman's body had turned up, missing a finger and an ear, in Montpellier, only a short distance from our home in Toulouse."

"You went looking for him?" Nadia said.

"Yes. I found him too, right where I thought he'd be. In a brothel."

"Only now he was a vampire."

Philippe nodded. "I didn't know anything about vampires, I'd never heard of them before. All I knew was my brother was different in a way I couldn't quite define. I begged him to come home. He refused. We argued, he lost his temper and he bared his fangs at me. I think he thought it would frighten me away."

"It didn't?"

Philippe chuckled, a quiet, sad, almost bitter response. "Just the opposite. Now I had even more reason to *'Save my brother's soul',*" he said, using air quotes to emphasise his naivety. "I spent the next few days watching him, following him. Finally, I confronted him again when I could see his attention had settled on a new woman. I couldn't bear to see him going down such a depraved path. Deep in my heart I believed him to be a good man, capable of having a happy and fulfilling life, if he was given a chance to redeem himself."

"That's when he made you a vampire." Dray assumed.

"It was. Reluctantly of course. The last thing he wanted was to have his thirteen year old, kid brother tagging around with him for eternity. In the end he relented when I told him I had his souvenirs and he'd never see them again if he didn't make me a vampire like him."

"And the killings stopped."

"They did. I never let Nicholas out of my sight. Wherever he went, I went. If I wasn't in full view, I was in the shadows, but he always knew I was there. In the early days I didn't trust that he wouldn't fall back into his bad habits, nor was I confident I could stop him if he did. He was bigger and stronger than me, so I set out to rectify that. I spent every spare moment training, honing my skills as a fighter until my size no longer mattered. After that, things between us seemed to improve. I thought we were getting along quite well, most of the time, until Scorpion showed up again three years ago. It took years before I felt confident that Nicholas had reformed. And it only took that evil son-of-a-bitch the space of a nanosecond to undo everything. Maybe if I'd…"

Dray put his hand up to silence Philippe's impending verbal self-flagellation, eyeing him carefully for a long moment before speaking. "Philippe, you need to keep this in perspective. Your father had depraved sensibilities. He obviously fostered those same base needs in Nicholas, but who's to say they weren't already there. Scorpion sired him, making him a vampire because of those same depraved desires lurking inside him. You can't change a man's basic make-up just because you will it to be so. Nicholas is a sociopath, he always was and always will be. It's not your fault and it's not your father's either. Okay, your father is probably to blame for Nicholas acting out on his sadistic thoughts instead of just spending his life fantasizing about them, but those tendencies are ingrained into his nature. You can't change that."

Philippe nodded but didn't speak.

"What happened to your mother and sisters? I'm sure it would have been hard for them with no man left in the house. Your dad was dead, they thought Nicholas was too, and then suddenly you were gone as well. What happened to them?" Nadia asked.

Philippe's frown smoothed out and the corner of his lips curled up into a half smile. "I compelled a widower with a largish fortune from a nearby town to pay my mother a visit, under the pretext that he had known my father. Within months they were married. Through him, my sisters met a couple of very nice young men and were married too. I'm pleased to say they all had long and very happy lives."

"I'm so glad to hear it. At least something good came out of what happened."

"It has. The universe works in mysterious ways. If it wasn't for my brother, I never would have lived long enough to meet you." Philippe squeezed Nadia's hand, leaning forward he took her lips in a brief, but attentive kiss.

As their lips parted his attention shifted toward the door. Soft footsteps could be heard climbing the steps to the landing, and without hesitation Dray rose from his seat to open the door.

"Boss," Hawke greeted, clasping his forearm.

"Dray," Anna said, reaching up on her tip-toes to give him a kiss on the cheek. "So, we're off on a road trip to the manor. That's a whole hour away, how many guns do you think we'll need?" she asked in a hopeful tone, opening her jacket to reveal an arsenal of weapons.

Dray couldn't help but grin. "Hopefully none."

17

"I'll drive," Anna announced cheerily.

"Not this time you won't, you're still adjusting to driving on the left-hand side of the road. If there's any trouble, and I'm not saying there will be, but if there is, we need someone driving who's not going to *cause* an accident," Dray stated.

"Don't worry pumpkin, that means you'll have two free hands to manage the weapons," Hawke told her, knowing it would perk her mood up instantly. And it did.

"Um, actually, wouldn't it be better if we took two separate cars?" Nadia proposed.

"Why?" Dray asked.

"Well, if there is any trouble, if Hawke and Anna are following behind us, they could deal with the problem before it reached Philippe and myself. And, what happens if there's car trouble, we can't just wait around on the side of the road like sitting ducks until help arrives, can we?"

Hawke shrugged. "She has a point."

"Fine. But, keep them in sight at all times," Dray said, spearing Hawke and Anna with an *'or else'*, glare.

"No problem boss," Anna grinned. "But where do we get the second car from?"

"Nicholas' car is still in the garage, we could take that," Philippe offered. However, there was the minor problem of finding the spare set of keys. He knew Nicholas kept them in his bedroom. Unfortunately, they would need a metal detector to find them under the tonne of rubble now littering the room after Philippe's earlier hissy-fit.

"And you can drive," Nadia told Philippe.

"What? No. I don't think so. I've only ever driven once before and that ended with the car being towed away after an accident," he protested.

"Of course you can. I'll be your instructor. Once we get out on the motorway it's an easy drive all the way to the manor. Besides, I'm *really* tired. I wouldn't mind taking a nap while you drive." Nadia let out a huge yawn to emphasise her point, covering her mouth with a hand to disguise her devious smirk.

Of course, Philippe's unwillingness to get behind the wheel was quickly replaced by eagerness. Upon seeing Nadia's considerable fatigue, it wouldn't matter if he only had one leg, no arms and was legally blind, he still would have insisted on driving. She had to admit, as irritating as it was sometimes, a male's ingrained concern for his *mate* could work in her favour.

It took a group effort to sift through the debris in Nicholas' room, but eventually they found the keys to the car. A bronze coloured, Vauxhall Insignia Turbo 4x4. Practical, yet still classy. Its practicality in terms of safety wasn't something that Philippe had really thought about before. Its versatility in difficult driving conditions was a definite bonus, as were the extra safety features such as the multiple airbags. However, considering the circumstances, he would have happily traded the classiness of the car for even more 'anti-Nicholas' features, i.e. bullet proof glass, armoured tank thickness in the car's exterior panelling, and a five thousand horsepower engine like the Devel Sixteen Hypercar. But this would have to do.

Philippe opened the driver's door, nervous energy flooding his senses. He wasn't sure what had him on edge more, the thought that Nicholas might be out there waiting for them on the road somewhere or being responsible for getting Nadia to the manor in one piece with him at the wheel. Either way, the trip to the manor could easily end with the car in a ditch and Nadia injured, or worse. At least Nicholas' car had one major advantage over the piece of junk he'd driven before. With an automatic transmission, there were no gears to deal with. That should make the drive a bit easier, he hoped.

Philippe started the car and eased out of the garage and onto the road. As anticipated, his apprehension made his navigation of the car a little clunky. Although, his anxiety was relatively short-lived. By the time they reached the motorway which linked Oxford to Cadley, he was much more confident. Very fortunate and necessary too, Nadia thought, considering what she had planned for the remainder of their trip. Contrary to what she had told Philippe, taking a nap was the last thing she planned on doing.

Nadia let out a series of well-timed, contemplative sighs.

"What's on your mind?" Philippe asked, concerned she was still upset with him for insisting she go to the manor earlier than they had originally planned.

"Nothing. I'm just disappointed we won't get any more time alone together," she pouted.

"Of course we will," he reassured, reaching across to squeeze her hand and offering her a smile.

"No, we won't. Not really. Not when everyone has super-human hearing like yours. Every time you slide that huge flagpole of yours between my thighs and drive it home, deep inside my hot, wet pussy and make me scream your name, they'll all know about it. We'll have to endure the embarrassment and humiliation of knowing they'll hear every moan and gasp of erotic delight."

"If you keep talking dirty like that, it's going to get embarrassing long before we give them a chance to *hear* what we're up to," he said adjusting the bulge behind his zipper.

"How?" she chuckled, enjoying the power she was wielding over him.

"If you keep saying stuff like that, my *flagpole* will be raised high enough that everyone will notice as soon as I get out of the car when we get to the manor." That prospect wasn't the least bit appealing as far as he was concerned. He had already displayed his wares for Mrs Philpot and Cassie once, and he had no intention of doing it again.

"Okay, I'll stop talking. How about I do this instead?"

Philippe was about to ask her what *this* was, but the only thing that left his lips was an uncensored moan. Carnal pleasure spiked by surprise, rippled through his body, tightening every muscle on his frame as Nadia reached across and cupped his hardening manhood. Her nimble fingers unfastened his jeans, wrapping them firmly around the base of his iron-hard flesh. Slowly, she began stroking the velvety warm shaft, tugging at it gently until Philippe's hips flexed with the rhythm of her caress.

"Do you like this?" she asked tentatively.

"Shit yeah, but you'd better stop before we have an accident," he told her in a strained voice. Of course, Nadia had no intention of stopping. If this was going to be the last time she had Philippe all to herself for the foreseeable future, she was going to make the most of it.

Dipping her head, she licked the pulsing vein along the length of his thick shaft, following its path upward from the base to just beneath the cap at its apex. Her warm breath over the moist trail sent another rush of blood to Philippe's groin, and a jolt of lust straight to his balls.

"Oh Christ!" The oath ripped from him as his head slammed back against the seat, sucking in a sharp breath.

Philippe pushed his fingers through Nadia's hair, gripping it lightly in his fist in anticipation of her wickedly sweet lips coming closer to the wide, blunt tip.

Nadia's hunger grew at the sight of his uncensored pleasure. Her gaze locked onto his moistening tip. With a slow swipe of her tongue, curling around it, she explored its contour.

"Nadia, sweetheart, you really need to stop now," he almost begged. But even as he pleaded for mercy, his hips flexed involuntarily into her caress, urging her on to explore more boldly.

Silken lips parted, allowing the blunt tip of his turgid stalk to enter the wet heat of her mouth, her lips closing over the whole head.

The sight of her taking him, swallowing the crest between those parted pink lips as her gentle hand gripped his shaft, drew a strangled cry from Philippe's lips.

Sweet Jesus!

Pleasure rippled from his engorged shaft to his tightening balls like an electric shock.

Nadia tasted him, slowly at first, but then the sweet heat of her mouth began drawing on him. Sucking delicately, then with erotic confidence. As the reins holding back his lust began to fray, she sucked at the flesh stretching her lips and filling her mouth. Sweet, wet heat surrounded the brutal sensitivity of his crest, working over it with hungry flicks of her tongue.

Restraining the shallow thrusts between her lips, Philippe couldn't help revelling in this intimate acceptance. Pleasure tightened through his body, drawing his testicles higher, his cock throbbing with the rising need for release.

Philippe gripped the steering wheel tighter, finding it almost impossible to concentrate on the road ahead, his attention oscillating between the endless white line ahead and stolen glances at the erotic, and much more appealing vision taking place in his lap.

Nadia's lashes lowered with drowsy eroticism over her pale grey eyes, her lips drawing on him, tongue flicking against the underside of his turgid crest, lashing along the slit at its rim to its weeping peak, pushing him ever closer to the edge of oblivion with every stroke.

The feel of the silky head of his steel-hard length, throbbing furiously as she sucked at it, drew a moan from Nadia's lips. Working her tongue over it as she drew it in and out of her mouth, his hips jerked when it hit the back of her throat. "Ah, fuck," he cried out, his voice hard and gravelly with his desperate need to keep control, not only of his own body, but also the car, and his face contorted with a grimace of tortured pleasure.

Philippe took the bend in the road so sharply, the wheels squealed in protest.

Hawke and Anna drove at a respectable distance behind. Not so close that they could lip read Philippe and Nadia's conversations, but close enough to catch up to them in an instant at the first sign of trouble.

"When Philippe said he sucked at driving, he wasn't kidding," Hawke said.

"You'd drive like that too if you were being distracted in the same way he is right now," Anna told him.

"What do you mean by that? I'm never distracted, my mind is always focused on the job, even with a beautiful woman beside me," he told her proudly.

"You think so, ha?" Anna's smug grin suddenly made Hawke less sure of his statement.

"I know so," he answered much more confidently than he was feeling right at that moment. Anna leaned across the seat and gripped her hand over the flaccid bulge at the front of his jeans and felt it twitch. Hawke gripped the wheel more tightly, but he kept his eyes on the road. "Are you saying that Nadia is…"

"Giving Philippe a head job? Of course she is. Didn't you pick up on the clues back at the apartment? She couldn't have been clearer about her intentions if she'd flashed a neon sign."

"Really? I heard her say she was tired and wanted to sleep in the car on the way."

"You should've been listening to what she *wasn't* saying."

"Now you've lost me. I thought I was. When she said she was tired, I thought she was trying to say that Philippe had shagged her to exhaustion. And I have to tell you, when she said that, I felt mighty proud of the guy."

Anna laughed and shook her head. Were all men so totally clueless when it came to understanding women's subtle communication, she wondered as she pulled her hand away and sat back in her seat.

"What, you're not going to play too?" Hawke asked in dismay.

Rolling her eyes, Anna gave him a cheeky grin. "No. We're working."

"I thought you were good at multi-tasking?" Hawke's eyes almost pleaded with her.

"Oh, I am. But you're not."

"You're a cruel woman. You get me all excited and then leave me hanging."

"It's called sexual tension. Consider it foreplay. A little bit of teasing now will make the sex later, explosive," she said, waggling her eyebrows at him suggestively.

"When you put it like that…"

Releasing his vice-like grip on the steering wheel, Philippe reached down and gently pushed Nadia's shoulders back. "Stop." he choked out. "You need to stop now."

The sensations below his waist were reaching fever pitch. They were ready to take him over, submerge him under a tidal wave of high-octane ecstasy.

Gritting his teeth, he grimaced. "Nadia, please, you need to stop…" he said, his voice husky with arousal.

Nadia wasn't listening. She was busy working her lips and tongue over his hardened flesh with feminine hunger. That wicked little tongue licked and stroked, rubbed at the underside of the throbbing crest, teasing that ultra-sensitive spot just below it, which he didn't even know he had.

It was exquisite.

Glancing down at her, watching her lips moving over him, her expression flushed and filled with pleasure and need, he could feel himself unravelling.

The car swerved across the road in a sudden jolt as Philippe made a hasty correction back into the correct lane. The sudden sideways movement of the car, sent Nadia lurching forward into his lap further, and her hot little mouth took more of his length with the sudden jerk.

Holy mother......!

All at once the car pulled off to the side of the road and came to a screeching halt, Philippe's hands leaving the wheel to grip Nadia's face in an attempt to lift her away. His release was boiling in his balls, threatening to slip his very tentative control.

"Enough. Please, you have to stop. Now!" In distress, the last word slipped past his vocal cords a couple of octaves higher.

Nadia's pale eyes looked up into his face and her whole body practically melted from the red-hot flames of desire burning in his intense gaze. A languid flutter of her lashes and the heat of arousal darkening them, her determination solidified. *Stop now? I'm just getting started*, she thought, intensifying her mouth and hand action.

It was too much. Philippe couldn't stop himself. Letting out a hoarse cry, every muscle in his abdomen clenched and his hips jerked, as he ejaculated into her hungry mouth.

Dray waited until the two cars disappeared into the distance before pulling his phone from his pocket and dialling Saladin.

"Dray," Saladin said as he picked up.

"Has Marek arrived yet?" he asked brusquely.

"Are you asking because you genuinely don't know, or are you pretending not to know and are actually down the street watching the house in the hope of seeing Shani?"

A low growl rumbled from the pit of Dray's stomach at the accusation. "I've been busy. Is he there yet or not?"

"Busy how? Cranking out a few reps on a nice young blonde or brunette from the club? Because if so, I'm glad to hear it. Obsessing over a woman you can't have isn't healthy." *Anyone except Vanessa.*

"You'd know all about that," Dray bit back. "No. I've been busy dealing with a situation at Philippe's."

"What kind of situation, did something happen to Nadia?" Saladin's taunting tone suddenly turned harsh with concern.

"No, but I've sent her and Philippe to the manor with Hawke and Anna as escort." Briefly, Dray outlined the grizzly gift left on Philippe's doorstep and the equally disturbing phone call that followed.

"Okay, thanks for the heads-up. I think I'll hold off telling Teagan about it until we get word from the manor that they've arrived safely. And yes, Marek's here. He arrived about a quarter of an hour ago. I'll keep you posted on what Shani comes up with on his binding stone. With any luck it might lead us to both Nicholas and Scorpion."

"It better. We're running out of fucking options, Saladin. The psychopathic duo have been one step ahead of us all along. The more time they've got to put a plan together against us, the more chance they've got of succeeding."

"I'm well aware of that. I wrote the book on war tactics, remember?" Saladin told him in a dry tone, his good mood having taken a dramatic dive down the crapper.

Dray grunted back a reply. "Call me with the outcome," he said, and promptly hung up.

Saladin took a deep breath to settle the rising anger building inside him before re-entering the lounge room.

"Is everything okay?" Teagan asked him as he quietly closed the door behind him.

"Great. Dray was just checking in." Saladin cursed inwardly at his own stupid thoughtlessness the moment the name, *"Dray"*, left his lips, and Shani's olive complexion blushed a pretty shade of pink.

"Is he coming here today?" Shani asked tentatively.

"No. He's taking care of another matter."

"Oh, okay, I guess we should begin then. Marek, can I see the picture of your stone on your phone please?" Shani tried to pretend she wasn't affected by the mere mention of Dray, but she couldn't stop her hand from shaking just a little as she held it out to take Marek's phone from him. She was glad that Dray wasn't coming, nor could she help feeling disappointed. There must be something mentally wrong with her, she thought. What else could explain her incredible need to see him, be near him...touch him? Even after what happened at the club the night before, what she walked in on between Dray and that tramp, she still felt an irrational desire for the man which she could neither eradicate nor act upon. She wanted him so badly it physically hurt.

Shani's stomach rolled into a tight knot of regret.

It was the conundrum of her cruel life. She had met the man of her dreams but was already married to a man who made her reality into something akin to a nightmare.

Well, there was no point dwelling on what she couldn't change.

Marek made no comment as he passed Shani his phone, yet his eyes conveyed his concern at the slight quiver in her hand. This wasn't a situation she was unfamiliar with however, and covered her anxiety with the ease of an expert having had many years of practice.

Shani's smile was smooth and carefree. "Let's see where your binding stone is, shall we?"

Staring at the picture of the sapphire set in the ornate gold ring, Shani let her mind wander through the familiar labyrinth deep inside her mind. An intuitive pathway she had treaded countless times which always led her to the lost articles.

Until now.

It seemed inconceivable. Not only couldn't she find Nicholas using articles imprinted with his personal energy, it seemed she couldn't find a missing ring when the owner was standing in front of her, giving off more than enough energy for her to tune into and track it.

"I'm not getting anything. Nothing at all. I'm sorry, I don't know what the problem is."

Both Saladin and Marek cursed at the same time and shared a look that made Teagan nervous. "You don't think this is Morganna's doing, do you?" she asked.

"I wasn't one hundred percent sure before, but I think we can consider the debate of whether or not she's working with Scorpion and Nicholas, resolved. Besides you, Morganna's the only one powerful enough to put a concealment ward around someone."

"Are you sure, maybe my gift has just gone on the fritz a bit?" Shani offered.

Marek's snort of laughter was filled with bitter contempt. "Saladin's right. We also can't forget that Scorpion was wearing Morganna's amulet the last time we saw him during that battle in Alabama. Normally, Morganna doesn't share anything with anyone. She is paranoid and self-serving. She must have a very good reason why she's working with Scorpion and Nicholas, and if she thinks they will benefit her in some way, you can rest assured she will be keeping a close eye on her investment. If...sorry...when, we find Nicholas and Scorpion, Morganna won't be far away."

"Isn't that good? You can get them all at the same time, right?" Shani asked, a little confused.

"In theory, yes. In reality, we could have some very big problems. Scorpion is a psychotic vampire, at least several centuries old, who we know nothing about, other than he has been manipulating his way up the greasy pole of the Guild's empire for the past few years. He's also deliberately sired numerous other vampires who he believed would wreak havoc on the world, including Nicholas. As for Nicholas, he drank a potion which has made him stronger and faster than any other vampire, to an unknown degree. He's also mastered invisibility using the ring of Gyges. Then there's Morganna...." Teagan was cut off before the end of her explanation.

"Morganna is as powerful as Teagan, probably more so. Teagan has only had a few years to learn how to master her power. Morganna has had one and a half thousand years," Saladin said.

"Thanks for the vote of confidence, honey. My sisters and I defeated her once already, in case you've forgotten," Teagan grumbled.

"That's not a day I'm likely to forget in a hurry, love. But I think you'll agree that Morganna underestimated your capabilities then, she's not going to be caught off guard a second time."

Teagan muttered under her breath although managed to refrain from openly contradicting him.

"So, what you're saying is, if anyone happens to come across that trio in a dark alley, run like hell?" Shani said.

"You betcha. Run like the hellhounds are on your tail, because there's a good chance they really could be," Saladin told her.

"Hellhounds are real too? Now you're just having a lend of me."

"Um, no, not so much. They're real," Teagan said in an apologetic tone.

"Considering the turn of events, I think we need to take a few more precautions. I wasn't going to mention this until after Philippe and Nadia arrived at the manor, but it seems Nicholas paid a visit to his apartment through the night." Saladin quickly put up his hand to silence the deluge of questions and threats he knew were about to spring from his wife's mouth. "They're fine, but Dray sent them to the manor with Hawke and Anna. And I think, considering your gift Shani, you should stay at the manor too, for the time being." Saladin told them.

"You think they might see Shani as a threat?" Teagan asked, her gaze levelled at Saladin, such that he knew she had every intention of discussing the matter of him concealing this news about her sister further with him later. Somehow, he didn't think it would matter to her that he'd only just learned about the incident himself. However, the make-up sex after their argument would be well worth any misunderstandings, he thought to himself.

"Shani did locate Nicholas' stash of trophies. Who's to say the evil trio won't try to eliminate her on the off chance she can get past Morganna's concealment ward." Turning to Shani, he added, " It'll just be for a few days, a week at the most."

"What if you don't find Nicholas and Scorpion by then?" Shani asked.

Saladin didn't want to lie, but he didn't want to sound pessimistic either. "There's only so many rat-holes they can hide in. We're going to flush them out, don't worry. Besides, they're also running out of allies since the incident with the drug dealers in Alabama. Any day now we'll get news of them being sighted somewhere."

"Okay, if you think it's for the best. Would it be possible if my cousin Yasmin, could come too?"

"Sure, I don't see why not," Saladin told her.

Marek's keen eye watched Shani carefully throughout this revealing conversation. Interestingly, she didn't seem too distressed by the disturbing news that she may find herself on a mega-villain's hit list. However, when she was told she had to go to the manor, her anxiety levels seemed to spike. At least, they did until she was told her cousin could join her. Marek's curiosity stirred. Clearly, she wasn't concerned for her own welfare, so why would Shani's apprehension about relocating to the manor be dependent upon her cousin's attendance.

Philippe drove down the long driveway and pulled up alongside the stairs to the manor's front doors.

It was a miracle. They'd made it in one piece. For all the stress of driving though, he couldn't get the smile off his face. If only every driving experience could be that enjoyable.

Climbing from the car, he quickly opened Nadia's door, even before she had time to remove her seatbelt and collect her handbag from the floor by her feet. Almost in the same moment, the manor's front door opened.

"Philippe, I've reconsidered our options and I'd rather take our chances out there with Nicholas than be stuck here at the manor with our family."

"Come on sweetheart, it won't be that bad. I promise." The words left his lips, but not even he believed them. He wanted to, but he didn't. Not that he was going to let Nadia know that though. One of them needed to at least pretend to have a positive outlook on their situation, and since he'd had the most practice at it....

Nadia's feet hit the gravelled driveway as Philippe removed his duffel bag from the backseat and hitched it over his shoulder. With each step closer to the house, Nadia let out a fresh string of grumbles and groans about turning around and going somewhere else, anywhere else. Philippe took her hand in his and for a brief moment she forgot what she was complaining about. The cool touch of his skin, the gentle strength of his fingers clutching hers, made all the misconstrued, unfathomed anxiety and frustration fade away into a grey void of nothingness.

Then Cassie and Abby appeared in the doorway, bringing with them a huge jolt of reality.

"You're here. Great. We've got so much to talk about," Cassie called as the two women hurried down the front stairs to meet them on the wide, slate path between the house and adjoining gardens.

"Take a deep breath, and just keep smiling," Philippe whispered to Nadia, doing his best to follow his own advice. Nadia squeezed his hand a little tighter and somehow managed to broaden her fake smile.

They each shared a brief hug in greeting and when Nadia opened her mouth to speak, her words were abruptly halted, mid thought.

"You did the deed on the way here, didn't you?" Cassie blurted out excitedly.

"What? No! Why would you say that?" Nadia answered, trying her best to sound offended.

"Oh, please, you only need to look at Philippe's cheesy grin to know it's true."

"No, it's not," Nadia insisted more forcefully, but immediately turned toward Philippe looking for the evidence Cassie was referring to. Her exhaled breath came out almost as a groan of acknowledgement. There was no hiding those post-orgasm glazed eyes, or that satisfied grin he was sporting from ear to ear.

"Ha! I knew it," Cassie boasted with way too much enthusiasm for Nadia's liking.

"No, we didn't have sex!" *Well, not in the strictest sense of the word.* Nadia insisted again.

Looking from Nadia to Philippe, Abby began to chuckle. "She's not lying. They didn't have sex," she told Cassie.

"Thank you," Nadia retorted, crossing her arms beneath her breasts haughtily, feeling rather vindicated.

"But you did give him a head job while he was driving."

"Abby, that's not fair. Stay out of my head."

"I wasn't in your head. I was in Philippe's," she answered, barely containing her amusement. "Besides, even if I couldn't read your minds, you can't deny it. Look at you, your hair is all messed and Philippe's shirt is only half tucked in,...and he's still got a boner."

Philippe cleared his throat uncomfortably, swinging the bag from his shoulder to cover his groin.

Nadia gasped again in horror. "No! Seriously?" she said, quickly smoothing down her hair and straightening her dress. "Crap. Do you think anyone else will notice?"

"Anyone? No. Everyone? Yes." Cassie eagerly answered.

"Oh, this is too much. See Philippe, *this* is why I didn't want to come here," she huffed as she stomped up the stairs past Cassie and Abby. As she did, Abby's nose tilted in the air ever so slightly, catching Nadia's scent.

"And....you're *Mated!* Yes. Yay me, I won! Pay up. You owe me ten quid," Abby told Cassie, as she did a little victory dance.

"Crap, really?" Cassie asked, looking hugely disappointed.

"Yep, pay up. They're *mated*." Abby laughed.

Nadia stopped in her tracks and turned on the two women. "What, you bet on us?" The hard edge to Nadia's voice would have alerted most people that they had crossed a personal line, which in turn should have prompted them to shut up. Sadly, there wasn't a single person at the manor who understood the definition of boundaries.

"Of course we did. Guessing how long it would take the two of you to be *mated* has been the hot topic of the house for the last couple of days. I thought, considering how new sex is for you both, that it might take a week or so, because you'd be too busy doing the nasty, to get down to the business of *mating*. But Abby bet it would be on your first time." Cassie pulled the £10 note from her pocket and handed it over. Nadia's jaw almost dropped off its hinges. Although really, why was she surprised? "Don't worry I'll get it back again when your dad gets here," Cassie added confidently.

"What do you mean by that? Did you also bet on my dad's reaction to me and Philippe?" Cassie and Abby both nodded. Nadia's shoulders slumped as she hung her head low, slowly shaking it in dismay.

"Don't worry love, it'll be fine. You'll see," Philippe told Nadia as he wrapped a comforting arm about her shoulders. Over the top of her head he whispered to Abby, "I want in on that bet."

"I heard that," Nadia grumbled against his chest, but at the same time it seemed to break the tension. *Damn it, if you can't beat 'em, join 'em.* "I've got £10 that says dad will frown, growl and then pretend to be happy about it."

"I think there'll more likely be frowning, snarling and the breaking of a few bones…then he'll pretend to be happy about it," Kaitlyn said as she stepped through the doorway.

"I suppose you've put money down too?" Nadia asked dryly.

"Naturally. Life around here's pretty dull. We need something to keep us amused," her sister replied.

Nadia snorted out a laugh. "Dull? Right. Compared to what? Armageddon? There's practically an apocalyptic event here nearly every other day."

Kaitlyn shrugged her shoulders. "Pfft, sure, but none that are fun. Watching you and Philippe tip-toe around dad will be fun. Watching you trip over the kids plastic toys and fall arse-over-tit again, that's fun," Kaitlyn grinned, knowing exactly how to push her sister's buttons.

"Damn, I should have thought of that before I made the kids put away all their toys. There's nothing inside to trip over," Cassie said, feigning disappointment.

"I don't want to ruin this warm, fuzzy moment, so I'll refrain from any actions, but just so you know, I'm mentally giving you all a rude gesture," Nadia told them flatly.

"I saw that," Abby piped up, tapping her temple with a finger.

"Good. Now, who do I give my tenner to for the bet?" Nadia asked.

"Megan," they all answered together.

"Even Megan's in on it?" Nadia shook her head as she let out a deep sigh of resignation. It was official. Her personal life was never going to be personal again.

Pushing Philippe out of the way, the girls all surrounded Nadia as they walked her toward the open doorway.

"So, come on, dish. Was it bone shaking good? I bet it was. Vampires seem to have a natural knack for sex, I think it's one of their super powers. Especially the ones with big schlongs," Cassie winked.

Nadia's eyes widened with an expression of shocked horror. However, as genuine as her surprise was for Cassie's line of questioning, she couldn't quite cover up her pride at her *mate's* endowment status. "You don't know what Philippe's *penis*, looks like," she exclaimed, feeling a little uncomfortable talking about his man parts, especially with him standing right behind them.

"Not exactly. But he did come into the kitchen with his '*morning glory*' tenting his track pants, remember, and it was a pretty big tent he was making. I'm afraid it was one of those mental impressions you don't forget in a hurry." Cassie waggled her eyebrows a couple of times to emphasise her meaning.

Nadia groaned, spearing a desperate look over her shoulder at Philippe for help. His embarrassed look said it all. A second later, he disappeared in a flash of speed.

"We've made up the suite in the west wing on the second floor. We thought you'd want some privacy," Abby yelled out to him as he disappeared, leaving behind a vacuum of air. "We've moved all of your things from your old room in there too," she added to Nadia.

"The second floor, west wing?" Nadia asked incredulously.

"Yep. You'll love it. It's got extra sound proofing in the walls. You'll have all the privacy you need."

Nadia wasn't sure if she was grateful for their thoughtfulness or mortified. "What about *your* toys, are they still in their too?"

"Of course not. Alex moved them all to our *pleasure dungeon* ages ago. Well, most of them. It still has a couple of essentials in there, but only in the bathroom. We left the bondage chains and cuffs in the shower stall. Don't worry though, we have a new, bigger and better set-up in our bathroom, so you don't need to worry about Alex and I barging in on you to use your equipment," Abby assured confidently at Nadia's panicked expression.

Our equipment? I think not! "That's comforting to know. FYI, Philippe and I will *never* use any of that stuff," she stated with a dramatic flick of her hair as she marched defiantly past the stained-glass doors, and into the manor's enormous foyer.

"If you say so," Abby chuckled.

"Well come on girlfriend, we're waiting for some details," Cassie probed, directing the conversation from one uncomfortable topic, back to another.

"I am not going to recap my sexual exploits to you or anyone. I will however, say that I have no complaints." Nadia blushed with a coy smile.

A moment after the front door closed, Hawke and Anna stopped their car alongside the manor's oversized garage.

"So, now that we're officially off duty, are you up for playing a bit of tonsil hockey?" Hawke asked in a hopeful tone.

Anna scrunched up her nose as though contemplating his offer. "Tonsil hockey is good, but I'd really prefer a bit of thigh wrestling and gland-to-gland combat."

"Your wish is my command," he answered, reaching across the seat for his *mate*.

"Ah huh," she t'sked, pushing his hands away. "There's just one catch," Anna said.

"What?"

"You'll have to catch me first. Just so you know, I'm not going to make it easy for you."

Hawke's eyes sparkled with delight. "I love it when you get nasty."

18

The sun had fully set by the time Saladin's car rolled down the long driveway with his cargo of uncharacteristically quiet women.

"This is it, we're here?" Shani asked. Where here was however, she had no clue. Once they left the main road a few miles back, she felt like they had been driving in circles down laneways and narrow roads, which somehow led them to this wide, gravel driveway. A canopy of bare branches from the old oak trees wove an intricate net above them along the long avenue, the night sky twinkling in and out of view as they passed beneath.

"Wow," Yasmin added.

"Yep, this is it. Havenswood Manor," Saladin's tone lacked the sense of awe that Shani and Yasmin's did, as they rounded the final bend in the driveway and the manor came into view. Although, he couldn't deny he felt every bit of their anticipation. Just not for the same reasons.

The Alliance was gathering in and around Cadley once again in preparation for yet another battle with their enemies. They had struck a damaging blow to the Guild in Alabama, severely denting their infrastructure and eroding the Guild's ties to the underworld crime gangs. But Saladin was under no illusion that their true enemy hadn't suffered anything more than an irritating inconvenience. The Guild maybe a raging bull with dangerous pointy horns, belching its poisonous hatred in every direction. However, the real danger was the tiny parasitic tick, hidden in the folds of that enormous arse. A parasite that could cause paralysis and death before you were even aware of its presence. Maybe it was a crude analogy, but with Morganna, Scorpion and

Nicholas teaming up together, the Alliance had a serious tick problem on their hands. The question was, from which hidden quarter were the evil trio going to emerge, and how much collateral damage would they leave in their wake?

Saladin shuddered at the thought. War was nothing new to him, nor was death. As a human he had been born a Kurdish Muslim, raised to fight, to lead battles as the Sultan of Syria and Egypt. His battles and conquests against the Crusaders were legendary. But the battles he fought back then, although brutal and bloody, weren't even in the same ballpark as their current enemy. How do you defend yourself against an enemy you can't see coming, have no way of tracking, and have no clue about their capabilities.

Shani shifted in her seat to get a better look at their destination.

It was too dark for her to see anything beyond the manor's exterior, illuminated at ground level by a string of solar lights along the slate garden path, bordering the length of the building. Despite the poor light, Shani could see it was large enough to rival Buckingham Palace. A little more rustic, although still quite regal. Smooth, pale stone walls extended upward three floors above ground level, ending with a mixed blend of roofing. The vertical walls ended abruptly with circular turrets at each corner of the building, connected by long walkways between, like an old-fashioned battlement. Beyond however, were areas of flat and pitched roof, as though extensions had been added to the manor at different times in history. Dotted along its length were soft plumes of smoke rising from the numerous chimneys.

Beside the manor, the pathway bordered perfectly manicured garden beds, beyond which lay even more sprawling gardens. The faint outlines of bushes and shrubs disappeared into the darkness in all directions, ending at the heavily wooded forest cloaked by the dark shadows of nightfall.

"Wow, I can't wait to see this place in daylight," Yasmin said.

"Me too. How big is the property?" Shani asked Saladin as he brought the car to a stop.

"That depends on who you talk to. The manor's house and grounds cover about twenty acres. But originally Savernake Forest also used to be part of Alaric's land. Over the centuries the Shire has conveniently *lost* the documentation of ownership and have assumed ownership of the land. If you include the forest, Alaric owns approximately four and a half thousand acres, which is about eighteen square kilometres of land," Saladin answered.

"Why doesn't he claim the land back?" Yasmin asked curiously.

"No need. The forest has always been open for everyone to use and enjoy, and since the Shire maintains the forest's upkeep, that's one less thing for Alaric to worry about. If he ever needed to, he could easily claim it back."

"Isn't he afraid someone might destroy it? I thought it was some sort of sacred forest," Shani queried.

"It is. The Elder Tree, which is at the heart of the forest, protects this land. The forest will never be cut down or defiled, the Elders wouldn't allow it. Nor can anyone with harmful intentions of any kind set foot inside the forest. At the first sign of trouble the guardians of the forest will know and be ready to defend anyone or anything inside the forest's parameters if necessary."

"Who are the guardians?" Yasmin asked.

"The forest has several. The lycans patrol the forest here on Earth, on this dimensional plane, and the nephilim protect it in Fey."

"Savernake Forest exists in two planes of existence?" Yasmin asked. She was trying to understand and accept what Saladin was saying, but it went against the laws of nature and the universe, as she knew them. A very narrow view of the universe, she was beginning to realise.

"Not exactly. The Elder Tree exists simultaneously on *three* planes, here on Earth, Fey and in the Higher Realms, and it's surrounded by a different forest in each dimension. Here, it's in Savernake Forest, and in Fey, it's in the nephilim forest called Coed Caer Ffin, which literally translates to *Border Fortress*. If you're ever in trouble, get to the forest and you'll always be safe."

"No doubt all this probably seems a bit overwhelming at the moment to you, but don't worry, just remember that everyone who lives here at the manor are all just regular people like you," Teagan said, giving Shani and Yasmin her best reassuring smile.

Carrying their bags inside, they left them by the front door and followed Saladin and Teagan through the long, wide corridors of the manor, toward what Shani assumed was the kitchen. The smell of recently cooked food was growing stronger the further into the manor's interior they walked.

It seemed she was right. As they pushed open a swinging door they stepped inside a huge kitchen, not too unlike the one in her own house back in India, she thought.

"Hey, Alex, what are you doing?" Teagan asked curiously.

"Staring at the clock and wishing for it to turn 9:00pm."

"Why?"

"Because then it will be the kids bedtime, and I really wish it was the kids bedtime. They're driving me crazy."

"You know, you can just tell them to go to bed now if you want," Teagan said.

"And that works, they just go to bed because you tell them to?"

"Not usually, but it's worth a try. It's better than standing there staring at the clock. Anyway, how did you get the job of looking after the kids, I thought you were banned. Where's Cassie or Kaitlyn?"

"They're all having a girls night at the pub, so I volunteered. I've been *encouraged* to try to be a more responsible adult, but it's exhausting. I really don't think I'm cut out for it."

Teagan tried to hide her grin. If there was anyone less cut out to be a responsible adult, it was Alex. But, he was trying, sort of. She had to give him credit for that.

"If you're supposed to be looking after them, where are they?"

"Follow the noise, you'll see," Alex advised.

"Why, what did they do, or should I be asking, what did you do?" Teagan asked suspiciously. If she was right, the kids probably weren't behaving any worse than any other day, except if Alex was trying to be *responsible*, he probably had no idea how to manage them without making their behaviour more mischievous, as he usually did. While everyone else tried to contain the kids enthusiastic/creative minds, indoors at least, Alex was usually the one encouraging them to push the boundaries of acceptable behaviour just a little farther.

"Follow the noise," Alex repeated.

"I can't hear anything," she told him, looking out the kitchen doorway in the hope of some clue to the direction they might be.

Saladin pointed up at the same time Mrs Philpot appeared in the doorway, "You'll find them playing on the staircase in the east wing.

They insisted on helping Megan and I set up the rooms for our new guests, although I believe they may have become a little distracted," she said, smoothly switching her exasperated tone to a cheery one when she spotted the guests in question. "Hello, I'm Edwina Philpot, the housekeeper here. And you must be Shani and Yasmin."

"Yes, it's a pleasure to meet you," Shani replied politely, and Yasmin seconded the greeting.

"Likewise. I hope you have a pleasant stay with us. The kids or Megan would be happy to show you to your rooms while I try to remember why I came in here," she grumbled, scratching her head. "Don't ever get old love, it really sucks. I can remember every word of a song from 1954, but I can't remember why I came into the kitchen," Mrs Philpot complained.

"I'll do my best," Shani smiled.

"You know what's sad? Once upon a time my bed was somewhere I used to go to sleep. Now it's a magical place where I go to remember everything I was supposed to do earlier in the day....Ah, yes, I know why I'm here, I needed to get some duct tape," she announced enthusiastically, marching quickly across the room to rummage through the kitchen drawers. All the while continuing to mumble away to herself as though still involved in conversation, ending her vocalised internal dialogue with another complaint about how often she also needed to give herself a pep talk these days too.

"Should I ask what you need duct tape for?" Saladin asked.

"Probably not love," she answered, waving away the enquiry.

"Mrs P, you know it's okay to talk to yourself. It's even okay to answer yourself, but if you ask yourself to repeat whatever you just said, I think that's when you might have a problem," Alex told her cheekily.

Mrs Philpot let out a hearty peel of laughter, her large bosom jiggling as her whole body got caught up in her humour. "Oh Alex, you're a cad, a lovable one though," she told him, giving his cheek an affectionate pinch.

"So, tell me Alex, what do the voices in your head tell you?" Saladin asked.

"Don't knock my imaginary voices, they may not be real, but they come up with some great ideas."

Mrs Philpot roared laughing again. "Go find Megan and the kids, they'll help get you two settled in," Mrs Philpot told them, between receding chuckles. "Have any of you had dinner? I can put a quiche in the oven for you if you haven't."

"We're good, thanks Mrs P. We grabbed some burgers on the way here," Teagan told her.

"Okay love, but if you get peckish, Megan's been cooking up a storm, the fridge is full, help yourselves."

"Hey, if you guys are going up to the kids, how about you tell them it's their bedtime," Alex suggested.

"No chance Alex. If you volunteered to be responsible for them tonight, you can deal with them," Teagan smirked.

"Fuck a duck! Ah, I mean damn it. Shit, sorry. I'm trying to turn over a new leaf, I really am. But fuck, it's harder than I thought it'd be. Fuck! Sorry, I didn't mean to say fuck...again. Fuck!"

"Alex, shut up and everyone will be happy," Saladin told him.

"Don't take anything that Alex says personally. He's fluent in sarcasm, movie quotes and being an arsehole," Teagan interjected with an affectionate grin in his direction.

Shani and Yasmin both tried to cover their smirks. Alex seemed a little odd at times, but he meant well, of that Shani was sure. However, it did appear his sarcasm wasn't just limited to verbal foot-in-mouth disease and poorly timed social faux pas. He also seemed to have a collection of very aptly contrived, humorous T-shirts. Like the one he was currently wearing: *I would like to apologise to anyone I haven't offended yet. Be patient, I'll get to you shortly.*

"Why don't you girls go upstairs, I'll see you a bit later," Saladin told them, giving Teagan a quick peck on the lips. Teagan didn't need to ask the question about where he was going, Saladin was quick to offer the information before she could get the words out. "I received a message from Oliver. He wants to discuss what's been happening and hopefully put some security in place for Mrs P's party on the weekend."

"Okay, but fill me in later, yeah?"

"Of course." Saladin kissed his wife again and marched out the kitchen's back door into the vegetable garden and down the path which led to the shortcut across the gardens and into Savernake Forest.

"Okay, why don't we go find Megan and the kids and get you two settled in your rooms," Teagan said.

"Sounds good to me," Shani replied.

"I'm following you, lead the way," Yasmin added.

As Teagan led them down yet another corridor towards the east wing staircase, she gave them a brief overview of the facilities that they were welcome to use. The gym and swimming pool down in the lower level, the library and games room/ginormous lounge room. Plus, the conservatory, if they felt like chilling out in the indoor tropical garden setting, instead of braving the wintry cold of the outdoor gardens and forest.

Teagan continued to talk although neither Shani nor Yasmin appeared to hear more than about half of what she was telling them, their attention snared by the rustic beauty of the old house. Beautiful tapestries and paintings lined the walls, some by unknown but very talented artists, and others by artists like Rembrandt, Van Dyke and even one by Leonardo Da Vinci. Priceless Persian rugs covered the timber flooring, while ornate cornices and ceiling roses comprising intricate silver leafing, covered the high ceilings.

"If you think this is impressive, wait until you see the ceiling in the lounge room. It's thirty foot high and covered in frescoed paintings that put the ceiling in the Sistine Chapel to shame," Teagan told them in a blasé tone.

"How long has Alaric owned this house?" Yasmin asked.

"I'm not sure exactly, I think he was made a guardian of this land pretty much as soon as he was made immortal. But, I think he didn't start building the manor until about eight or nine hundred years ago. He doesn't talk about his past much though. What I do know, Saladin has told me, and I don't think even he knows all of Alaric's history, and he's Alaric's oldest and closest friend."

"Isn't he also Alaric's oldest vampire child? Um...what do you call it...?" Shani asked, trying to find the word she heard used only days before by one of the other vampires at the club.

"Progeny."

"Yes, that's it. Isn't Saladin Alaric's oldest progeny?"

"His oldest *living* progeny. Yes. There were others, but they were all killed long before he turned Saladin."

"Why?" Yasmin asked.

"Various reasons, from what I've been told, the majority of them were killed by Alaric himself."

Shani and Yasmin both gasped in shock. "But he seems so nice. Why would he kill his own progeny?"

"I'm sure it wasn't something he wanted to do. I think in the early days he created a few vampires either without realising it, or because he was lonely? I'm not really sure. I do know from Cassie though, that in the early years he was very angry with the Elders and with the world. For centuries, Alaric was talked about through the supernatural community as being the scary boogieman. Except, back then he wasn't known as Alaric, he was known by his angelic name, Sammael. New vampires were told stories about him to scare them into behaving responsibly and not end up on *Sammael's* hit list for extermination."

"I get it, he definitely gives off a scary vibe, but he doesn't seem like the type to instil that kind of fear deliberately. Are you sure the story wasn't made up just to scare them without any real basis to it?" Shani asked.

"I'm sure. These days Alaric is a much different person than he was a couple of thousand years ago. After he killed off his progeny, he became a recluse for centuries, only coming out to watch over his descendants. Discretely. That's how he met Saladin. They became friends, and when Saladin was dying, Alaric gave him the choice to become a vampire too. A few hundred years later they came across Narayan, and only about seven years ago, Alaric found Abby."

As they neared the east wing staircase, the noise Alex was referring to began to filter through to Teagan, Shani and Yasmin's ears.

"What are they doing?" Shani asked.

"I don't know, but I'm pretty sure I can figure out why Mrs P, needed duct tape. It sounds like they're doing their best to put holes in something," Teagan growled, putting more speed in her step to reach the staircase.

Oh. My. God!

There on the landing between the first and second floors, all hell was breaking loose with what could only be described as a clash of the mini-titans.

Teagan threw her hands out in front of her, freezing everything in mid motion. Well, almost everything.

Before them were the three children and Tilly. Finn, inside his protective purple bubble was unaffected by Teagan's magic, continuing his duck and roll manoeuvre. While Riley, although momentarily frozen in time and motion in midair, twitched once before the spell on him was broken. His vampiric fangs fully extended and his angelic wings resuming their flapping to avoid a collision with Tilly.

"Wow, interesting," Teagan exclaimed in awe of how ineffectual her power was against theirs.

In contrast to the two boys, both Grace and Tilly remained in suspended animation, facing off their pint-sized enemies. Which, when taking in the whole battle scene, was extremely fortunate since Tilly had transformed herself into a hellhound and was dripping acidic drool onto the priceless rug. While Grace stood at the rhinoceros-sized hound's side, poised for a fight, her own pair of vampiric fangs and a sharp set of taloned nails were extended, ready for combat.

Teagan waved her hand again and broke the spell holding the remaining two of the mischievous four. With a click of her fingers, a flash of blinding light caught their attention and they stopped, turning to face the source of the flash.

"Aunt Teagan," they all exclaimed excitedly, suddenly forgetting about their fight.

"Who wants to explain what's going on here?" Teagan growled, looking down on them with an angry scowl. The children looked around at the damage they had caused to the walls, carpet and staircase, quickly dropping their eyes remorsefully. All except Tilly, who had locked her hellhound gaze on Shani and Yasmin.

"I think I want to go home now," Yasmin squeaked and swallowed the lump of terror that was quickly rising, threatening to bring about a fight or flight response.

"It's okay. Tilly won't hurt ye, will ye Tilly?" Megan called as she hurried along the corridor.

Tilly turned her head to look at Megan, letting out a snort of defiance but dipping her huge head with reluctant penance.

"Tilly, change back, yer scaring our guests." Tilly barked and made a series of grumbling noises in reply, to which Megan once again berated the huge hound. A moment later, the air around Tilly seemed to shimmer. In the space of a second, the giant hellhound was gone and Tilly, the playful Irish Wolfhound, had taken her place.

"Alright, who wants to explain what was going on here?" Teagan looked each child in the eye until finally they all began to speak at once.

"Hold up. One at a time. Grace, what happened?"

"We were watching the Lego Movie with Uncle Alex and he got bored. So, he told us we should play a game like cowboys and Indians or doctors and nurses. We don't know how to play doctors and nurses, and no one wanted to be a cowboy because we all like Indians. So, we decided we should play angels and demons. Finn and Riley were the angels and Tilly and I were the demons."

"That makes sense, kids role-play what they know," Yasmin piped up, stepping out from the relative safety behind Teagan.

"Well, next time, can you wait until daytime and play outside. Look at this place. And...you can all explain to your parents what happened."

"Yes ma'am," they all grumbled, their shoulders slumping and eyes cast down in disgrace.

"Good. Now go back downstairs. You can all spend some more time with Uncle Alex before bedtime." *I think he deserves a bit of punishment too*, Teagan added to herself.

"Teagan, you told us everyone here at the manor were just regular people like us." Shani said, watching on in awe beside her cousin. Right before their eyes, Finn's protective bubble dissolved, Riley's wings disappeared and his fangs retreated back into his gums. As did Grace's. The three of them returning to look like the three sweetest, butter-wouldn't-melt-in-their-mouth, most harmless children on the planet.

"Ah, yeah. I might have understated things a little. But hey, it could have been worse."

"Worse, how?" Shani asked dubiously.

"You know Finn's dad is Raif, right?"

"Yes."

"Well, Finn is only three years old, so if he'd shifted into his dragon form, he would have been about as big as Tilly was as a hellhound."

"Okay, I think I'm grateful I didn't see that. As it is, I think I might need some intensive therapy until I can convince myself all that didn't just happen." Yasmin said.

"What if Finn was older?" Shani asked.

"His dragon would be bigger," Megan said.

"How big does an adult dragon get?" Yasmin asked.

"Did you see the *'fake'* footage of a dragon flying over the Jefferson Tower in Alabama a few weeks back?" Teagan asked.

"Yeah, we did. It even made it on the news in India. It was special effects for a movie that put the city into a panic, wasn't it?" Shani replied.

"Nope. That was actually Wade, Raif's brother," Megan stated.

"You're kidding. That was real? That dragon was *real*?"

"You betcha."

"Wow, he was huge. Just out of curiosity, I know the wyvern are tall in their human form too, but are they, you know...well proportioned?" Yasmin asked, crafting her words and tone to mask the meaning of her query from the youngest members in their midst.

Teagan chuckled. "My sister Kaitlyn, who's married to Raif, tells me they're *very* well-endowed."

Grace suddenly became excited as her sensitive ears picked up noises downstairs, that once again passed by Teagan's regular hearing.

"We have more visitors. Come on, quickly," Grace urged fervently, grabbing Teagan by the hand and dragging her downstairs with everyone in tow.

"Hi, I'm Megan?" Megan said, introducing herself to Shani and Yasmin as they took up the rear. "Don't worry about all this craziness, after a couple of days it'll all seem quite normal," she reassured with a chuckle.

The kids ran ahead, eager to accost the new visitors, while the girls struck up a conversation which even Shani and Yasmin considered to be relatively normal....Mrs. Philpot's upcoming centenary party.

From down the hallway, they could hear the kids squeal with delight as they greeted a room full of deep voiced, gruff sounding men.

Teagan led them toward the over-sized lounge room. Inside was a growing number of tall and incredibly well muscled men. Some, Shani and Yasmin had seen before, and others they hadn't.

Stepping forward from amongst the group, Saladin introduced Shani and Yasmin to each and every person in the room. Not that Teagan took that much notice. She was more interested in the dark moods and concerned frowns etched into each of their faces.

Oliver may have come to meet with Alaric about the party preparations, since it was being held in his family's pub, the Drunken Duck. Considering however, he had brought with him the senior members of his clan, plus half the lycan military including his son Callum, Mrs Philpot's grandson Marcus and their recently acquired new Special Ops Commander, straight from Alabama, Gary Sanders, this wasn't going to be a simple meeting about seating arrangements and decorations. The topic of discussion was probably going to follow along the lines of weapons and contingency plans.

Even Sebastian had been called home from one of the Alliance secret recon missions, much to Megan's delight. Marek was also there, along with Don Eckhaus, the South African lycan leader. It seemed everyone had arrived except for Dray.

Shani began to feel a little overwhelmed as more people continued to arrive. Fortunately, the last group were familiar faces she had already begun to think of as friends. Cassie, Kaitlyn, Paige and Abby. Plus, Nadia and Philippe.

This really was a new world she'd found herself in, yet not an unwelcome one. As strange as it sounded, she really felt like she fitted in here among these people. Shani shot a sideways glance toward her cousin. Yasmin didn't look quite as comfortable, but Shani could tell there were some attributes Yasmin found very appealing, i.e, the lycan men's muscular physiques.

Shani heaved a heavy sigh. If only she was free to look at other men too, like her widowed cousin.

"Shani, can I talk to you for a minute?" Marek asked, catching her off guard in her moment of self-absorbed wallowing. His casual smile and smooth manner disguised his underlying curiosity well.

"Sure, is it about your binding stone? I'm really sorry I wasn't able to get a read on it. I could try again for you if you like, but I don't think it will do much good," she apologised.

"No, it's not about my stone. I just wanted to check if you're alright. You seemed upset when Saladin told you you'd have to stay here at the manor for a while. Is there something bothering you, because if there is maybe I can be of some help."

"Everything's fine. Really," Shani pasted on her best smile, but Marek wasn't buying it. *Shit!* This wasn't a can of worms she had any interest in opening, thank you very much. It was time to change tack, shut down this line of questioning. "You're not really interested in my life, so there's no need to pretend you are. I promise I won't hold it against you. *I'm* not interested in my life, so I don't expect anyone else to be either."

"Oh? You might be surprised what interests me," Marek told her.

"My life is boring. Every day is the same, a busy succession of nothings. Does that satisfy your curiosity?"

"Not even close, but I won't push you to tell me the truth. After all, trust must be earned. If anyone understands that, I do."

Shani didn't know how to respond to that, so she nodded. "Excuse me, I think my cousin is looking for me," she said, stepping away politely without looking him in the eye, still, she could feel his gaze following her as she made her way across the room. Coming to stand at Yasmin's side, Shani smiled and pretended to be interested in the conversation she was engaged in, with....with....nope, she couldn't remember his name.

"Do you have anyone in your life?" Yasmin asked.

"No, not these days. There was someone but that's all over with now. The restraining order was very specific," he stated with a deadpan face. Yasmin stared for a moment to assess the efficacy of his statement.

"I like you, Sanders. You're funny," Yasmin laughed.

Gary Sanders shrugged. He was telling the truth, but hey, no need to burst her bubble if she wants to believe otherwise.

Shani barely heard any more than that. Everything around her sounded like, blah, blah, blah this, and blah, blah, blah that. She did notice however, how in sync all the couples seemed to be together. Her eyes roamed from one couple to another, coming to rest on Alaric and Cassie.

Alaric's broad palm absently stroked up and down Cassie's back as she leaned in closer to him. The gesture was simple, of no consequence. All the same, for Shani witnessing their bond, that intimacy was as difficult to watch as an act of violence. Shani blinked quickly to stop her eyes from welling.

She really wished her husband was as loving and as caring as Alaric was, as all of these men were to their wives and partners. Or even better…she wished she was free to be with Dray. What would it be like to feel his arms about her, or his fingers caress her, his lips kissing her…

Shani looked away in a futile attempt at banishing the thought from her mind, but everywhere she looked she saw the same show of affection and her heart sank. Quietly she left the crowded room and made her way to the relative seclusion of the kitchen and a freshly brewed pot of tea. But even there, there were reminders of what she would never have.

"Oh, hey, sorry. I didn't mean to interrupt you," she said to Philippe and Nadia, doing a quick about turn to walk back the way she came.

"You're not interrupting anything," Nadia assured. "I was just explaining to Philippe how I've been on a low carb diet all my life. Whenever I'm feeling low I eat carbs."

Philippe and Shani both chuckled, but only Philippe received a scathing scowl in return. He opened his mouth and then shut it again. Even though he knew she meant her comment as a backhanded joke at herself, it seemed he wasn't supposed to laugh.

"I think I might take a walk outside," Shani said, letting her finger point the way to the kitchen's back door and the peaceful sanctuary of the garden. As the door closed behind her, she leaned against it as though it was the only thing keeping her upright, the thick timber filtering Philippe and Nadia's conversation down to background noise, as she dredged up the energy to venture out into the darkness.

"It's not funny. Look at me, I'm overweight and I want to be skinny. So, I've decided it's time for a change. I'm going on a real diet. I'm going to diet until I'm on the cusp of organ failure, and in a month's time I want my body to have all those hard bulgy bits," Nadia proclaimed, although her enthusiasm came out more like an angry rant, almost daring Philippe to tell her otherwise.

"They're called muscles," he said matter-of-factly, not foolish enough to make the mistake of laughing a second time.

"Right, lots of muscles, with veins popping out all over. I want to be so slim and fit, I'll be like an X-ray with a pulse."

"Good for you, but have you considered that I like you just the way you are?"

"Is that important?"

"I guess not. It's all about how you feel. What will being slim do for you? Will it give you a longer life expectancy? I don't think so, you're as close to being immortal as I am. Would becoming slimmer make more men take notice of you? Maybe, but that's not necessarily a good thing, I might have to kill them for ogling you. Will it give you greater self-esteem? That question, only you can answer. I know you've always struggled with the idea that somehow, you're inferior to your sisters. But really, look at them, they're all different in their own way just like you, and they all have their own issues to deal with. You might be surprised to learn that they all envy you too. So, what's your motivation to get on this fitness kick?"

"They do? My sisters are envious of me?"

"That's what you got out of my pep talk?"

Nadia nodded guiltily. "I know it's shallow, but I've always been the ugly duckling in the family with a lame natural druid gift and virtually no magical abilities. But, I had no one to teach me, while they all had our grandfather to teach them."

"Nadia, sweetheart. You had what they only wish they could've had. Elise never knew either of your parents until she was sixteen. Your other sisters barely even remember your mother. And the man they were led to believe was their father abandoned them when your mother died. Your grandfather raised them, but he didn't give them hugs at night or dry their eyes when they scraped a knee. He drilled them every day about their druid legacy. Learning magic for them wasn't something they wanted, it was expected. Now, they're all still trying to get to know the one parent that they didn't know they even had until five years ago, and you've known him your whole life. You might feel like the fish out of water around them sometimes, but they're the ones who are envious."

"When you put it like that....maybe my life hasn't been so bad after all," Nadia said on reflection.

"You also have a man who loves you very much just the way you are, and who would do anything to protect you and make you happy."

"You know that goes both ways, right?"

"I do," Philippe told her with a sly grin. Leaning down he kissed her lightly on the lips.

"I hope you have the same reply when you're standing at the altar with my daughter," came a humourless, gruff voice from behind.

Philippe closed his eyes and inwardly cursed.

Gustav.

19

The happy feel good moment between Nadia and Philippe seemed to dissolve like sugar in tea at the sound of Gustav's voice. It was surprising how easily he managed to sneak up behind them. For such a big man he moved almost as quietly as a vampire.

"Is there something you'd like to share with me?" Gustav asked, his low, even tone cutting through the air like a knife, as he looked first at Nadia before locking his hard gaze onto Philippe.

Philippe stared into Gustav's unblinking glare, realising that voicing his personal opinion at that moment probably wasn't a healthy choice. Healthy for him that is, going by the guttural snarl projected in his direction. Philippe swallowed a nervous lump in his throat and stepped back.

"Yes, we're *mated*. Get over it," Nadia snapped, her voice dipping several degrees colder.

"So I've heard. And, when were you planning on telling me?" Gustav replied with a deep growl in his voice.

Nadia regretted her whiplash tone, but she'd had it up to her ears with her overbearing and interfering family. Not that her equally overbearing father seemed affected by her crabby mood, his facial expression never altering even a twitch, which only made her more annoyed.

"Right about now," Philippe told him, exerting confidence he didn't feel.

Gustav glared at Philippe for long seconds, his eyes conveying the storm brewing behind them, before turning his attention back to his daughter. "Are you happy?" he asked her simply.

"Yes. Very," she replied much more contritely.

"You're ready to spend the rest of your life with him?"

"I am."

Gustav turned his attention back to Philippe. "You will be marrying my daughter." It wasn't a question, it was a statement of fact.

"Definitely." Philippe agreed quickly.

"Have you asked her yet?"

"No Sir. Not yet." The way Gustav was looking at him, Philippe suddenly felt like he had failed in his duty somehow, even though he and Nadia had been a couple for less than twenty-four hours.

Gustav speared another look between Philippe and Nadia who were now clinging to each other for comfort under his scrutiny, before letting out an uninterpretable grunt and left the room.

"That went well. Not awkward at all," Philippe said.

"It went great. I think I just won ten quid," Nadia laughed, doing a mental check. Did her father frown? *Check!* Did he growl? *Check!* Did he then pretend to be happy? *Check!* No broken or dismembered limbs? *Nope!* Then, yep, she had won the bet.

A moment later Gustav re-entered the kitchen, his expression no longer angry, yet the crease in his brow was no less severe.

"Philippe, can I have a word with you…please…Outside."

Philippe's shoulders slumped. He knew his acceptance wouldn't come so easily. *Now for the broken bones*, he thought.

"I'm coming too! Anything you have to say to Philippe, you can say in front of me," Nadia told her father defiantly, shoving her hands on her hips. It was either that or rub her sweaty palms on her thighs. She thought they had his blessing, now she wasn't so sure. Nor was she sure how she felt about that. Angry? Disappointed? Frustrated?

Angry. Definitely angry. She had three older sisters already *mated* and he never behaved like this with any of them. Why was he singling her out with his heavy-handed, overbearing, controlling behaviour? *Because, as Philippe pointed out, you are the only one he was able to raise. You're the only one he feels as though he has a right to have a say in your life,* she answered her own question silently. And damn, didn't that just flip her mood switch. She really wanted to stay mad at him. Instead, now she was starting to feel sympathy for him.

"Not this time. I want a private word with your man."

Your man! Those two words of acknowledgement caused a lump of emotion to lodge in her throat. Whatever her father had planned with Philippe, killing him wasn't on the agenda, of that she was certain. Thank God for small mercies.

"If you break any of his bones, I won't talk to you for a month," she growled. *Coz I'll lose the bet.*

Philippe drew in a long breath. "Okay, let's get this over with."

Nadia hugged herself in frustration and held her breath as her father and *mate* disappeared into the darkness.

Out in the gardens Gustav stood eye to eye with Philippe, his back ramrod straight as he rolled his shoulders and cracked his knuckles.

Philippe wasn't sure whether to prepare for a fight or stand there like a stuffed dummy and just accept whatever beating Gustav wanted to payout on him. However, as it turned out, kicking Philippe's arse wasn't on Gustav's agenda.

Philippe watched silently as Gustav pulled a small box from his pocket and opened it. He stared at it for a moment, his expression a mix of resignation, sadness and relief. An interesting combination for sure, but not one he would have expected from this hard-arsed lycan.

Then, as Gustav held the box out toward him, Philippe saw its contents and understood.

"This was the ring I gave Nadia's mother just after we were *mated*. I don't need to tell you the story about why Debra and I never married, I'm sure you know it as well as anyone else. We were forced to live a lie for years to protect the girls from their own grandfather, the same man who ended up raising all of them...except Nadia. In our hearts though, Debra and I were married, and she never took this ring off. Ever. When she died, her fake husband was going to pawn it for cash. I *persuaded* him to give it back to me, and I've kept it close to me ever since."

"And you want to give it to me? Why?" Philippe asked as he took the gift.

"I want my daughter to have it. I heard what the two of you were talking about before. I can't tell you how much guilt I carry around every day about how my girls were raised, without a mother, and all of them without a proper father. I failed them, I know that. And there's no justifying it by claiming it was for their protection. I should have found a way to be there for them. Maybe then, Nadia wouldn't feel like the *ugly duck* against her sisters, their mother might still be alive today too and all our lives might be different."

"Maybe. But everything happens for a reason Gustav. Just because you don't know why things happened the way they did, doesn't mean you failed. Because of the events of the past, all but one of your daughters have now found happiness with their own *mates*. Who's to say that would've been possible if you'd chosen a different path," Philippe told him. Looking down at the ring in his hands, a small smile quirked up one corner of his lips. "You know, I honestly thought you were pulling a knife from your pocket to cut off my balls," Philippe half joked.

"The thought did cross my mind. But I wouldn't use a knife." Gustav made a gesture with his hand that made Philippe's nut sack reflexively suck back up into his abdominal cavity.

Yikes. "Good to know," Philippe replied a little uncomfortably.

"Welcome to the family, Son," Gustav said in his native Ukrainian, a second before wrapping his huge arms around Philippe and squeezing, hard.

"What the hell dad? I said no broken bones," Nadia griped testily. Waiting patiently wasn't one of Nadia's best virtues, and clearly the wait to find out if Philippe still had his limbs attached was too much for her.

"It's not what it looks like," Philippe managed to squeak out with what air remained in his lungs. "Your dad wanted to give me something. Actually, he wanted to give me something to give to you."

Nadia stopped still at the sight of the small box in Philippe's hands. She had seen that box on her father's dresser beside her mother's picture for years.

"What? Are you serious? You want me to have *this* ring? I didn't think you'd ever want to part with it. It's the only reminder you have of my mother," she blurted out incredulously, her voice tight with emotion.

"Wrong. I have five daughters who remind me of her every day. I don't need to keep the ring. I know she'd want you to have it." Satisfied pride gleamed in his eyes as he stared down at Nadia's smiling face which had silent tears streaming down it.

"I think I should leave you two love birds alone now. I believe you have something to ask my daughter." Gustav quirked an eyebrow up in Philippe's direction, conveying something crossed between a not-so-subtle prompt and an *or else,* order. Not that Philippe needed any encouragement, he was totally on-board with the plans his future father-in-law was advocating.

"Thanks dad. For everything," Nadia stretched up to give her father a kiss on the cheek and hugged him tightly. Gustav reciprocated the warm embrace, laying his cheek against her head, soaking in the scent and feel of his daughter one last time before relinquishing his duty of care and responsibility in her life to her *mate.* He always knew this day would come, but somehow it still came too soon.

Silently Gustav retreated back inside the manor, leaving Philippe and Nadia outside under the starry sky of the brusque wintry night, his heart a little lighter.

"Well?" Nadia prompted impatiently, eliciting a chuckle from Philippe.

"Well, what?" he replied, deliberately frustrating her. Why? Because he loved the way her cheeks blushed and her eyes sparkled when she got annoyed. And it was fun. "Oh, you mean you want me to give you the ring. No, not just yet," he teased.

"Philippe, unless you want *me* to cut off your balls, stop messing around."

He couldn't help it, he let out a hearty laugh. "Fine, but not until you answer me one simple question."

"Oh, what's that?"

Philippe dropped down on one knee, the vision of her in the moonlight etching into his memory forever as he asked, "Will you be my wife?"

"Of course I will," she squealed happily, tears streaming down her face as she threw her arms around him, kissing him until she was almost turning blue from lack of oxygen.

Philippe couldn't remember a time in his life when he had been so happy.

"So, what are we going to do?"

"With you now wearing that ring, and me still shit scared of your father, I believe we'll be getting married as quickly as possible." When

Nadia's eyebrows shot up, Philippe quickly amended his statement. "To my overwhelming delight."

Nadia's lips quirked up in a cheeky smile. "I meant, what are we going to do right now?" She stretched on tip toes and brushed her lips across the pulse thrumming in his throat. When his reaction was a blank, clueless face, she let out a frustrated huff, and proceeded to make her proposal a little bolder, in a gesture Philippe was guaranteed to understand. She pulled her top to one side, pushed down the cup of her bra, and gave him a sensual flash of a voluptuous breast, pinching the dusky nipple between her fingertips.

Philippe's moan was instantaneous, so too was his response. His lips covered hers, his tongue breaching the opening and stroking against hers with an erotic caress. White-hot pleasure whipping through her whole body, a vibrant explosion of need sending her senses reeling.

She couldn't catch her breath.

She didn't want to catch her breath.

"You're in trouble now."

"Why's that?"

"You've given me an everlasting mongrel from just one tittie flash."

"I didn't know my titties were so powerful. I wonder what powers my pussy has?"

"I have plans to find out," he growled.

The way Philippe saw it he had two options. Either he took care of the perma-erection he had rocking, or he went back to the group gathered in the lounge room, sporting a baseball bat in his pants. Not a good advertisement unless he was trying to sell tickets for a skin flick, which he wasn't.

Impatient to get his *mate* naked, Philippe wasn't willing to wait for her much shorter legs to walk the distance through the corridors of the ground floor to the west wing staircase and up the two flights of stairs to reach their suite. Instead, Philippe picked Nadia up in his arms and powered up his full speed to reach his destination in a matter of seconds.

"Wow, what a rush. I don't think you've carried me quite that fast before, at least not while I was sober," she joked.

"I've never had so much incentive."

"So, what do you have in mind now?" Nadia asked in a sultry tone, slowly dragging a finger down his chest, through the valley between his well defined pecs, continuing lower across the hardened muscles in his abdomen. Wow. Just, wow! How did it happen that her life had changed so much in such a short period of time, Nadia wondered.

Light from the fire on the far side of the room bathed Nadia in soft hues of yellows and oranges. He'd never seen anyone so beautiful.

"Shh. Enough talking, come with me." Philippe said, leading her towards the sofa near the fireplace.

"Whatever you have in mind it better not involve those chains and handcuffs in the shower," Nadia told him firmly.

Philippe's snicker was neither confirmation nor denial of her request, which made her a little nervous. Not that she needed to be. Philippe's brain seemed to be hardwired to only want to bring her pleasure, not distress. She made a mental note to arrange for the remainder of Alex and Abby's BDSM equipment to be removed permanently from *their* suite as soon as possible, before he got any bright ideas.

"The only thing I want you bound to for the foreseeable future are my hips," he told her as he came around behind her. Philippe's breathing quickened, a feather-light caress against the back of her neck.

His hand slipped under her top and cupped the heavy weight of her rounded breast, squeezing her nipple to a tight bud between his fingers. She leaned her head back onto his shoulder. He kissed her neck, licking and nipping hungrily at it and revelled in the erotic moan it elicited from her lips.

Nadia felt a tug on her shirt. Something clickety-clacked onto the floor, like a string of pearls breaking free of their string, followed by another tug of her skirt and the sound of something ripping. Nadia glanced down at herself and gasped. In less than a second she had gone from fully clothed to naked, except for her knickers and the shoes on her feet, and she hadn't moved a muscle. Not that she was complaining, especially when a second later Philippe was standing before her, clothed in a mirror image, minus the shoes.

Nadia's hand fit snugly into Philippe's larger palm, his gentle but firm grip leading her over to the sofa where he took a seat. Her eyes gravitated automatically to his erection, jutting hard against the fabric of his snug fitting boxers, evidence of just how much she affected him.

"You have no idea how much I want you right now," he whispered as she straddled his thighs.

"I'm getting an inkling, but please feel free to show me," she chuckled, nuzzling her breasts closer to his face.

Philippe's lips drew her nipple into his mouth, the sharp nip of his teeth sending shards of sharp pleasure to clench her womb. Nadia's gasp became a moan as he shifted his weight beneath her, opening her up to him for better contact against all that moist heat he could scent weeping from her core, and bringing his hard shaft into contact with her clit.

His gentle touch became more aggressive, increasing the pressure in all the right places as his hands roamed her body. The pleasure built as she began to rock her hips against him, making them both frantic for more. They weren't even completely naked. If they were, he would already be inside her, filling her with deep, powerful thrusts and relieving this burning need that was threatening to overwhelm him.

Philippe kissed his way back up to Nadia's sensitised breasts to taste her lips once again, wanting her so badly his own body shook from the effort to keep his movements slow and even, his pulse pounding in his ears in tandem with the throbbing pulse in his groin. He was so hard he knew he wouldn't last long once he breached her slick entrance. He'd waited too long, wished too hard for this day to come.

It still felt surreal, but his dream of having Nadia as his *mate* was no longer mere fantasy, but reality. And, soon she would also be his wife. Life just didn't get any better than this.

At that moment Nadia jumped from his lap and he couldn't stop the groan from the loss of contact.

Nadia quickly pushed her panties from her hips and kicked them off. Once again, her eyes locked onto Philippe's groin. A small patch of moisture had dampened his boxers where the tip of his cock had leaked, and she licked her lips. Only hours earlier she had wrapped her lips around that weeping tip and sucked it dry. She would have been tempted to do it again now, if she wasn't so desperate to have that hard length filling her body.

Following Nadia's lead, Philippe discarded his shorts, his shaft springing free of its tight confines, jutting high and proud of his body.

Nadia straddled his hips once again, slowly lowering herself down.

Gripping his thick girth, Philippe positioned it against her wet and needy opening. His eyes meeting hers as she slowly sank down, sheathing his hard length inside her enveloping channel. So warm. So wet. So tight and ready for him. Philippe couldn't hold back a growl of appreciation and shuddered anew when her inner walls suddenly clamped down on him harder in response. "So good," he said, his voice barely more than a husky whisper.

Nadia moaned when his lips slid over her jaw to her neck, his hands guiding the smooth movements of her hips, his own hips moving with strong, sure thrusts as he pumped his shaft inside her slowly.

Sensitive tissue parted with his dominant ministration, impaling her with each rocking movement of his hips, her inner walls clenching around his erection on each retreat and thrust. He caressed her with heavy strokes through her slick inner flesh, as his hands and mouth did the same to the rest of her body.

As the friction between their bodies built, Nadia rode him with her head thrown back, revelling in the erotic moment. So, he let her pick the pace, steadying her with his strength. Philippe sat back with his feet braced apart and gave her free rein, watching as she took control, it was so God damned hot, he was ready to explode witnessing her passion. Nadia's ecstasy filled eyes meeting his with an unspoken plea as she tilted her head to the side, exposing her neck to him. Nothing needed to be said. With a swiftness that surprised even himself, his fangs descending with a *snick*, and latched onto the pulsing vein offered. Long hard pulls of her crimson nectar combined with her slick tight walls riding him, hardened his cock to the point of pain. It was too much, the sensations overwhelmed him.

With a guttural growl, Philippe took control and slammed her down onto him, over and over.

Nadia began to shake with pure unadulterated need. "Oh, fuck yeah. Make me come," she pleaded.

A frown tugged at Philippe's lust filled face as he directed all his focus into doing just that.

As the first waves of orgasm erupted inside her, Nadia felt his thrusts change, become harder, shorter, and then he jerked beneath her, an animalistic growl rumbling from his chest a second before she felt the first pulse of his semen jet deep into her womb. He tensed as he came, shuddering as his cock pulsed and jerked inside her, and held her even tighter.

"I could really get used to this," she told him breathless and boneless, resting her full weight against his warm body.

"Sweetheart, we can do this every day for eternity."

"I know. I can't help feeling like I've won the lottery," she chuckled. "Wow, I'm tired. I could really use a nap," she said with a huge yawn.

"I'd love nothing more than to tuck you into bed right now..."

"I bet you would," Nadia quipped happily, rolling her hips over his, noting how hard he still was, then did it again when he let out a tormented groan. He could go again another six times and not break a sweat, but after only two hours sleep the night before, and a rather emotional day, Nadia was beat.

Philippe gently lifted Nadia off his lap and sat her on the sofa as he got to his feet. "As I was saying, I'd love nothing more than to tuck you into bed right now, but...we really should go back downstairs. Everyone's here to discuss what to do about Nicholas and Scorpion, and since..."

"And since we're the ones that are affected the most by whatever is decided, we need to be there for the decision making," Nadia finished, letting out a long sigh of understanding and resignation.

"Yes," he answered. Nadia watched as Philippe's countenance suddenly stiffened at the mention of his brother, while in contrast, his stiff erection sagged to become a pleasant memory.

"Okay, but promise me you'll tuck me into bed later?"

"I'm looking forward to it. Tonight, and every night from now on," he agreed, leaning down to kiss her in a short but sensual kiss.

"Come on. We'd better get back before people notice we're missing." Gripping Philippe's hand, Nadia pulled herself up onto shaky legs and looked about for her clothes. Ah, right, not a good idea to wear the same outfit. She could probably wear the buttonless shirt again, if she wore it as an over-shirt. But her skirt was probably going to be more useful as a cleaning cloth. At least the half of it she could find would. There was a high probability that the other half had fuelled the fire in the hearth.

"You go ahead, I just want to fix my hair a bit. If I go down there like this everyone will know what we've been up to," she told him as she rummaged through the dresser drawers for clean underwear and a new outfit.

Philippe held back his smirk. Every vampire and lycan in the room would know what they had just been doing. The scent of sex clung to them like a sensual stink bomb. Not that he was going to tell Nadia that. She'd never come back downstairs. Ever. "Alright. I'll see you in a few minutes."

Philippe stepped into the hallway and closed the door. Thoughts of his brother and recent events crept into his mind. As he followed the corridor to the far end, it took him past Nadia's old room, he couldn't resist the temptation to go inside.

It looked the same as it always had, minus Nadia's personal possessions on top of the dresser, or slippers beneath the bed which were now in their new suite. But the emotions and vivid memories this room brought back were painful and raw. As a direct consequence of his brother's actions, he had watched Nadia die an agonising death in that bed just a few short weeks ago.

Now, only this morning, Nicholas had threatened her life again.

"I thought I'd find you up here, are you okay?"

The familiar voice at his back jolted Philippe from his stupor.

"No, not really. Nor do I think I will be again until Nicholas is dead," he told Narayan.

"Maybe it isn't wise for you to be in this room. Reliving the past trauma of what happened here isn't necessarily a good thing. It can cloud your judgement of the present and the future," Narayan said, looking about the orderly room filled with dark, unseen shadows.

"I can't forget what Nicholas did to Nadia."

"Nor should you. Holding onto your memories is important, but holding onto all that negative emotion attached to them, isn't healthy. If you're too focused on your anger, you'll leave yourself open for another attack, or you'll make a mistake. Maybe both. To keep things in perspective you need to calm your mind. Find that place deep inside you where it's still, where you can think without feeling."

"I have a confession to make, Narayan. I don't know if I have the capacity to find my inner Zen right now."

"Yes, you do. You just need to know where to find it. Ask yourself, what it is that quiets the demons inside you," Narayan told him.

"What will quiet my demons? Catching up with my brother and ripping him limb from limb, very slowly. That's what. I want to draw out his pain for as long as possible before I kill him. And you know why?" Philippe didn't wait for Narayan to answer. "Because he doesn't deserve such an easy ending as death. At the same time, I can't bear the thought of him still existing in the world." Philippe's tone was hard, brittle with hatred.

"Be careful you don't destroy your own soul in the process of sending his to the Underworld."

"I wasted so many decades on my brother, believing I had somehow miraculously changed him. All the while he was just biding his time, waiting for a chance to act out on his psychotic fantasies."

"You haven't wasted anything. Life teaches us many things. Some lessons are painful, some lessons are painless. And some lessons are priceless. But there's no point dwelling on something you can't change, you did the best you could with the knowledge you had available to you," Narayan pointed out.

Somewhere in the back of his mind, Philippe recognised the similarities between Narayan's speech to him, and his own speech to Gustav about accepting that the universe has plans for our futures regardless of our current understanding of them. However, accepting the lesson wasn't so easy when it was directed back at him.

Philippe nodded woodenly, unable to let go of his fury. "If he tries to hurt Nadia again…" he left the thought unfinished.

"No one is going to let that happen. Now, come on, I believe you have an announcement to make, and if you don't hurry your *mate* will be left to make it without you. Trust me, you don't want Nadia's sisters or the other women in this house grilling you about why you missed the announcement of your own engagement," he told Philippe, slapping a consolatory hand on his shoulder.

"You know already? How?"

"Hmm, I have my ways," Narayan winked. Turning on his heel, he exited the room, waiting in the corridor a second for Philippe to follow.

20

The days passed quickly for Shani and Yasmin at the manor with all the hustle and bustle of pre-party arrangements. Much too quickly for Shani's liking. She enjoyed the friendly atmosphere of the manor. Most of all she enjoyed the seclusion and peace and quiet of Savernake Forest. Each day she and Yasmin took a walk through a different part of the woods. However, as much of the forest they had covered, they never once managed to find the Elder tree which was said to be at its heart. For a tree supposedly as tall as the Eiffel Tower, it should have been easy to locate. As they quickly learned, that wasn't the case.

Not that it really mattered she figured, tomorrow she would be leaving here forever anyway. The job she was paid to do was complete, and since today was Mrs Philpot's big party, there was nothing left to keep her here. Tomorrow she would go back to London with her cousin and await Saadir's call instructing her when to go home.

Shani let out a wistful sigh. She may be forced to return to India, but she was definitely leaving part of her soul behind here in England. How strange it was, she thought. She had never even kissed Dray, and had known him for only a couple of weeks, if you didn't count all the work related emails they sent each other over the last year or so. But, she felt more connected to him than she had to anyone else in her entire life.

"Shani, I have an outfit which would look stunning on you." Abby held out a beautiful crimson coloured, figure hugging, sleeveless dress. "It might be cold outside, but inside the Drunken Duck Pub with its open fires burning and cosy atmosphere, there'll be no need to rug up," she told her.

Shani looked at it with admiration. She would love to wear it, it truly was stunning.

"Thanks, but no. I like to keep my arms covered." she replied gracefully.

"Is it a religious requirement or something?" Abby asked curiously.

"No. It's just me. I don't feel comfortable exposing my skin." Shani turned away to pick up the slightly modified (with sleeves) traditional Indian, gold and jade wrapped silk sari which she'd brought with her, effectively cutting off the conversation. Yasmin gave Abby an apologetic smile but didn't elaborate on her cousin's behalf.

Abby examined Shani a little harder. Maybe it was rude of her to do so, but she couldn't resist the urge to push into Shani's mind and retrieve the answer to her question. "Oh my Lord. Your husband beats you!"

Shani turned around so fast, she almost lost her balance. "Please don't tell anyone. I didn't want anyone to know," she pleaded, her calm façade shattering in an instant with panic and embarrassment.

"You know we have ways to deal with people like him, right?" Abby growled.

"Yes. But no. You can't fix this, it's....complicated."

"Why? Is your husband the boss of the Indian Mafia?" Abby asked jokingly, although she didn't find Shani's situation the least bit funny.

"Not quite. He's the son of the Indian Mafia Raj," Shani replied regretfully.

"That's not all," Yasmin said.

"Shh. There's no need to share every sordid detail of my life," Shani growled.

"Yes, there is. If anyone can help you get out of your situation, these people can." Yasmin swatted away Shani's hands when she attempted to silence her, side stepping her cousin and speaking quickly to expose the rest of Shani's secrets while she had the chance. "Shani's only been allowed to come here to England because Saadir needed her out of the way for a few weeks. Shani can't have kids...." *Because of what he's done to her*, she wanted to add. "Which poses a problem for him. To keep his family's criminal empire going he has to produce at least one heir. So, he's deliberately knocked up some poor woman. I believe he's planning to put Shani's name on the birth certificate as the mother, and pay the woman off for her silence and to stay away from the child after it's born."

"Oh my God. You're serious," Abby gasped in shock. One look at Shani and no one could deny it was the truth. For the first time Abby could see the mask she lived behind crumble away to dust, leaving behind a frightened woman, destitute of hope for her future.

"Very," Yasmin replied with a sad smile, gripping her cousin's hand with moral support.

Abby wanted to be nosy and probe her for more answers on the subject, either by Shani's voluntary verbal admission, or by delving into her mind directly, but unfortunately the opportunity was lost with the approach of more of the household women.

"Please don't tell them," Shani begged Abby as the gaggling, laughing voices grew nearer.

"I promise I will never tell the other girls anything."

"Or Dray. Please, don't ever tell Dray," Shani added, feeling the need to expand her wishes.

"Promise." Abby crossed her heart with her fingers. She was tempted to cross her fingers behind her back, as she was crossing her heart, to give herself a loophole in her promise. Not that it was necessary, she realised. Her promise was quite specific, she couldn't tell any of the women in the house or Dray. Shani didn't mention anything about not telling Alex, Saladin or even Alaric. However, she would need to choose her timing and method very carefully. Any one of those three would likely rush over to India and rip Shani's abusive toad-of-a-husband, limb from limb and start a war with yet another underworld crime organisation. As if they didn't already have their hands full with the Guild, Morganna, Scorpion and Nicholas.

Shani visibly relaxed. "Thanks. I'm sorry. I don't mean to appear over emotional, I guess I must be having one of those hormonal days," she tried to joke, playing down her anxiety and misery.

"You've been having one of *those* days, for about seven years now," Yasmin chided.

"What can I say, I have a bit of emotional baggage." Shani replied, spearing her cousin with a *shut up or else* glare. Not that Yasmin was paying any attention.

"A bit? You'd need an industrial sized forklift for all your baggage." Yasmin told her.

"Okay, so my life sucks. I'd like to think that being Hindu gives me some advantages though. If I suffer in this life, then I'll benefit in the next."

"How do you figure that?" Abby asked.

"Well, if I suffer through this life being married to Saadir, in my next life I'll find myself married to a well hung, muscle man with wings," she replied light-heartedly.

"Hmm. You know, Dray is likely going to still be around when you come back for your next life. He may not have wings, but I'm pretty sure the guy must be well hung...if his huge muscles are proportionate in size to other body parts," Yasmin told her, waggling her eyebrows and laughing at Shani's blushing cheeks and ineffective heated glare.

Oh, Dray is definitely well hung. The erect length he pulled from that skanky whore, Vanessa's body, was testimony to how unmistakably large he is, Shani thought with a pang of regret. Although, she wasn't sure what she regretted more. Seeing Dray having sex with that woman on his desk, or the revolving fantasy which plagued her dreams of her locked at the hips with him instead.

"My life may not be perfect, but I shouldn't complain. A lot of people are worse off than me."

"Right. Money may not be able to buy you happiness, but it's more comfortable to cry in a Mercedes than on a bicycle." Yasmin may have made the remark in a jesting tone, but the sympathy in her eyes was proof she wasn't any better at covering up her emotions than Shani was.

"I heard there's a party on," Brin called out a second before she stepped into Abby's bedroom. "And you must be Shani and Yasmin. I'm Brin," she greeted, looking between the two cousins for some sign as to which one was which.

Both Shani and Yasmin bowed respectfully. "I'm Shani, and this is my cousin, Yasmin. It's a pleasure to meet you," she said, openly staring at her. Shani had met Brin's brother, Raif, and knew that wyvern were generally very tall...and tanned, their natural skin tone only a shade or two lighter than her own. But what struck Shani most about Brin's appearance was her hair. Thick, waist length waves of the most incredible rich shade of deep red, she had ever seen.

"Please don't bow to me, I'm not royalty or anything," Brin laughed, reaching out to hug each woman in turn.

"I'm sorry, but I thought you were the sister of the Avengard wyvern's High Lord. It's our custom to greet nobility with respect," Yasmin said.

"Yes I am, but there's nothing noble about me. I just scrub up quite well on special occasions. Or, I will shortly if there's enough room for me to get changed in here too with you guys," Brin said.

Yasmin looked about Abby's suite. It was large enough to hold a circus. In fact, some of the accessories in the room looked like they belonged in a circus, e.g. The very unusual looking swing and hoists attached to the ceiling and walls at the back of the room. Not that she was going to ask what they were used for. She and Shani had been in the house long enough to know that Alex and Abby's pleasures were not what most people would indulge in. Yasmin couldn't help wondering though, if they considered the *toys* here in their bedroom to be *tame* enough for public viewing. If so, what did they keep in their pleasure dungeon down in the underground level of the manor? No, scratch that thought, she really, really didn't want to know.

"Of course. There's plenty of room," Abby replied, pushing a pile of clothes aside on the bed to make room for more.

"Great. I just need to get my bags, I left them downstairs. I'll be back in a sec."

At that moment Shani's phone started bleating its dreaded tone. "I'm sorry, I have to take this," she said, almost bowling Brin over in her haste to get out of the room. While Shani turned in one direction walking up the hallway further, Brin headed in the opposite, retracing her steps back towards the drawing room on the ground floor. As she reached the bottom of the staircase in the main foyer, the front door swung open and her good mood evaporated.

"Hi Callum, how are you, it's been a while," she said politely, her eyes hardening to spear the person entering behind him with daggers. "Marcus. What rock did you crawl out from?" she snarled.

"What are you doing here?" Marcus asked between gritted teeth.

Your grandmother invited me to her party," she replied haughtily.

"And is that what you're wearing?" Marcus sneered, looking her up and down, his tone just shy of being openly hostile. He wasn't going to admit it, but he really liked the way her full breasts pouted at the top of her sweater, and the way her jeans hugged her curves, he was in danger of developing an instant boner. Which of course, was the real reason he was now in a shitty mood. He hated Brin. He wanted nothing to do with her…Ever. But his body had other ideas, which really pissed him off.

"Don't tax your tiny pea-sized brain about it. I'll be wearing something more appropriate for the party," Brin replied as calmly as she could. What she wanted to add was, *'When I peel the flesh off your carcass and dye it a prettier shade.'*

"I don't know what your issue is with each other, but get over it. Marcus, today is about your grandmother, don't do anything to ruin it. Okay?" Callum berated. He may have directed his comment at Marcus, but he shared his disapproving glare between the two of them.

Marcus locked stink-eyes with Brin as he sauntered away with all the calmness and superiority of someone who could see the future and had the answer to the age old question to the meaning of life. Well, she hoped he enjoyed his moment of superiority, it wasn't going to last.

Marcus marched toward his grandmother's room on the far side of the kitchen, which had once been the servants quarters. These days his grandmother had the entire wing to herself. Needless to say, he still had his head up his arse thinking about all the ways Brin affected him, and barged right into her room without thinking.

"Ohmigod Gran, put some clothes on," he yelled, quickly covering his eyes and turning around the other way.

"You should've knocked dear. Don't worry, I'll be ready in a few minutes," she replied, calmly going through her wardrobe of clothes for the particular dress she had bought for the occasion.

"Sorry," Marcus apologised, his cheeks turning a mild shade of pink.

"Seeing your gran mostly naked isn't half as disturbing as your three year old showing you a picture of Sponge Bob with a dick in his mouth." Narayan complained as he and Callum appeared in the doorway, both careful to look the other way.

Callum chuckled. "Where did he get that?" It was a rhetorical question, the answer was obvious. "Alex!" they both answered simultaneously and laughed.

"Fortunately, Riley thought it was a banana, not a dick." Narayan said.

"How did he get it?"

"It was in my comic collection," Alex answered innocently, as though everyone had a collection of pornographic comics. Stretching up, he peered over their shoulders from behind. "Wow, Mrs P, nice jugs."

"Nice of you to notice," she grinned cheekily, puffing out her chest a little more.

"Gran would you *pleeease* get dressed."

"Oh, stop you're grumbling. If no one else is offended by my lack of attire, then you shouldn't be either. From my point of view, it's not every day I get handsome young men looking at me, is it?" she chuckled as she pulled a dress over her head. "Be a dear and zip me up would you love?"

Marcus moved forward reluctantly, but was pushed aside by Oliver, who had also now joined the group of men in the half naked housekeeper's doorway. "Let me. I recall a time, back in the day, when I wasn't trying to get you into a dress, but out of it."

All eyes turned to Oliver with a mix of amazement, shock and horror. The last expression was reserved for the two youngest in the group, Marcus and Callum.

"What did you say?" Marcus almost choked on the words.

Mrs Philpot and Oliver both watched as the cogs ground together slowly in their brains.

"You two were an item?...I don't believe it," Callum stuttered with enough horror in his tone to deflate even Mrs Philpot's bubbly countenance.

"Fuck me!" Marcus blurted out.

"Holy crap. Um...sorry, I didn't mean to offend either of you, I just can't believe it. What happened?" Callum apologised numbly.

"I discovered that chocolate makes your clothes shrink?" Mrs Philpot answered with a chuckle.

The how and why she became the size she now was, wasn't the question Callum was asking, but she couldn't resist dragging out the boys suspense. She hadn't had so much fun in ages.

Callum and Marcus continued to see-saw their stares between her and Oliver, their jaws gaping open.

"Chocolate, it makes your clothes shrink," she elaborated. "I was on a chocolate diet for years. Did you know that the word diet is actually an acronym for, *Did I Eat That?* I was also on a seafood diet, *See Food And Eat It,* girl. It took a lot of dieting and quite a few years to get to the size I am now." Mrs Philpot's hearty laugh was infectious, making her large breasts jiggle up and down.

"What?" Marcus spluttered incredulously, not sure whether he wanted to drill out his ears or sign up for a lobotomy to rid himself of the visions now occupying his brain.

"You and my dad...? When?" Callum pried, now staring at his father as though he had suddenly become a complete stranger. "You could have been my mother." The words practically squeaked out, restricted by the tight bands of astonishment wrapping around his chest.

"Oh, no love. It was only a childhood romance, that's all dear. I met Tom and your dad met your mother, Claire."

It wasn't the fact that Oliver looked barely over thirty, while Edwina Philpot looked seventy, that Callum was having a hard time getting his head around. It was the simple fact that for all his life he had looked up to Mrs P, as a surrogate grandmother. It never occurred to him that at any point in history, she and his father could have been a couple. It was inconceivable.

Except...the laws of nature as it existed for lycans made it a very real possibility. After all, Oliver had celebrated his one hundredth birthday only a couple of years before.

Every race had their limitations. It was the universal law that everything that had a beginning, must also have an end. And while lycans could live up to the age of around five hundred, not all of them did. When the nephilim and wyvern were banished from Earth, and the Elders created the lycans to be the replacement guardians, they were created to fit in with regular humans much more easily. That is, only male lycans produced an anti-ageing hormone which was shared with his *mate.* Thus, she too would live as long as he did, regardless of whether she was a lycan or human. But, that hormone was only produced if he shifted regularly into his wolf form. If he chose not to for any reason, he would begin to age at a regular human rate.

In Mrs P's case, her mate was killed almost fifty years ago. She had retained her youthful looks for a few years, but the lingering hormone in her veins diminished and age soon caught up with her.

"Wow, I never would have picked you two bumping uglies," Marcus snorted out. When all eyes turned to stare at him, he realised he'd said that out loud. "Crap. Sorry." *Note to self: Just because a thought pops into my mind, doesn't mean it should come out of my mouth.*

"You know, there's nothing wrong with dipping your toe into several pools before deciding which one is the right temperature for you," Narayan said, cutting through the awkward silence in the room.

Oliver cleared his throat. "Couldn't have said it better myself."

"Come on Gran, finish getting ready, you don't want to be late for your own party. Do you know what you want to say in your speech?" Marcus asked, changing the subject.

"Speech? I can't make a speech," Mrs Philpot argued nervously.

"Sure you can. Just say something like, I would like to thank my arms for always being by my side, my legs for always supporting me, and my fingers....because I can always count on them." he told her, making the old housekeeper laugh.

"If I have to make a speech, I might just have to use that line." She chuckled. "Marcus dear, could you hand me that thingy," she said, pointing to her dresser. You know you're getting older when you start using the word 'thingy' to describe something because you can no longer remember what it's called, she thought to herself with a mild degree of frustration.

"You mean your phone?" he asked.

"No. The other thingy. The one in the little box."

Marcus picked up the little box and opened it. It was her hearing aid.

Mrs Philpot walked proudly with her troop of escorts out toward the kitchen. Her movements might have slowed over the years, but her mind was still pretty sharp, except for the forgetfulness.

"Cassie love, what are you doing?" Mrs P's brow raised with a pitched eyebrow.

"Helping," she answered enthusiastically, doing her best to discretely cover up the evidence of just how she was helping.

Cassie was resigned to the fact that she would never be a good cook, but she did try. And this had to be one of her better efforts. She had managed to melt chocolate in a double boiler without hurting herself. Sadly, her attempt at making toffee didn't go so well. No one got hurt, although there was a good chance that several of the floor tiles would need replacing. Who knew that spilling molten sugar onto cold tiles would have the same effect as pouring quick set lava over it. That stuff wasn't coming off anytime soon. But she didn't blow up the kitchen....again. So that was a bonus, right?

"Does Megan know you're in here?" the housekeeper asked suspiciously. Although the kitchen had always been Mrs Philpot's pride and joy, she had happily relinquished the domain to Megan, who enjoyed the art of creative cookery even more than she did. In truth, Mrs P, was relieved to be able to share the burden of feeding this growing household. She was beginning to feel more weary as the years crept by.

"Not exactly. I said I was going to get some extra snacks for the party, I might have forgotten to mention that I'm going to make them," Cassie confessed.

Mrs. Philpot shook her head and kept walking, barely glancing at the evidence of Cassie's lack of cooking skills.

"You feeling alright Mrs P? You're not yelling at me."

"No love. It's your kitchen, you can do to it whatever you like," she replied happily.

"Okaaay...Who are you and what did you do with the real Mrs P?"

Mrs Philpot let out a hearty laugh, linking a hand through the crook of Marcus and Callum's arms as they walked on either side. "Today is the first day of the rest of my life. I intend to make the most of every good thing it has to offer. Who knows, I might even find a pool to dip my toe into," she laughed. Although, she was the only one. Both Callum and Marcus shared identical horror stricken expressions, and Oliver who followed behind, broke into a coughing fit.

"Did I miss the joke?" Cassie asked.

"No!" All the men replied simultaneously.

They didn't wait for anyone else to be ready before leaving the manor, or they might have been there for another few hours. And, since they had all volunteered to be Mrs P's official escort for the day, it was their duty to ensure she arrived at her own party ahead of her guests.

It was a wise move for sure. Especially if they were going to wait for Nadia. She stood at her closet for an hour staring at the options she had to select from. Unfortunately, her sisters had very kindly updated her wardrobe over the past few days and now she didn't know what to wear.

In the end, she came to the conclusion that it was best just to put on something. Anything. Then she applied some makeup, and hoped that the smoky eye shadow she had chosen made her look alluring and not like a victim of domestic violence. It was hard to tell how much was too much, with her eyesight set to the *spectral phantom zone*. For all she knew, that demure shade of grey was in fact iridescent green, and the soft um….brownish dress was purple.

Not that she needed to be *too* concerned, if it turned out her colour co-ordination was completely off kilter, her sisters would rectify things pretty quickly. In situations like this, Nadia was grateful she had so many interfering busy-bodies hovering around her all the time. They drove her crazy sometimes, but she also knew it was their way of saying, *I love you.*

"How do I look?" she asked Kaitlyn.

"Not like a patchwork quilt at all. You look great." Nadia's sigh of relief made her sister chuckle. "I have to tell you, whether it was a fluke or not, you've outdone yourself, you really do look good."

"Thanks, I think," Nadia replied.

"You're not going to do what you did at the last party we went to, are you?" Elise asked.

"If you're meaning how I felt up Rhonda Freedman's husband…which I still *don't* remember doing by the way…then, no. I have my own *future* husband to feel up," Nadia squealed happily.

"You don't say," Elise chuckled. "Is this a normal kind of happy or have you already snuck a few nips of the cooking sherry?" Elise teased.

Nadia rolled her eyes but couldn't dredge up the necessary enthusiasm it would require to turn her grin into a frown.

Her excitement was cute and contagious.

When someone is in love, they want the whole world to be in love too.

If only I had that option, Shani wished. Her own reality was much different. Feelings were messy and emotions were dangerous. Nonetheless, despite knowing the trap they posed, it wasn't too difficult to realise she was sinking quickly in emotional quicksand, and she was totally unprepared for it.

It seemed however, that her issues around her feelings for Dray were about to become insignificant. In bleak contrast, the ones she had for Saadir were about to become much more complicated.

"Is everything alright?" Yasmin asked as she re-entered the room. Shani's stricken expression answered the question for her.

"Come on everyone, we're going to be late," Abby said, ushering all the women from the room.

"Aren't you coming too?" Megan asked.

"Yep, I'm just going to clean up a bit first," Abby replied, practically closing the door in Megan's face, leaving only Yasmin and Shani in the room with her.

"Well, what happened?" Yasmin asked nervously.

"Saadir has booked me on a flight back to India tonight. The baby was born this morning. It was a girl," Shani told them, half in a daze.

"I thought it was supposed to be a boy," Yasmin replied in disbelief.

"That's what he believed. The woman told him it was a boy. It seems she lied….And now she's dead."

"Dead? The woman or the child?" Yasmin asked.

"The woman. I doubt I'll ever be able to prove it, but I'm pretty sure Saadir had her killed."

"Why, because she lied to him?" Abby probed.

"Maybe. Although…I have a feeling he was planning on killing her anyway."

"What for? He doesn't want anyone to know he fathered a child to his mistress?"

"To tie up loose ends."

"So now what? You're officially a mother, your name's on the child's birth certificate?" Yasmin queried.

"I believe so, yes," Shani answered miserably.

"And if you don't go back?" Abby asked.

"It's not in Shani's long term interest to go against Saadir's wishes. He has many friends in low places, and not just in India," Yasmin explained.

"It isn't right," Abby argued.

"Maybe not, but this is the life I was dealt," Shani lamented sadly. Putting on her shoes, she also affixed her well rehearsed, cheery smile, and left the manor for the party.

21

"You're seriously *not* wearing that T-shirt," Alaric told his brother-in-law.

Alex looked down at himself and the T-shirt in question which read: *My idea of help from above is a sniper on the roof. I'm here to kick arse and chew bubblegum, and I'm all out of bubblegum.* "What's wrong with it? At least I'm wearing a shirt."

"There will be a lot of kids at this party. Don't you have anything that won't prompt awkward questions?"

"This *is* kid friendly, all kids love bubblegum," Alex stated innocently.

Alaric rolled his eyes but said no more. There really wasn't any point arguing. Alex would probably just start ranting a diatribe of words complicated enough to confuse a Mensa candidate or, he would change the shirt for something even less appropriate.

"Hey, pot, kettle, black, bro. I hate to say it but that Hawaiian shirt really isn't you. On someone your size, that much splashy, psychedelic colour and pattern is likely going to cause someone to have an epileptic fit."

"You think? But I like this shirt." Alaric almost pouted as he looked down at himself, holding the shirt out from his body in an attempt to see it from someone else's perspective.

"I like disco balls, but I wouldn't turn my shirt into one. Bro, you look like a living, breathing migraine aura."

"I'm guessing that's not good." Normally, Alaric ignored ninety-five percent of whatever came out of Alex's mouth, filtering the other five percent. For once, he found himself taking his opinion to heart. Alex's taste in clothes regularly pushed the boundaries of propriety into vulgarity and poor taste, so for him to say the shirt was a bit too loud, he was willing to take his comments seriously. "I'll be back in a minute," Alaric told him.

In fact, the trip from the Drunken Duck pub to the manor and back again took exactly one and a half minutes. Most of that time Alaric spent staring into his closet deciding what to switch the colourful shirt for, settling on a simple black T-shirt. Hey, if you can't beat 'em, join 'em. At least his didn't have a controversial slogan splashed all over it.

"Better?" Alaric asked.

"Much. I'll have you converted into becoming my *Mini-Me*, any day now," Alex grinned, slapping him on the shoulder.

Alaric cleared his throat uncomfortably. "If that's a reference to Austin Powers, I'm going to choose to ignore it."

"Who knows, a black T-shirt today could lead to a set of handcuffs on your bed head tomorrow. Don't knock it until you try it. You might like being my Mini-Me."

"Fuck off Alex. You're really starting to piss me off, *again*. If you don't walk away right now, I'm going to have to remove one or two of your body parts, starting with your tongue," Alaric growled.

"Cool your jets there bro," Alex answered, unperturbed by the threat.

"Alex, I'm serious. Fuck off!" The temperature in the warm pub took a sudden dip as Alaric's power flared to life. "And stay away from trouble. By that I mean don't hang around with the kids. We don't need any disasters to clean up today," he tacked on.

"What? Are you saying I'm a bad influence on the kids? I'll have you know I babysat Grace, Riley and Finn a few days ago without any problems. We watched the Lego movie."

"And then you suggested they act out a role playing game."

"Yes. I suggested Doctors and Nurses, but none of them knew how to play that."

A fact that Alaric was very grateful for. A six-year old and two three-year olds shouldn't know how to play Doctors and Nurses, especially not Alex's version. "But then you got bored and left them to their own devices after putting the role playing idea in their heads. Now we have another wing of the house that needs repairs."

"Yeah. My bad. Okay, I get your point. I'll stay away from the kids today," Alex promised, crossing his heart.

"*All* the kids," Alaric said.

"There are more than fifty kids here today. Seriously, all of them? That's going to be tough."

"Do your best." Alaric growled, drilling him with a heated glare.

"Fine. How about I stick to the bar?"

"You do that."

Shani stood alone at the bar waiting for her champagne cocktail, her eyes roaming the sea of faces. Many now looked familiar to her, but there were just as many at the party she had never seen before. Not that she was all that interested. There was only one person she wanted to see. And there he was at the buffet table. The man who she had every intention of wasting as much time as possible, having illicitly spectacular carnal relations with....In her dreams.

As though he could feel Shani's eyes on him, Dray turned.

They stared at each other for a long moment. Dray's stare so intensely neutral, she couldn't help but wonder what he was thinking. Was he thinking about her, the meaning of life, the lint on his jacket? She would probably never know.

Dray's breath caught in his chest at the sight of her. She was stunningly beautiful. Her plump red lips made him want to reach out and grab her by the neck and kiss her as hard and deeply as he could. Not that he could ever do that. He *wouldn't* do that. He'd made a promise to himself and Saladin that she was off limits, and he intended to stick to that decision. No matter how much he wanted to...*Dammit!* He had to think of something else quickly before he did something inappropriate. *Think of anything else. Swimming in a pool of urine. Having a tooth pulled without anaesthetic. However, not even thinking about eating that disgusting Scottish dish of a sheep's stomach filled with barley and offal, which Megan sometimes cooked, was enough to make him break eye contact with her.*

The sexual tension between them only thickened. It was like a rope that pulled at him. With no conscious input from his brain, his feet began to move across the room toward her.

"I'm sorry if I ruined your moment with Vanessa. I have very poor timing. Can you forgive me?" she blurted out anxiously as he came to stand in front of her. Okay, so it probably wasn't the opening line she should have used. Maybe, *Hi, how have you been?* might have been better, but once the words left her mouth it was too late to take them back.

Besides, she didn't have time for idle chit chat, she was on borrowed time so why not open the conversation by addressing the volcanic crater between them.

It was pointless avoiding the topic just so they could pretend it didn't happen. In the end, denial doesn't cancel out the truth, it just makes it more painful to deal with. And the truth was, she was the one in the wrong, thinking she could just barge into his office without knocking. Even if the spark of attraction between them was real or just a figment of her imagination, Dray was still a free agent, free to have sex with anyone he wants to.

And, since she was going to be on a plane back to India in a little over eight hours, and there wasn't likely to be any chance of ever seeing him again, the last thing she wanted was to part with any bad blood between them.

Shani tilted her head, giving Dray a long once-over look. As fragile as Shani appeared, she looked at him with a steady eye, clearly indicating she knew how to sift through any bullshit.

Opening his mouth...he promptly closed it again. He wasn't a touchy-feely kind of vampire at the best of times, unless it was between the sheets with a hot little sex kitten, which of course is what kinda got him into this mess. But, when it came down to expressing his emotions, he became as articulate as a grunting baboon.

Why was it that briefing a room full of people on world changing issues came as easily as breathing, but telling Shani something as simple as, *I'm* sorry, tied his tongue and brain into knots. He lifted his hand absently to scratch his head and only then realised he was still holding a plate from the buffet table. Placing it on the bar beside them, he refocused his thoughts.

Dray hesitated another moment before answering her. He didn't want to lie. He didn't want to tell her the truth either. Her question was simple, yet his answer held layers of complexity he wasn't willing to share. Regardless, the words that left his lips felt like a lie, a bit.

"No, I'm sorry Shani. I never meant to upset you." That part was true. "I guess over the years I've forgotten how to behave properly. My life revolves around the club and the Alliance. I don't get out much to socialise. So, when I have certain *needs*, I rely on the services of females at the club like Vanessa." That part was true too, although what he really wanted to say was, *I only had sex with Vanessa because I was going crazy from wanting you.*

"Services? You pay her, she really is a whore?" Shani's whispered voice held a note of surprise.

Dray almost smiled. "No. I don't pay her, that's not to say others don't. Sadly, I don't think she's bright enough to realise that if she is offered money after having sex it's because they think she's a prostitute. She probably thinks it's because they like *her*."

"Hmm, I can see how that could be easily confused," snorting out a forced laugh. She wanted to feel sorry for Vanessa, she really did. But, she just couldn't.

Shani eyed off the cream buns on the plate Dray had placed on the bar.

"I heard about the present Nicholas left for Philippe the other day. Are you any closer to catching him yet?" Shani asked as she absently took a cream bun from the plate.

"Not yet," Dray answered distractedly.

Shani looked at her fingers, covered in sugary cream oozing from the bun and wondered what to do with them. She didn't have a napkin, so did she wipe them on her clothes? No. That was too messy. Did she lick them clean? Yes, it was mildly embarrassing but slightly more acceptable. As she lifted her fingers toward her mouth, Dray gripped her wrist and drew her hand away from her lips.

"That was my bun, I believe I'm entitled to some of it," he told her as he bent his head down and sucked her fingers into his mouth, lapping at the cream with slow, deliberate enjoyment. He didn't consciously intend to do that, it just kind of happened, and once he started he couldn't stop himself.

Shani's knees began to shake. Her entire body shivered with pleasure. Never had she experienced anything so erotic in her life.

Raising his head, Dray held her gaze. "Do you make a habit of grabbing someone else's buns?" he asked, his voice a husky tease.

Grabbing his buns? Shani's eyes dipped down, her head tilting to the side until she could see his muscular *buns*. She nodded helplessly, not wanting the sensations to stop. Nor did she have the strength to pull her hand free of his grip.

As the rusted cogs in her brain reluctantly cranked back to life, Shani quickly shook her head. "No. I'm sorry. I didn't realise your buns were spoken for."

"They're not. But yours are." There was no mistaking his meaning in the innuendo, and the truth in that statement was like a slap in the face. Shani stiffened, sucking in a sharp breath as she pulled her hand free of Dray's grip. It was a double whammy of torment. The sting of his words left a wound on her heart, and the loss of his touch caused a ripple of pain that felt like a punch to the stomach.

Dray wanted to kick his own arse so hard he could eat his own shoelaces. He must be suffering some sort of brain fade, a mini stroke or an aneurysm or something. He didn't behave like this. He never did or said anything that wasn't thoroughly thought through first. Except, when he was around Shani, he went from one blundering balls-up situation to the next.

Turning her head away from him, Shani tried to ignore him.

She tried, tried so hard just to wish it all away. Her past. Her future. And now she even wanted to wish away her present. It was all too hard.

Shani took a mouthful of her drink to buy herself some time before answering, but there was only so much time you could hold a liquid in your mouth without swallowing it. With forced effort, she swallowed. *Bite your tongue,* she told herself. She had to remain silent. It wasn't in anyone's best interest to tell the truth. But the temptation to tell Dray about Saadir, about how he treats her, and about the baby she was about to go home to, was almost too much to bear. Really though, what would sharing her truth achieve? It would only create more complications, that's what.

Clutching her hands together in front of her Shani held her outward composure, her fingers tightening together as she fought the need to cry.

"Shani, I'm sorry," Dray apologised awkwardly. "I didn't mean it the way it came out."

"No don't. Please don't apologise. Excuse me, I think my cousin is looking for me." Shani collected her champagne off the bar and quickly headed for the other side of the room.

That was great, not awkward at all, she told herself stiffly. It would be even better if one day she could meet him without being on the verge of self-combusting from sexual tension, or falling to pieces over some misconstrued indiscretion or inadvertent blunder. Sadly, today was not that day.

"Did I see you talking to Dray?" Yasmin asked.

Shani's shoulders slumped, she felt so tired. "Yes," she answered drearily.

"Did you tell him how you feel about him?"

"No."

"Good. Be strong and stick to your guns, and don't look into those big brown, gorgeous eyes of his. You'll crumble and that won't be good for your long term health."

"I know," Shani grumbled miserably.

"Now. Come on. Do this with me. Please?"

"It's pandering, undignified and...and bite me."

Yasmin laughed. "Come on. Doing the chicken dance isn't that bad. Look, all the kids are loving it."

"They're seven. I'm twenty-seven," she grumbled. Shani pulled her best wounded-baby-deer face, but it seemed that over the years her cousin had become immune, the crevice in her brow furrowing even further. "Oh, fine," she huffed.

Dray brooded gloomily as he watched Shani from the bar, following every move she made, watching every facial expression, listening for every word she uttered.

"I hear you've been having a few issues recently. The love bug bite you on the arse?" Gary Sanders probed as he took a glass of whisky from the barman.

"I need to be bitten by the love bug about as much as I need a bite from a black widow spider," Dray snarled.

"Is there a difference?" Sanders replied.

"Not as far as I can tell."

"Fuck 'em and leave 'em. That's what I say."

Dray would have agreed with him a couple of weeks ago, whole-heartedly. Today? He wanted to agree but now it wasn't so simple. He hadn't bonded with Shani, although that didn't mean he felt free to be with anyone else. His mind and heart were in turmoil. Logic versus compulsion. Love versus sanity. Inside he was a twisted mess of confusion.

"If I were you, I'd forget any fancy notion about starting a relationship. You know, the grass often seems greener on the other side because it's been fertilized with bullshit. Relationships bring you nothing but trouble."

"Sanders, if you want to keep breathing, I suggest you go elsewhere." Dray's snarl shifted into barely veiled hostility, his top lip curling to expose a fully descended fang, his hard eyes glittering with pent-up frustration desperate for an outlet.

"Fine. I'll go outside. It's nearly time for me to take guard duty anyway."

As Sanders marched casually out the front doors, he was surprised to see that the crowd of guests was still continuing to steadily grow. Most had arrived on time, although there were always the stragglers. Nadia and Philippe being amongst the last to make an appearance.

"Ohmigod. This place is alive with plastic. I need a seeing eye dog to get around here." Distress tightened Nadia's voice to almost a squealing pitch as she bumped into one chair, side stepped it straight into another one.

"No you don't," Philippe answered happily, swapping hands he used to hold hers, threading his free hand around her waist to guide and steady her through the minefield of plastic chairs and tables, and around the giant plastic jumping castle in the Drunken Duck's car park. "Callum has assured me that inside the pub there's no plastic anywhere. So long as you don't go outside on your own, you'll be fine."

"Fine? Do you know how frustrating this is?" she grumbled in reply and held onto his hand for dear life. Inwardly, Nadia resented her new status as an *Ei'Ambriath*. Why the angels were so excited about her becoming like her sister, she couldn't understand. Because she wasn't like her sister. Paige still had full use of both her eyes. She could see the world normally like everyone else, and she could also see the astral plane. Only, she got to choose how and when she viewed the world in its different forms. Nadia didn't. She was stuck with the astral view permanently, which really sucked.

Nothing looked the same anymore. Grass was still green, but the sky often looked yellow, depending on how much cloud covered it. Plants seemed to shimmer with the auras that surrounded them. Animals too appeared different, their auras were often large and interconnected with one another, as though they were thinking as one, particularly birds. People however, were much more complicated. Their auras had multiple colours, all swirling together in complex, compacted layers. Sometimes it was confusing and difficult to see the person beneath.

Nadia tried to think what else she had in common with Paige as an *Ei'Ambriath*. She came up with nothing. Well, maybe she did, but that would depend on whether or not Paige could separate a vampire's soul from their body, like she had done to Vanessa at the club. That was mildly impressive she supposed. Although, Nadia couldn't see much practical advantage to it. Not unless you count scaring the crap out of that skanky bitch enough to make her run screaming from the club. If Vanessa never went back to the club, then maybe Nadia could count the ability as being of benefit.

"Aunty Nadia, will you come and play in the jumping castle with us?" Grace asked, putting a whiny twang of desperation into the request in the hope of swaying Nadia into acquiescing.

"Sorry sweetheart, I think I'll pass this time, but why don't you ask someone else?"

"Like who?" Grace asked, looking about the crowded car park and seeing no one in particular.

"Umm, I don't know, why don't you ask one of the big burly lycan military men like Mr Sanders," Nadia suggested, spying the surly looking man watching the crowd of kids like they were mutant creatures ready to morph into some kind of deadly monsters.

Philippe cleared his throat to cover his laugh. After spending a bit of time with the special ops soldier in Alabama, he was tempted to hang out in the car park for a bit longer just to see how the big guy might react when the horde of kids suddenly descended on him.

And how do you stop them? You can't. Not once the idea has been put into their heads. It was as useless as trying to monitor how much sugar they each consumed at a party. If they weren't given easy access to it, they simply took the contraband secretly by any means possible. The party had only just begun with many more hours of fun to come, but already the kids looked like they'd consumed enough sugary treats to power a small town for a week. In comparison, the same amount of sugar would probably cause an adult to have an adrenaline fuelled heart attack or put them into a diabetic coma. Even if some of the kids weren't naturally born with extra abilities, at the rate they were consuming sweets, their blood sugar levels would give them all the strength of ten men.

Hence, the jumping castle to expend at least a portion of their hyperactive energy rush.

"Okay." Grace hugged Nadia, letting out an appreciative squeal high-pitched enough to shred the nerves of anyone within ear shot and set off the neighbourhood dogs howling.

"I think this is going to be a long day," Nadia grinned.

"Especially if you're one of the lycan military guys. That was cruel, giving Grace the idea to get them involved in playing with the kids."

"Ahh, it'll be good for them. They're all too serious." Nadia pursed her lips, reducing her broad grin down to a smirk, her pale eyes glittering with mischievous delight.

Even as he laughed, he shook his head, making a mental note to take a peak outside in about, oh…half an hour or so.

"Philippe, can we not go inside just yet."

"Sure, but why, is something wrong?" he asked, his brow creasing with mild concern.

"Is there anything wrong with wanting to have you to myself for a few more minutes?"

"No. But I know you, Nadia. Anxiety about your navigational issues aside, something's bothering you. If you tell me what it is, maybe I can help," Philippe told her as he led her away from the pub and its noisy car park/kids playground, towards the seclusion of Savernake Forest nearby.

"Really. It's nothing." Nadia remained silent until they had walked some distance into the forest, coming to a stop beneath the overhang of an old oak tree's leafless, wintry branches.

"Now, spill. What's on your mind and don't give me any bullshit, I'll know if you're lying to me." His no nonsense words sounded harsh even if they were spoken with love. Philippe hated that anything might have upset his *mate*, and he felt compelled to eliminate the source of her anxiety, no matter how big or small an issue that might be.

Nadia's shoulders slumped on a heavy sigh. Yeah, there was no point lying, Philippe had always been able to read her like a book.

"It's nothing really. I'm just frustrated. I feel so useless."

"How?"

"I don't know. I guess I was hoping that becoming an *Ei'Ambriath* would give me some cool powers like my sisters, you know? Something that would make me a formidable opponent against the Guild or....or..."

"Nicholas?" he asked.

"Yes. I hate it that my *gifts* are still so passive. Believe me, I'm not jealous of my sisters, not really. At least, not anymore. I just wish I could do more than just understand languages and see auras. I don't want to be sidelined with every battle we have to fight because I'm a burden."

"You're not a burden Nadia," Philippe assured her with a gentle stroke down her cheek with his cool fingers.

"Yes, I am and don't pretend otherwise. Unless another mysterious ancient book is found that needs interpreting, no one's going to let me get involved in anything dangerous." Having said that however, Nadia doubted they'd let her read any more mysterious books either. Not after what happened to her from reading the last two. First there was Morganna's grimoire, reading that book actually killed her. And when she read the Book of Thoth, that resulted in Megan becoming the conduit to the angels and communicating with animals. Okay, so Megan holding the Cintamani stone had a part to play in that, but it wouldn't have happened if she hadn't read that book.

Philippe wished he could tell her otherwise, but she was right. With her abilities as they currently were, no one was going to let her get anywhere near danger, especially not him. Just the thought of something happening to her sent him into a tail spin.

"How about I make a deal with you. After you've had more time to learn what you're really capable of, we'll reassess things. It's only been a few weeks, you're still adjusting to being an *Ei'Ambriath*. Paige has been one for nearly four years, and she still doesn't know everything she's capable of. Keep in mind that you and Paige are two of a kind, you don't have anyone who can explain what you need to know. You'll just have to figure it out as you go."

"I know that, it doesn't make it any less frustrating though."

"Would it help if I provide you with a temporary distraction?" Philippe winked.

"Maybe." She leaned into him, her breasts pressed firmly against his chest. He closed his eyes as her hand glided lightly over his ribs, across his hips and down further, finally cupping her hand over the bulge at the front of his trousers, adding pressure as she rubbed along the length of his rapidly hardening shaft.

Philippe groaned. "I thought I was going to distract you."

"I can stop," she offered cheekily.

"No. Definitely not." He looked down at Nadia's dress with a more discerning eye. If it wasn't so chilly he'd rip that dress off her in a heartbeat. However, that full skirt could serve two purposes. It was long enough that it would keep her warm even with her legs wrapped about his waist as he pounded his hard length into her. Secondly, it was one of his unfulfilled bucket list fantasies. He had always wanted to be able to lift up a girl's skirt and have passionate, heat-of-the-moment sex. Well, he'd fantasised about doing it with Nadia.

Leaning down, he took Nadia into his arms, crushing his lips against hers. There was no slow build up to the hot, passionate kiss. That's where the kiss started....and ended.

The buzz of Philippe's phone began to ring in his pocket. He ignored it.

Nadia released her hand from what had now become a healthy erection, straining forcefully against his zipper.

"Shouldn't you get that?" Nadia asked, breaking from their kiss, her rosy, swollen lips and sensually glazed eyes making him think that yes, he really should get the phone....so he can smash the thing to pieces.

His phone went silent and he resumed things where they left off.

A moment later it started again.

"You'd better get that," Nadia suggested.

With a string of curses, Philippe reached one hand inside his pocket, the other he used to adjust the placement of the flagpole in his pants. Not that he needed to, it deflated almost instantly when he answered the call.

"Fuck. Okay, I'm on my way."

"What's happened?" Nadia asked warily.

"That was Dray. The alarm at my apartment just went off."

"Do you think it was Nicholas?"

"That's my guess."

"I want to come too. I know, I know, I can't. That doesn't mean I don't want to be there, even if it's just for moral support." Nadia told him.

"Don't worry. I won't be going alone. Dray, Alaric, Saladin and Hawke are coming too." Philippe's smile, while he intended it to be reassuring, almost broke her heart.

What if Nicholas really did trip the alarm? No doubt he has some sort of trap set for his brother.

What if Scorpion was waiting for him too, or even Morganna?

What if Philippe and the others weren't strong enough to defeat Nicholas?

What if Philippe never came back?

Philippe must have been thinking the same thing because the kiss he left her with was passionate and full of desperation. Not the kind of desperation that comes with intense arousal, but the kind that comes with good-bye's.

Breaking the kiss their eyes locked, a thousand unspoken words between them conveyed through a single look.

"I'll be back as soon as I can," he told her.

A moment later Nadia stood alone beneath the old oak tree, her heart as empty as the tree was barren of leaves.

"The trap's set?" Scorpion asked Nicholas.

"And fool proof. My brother's a fool which is proof that he'll fall for it hook, line and sinker. So will Nadia. She's an even bigger fool than he is. That's probably why they're now *mated*, they're perfect for each other."

"If this plan of yours doesn't work...."

"It will," Nicholas assured."

"If it doesn't work, you won't get another chance. Not for a while anyway. We have other plans to take care of, much more important than your squabble with your brother. I'm only indulging you this now, because of all my progeny, you're the only one whose turned out to be worthy of my gift."

Nicholas' chest puffed out at the compliment. The fact that Scorpion was complimenting him on his psychopathic tendencies and not on any humanitarian traits, was a testament to the fact that he deserved Scorpion's praise. It took one to know one.

"Like I said, it's fool proof. With the help of modern technology and a bit of emotional manipulation, it can't fail," Nicholas gloated.

22

Nadia made her way through the forest with as much speed as she could muster, which really wasn't all that fast considering she was restricted by her limited eyesight. She still doubted her ability to read her surroundings with the same clarity she used to. Especially when she reached the edge of the Drunken Duck's car park and the gauntlet of everything plastic which stood in her path. It seemed she had reached an impasse. She didn't want to go back into the woods and wait for Philippe to return, but reaching the front door to the pub seemed like an impossible task.

"Aunty Nadia, have you come to play in the jumping castle?"

Nadia looked down into Grace's smiling face, her own grin almost as broad from relief. "No, sorry. I could use your help though." Grace's excitement and enthusiasm was adorable, and contagious. "I want to go inside, but I'm having trouble getting through the car park. Can you guide me?"

"Is it all the plastic?" Grace asked, her excitement receding a little, although her enthusiasm remained unaffected. "Mum told us to put all our plastic toys away because you can't see them. You can't see the jumping castle either?"

"No. I'm afraid not. I can't see any of the tables or chairs out here either," Nadia confessed.

"Really? That sucks balls."

Nadia nearly choked on her laugh. "Did uncle Alex teach you that phrase?" Nadia asked. Grace nodded, her grin broadening.

"Let me give you a tip. If you don't want to get into trouble from your mum or dad, don't repeat anything you hear Uncle Alex say, okay?"

"Okay."

"Now, how about some help to the door?" Nadia held out her hand for Grace to take the lead and guide her through the minefield around her. Despite the six-year old's eagerness to help, she didn't move. Instead, she fixed her gaze on Nadia curiously.

"But why can't you see plastic?" Grace asked.

"I don't know. Because it's synthetic, not a natural part of the world maybe? I really don't know."

"But, if you can see all the things around the plastic, doesn't that mean you can see where the plastic is too?" Grace's question on the surface made little sense. Yet, when Nadia examined the basis of the question, it made perfect sense. Looking around the car park Nadia could see people sitting on what looked to her to be nothing. Platters of food and drinks sat suspended upon blank spaces in midair.

If she focused her sight on those blank spaces, Nadia noticed that there was a slight haze in the vague shape of furniture. She wasn't about to get overly excited about the breakthrough, the effort to see those ambiguously faint outlines strained her eyes enough to give her a headache, but it was a start. A very promising start.

"You know, maybe with a bit of practice I will be able to see plastic soon too. In the meantime, how about you help your very grateful aunty to the door?" Nadia smiled.

"Okay."

Grace took Nadia's hand and led her in a zigzag path through the obstacle course, her eyes focusing on the hazy patches they were side stepping.

"Sure you don't want to come in the jumping castle?" Grace asked once again as they passed the giant, air filled plastic cushion.

"I'm sure," Nadia chuckled. It was then that she noticed Sanders. She had prompted Grace to get the lycan soldiers involved in entertaining the kids, although she never believed for a moment they would actually do it. Nonetheless, there was Sanders, surrounded by a group of children. Reading a book to them.

Listening to Sanders read to the kids was creepy as hell and sent chills down Nadia's spine. It was like listening to a fairy tale being read by a kidnapper reading out a ransom demand. His deep voice, gruff with crusty attitude. Not that the kids seemed to mind. In fact, they found his style of reading very entertaining. Nadia couldn't hold back a snicker. He didn't look to be enjoying the experience nearly as much as his audience.

"You didn't tell Mr Sanders it was my idea to play with you kids, did you?"

"No. I can if you want me to though," Grace answered cheerily.

"Ahh nah, that's okay. Probably not a good idea," she shook her head.

"We're here," Grace told her in a sing-song tone as they reached the pub's front door, much to Nadia's relief. "Do you need me for anything else?"

"No, thanks. I owe you one."

"So, you'll come in the jumping castle later?"

Nadia laughed, she had to give her credit for persistence. "Another time. I promise." Giving Grace a hug and a kiss, she left her niece to go back to playing. Entering the pub she made a b-line for the bar.

One shot of tequila wasn't enough to calm her nerves, although she didn't dare drink any more than that. Her reason for limiting her alcohol intake wasn't to avoid the chance of making a fool of herself at the party, which would be a first for the record books. She simply wanted to keep a clear head while she waited for news from Philippe. That didn't mean she wasn't tempted to order another drink, she really did want to. All it would do though, was dull her senses, it wouldn't relieve any of her anxiety. So, keeping things in perspective, she opted for a soft drink instead and sat at the bar for a while longer, watching everyone interact.

All the while she watched the minutes tick by. Ten minutes. Twenty minutes. Thirty…Forty…Fifty minutes. She watched the change-over of the guards outside. She watched the laughter and carefree revelry as the music played and people ate and drank. Nadia also watched the awkward interactions and predictable outcomes between the less amiable guests at the party. One pair in particular caught her attention.

Marcus stood at the back of the room, arms crossed and his face like thunder. He decided to ignore the dumbass part of his brain that was turned on by the distracting sight of Brin's breasts in her low cut dress.

"Damn, someone shit on your favourite…?" Callum began.

Marcus held up a finger to silence his best friend's next word. He knew he was going to say *bunny rug,* and if he did, Marcus was going to bitch slap him into the middle of next week.

"I don't want to talk about it."

"Does it have anything to do with Sanders talking to Brin?"

"I said, I don't want to talk about it."

"I don't get this love/hate thing the two of you have going. Did she cut off your balls in another life or something?" Callum asked, shaking his head, bewildered. He wasn't expecting an answer and so wasn't disappointed when he didn't get one.

Marcus hovered in the background, watching, listening in on Brin's conversation. He was like a moth to a flame. He knew he shouldn't get too close or he was likely to get burned, but he just couldn't help himself.

From the corner of her eye, Brin could see Marcus pacing in the background. Even from a distance she could see his frustration and annoyance eating at him, his indignant stare practically boring a hole through her forehead. It stung a little knowing how much he hated her, and to be honest, she didn't even know why. Nonetheless, his behaviour seriously pissed her off. He couldn't even pretend to like her, not even for a few hours? Well, if that was the way he wanted it, so be it, she thought.

"Is it true that all lycans are well-built....down there?" Brin asked in a loud, clear voice, using her eyes to point at the body part she referred to.

Sanders' chest puffed out, a glint of pride backlit his eyes as he viewed Brin with a little more carnal interest. "I believe I'm a little above average in that department," he told her. "I can't say I've ever actually measured it, but my cock is probably about nine and a half, maybe ten inches when I'm fully erect. I'd be happy to show you. You bring the tape measure, and I'll provide the post-examination entertainment," Sanders answered.

"Jesus." Brin said.

"Is that a *happy* kind of *Jesus or an Ohmigod, too much information, kind of Jesus*?" he asked curiously.

Anna laughed. "I think that was a *Jesus, come to mamma, kind of Jesus. But don't get a swelled head about it, been there and done that with you, remember?*" It seemed like a lifetime ago that Sanders had been her DEA partner and part-time romp between the sheets. "*You're not that big...at least not compared to Hawke. I'd say you're just on the 9 inch mark,*" she answered on Brin's behalf whose cheeks had suddenly turned a shade darker than they had been a minute earlier. She had to concede it was her own fault, seriously what reason did she have for asking such a pertinent question other than to piss Marcus off.

Behind them, Brin could hear a low rumbling growl. When she turned to see what, or more accurately, who was making that noise, there was no surprise to find it was Marcus. He was glaring straight at her, his lycan eyes blazing a volatile golden colour and his top lip curling back in a snarl.

Brin huffed out an irritable breath, shoving her hands on her hips, she turned to face him. "What, are you offended I was interested in Sanders' manhood and not yours?" she demanded haughtily, raising her best bitch-brow, a snarky extension of her taunting words, combined with her best frosty glare.

Brin's question seemed to snap Marcus out of whatever brain fade he was having, his eyes returning to their normal chocolate brown, however, the snarl remain firmly imprinted on his lips.

"You. Just being in the same room as you offends me," he bit back.

"Ahh oh. Wait for it. There's a shit storm coming," Elise said under her breath, nudging her sister.

"Umbrella anyone?" Teagan replied, equally as tensely.

Marcus knew he'd said the wrong thing the moment Brin stilled. Her chin lifted so slowly there was no doubt she was winding up to come at him with both barrels. Marcus was the deer caught in the headlights of an oncoming car, and there was no escape.

Fuck! Why didn't he keep his big mouth shut.

He sucked in an uneasy breath as his eyes met hers, and there it was. That primal stink eye, deadly and unforgiving. He could feel his balls shrivelling up to the size of peas in an instant.

For a moment, her eyes simply widened, shocked anger filling her gaze just before she laughed mockingly, anger flushing her face. Taking a step back he realised too late just how pissed off Brin was when her knee connected with his groin.

Marcus collapsed to his knees clutching at his man tackle.

Turning on her heel, Brin walked away leaving him bent over on the floor. Her first couple of steps were casual and slow, but then she almost broke into a run in her need to get away from him.

What the hell just happened? Marcus' heart pounded in his chest hard enough to crack a rib. His hands shook and his thoughts seemed to scramble inside his skull. The battered state of his manhood concerned him, but not nearly as much as his uncensored growling outburst.

For the first time ever, his inner wolf had taken control of his body without his permission, and it scared the crap out of him. *But why?* He asked himself the question. Deep down he knew the answer, he just didn't want to acknowledge it. It was the same reason why every little detail about her seemed to be magnified a hundredfold to him. From the slight sprinkling of freckles on her exposed arms and her nose, to the way her long, burnished-red hair shone in the sunlight, the long strands appearing to be almost peppered with gold dust, while others were as vibrant as living flames. Her darker tarnished eyelashes curled at the tips. *He* wasn't offended by Brin's curiosity towards Sanders' manly attributes. *His wolf* was. *It* had tried to exert its domineering will to drive her away from Sanders. His wolf didn't care that he hated the woman…with a passion.

Hell's hairy balls, this wasn't good. Not fucking good at all. He had managed to avoid being in the same vicinity as Brin for the past few years, but try as he may, he just couldn't avoid her all the time. Damn it! Still, he was determined. That cursed prophecy about her *was not* going to involve him.

"Whatcha doin', searching for your dignity?" Callum quipped.

"My dignity is long gone. I'd settle for finding my left nut. I think it might be lodged in my oesophagus." Marcus answered with a groan.

"If you want, I can get you an ice pack," he offered.

"No thank you. If Brin ever decides to come out of the bathroom her icy glare will work just as well."

"Fine. Whatever. You asked for that you know," Callum told him as he helped Marcus to his feet.

"Yeah, I know. I think I've got a fucking screw loose." Callum agreed whole-heartedly, which only proved his assumption. There really was something seriously wrong with him.

Brin exited the room, her back straight and head held high. The rapid thumping of her heart went unheard by anyone but her own ears, while the violent trembling of her legs went unseen, or at least she hoped so. She had no idea where she was going until a little plaque on the door in front of her caught her attention. The ladies bathroom. The perfect place to barricade herself in and hide out until she either calmed down or she was sure Marcus would have left the building.

As the door slowly closed behind her, Brin leaned herself up against the wall, pressing a palm to her chest to calm her erratic heartbeat, not that it did anything for her hyperventilation.

Just as the door fell back into place it swung open again. Through the doorway stepped a woman with long dark hair pulled back in a French braid. Long slender legs, small waist and shapely bust filled out her little black dress to perfection. Brin groaned inwardly when the woman's golden brown eyes, filled with curious determination, locked onto her.

"Hi, I'm Holly, Marcus' sister," she said, holding out her hand in greeting, a gesture Brin declined to return.

The silent groan Brin had been holding in, escaped its containment with an audible moan of dismay. Great. All she wanted was a bit of solitude to wallow in self-pity for a while. Instead, she was going to have to endure a lecture from Marcus' interfering older sister. Just great!

"What's with the two of you?" Holly asked.

"Nothing. We have a mutual dislike of one another, that's all."

"Did my idiot of a brother do something to offend you? Sorry, let me start that again. What did my idiot brother do to offend you?"

Brin almost laughed. Maybe this wasn't going to be the lecture she thought it would be. At least Holly seemed to know her brother well enough to realise he was capable of stupid behaviour.

Brin was determined to remain silent, contain all her thoughts and frustrations within the walls of her on head, but somewhere along the way she seemed to suffer an emotional response without any input from her brain, resulting in a case of verbal diarrhoea.

"It's been like this between Marcus and I ever since the first time we met at Havenswood Manor. He walked in, unzipped his pants and pulled his penis out in front of me, hard as a rock it was. And, proceeded to tell me how he'd like me to *gnaw on his bone*." Brin told her with a humourless laugh.

Holly almost choked, caught somewhere between a laugh and a gasp of horror.

"He really did that?"

"He sure did. And things have gone downhill from there." Brin conveniently managed to forget to mention the most important part of that story. The part where Marcus was acting out impulsively because of the potent scent caused by Kaitlyn's mating heat which had permeated every inch of the house at the time.

"I see how that could have started things off badly between the two of you. Although, you know, the law of averages means that at some point the two of you are going to find you actually like each other, and then where will you be?"

It was Brin's turn to choke out a horrified laugh. "What? Never. That will *never* happen."

"I wouldn't put money on that if I were you."

"Why do you say that?"

"Because I know my brother, and the way he watches you so closely…well, let's just say that *no man* watches a woman that closely who he's not attracted to," Holly smirked.

"You're seeing things that don't exist," Brin told her very decisively.

"Am I? You know, love can be unpredictable, unexpected, and even unbearable at times. Strangely it can easily be mistaken for loathing."

"Not this time. There's only mutual loathing between Marcus and me."

"Hearts are wild creatures, that's why our ribs are cages," Holly joked but Brin clearly wasn't in the mood. "Either way, I guess we'll see in time, won't we."

I don't think so, Brin thought to herself although chose not to comment and risk starting up an *I'm right and you're wrong* conversation. Instead she said, "You sound like you know something on that subject."

"Not firsthand. I learned that lesson through my mother. You may not know this, but Marcus and I spent more of our childhood at the manor with our Gran and Alaric, than we ever did with our mother. For a long time she had this love/hate relationship going."

"With your father?" Brin asked.

"No. Our father was an arsehole plain and simple. He was never our mother's *mate.* They met when they were young and married before they really got to know each other. Despite the fact they had nothing in common, and he sometimes beat her, she believed that she had a duty to stand by him. The problem was, one day she met Mr tall, dark and handsome who she fell instantly in love with. Of course, she couldn't admit it to anyone, especially not herself or she'd also have to admit that she'd made a screw-up of her life by marrying my father. So, every time she saw Bowen, she'd pick an argument with him. It kept him at a distance for a while but not forever. After a couple of years it became obvious that the angst they were arming themselves with to keep each other at arm's length, was also the thing that kept drawing them together, until one day things eventually came to a head and they admitted their mutual attraction."

"Did your mother split from your father and hook up with Mr tall, dark and handsome?" Brin asked.

"Pretty much. My point is though, the aggravation between you and Marcus seems to be excessively out of proportion to the provocations, so maybe there's more going on than you want to admit. If I'm right, and I'm pretty sure I am, eventually things are going to come to a head between the two of you. Sadly, I think my brother's too much of an idiot to understand his own feelings, just like my mother."

"You're wrong," Brin denied, but strangely Holly's words had a prophetic feel to them. Ahh, no. On second thoughts, definitely not. A prophecy already existed about Brin and her true *mate*, and in no way did it describe someone like Marcus. Although the prophecy did involve a lycan, her intended *mate* is supposed to bear the mark of a dragon, something akin to a birth mark, or so she had been led to believe. Fortunately, Marcus carried no such mark.

"We'll see," Holly grinned. "Come on, let's join the party. Don't worry, I can guarantee Marcus won't be game to cross you again. At least not today," she reassured.

Holding the door open, Holly waited for Brin. Walking side by side, Holly hoped she was right about Brin and her brother. She really liked this wyvern woman and could see them becoming good friends.

"I need a drink," Brin grumbled.

"Great idea. We should toast to my Gran's centenary and your future possibilities," Holly proudly declared.

Somehow, despite Brin's dour disposition, she found herself being swept up in Holly's enthusiasm. One glass of champagne became two, and by the third one, Holly's prediction had come true. The two women were well on the way to becoming best of friends.

All the while Nadia sat at the bar watching the minutes tick by, waiting for a call from Philippe.

Again, she focused her attention on others in the room. The ones she couldn't actually overhear were the ones that interested her the most. They gave her imagination something else to focus on other than what Philippe might have encountered at his apartment.

Nadia focused her attention across the room on Shani, and wondered what it was that had her looking so distressed.

"You should just leave Saadir," Yasmin told her.

"Yasmin, I think you've been living in England too long. You know that's not possible. He'll never grant me a divorce, and if I left him, he'd automatically assume I was leaving him for another man."

"You would be. Dray."

Shani let out a heavy sigh. She really wished that was true. "I can't. You know Saadir. If he thought I was with another man, he'd send someone to hunt him down and kill him."

"He won't kill Dray. Although, I'm pretty sure that Dray would kill whoever Saadir sent after him."

"That's my point. Saadir's hitman won't be seen or heard from again and Saadir would send someone else to do the job. When he didn't return either, he'd start digging into Dray's background more thoroughly. Eventually he'd discover what Dray really is, and everyone else. That's when things would get really bad. I'd like to think that these people have become our friends. Unfortunately, Saadir could easily become as big a threat to them, to all of them, as the Guild. I can't take that risk."

"What if you don't need a divorce? What if you take Abby up on her offer to *deal with Saadir,* another way?" Yasmin said, adding air quotes to emphasise her meaning.

Shani would be lying if she said she hadn't considered that option. In reality though, it really wasn't an option either.

"You know that won't help. Saadir's *business colleagues*, would only cause trouble then too. Besides, there's still the matter of the child."

"Are you sure you can handle all this on your own?"

Shani's laugh was harsh, almost bitter. "No, but what other choice do I have? None."

"Does he really expect people to believe you're away at the moment to convalesce in the last few weeks of your fictitious pregnancy?"

"They'll believe him because he's told them to. What other reason do they need?"

From another corner of the room, another pair of eyes watched the cousin's discussion.

Despite his height of six feet, five inches, Marek blended into the crowd seamlessly. So well in fact, that he was able to remain close enough to Shani and Yasmin to eavesdrop on their conversation.

It hadn't slipped his notice either that Abby had spent much of her time throughout the afternoon hovering about the pair, and her look of concern wasn't her customary expression. Something was seriously wrong in paradise between Shani and her husband, and he was determined to find out what it was. If Shani wasn't going to open up to him with the truth, maybe Abby would.

Nadia let out a tense breath as she looked about the room for the five hundredth time. So many stories being exchanged, so much happy cheer. She only wished she could feel as carefree as everyone else.

"Hey sis, have you heard anything yet?" Teagan asked, joining her at the bar.

"No. Nothing. You?" Nadia answered, checking her phone for the thousandth time.

"No. I left my phone back at the manor."

"It's been over an hour. They should be there. Why haven't we heard from them?" Nadia's anxiety was beginning to get the better of her, irrational pessimism taking a foothold in her imagination over the more logical explanations."

"I'm sure everything's fine. They'll call soon."

"I can't stand this waiting. What if something's happened?"

"Have you tried calling Philippe?" Teagan asked.

"No. If there is a problem, I don't want to distract him." That problem being Nicholas.

"Call him now. Just to put your mind at rest."

Nadia did just that. She hit speed dial on her phone, but Philippe didn't answer. Her anxiety suddenly doubled. "He had his phone when he left. Why isn't he answering?"

"I don't know. I'm sure there's a logical explanation. How about I go find Cassie and get her to call Alaric. I know he's got his phone on him."

"Yes. And hurry back, the waiting is killing me."

Teagan had only been gone thirty seconds when Nadia's phone buzzed with a message.

Thank God, she thought with relief when she saw Philippe's name come up on the screen.

Her relief turned to horror a moment later when she opened the message to discover a photo of a blonde haired man tied to a beam, beaten and bloody. Beneath were instructions: *If you ever want to see your mate again, come to the church ruins off Durham Creek Road. Be there within the hour or he dies.*

Holy hell. Philippe!

Philippe climbed into the backseat of the Hummer beside Saladin and Alaric. He barely heard what Dray was saying as Hawke started the car, his mind was lost in dark thoughts of retribution. He was so sure he was about to get his chance to finally rid himself of his brother's evil stain on his soul, only to discover he wasn't there waiting for him. Disappointment didn't begin to cover how he was feeling right now. His insides were a mish-mash of regret, anger, frustration…and fear.

It was strange though, for a short time just after they arrived, he could have sworn he felt his brother's presence. Clearly that was only wishful thinking.

The sound of Alaric's phone going off in his pocket jolted Philippe back to reality.

"Hi sweet cheeks…Yes…No, it looks like it was just a false alarm. Is everything alright there?…Okay, great. We're on our way back now. See you in an hour," Alaric told Cassie.

Philippe could have listened in on Cassie's end of the conversation too, but he didn't want to. What he wanted was to get back to the party and to his own *mate*.

The drive from the Drunken Duck pub to his apartment had felt excessively longer than usual. And the trip back felt even longer. Ice in Antarctica would have melted faster. Still, Philippe couldn't shake the nagging feeling that something wasn't right. It was no coincidence that his apartment's alarm had gone off randomly today. Something or someone had set it off deliberately.

Nicholas was playing some sort of fucked-up game with him, except his brother didn't seem to want to enlighten him with the rules.

They had only been on the highway for a few minutes when Alaric's phone rang again.

"What's up, is everything alright?" he asked. The concern in his voice caught more than just Philippe's attention, every man in the car tuned into the conversation instantly.

"We can't find Nadia. We've searched everywhere. She's not here." Philippe heard Cassie say.

Philippe's world teetered on the brink of an abyss. *Nicholas has her!* He knew it in his soul. It all made sense now, how he was feeling. The anxiety and frustration were his own, but the fear he felt was Nadia's. *Fuck!* Why didn't he realise it before.

"Stop the car. Now!" Philippe demanded. "He's got her. I have to go."

Without question or hesitation, Hawke hit the brakes. As one, they all piled out of the car.

"Can you find her?" Alaric asked.

"Of course, she's my *mate*," he replied angrily, his anxiety rising to a new high. He stilled for a moment yet found it hard to focus on her location, his inner turmoil wreaking havoc on his senses, which only drove his frustration and fears even higher.

Closing his eyes, Philippe drew in a few deep breaths. Narayan's words replayed in his head, *"Holding onto your memories is important, but holding onto all that negative emotion attached to them, isn't healthy. If you're too focused on your anger, you'll leave yourself open for another attack, or you'll make a mistake. Maybe both. To keep things in perspective you need to calm your mind. Find that place deep inside you where it's still, where you can think without feeling."*

"I can do this." His internal dialogue spoken out loud was a verbal affirmation of his resolute thought. *I have to do this!* He added silently.

Philippe took a few more deep breaths. With each one he released more of his emotional baggage until his senses overtook the clutter in his mind. He could feel the bite of the cool breeze on his skin, could hear the chatter of nearby birds and animals, and could taste the coming snow on the air, its scent as subtle as the sun's rays on his skin through the thick cloud cover. But it was the pulse of his *mate's* blood humming through his veins, permeating every cell in his body, that centred his soul with the calmness and focus of a seasoned soldier.

"Where is she?" Saladin asked through snarling lips.

"She's only a mile or two east of Cadley."

Not willing to waste another second, Alaric, Saladin, Dray and Hawke disappeared in a blur of speed behind Philippe, leaving their vehicle abandoned by the side of the road.

23

Nadia entered the grounds of the church ruins. Neglected over time she stepped carefully through the knee-deep long grass, aware that beneath it lay more than just the occasional hidden rabbit hole to snare her foot. She was also walking through the old church graveyard. Moss covered headstones were long forgotten in the old graveyard. Not all were still standing, of those that were, some were broken, while others tilted precariously, just waiting for a stiff breeze to push them over completely. Those that had already fallen had been buried beneath the tall grass. Vegetation had taken over everything. The stone wall which bordered the church grounds still stood, testament to the craftsmanship of centuries past, although even it had been reclaimed by nature. Ivy and rose vines wove their way through the cracks and crevices between the stones, layering them in greenery and colour. However, at this time of year, the thick webbing of bare thorny roses made the church yard seem even more forbidding.

Considering Nadia was there to *#Rescue* Philippe, her skeletal surroundings only increased her anxiety. Rescue Philippe from Nicholas? What a joke. She couldn't rescue herself from a wet paper bag. What choice did she have in coming though, none. Nicholas had Philippe, she had the evidence of it on her phone. Maybe she couldn't rescue him as such, but maybe if she was really lucky she could buy him time to escape.

Nadia let out a heavy sigh of regret as she navigated her way around one of the old headstones. She had been looking forward to marrying Philippe and having an extraordinarily long life with him.

Looking at the situation she was walking into now though, that wasn't likely to happen. If she got to live out the rest of the day it would probably be a miracle. Regardless, if she could help Philippe escape, and hopefully kill his psychotic brother, her sacrifice would be worth it.

She thought initially that getting through the maze of plastic furniture in the pub's car park was going to bring on a major panic attack. As it turned out however, with the right kind of incentive she was able to make out the man-made synthetics well enough to navigate around them and avoid attracting attention. A minor miracle.

What she needed now was a slightly bigger miracle. Okay, so *slightly* bigger didn't quite cover it. Colossal, humongous, a miracle of epic proportions would be more accurate. Regrettably, beggars can't be choosers. At this point she'd settle for a boy scout with a lifesaving merit badge.

It was then, while wallowing in self-pity and contemplating her imminent demise, that she noticed something behind one of the headstones. A hazy figure seemed to fade in and out of view. Could it be a ghost, or was stress making her eyes play tricks on her, she wondered. It looked like a person, but there was no substance behind the layers in the aura. Strangely, she preferred the idea of a ghost haunting her than the alternative that she was losing her mind. At least a ghost was company, assuming it was friendly. Then she thought, what if this was just part of Nicholas' trap?

Freaking hell. Who needed Nicholas to kill her, Nadia was ready to hyperventilate her way into one of the graves all on her own. The only thing that kept her placing one foot in front of the other was the knowledge that inside that run down church, was Philippe.

Stepping through the archway of the church into the vestibule, Nadia looked about nervously before entering the chapel. The room was big enough to park a bus, yet despite all that space, she felt as though there wasn't enough room to breathe.

Before Nadia could step more than one foot inside, a hand grabbed her and dragged her back, the force exerted on her arm was excruciating. She would have screamed only before the shock of what was happening allowed the fight or flight response in her brain to kick in, she was struck a hard blow to the head, dazing her for a second. Pain exploded through her head as the first blow was followed by another, and harsh fingers gripped her about the throat, effectively cutting off her air and her ability to scream.

"Bitch!"

She knew that voice. It held a harder edge to it than she remembered, but there was no mistaking who it was.

Nicholas gripped her hair painfully at the scalp and pulled her back toward the chair beside the altar. The same one from the photo he had sent her, the one that had Philippe's beaten and bloody body tied to it.

Except…it wasn't Philippe in that chair, it was someone else entirely who unfortunately for him, had an uncanny resemblance to Philippe.

Oh crap, this couldn't be happening. Where was Philippe?

Nadia reached up, her fingers clawing at the hand about her throat, but it was no use, Nicholas' grip only tightened further, cutting off her air until she blacked out.

"What's the plan?" Hawke asked, drawing his semi-automatic Glock from its holster beneath his jacket, flicking off the safety. Beside him, Saladin unsheathed a pair of razor sharp katanas.

"Punch Nicholas' ticket," Dray answered.

Alaric tipped his nose into the air, a hint of something on the breeze caught his attention. It was subtle, yet familiar. Annoyingly, he just couldn't place where he recognised that scent from.

Something wasn't right.

Silence surrounded them. Complete and utter silence.

"Do you sense that?" Saladin asked.

"How can you miss it. Every hair on my body is standing on end right now," Hawke replied in a hushed voice.

Adrenaline spiked through Philippe's veins, he spun in a circle, sharp eyes taking in every untrampled blade of grass, every undisturbed leaf, and found only one set of footprints.

Nadia's.

Fear seized him. Thoughts of Nadia had him thinking he was in fact suffering a case of mental seizures. He could barely think straight.

One thing he knew for certain, if he went into that church distracted, he wouldn't need to worry about what he was going to do afterwards, because he would be dead. That was not an option. The only one dying today was Nicholas, slowly and very, very painfully. Every muscle in his body tensed, eager to rip his brother a new hole, or fifty.

Philippe felt like his passive aggressive behaviour had become his idling speed, which was a long way from the usual calm, collected composure he was used to. Taking a deep breath, he forced his tangled thoughts and emotions into the background, filing them away in a mental compartment to be dealt with at a later date.

Nadia's scent grew stronger the closer Philippe got to the church ruins.

Stepping through the stone archway onto the church grounds the group suddenly stopped, each spewing out curses as black as their mood.

Philippe turned around, his sword raised ready to take on whatever it was that had the others so riled up, but saw nothing.

"What's wrong?" he asked, gripping the hilt of his weapon a little tighter.

"We can't fucking move, that's what's wrong," Saladin fumed, tugging at his leg which appeared to have been super-glued in place.

"What the Hell?" Philippe growled.

"Our feet are stuck. We're not going anywhere. It looks like this party is only supposed to include you," Saladin told him, followed by another string of curses.

"Fuck! Fuck! Fuck!" Alaric's power burst from him in a flash of icy wind, but it appeared that even his power wasn't strong enough to break free of the binding spell that surrounded them. All he succeeded in doing was cementing a crust of ice to his own body, which in turn only pissed him off further.

"No guessing who's behind this little surprise. Doctor Evil and Ivana Humpalot," Dray spat the names as though even speaking of them, *Scorpion and Morganna,* left a bad taste in his mouth.

"Was that a joke Dray?" Saladin asked, a little surprised.

"What if it was?"

"I'm impressed. You want to know what I think?"

"No," Dray replied curtly.

Saladin ignored Dray and told him anyway. "I think you need to be dropped into evil traps more often, it brings out the best in your personality," he told him with a broad smile, slapping Dray on the shoulder. Dray's only reply was a snarl and an angry glare, threatening enough to make a biker wet his pants. Of course, it only made Saladin laugh.

It seemed they really were stuck for the time being. Of all their enemies, only Morganna had the kind of power it took to cast a spell on the wide parameter strong enough to hold them so steadfastly immobile. And, if that was the case, the two of them were likely very close by, watching, waiting. It also meant that until the spell was broken, each of the men were sitting ducks if the evil duo chose to attack.

Likewise, Philippe was now the only member of their group able to enter the church. A moving target he maybe, but up against the likes of Nicholas, Scorpion and Morganna…he was woefully unequipped.

Fuck!

Philippe was torn, he didn't want to leave them out there defenceless, nor could he stand there another second knowing that Nadia was inside that church at the mercy of Nicholas' unhinged whims.

"Don't fucking wait around here, go and get your *mate*, we'll call for back-up." Saladin told him.

Even before the words left Saladin's lips, Dray was already pulling his phone from his pocket. Lifting it up he cursed. The binding spell blocked the cell reception. "Fuck. This just keeps getting better."

"I'll try," Philippe reached inside his jacket, but his phone wasn't there. He knew he had it when he left the party. He also had it when he first arrived at his apartment, it couldn't have just fallen out of his pocket. Philippe clenched his fists and cursed. Nicholas.

He hadn't imagined feeling his brother's presence. He really had been there…and he had pick-pocketed his phone. Was that how he lured Nadia here? No doubt it was. She wouldn't have left the party of her own volition, not unless she believed he had asked her to.

"Philippe, go. We'll figure something out," Alaric commanded. Not that Philippe needed any encouragement, he was halfway across the graveyard before Alaric could finish his sentence.

Inside the vestibule, Philippe slowed and then stopped as he crossed the threshold of the old chapel.

The inside of the church wasn't much of a surprise. It was your typical dusty, decrepit, ramshackle of a birdcage. Window frames bare of glass. Leaf litter strewn about the floor. It's supporting structures showed signs of neglect, time slowly crumbling away the stone walls. The roof was almost entirely gone, replaced by partial shade of an old oak tree beside the building and an abundance of ivy which clung to the rotting, wooden interior support beams. It appeared his brother had chosen a location that mirrored his own soul, Philippe thought speculatively. An empty wasteland just waiting to be torn down.

And there, in front of him, sat Nadia, her hands tied behind her back, her head down, her chin resting slack against her chest. The smell of blood permeated the air so thickly it almost seared his nostrils. In the same moment his eyes locked onto a dark, wet stain on the floor beneath her, reflecting the dim afternoon light as it filtered through the breach in the roof. It was a pool of blood, big enough to account for more than half a body's life-giving supply. Was it Nadia's? Had Nicholas killed her? A savage roar of fury ripped from Philippe's chest.

The sound of clapping echoed between the walls all around him. "Welcome brother. I'm glad you accepted my invitation," Nicholas drawled, a gloating swagger to his voice.

For a moment Philippe was stunned into immobility. Before him was someone he had known his entire life but didn't recognise at all. Nicholas' eyes were icy shards of enmity, curiously flat and devoid of any warmth or kindness. The brother he once knew no longer existed, in his place stood a cold-blooded serial killer, a snarl curling up one corner of his lip in silent challenge.

"What have you done to Nadia, you fucking arsehole?" Philippe demanded, but he dared not move toward her, not just yet. With his initial distress subsiding, his senses cleared easing his fear. That wasn't Nadia's blood surrounding her. Thankfully she was very much alive, the sound of her steady breath sent a ripple of relief through his soul.

"She's taking a little nap," Nicholas sneered.

"If you've hurt her in any way...."

"What, you'll kill me?" he laughed.

"Oh, make no mistake I plan on killing you, but if you've harmed Nadia, even broken a fingernail, I'm going to peel the flesh from your bones and feed it to you, before I kill you."

Nicholas laughed with an arrogance that made him sound like Santa Claus, although he sounded like *Ha! Ha! Ha!* instead of *Ho! Ho! Ho!* "I'd love to oblige you brother, but I think you have that backwards. The only one of us walking out of here is me." He shot Nadia a covetous look as she sat slumped on the chair. "I might have some fun with your *mate* first though."

"Time to make your peace with your soul brother, coz you're about to die," Philippe hissed.

Nicholas turned his head back in time to see his brother sprinting in his direction. Nicholas side stepped a fraction of a second before the blade of Philippe's sword found its mark across his throat. Nicholas easily knocked the blade from his brother's hand, sending it to the far corner of the chapel in a noisy clatter of metal on stone.

"This is one fight you're *not* going to win. Not this time. You might be bigger now, but you're still the same snot nosed little shit you always were," Nicholas taunted. To prove his point, Nicholas casually walked over to a wooden column supporting what was left of the roof's overhead beams and punched his fist right through it, shattering it into splinters. Above, the overhead beams creaked and groaned as their load bearing pillar shifted, but they didn't fall.

Holy crap! There had to be a movie in that: *Bruce Lee moonlights as a wood chipper.* "Impressive, but that timber isn't going to fight back."

In three long strides, Philippe was in Nicholas' face, landing an upper cut to his chin. Nicholas didn't attempt to block it, instead he took the hit and smiled. Philippe took another swing at him, and another, but Nicholas never even flinched as the punches found their mark. They had as much impact on him as a slap in the face with a limp lettuce leaf.

Then Philippe landed a punch that seemed to daze him for a moment. Reflexively Nicholas blocked the next punch and retaliated with his own. With each block Philippe made to Nicholas' attack, his brothers rage seemed to grow.

Punches and kicks were thrown by both in their vicious struggle, each man taking out their hatred of the other with every savage blow.

Receiving a bone crunching blow, Philippe was body slammed to the ground, his brother on top of him but he lost his grip as Philippe rolled, landing straddled on top of Nicholas, raining down punches. Nicholas took each hit, smiling up at his brother.

With one sharp shove, Nicholas threw Philippe off him, sending him flying across the room to land in a sprawling heap on the floor. Spitting blood, Philippe wiped his mouth. For the first time he knew he was no match for his brother, even if he had landed a few blows that caught Nicholas off guard, his brother's strength and speed surpassed his own threefold, which was really saying something.

Until this moment he had remained steady in his belief that his brother could never beat him in a fight. He had trained so hard for so many years to ensure he would always be better than his brother, just in case a day like this ever came along. His belief had been bolstered by the fact that his own strength and speed had increased since his second transition to become a vampire, having both Narayan and an archangel's blood in his veins. He thought the only ones stronger and faster than himself now would be Narayan and Alaric. As it turns out, he was wrong. He wasn't even in the same league as Nicholas and his chemically enhanced capabilities.

This wasn't good. Not good at all.

Nicholas watched his brother with malicious satisfaction. He revelled in Philippe's fear. The scent of it was like the sweetest perfume, teasing and tantalising his senses. He wanted more of it. He wanted the air about him to be saturated with it.

There was only one way to ensure that.

With a quick twist of the ring on his finger, Nicholas vanished from sight and he got his wish. Philippe's fear rose instantly.

"Show yourself coward," Philippe roared as he jumped to his feet, his eyes darting about for some sign of his brother.

"You hit like a bitch! Let's see if you die like one too." Nicholas sneered, thrusting out his foot he kicked Philippe backward fifteen feet and into the wall, causing a shower of dust and mortar from between the stones to cascade down upon him.

Nadia's senses returned as she came to from Nicholas' blow to her head and semi-strangulation. She didn't know how long she had been out, probably no more than a few minutes but it seemed a lot had happened in that time. Not only was she currently tied to a chair, the coppery smell of blood around her was overwhelming. She shifted on the seat, straining and stretching her muscles to see if anything hurt, wondering if any of that blood belonged to her. But, she felt fine. Maybe if it had been her blood, it seemed she had already healed, she thought with an inward smile. After all, she wasn't exactly mortal anymore. Losing her head or her heart would definitely kill her but other than that...?

Nadia suddenly remembered the guy who had been sitting on this seat before her, an innocent pawn in Nicholas' psychotic game. She would have shed a tear for him, if there wasn't still a chance she could very well end up just as dead as he was.

The floor beneath her shook. It sounded like a demolition team was hard at work to bring the building down around her. Opening her eyes she gasped in horror. Nicholas was coming at Philippe. Philippe's eyes darted this way and that but could not see the predator stalking him about the room with the ease and casualness of a spider trapping a fly. He must have made himself invisible, she surmised. Undetectable to Philippe's senses, to her though, he was as visible as the nose on her face.

Nadia fought to break her bindings, but it was no use.

Again, Nicholas came at his brother, and again Philippe went down, or maybe the ground came up to meet him, he wasn't sure. All he knew was one minute he was standing and the next he wasn't. Did he fall, or was he thrown down? It took a moment to decipher the difference since the contents of his skull reverberated back and forth from the force of his head's impact with the stone floor. Lights danced before his eyes and his ears rang so loudly he could barely hear Nadia yelling at him, and his limbs felt like dead weights attached to his torso. That was one hell of a swing his brother had there.

"Behind you. Six o'clock. Twenty feet," she called out.

Philippe shifted his weight and spun around one hundred and eighty degrees, swinging out his foot at the vacant air in front of him. It came as a pleasant surprise to feel his foot connect with a loud crunch. This time Nicholas was sent sprawling. A path of debris on the floor swept clear in his wake as his invisible body ploughed through it.

Philippe waited and watched for a few seconds, but he could not see nor hear any sign of his brother. Not until Nadia called out once again.

For a second Nicholas' easy demeanour dropped, letting his simmering rage surface. His dark eyes focused on Nadia with a sharp hatred she could feel like heat radiating from the sun on her skin. His lip drew back in a snarl. It was the only warning she got before he pulled out a pistol.

Philippe heard the crack of the gun, but he wasn't fast enough to stop the bullet. The world around him went into slow motion as he turned toward Nadia to see her head jerk backward and her body slump forward once again. A trickle of blood dripped from the wound in her forehead into her lap.

No!

A moment of panic gripped him yet subsided almost as quickly when her fingers twitched and he heard her heartbeat continue its staccato rhythm in her chest, loud and strong. *Thank God!* Relief was like a band-aid for his soul and his nerves. Fortunately, a bullet to the head was now nothing but a minor inconvenience for her body to heal. A little fact he'd prefer his brother not pick up on or he would probably make a more thorough attempt at killing her. What he needed was to keep Nicholas distracted until she recovered, and he could figure out how to set her free, preferably before his brother killed him too.

"Why for fuck's sake, did you want to go and do that?" Philippe asked looking around at the empty space around him. Under the cloak of invisibility his brother could have been standing only a foot in front of him, about to pluck out his eyeballs and Philippe would have been no less blind to his whereabouts.

"She was telling you where I am and it pissed me off." How did Nadia know where he was? He couldn't think of a logical excuse other than it was some sort of druid spell to *see the unseen,* or some crap like that. Either way, she was one problem now dealt with.

"That wasn't your preferred style of killing now, was it? I'm a little disappointed Nicholas. Didn't you take a course in creative killing or something?" Philippe said, pitching his tone thickly with a mocking jeer.

"Since when have you been interested in my hunting habits?" Nicholas was confused. This wasn't the reaction he was expecting after having just killed his *mate.* Philippe was calm, almost matter-of-fact about it. He was too calm. Maybe he had a touch of psychopath about

315

him too, and he just hadn't seen it before, Nicholas thought. Whatever the reason for Philippe's cool reaction, he didn't like it.

Hunting habits? Philippe thought angrily. Nicholas made murder sound like a sport. "Do you hear the screams of those you've killed when you close your eyes? Do you taste their blood on your lips?"

"Every day, and I savour every memory," Nicholas sneered. That remark got more of an emotional response from his brother than shooting his *mate* did. Philippe's top lip curled back, his eyes glittering with hatred as he swung around in the direction of Nicholas' voice, slashing at the air in front of him, contacting nothing.

Philippe felt a shift in the air to his right a second before his legs were swept out from under him, sending him crashing once again to the hard stone floor. He took his time getting to his feet, feigning weariness and injury. Behind the façade, Philippe's body hummed with a surge of adrenaline in his bloodstream, but this game of cat and mouse had to be played with precision and care if he had any chance of surviving long enough to save Nadia.

"So not cool brother. I always knew you liked to play dirty, but I never took you for a coward. Are you afraid the potion might wear off, and I'll beat you as I always do?" Philippe's taunt was met with silence. "Take off the ring and face me like a man. Brother to brother." He scanned his eyes back and forth across the room looking for any hint of where Nicholas might be.

Then, after a few seconds Nicholas twisted the ring on his finger and let himself become visible again, pacing back and forth at a healthy distance from his brother, halfway between himself and Nadia. Fortunately, Nicholas had his back to her and was totally unaware that she was coming to, again. Philippe arched his back and cracked his shoulders, standing taller. His face slid into a smile of malicious anticipation, his hard glare fixed on his brother. "I hope you're ready to have your arse handed to you because you're not leaving here alive," Philippe bit out caustically.

With a roar, Philippe charged at Nicholas, spearing his shoulder into his brother's stomach, lifting him off his feet and driving him backward several feet. Nicholas hammered him in the back of his head with his elbow, forcing Philippe to drop him. Stumbling a few steps, Philippe's vision blurred from the heavy blow to his senses. He gasped for breath and shook his head to clear the light show that seemed to dance in his vision.

Nicholas took advantage of Philippe's momentary disorientation, pouncing on him from behind, one hand gripped his chin, tipping his head back, the other he used to swipe his taloned fingertips across the soft flesh, slicing open his jugular vein in one easy strike.

Philippe let it fuel his rage.

With every ounce of strength Philippe had, he flung Nicholas off him and staggered back, putting a few metres of distance between them as he gripped a hand about his throat to stem the blood flow. Almost immediately the wound began to heal.

"I see your adult upgrade came with a few extra benefits," Nicholas bit out acerbically, his annoyance bubbling over. His plan was to inflict one slow-healing wound after another, concurrently breaking down his brother's will as he broke his body. Disappointingly, things weren't going quite as anticipated. Philippe was healing too fast for a regular vampire. As far as he knew only the true immortals like Alaric or Alex could heal faster than Philippe was currently demonstrating. Annoyingly, Nicholas seemed to have more questions than answers around his brother's sudden growth spurt. How it had even been possible, was top of his list. Philippe was made a vampire when he was only thirteen, he had been thirteen for one hundred and sixty years. He should have remained that way for eternity.

Undeterred, these turn of events in fact helped to motivate Nicholas to try harder, double his efforts, and his aggressiveness.

Rolling to his feet, Nicholas remained hunched over, spitting blood from his mouth. His snarl made him look feral, and like any rabid animal, Philippe intended to put him out of everyone's misery. Oh, he would love nothing more than to inflict the same amount of suffering on the bastard as he had on his victims, but enough was enough. Nicholas had to die. Now!

Achieving his goal however, was proving to be easier said than done.

Nadia shook her head and groaned, yet couldn't quite rid herself of the feeling of an entire brass band playing a concert in her brain at a volume that would drown out a squadron of military jets. Her whole head seemed to reverberate on her shoulders.

"Lass, you be awake?" The soft voice filtered through the cacophony in her head.

"Am I dead?" Nadia groaned, still dazed, her speech a little slurred.

"Not at present," the woman replied.

Nadia turned her head to face the owner of the soft voice. Blinking several times and stretching her eyes wide, the woman finally came into focus. She was a simply dressed, older woman of maybe seventy years. The style of dress she wore was from a much earlier era, maybe three or four hundred years ago going by the ankle length, full skirt of her brown woollen dress and plain linen bonnet. "Are you dead?" Nadia felt stupid asking the question, but she'd learned a long time ago that sometimes the craziest explanations were often the correct ones. At least they were in the supernatural world.

"That I am lass," she replied in an old English turn of phrase.

"So, you're a ghost," Nadia surmised. "Are you the one I thought I saw outside by the graves when I arrived?"

"Just so. You may call me Bessie."

"If I'm alive and you're a ghost, then how is it I can see you so clearly now when I couldn't before?"

"I don't rightly know, but it may have something to do with the bullet in your forehead," the woman told her.

"Ohmigod! That's right. Nicholas shot me!" As her brain healed, more memories came flooding back. Nadia went to lift her hand to her forehead and cursed beneath her breath when the movement was stopped by the rope still tied about her wrists. *Crap, Philippe!*

For a moment Nadia didn't know which compulsion gripped her more, the need to scream, the need to cry, the need to tug uselessly against her restraints or the need to help Philippe. It was the last one which started her thinking about the one before it.

Paige was able to converse with ghosts. She could also make their incorporeal spirits solid with her touch. Nadia had always wondered whether that came as part of her sister's natural druid gift of separating her own aura from her body or, what if….

"Bessie, I need your help. I want to try something."

"Sure lass, what do you need me to do?"

"I need you to come close enough for me to touch you."

318

"Why?"

Nadia huffed in frustration. "I have a hunch about something. Please don't ask me any questions now. Please, just do it."

Bessie did as Nadia asked. She stepped around behind her, reached down, fully expecting her fingers to go straight through Nadia's straining hands, but they didn't.

"Oh, my lord," Bessie gasped in shocked amazement and pulled her hands away, instantly reverting to being a spirit.

"It worked. Freaking hell, it actually worked," Nadia almost squealed with joy. "Bessie, please, I really, really need your help. I need you to untie me so I can help my *mate*."

Bessie looked up at the two men fighting, Philippe was clearly beginning to weaken under his brother's fierce attack. With a quick nod, the ghost did as Nadia asked.

Nadia rubbed her wrists and flexed her fingers to get the feeling back in her hands. Now what? How was *she* going to overpower Nicholas if Philippe couldn't? She had no idea. What she did know however, she wasn't just going to sit there and do nothing.

Just as she stood from the chair, Philippe took another bone crunching blow from his brother. With a moan of pain, Philippe willed his legs to move under him, straighten and unsteadily take his weight, lunging for Nicholas once again. One hand gripped him about the throat as his other curled at the fingers, preparing to punch a hole in Nicholas' chest and claw out his heart.

Nadia saw the glint of metal as Nicholas reached behind his back. Her scream momentarily shifted his attention away from his prey.

The dagger came out of nowhere and hit Philippe in the shoulder, severing the tendons that made his arm work. His hand suddenly useless, lost its grip on Nicholas' throat and dropped to his side.

"What the fuck?" Nicholas lost his momentum. In fact, he stopped still for a few seconds to process what he was seeing. Nadia was alive! She could see him when he was invisible and a bullet couldn't kill her? *What the fucking fuck?*

Philippe grabbed the hilt of the dagger with his good hand, gritted his teeth, and yanked the blade free of his shoulder with a string of curses.

The wound would heal quickly, but not fast enough if he wanted to keep one step ahead of his brother. And that is all he was doing at this point. Not a good situation to be in, especially now that Nicholas knew Nadia was still alive.

Philippe's reflexes had slowed as his energy waned. His body had sustained too many injuries to cope with in such a short space of time. But he took his opportunities when he saw them. With Nicholas' focus on Nadia, Philippe lunged forward with the blade he'd pulled from his shoulder.

Nicholas jerked his head back as the blade sliced so close to his throat, he could feel the shifting air on his skin. Philippe never believed the knife would hit its mark, but he did accomplish is goal, bringing his brother's wrath back onto him and forgetting about Nadia. For now, at least.

Philippe didn't realise it at the time, but that was the best move he could have ever made.

Everything happened so quickly. Nadia leapt from the chair and ran toward Philippe, her heart pounding hard enough to break a rib. Fear, anger and determination fused inside her like an iron forge. There was no way in this world, or any other, she would let Nicholas win. He had taken too much from too many already. He was *not* going to take Philippe too.

Nadia had no weapons, no special skills…except one.

With a war cry that made Philippe proud, she leapt onto Nicholas' back and gripped her fingers into the thin veil of light that was fused to his body. His soul's aura.

As with Vanessa when Nadia had wrenched at her aura, Nicholas let out a howl and began thrashing about, trying to shake her off. And he did. Unfortunately for him, Nadia never let go of his aura. As she was flung across the room, she ripped his soul from his body.

Philippe watched in panic. He couldn't see what Nadia had done, whatever it was though, had sent Nicholas into a full scale meltdown. If he didn't stop his brother right now, Nadia was dead.

The world seemed to go into slow motion as Philippe looked down at the blade in his hand. His brain and emotions checked out, all that was left was instinct and pure adrenaline. He'd never felt so calm, so in control.

Philippe was on his brother in a second. Pulling him back, he spun him around and in the same movement plunged the blade into Nicholas' heart. He thought it would only momentarily slow him, but it didn't.

Nicholas stopped and stilled, his eyes going wide with surprise. It was surreal to look down and see the knife protruding from his chest. For a moment he was both alive and dead. His heart had stopped beating, although his mind still functioned. Then the moment was gone. Nicholas watched in disbelief as the floor came up to meet him. There was no pain on impact. There was no feeling at all as the curtain closed over the remnants of his brain's function and joined his body in death.

As the light in Nicholas' eyes dimmed, his life receding into the dark void of death, Philippe was hit with an incredible wave of sorrow.

Philippe dropped to his knees as the strength in his legs gave out. For a moment he just stared at his brother's lifeless body sprawled on the floor in front of him, his mind seizing in shock at their ordeal finally being over. Then, reality sank in and he let out the most heart wrenching cry.

He'd killed his brother.

Despite all the bad blood between them, Nicholas was still his brother. His family. Philippe had been by his side for more than one hundred and sixty-six years. And now he was gone.

He didn't regret killing him. Not at all. He hated the man he had become, the monster who had lurked just beneath the surface of his charming smile. Instead, he mourned the loss of the brother he had always hoped he might become.

It was hard to refocus his mind around the swirl of emotions, to reconcile what he had done, what he and Nadia had both done. He felt....Numb. Happy. Relieved. And more sadness and regret than he imagined he would.

"Are you alright?" Nadia asked as she ran to him.

And just like that his moment of grief was over. The sound of his *mate's* voice, more precious to him than every good memory of his brother combined.

"I'm fine, and you?" Philippe scanned her for signs of cuts and bruises but found none.

"Is it over?" she asked sceptically, not comfortable being so close to Nicholas, expecting him to jump to his feet at any moment, even though she could see his disembodied spirit hovering about angrily only metres away.

"It is. He's dead. How did you get free?"

"A friendly neighbourhood ghost named Bessie untied me. As it turns out when I touch a spirit they become solid, just like they do for Paige," she grinned proudly.

"That's my *Ei'Ambriath*, or maybe we should call you the vampire slayer, huh?" he chuckled as he pulled her in close. Philippe felt the tension in his bones and muscles ease as she relaxed against his body. Every molecule ached after his battle with his brother. Not that he cared. Nadia was safe and that was all that mattered to him.

"Only bad vampires," she replied, hugging him tighter. "Oh crap, I don't think I should have said that out loud," Nadia gasped.

"What? You'll only kill bad vampires?"

"No, the part about my touch making spirits solid." Pushing herself away from Philippe she quickly backed up a few steps.

Philippe cursed, his eyes darting about the old chapel although failed to see whatever Nadia's gaze was fixed to. He could guess what it was though. His psychotic brother hadn't accepted defeat and was planning one last attack.

"Stay back, don't you touch me," she cried out as she continued to take steps away from her invisible predator.

"Nadia, where is he," Philippe begged helplessly. He had no more hope of tackling a spirit than he had of holding water in a sieve, but he had to do something.

Nadia jerked her hand back as though it had been burned. In the same moment the cause of her distress made his physical presence known. Nicholas gripped Nadia's hand, although his hateful glare was levelled at Philippe, yet another evil plan brewing in his mind. Nadia tried to shake her hand free but couldn't, his grip was too strong.

Philippe lunged forward and just before he reached them, Nicholas let out a blood-curdling scream. For a fraction of a second his body began to vibrate and then vanished. Unfortunately, Philippe's momentum kept him tumbling forward, knocking Nadia down onto the dirty floor, his much larger and heavier body covering hers. Regardless, he didn't plan on moving in a hurry. Beneath him she was safe. His eyes darted about the empty space, expecting to find his brother standing over them again, although found no sign of him. Still, he refused to move even when Nadia punched him in the arm.

"Philippe honey, get off me or you'll be cut off from sex for a month." That got his attention.

"What if he's still here?"

"He's not. He's definitely gone," she told him.

"Where?"

"The Underworld claimed him," a soft voice informed them.

Philippe nearly jumped out of his skin when he saw the elderly woman crouched on the floor beside them, holding Nadia's hand."

"You're Bessie, I presume?"

"I am Sir. Pleased to meet you. I can assure you, your brother won't be returning again anytime soon. No soul comes back from the Underworld."

"Are you sure about that?"

"Very. I've been walking these grounds for many a year sir, I have seen my fair share of souls descend to Hell."

"Thanks for all your help, Bessie. I don't know what I would've done without you." Nadia told her, her own energy beginning to wane now that the excitement of the afternoon appeared to be over.

"Anytime lass," the ghostly woman replied happily as she released Nadia's hand and faded from view.

Philippe helped her to her feet, the sudden shift to vertical causing a sudden pounding in her head. "Wow my head hurts," she said rubbing her forehead.

"He shot you right between the eyes," Philippe told her, poking a finger in the only remaining sign it had happened, a circular red mark right through her *third eye*, the centre where her astral sight was located.

"Really? I didn't think he was that good a shot."

"I thought he was going to crap his pants when he saw you get up again," Philippe smirked.

"Is Nicholas asleep or unconscious?" Saladin asked as he and the others entered the chapel, weapons drawn.

"Neither. He heard so much about rigor mortis, he thought he'd give it a try," Nadia joked.

"What? Why isn't he a pile of dust?" Dray asked sceptically, nudging his body with his size fourteen shoe.

"You'll have to ask my *mate* about that, although I believe it has something to do with the fact that she can separate a vampire's soul from its physical body," Philippe said.

"Fuck me dead. Remind me not to piss you off in the future," Hawke nodded to Nadia.

"You and me both," Philippe winked.

"Oh, trust me, if you ever piss me off Philippe, I have other methods of punishing you."

He chuckled softly and covered her mouth with his own, silencing any further conversation. His kiss began softly, tenderly, setting off bursts of pleasure that radiated through her entire body.

Nadia leaned in closer, wanting more. Philippe readily obliged, increasing the pressure of his lips before parting them further to meet her tongue with his.

Nadia didn't want the kiss to end. Cupping his face with her hands she held him close, but soon his mouth wasn't enough. Her hands slid lower, her fingers traced the contours of his neck, over the soft fabric of his torn and bloody shirt, continuing lower over his lower ribs to his taut abdomen. His own hands explored the soft lines of her body.

She would have continued lower, lost in the need to touch him, if he hadn't stilled suddenly, his hands coming to rest on her hips. His eyes darted about the room at their audience watching with a mixture of amusement and boredom.

"Um, sorry," Philippe apologised a little bashfully. Nadia too cleared her throat and took a step aside. "How did you get free of the spell?"

"We didn't, it was probably tied to Nicholas. When he died the spell was broken," Alaric answered.

"Can we get out of here now. I really don't want to be around Nicholas any longer, even if he is dead," Nadia prompted.

"Sure." Philippe led Nadia outside to the church's graveyard. As strange as it seemed, the prospect of meeting another ghost in this creepy old cemetery was more inviting than spending another moment inside that chapel with the physical remains of his brother.

As the minutes ticked by, Nadia and Philippe each relayed the events of the afternoon.

"Where's the ring of Gyges now? Did you take it off his body?" Dray asked.

"Fuck. I forgot about that. No, he's still wearing it," Philippe replied.

"I'll get it," Alaric said.

With long, quick strides Alaric re-entered the old chapel and froze. For a moment his mind went blank as it travelled back two thousand years in time.

"It can't be," he muttered. Whether he was trying to convince himself or the man standing in front of him, he wasn't sure.

Scorpion stood from his hunched position beside Nicholas' body, pocketing the ring he'd pulled from his finger. Alaric was too shocked to do anything more than watch. Beside him stood Morganna.

"You ready to go dear?" she asked cheerily, although the humour never quite reached her cold eyes. Morganna took Scorpion's hand in hers, her other gripped the amulet about her neck. A second later they were both gone.

Alaric numbly walked back outside and stopped in the doorway, his brain still trying to process who it was he just saw.

"Alaric, you alright? You look like you just saw a ghost," Saladin asked.

"I think I just did."

24

"Come on, we'd better hurry. Have a quick shower and we should get back before the party wraps up," Philippe told Nadia as they entered their bedroom. His tone was clipped short, unintentionally. While their clothes were torn and bloody, fortunately neither of them showed any lingering signs of their ordeal. However, now that the adrenaline from the battle had begun to wear off, Philippe's annoyance that Nadia had gone to the church at all, was beginning to take precedence in his thoughts. Logically he knew she believed she had no other option, but that didn't mean he was any less upset that she had gone. The fear of losing her had nearly driven him mad. What if she really had…Philippe couldn't bring himself to finish the thought, it was too distressing.

"It would be faster if we had a shower together," she suggested cheekily, her pale eyes sparkling as she watched him warily, the colours swirling in his aura were like watching a bubbling cauldron of emotions, and there was no way of knowing which one was going to prevail as they each fought for dominance. One thing she knew for certain, she wasn't about to let one of the negative, self-destructive emotions take precedence. Philippe had already dealt with enough of those. It was time to move on.

"Oh no. If we have a shower together, we'll never get back to the party," he replied, careful to keep his internal irritation in check.

"I don't think Mrs P will mind. I doubt she even knows we're missing."

"It's not Mrs Philpot I'm worried about. It's your dad. And I *know* he knows we're not there. I have to tell you Nadia, your dad might have accepted me into the family, but he still scares the crap out of me."

Nadia laughed, the soft tinkle of sound was music to his ears. He'd come so close to losing her again, yet despite everything, she'd come through the ordeal no worse for wear. It seemed he had some serious rethinking to do. She wasn't the helpless female they'd all believed her to be. Between them they'd kicked some serious supped-up vampire arse today. Without her, there would have been a very different outcome. In fact, he would *almost* go so far as saying they made a great team together, not just as *mates*, but also as partners in the field, just like Hawke and Anna. Almost. He wasn't keen on putting her skills to the test again anytime soon, he didn't think he could stand the stress.

"Come on, shower," Philippe encouraged her.

"I'm ready if you are," she told him in a husky, heated tone. Simultaneously Nadia unhitched the button on his pants and slid the zipper down just far enough to slip her fingers inside.

Philippe considered protesting and removing her hand, at the same time he was mesmerised by the lusty hunger burning in her eyes. And really, his first priority was her happiness, so how could he refuse her this indulgence if she wanted to fondle his…um…what was he thinking, he couldn't remember. The pleasure centre in his pants seemed to have cancelled out his higher cognitive functions.

The pulsing length beneath her fingers was hard and hot, and the sound he made as her fingers stroked lightly along its length heated her own body exponentially.

In contradiction, Nadia's cold fingers around Philippe's growing erection made him shiver. Philippe gripped her arms lightly to steady himself and noted that they too felt chilled.

"You're cold. You need to get in a hot shower and warm up," he told her.

"I could, but that wouldn't be as much fun." Nadia's eyes sparkled with devious delight, drawing a puzzled expression from Philippe's concerned face. Cupping her breasts she tweaked the taut peaks lightly. "What do you see?" she asked him.

"Heaven."

Nadia giggled, amused by his greedy gaze and choice of words.

"No silly, what do you notice about my breasts, how has the cold affected them?" she prompted again.

His eyes roamed every inch of pale skin, drinking in the sight with ardent admiration. "They're covered in goose bumps, and your nipples are contracted to tight peaks."

"And, what happens to the rest of your body when you're cold?" she asked, a hint of mischief in her voice.

"Your muscles contract and you shiver."

"Exactly. *All*... your muscles contract. Both the external ones and the internal ones."

Philippe's eyes lit up as his brain caught up with her train of thought.

Reaching down between them, Nadia slid the zipper of his pants down just a little more, enough to get her whole hand inside, wrapping her fingers around his rapidly swelling length. Philippe shivered again, half because of the fire her words were building inside his veins, and half because of her icy fingers around his erection.

"If I'm cold when you enter me, I'll be as tight as I was on our first time," she emphasised, tightening her grip on his heavy stalk, drawing a moan of anticipation from his lips. "My hot, wet walls gripping you, giving you the equivalent of a blow job while you fuck me. Our bodies moving against one another, building the friction until..." she left the thought open-ended.

Philippe's low guttural growl sent a rush of heat to her clenched womb.

"I can't think of a better way to get warm, can you?" she asked him.

"Is that what it would really feel like?"

"Wouldn't you like to find out for yourself?"

"Hell yeah, but can we do it in the shower please. I wouldn't be able to really enjoy myself unless I knew you were as warm on the outside as you are on the inside."

Nadia rolled her eyes but smiled. "Wouldn't that defeat the purpose of having sex while I'm cold?"

"Trust me sweetheart, I have no intention of giving the water a chance to warm you up before I have my way with you."

"Oh, in that case the first one in the shower gets to set the water temperature. My choice is extra cold," she said, giving his hard length another squeeze with her fist, effectively shutting down his higher cognitive function as his primitive southern brain was distracted. It only gave her a few seconds head start toward the shower but that was all she needed.

Just as her fingers closed around the bottle of shower gel, the door to the shower swung open and a naked Philippe stepped into the large stall.

"Uhh ahh, that comes later," he murmured, easily removing the bottle from her hand as he tested the water temperature. Not too warm and not too cold. Perfect.

Philippe playfully pushed Nadia up against the wall with his body, his thick erection pressing into her belly, the contact of skin against skin causing it to jerk in anticipation of an even tighter confinement. From the corner of her eye Nadia could see the thick chains on either side of her, the wrist cuffs on the ends dangling open, inviting their use. *No chance,* Nadia thought. Besides, she and Philippe were going to be far too occupied with something much more pleasurable than bondage, in oh, about twenty seconds from now. Okay, maybe less than that, she realised when Philippe lifted her up, wrapping her legs about his hips.

"You weren't kidding when you said you weren't going to waste any time," she squealed with delight when he lifted her from the floor.

"It's your fault, you've got me so damn horny," Philippe told her, reaching underneath to grip his turgid arousal and placing it at her entrance.

The swollen folds of her sex, silky soft and slick with moisture, opened like the most delicate petals as he pushed the blunt tip of his heavy length between them to reach her weeping centre.

Nadia's eyes met his and held them steady as he slowly slid inside her. She wasn't wrong about her inner walls feeling like a fist around him. It was warm and wet, and so damned tight he couldn't hold back a moan of appreciation.

Nadia was half in and half out of the flow of water, the combination making the circulating cool air in the shower stall feel even colder and she shivered. Her inner walls suddenly contracted around Philippe's thick length in response and his knees nearly gave out from under him. The only thing holding him up was the wall he had Nadia pressed firmly against. "Fuck. That feels so good," he groaned, his voice barely more than a husky whisper.

Philippe pressed his hips forward, his eye's practically rolling back into his head at the feel of her snug, slick heat sucking him deeper into her body, almost destroying him with pleasure.

Drawing back, he plunged inside her a little harder, a little faster. Then again. And again. Soon he was driving into her with deep, hard, powerful strokes, angling his body to give her the most incredible pleasure as his groin brushed over her clit with just enough pressure to make her body hum with sensation.

With her back against the cold tiles, another shiver rippled through her body, culminating in a further contraction of her already tight channel and sending Philippe's libido into a frenzy. Nadia gripped his shoulders to gain some leverage but it wasn't enough. Beside her the chains rattled from their forceful pounding against the wall. Instinctively, Nadia reached out and grabbed them, wrapping them around her wrists to steady herself further, grounding herself against Philippe's vigorous thrusts.

With Nadia's body secured, Philippe shifted his centre of gravity lower, his hands gripping the globes of her backside, angling his hips to thrust deeper, her welcoming body taking every inch of him until he was buried to the hilt inside her. Nadia's breath quickened as she met him thrust for thrust. "More. Please," she begged.

"As you wish."

Nadia's smile turned into a gasp as she threw back her head and convulsed in pleasure. As the first waves of orgasm erupted inside her, Nadia felt his thrusts change, become harder, shorter, and then he jerked beneath her. A primal growl rumbling from Philippe's chest a second before she felt the first pulse of his seed jet deep into her womb. His whole body shuddered with ecstasy, his thick girth pulsing within the grip of her tight inner walls like a hot, velvet vice.

Firework-like sensations rocketed through Philippe's body. "I'm not done with you yet. That was your punishment for going to that church."

"But…" Nadia wanted to defend her decision, but Philippe didn't give her a chance, hushing her with a finger on her lips.

"Now, I want to thank you," he told her between heavy, laboured breaths.

From the intense, heated look in his eyes she expected him to pounce on her and have wild, out of control sex, again. However, she couldn't have been more wrong. Instead, he switched off the shower, carefully dried her off and carried her into the bedroom and laid her gently on the bed. All the while those intense eyes just drank her in. His naked body straddled her thighs, pinning her in place as he began to gently caress her face, then her shoulders. Sliding down her body he gave her hips and stomach his attention. Then he teased the peaks of her breasts with the tips of his fingers, pinching them lightly, tenderly, all the while he made a point not to touch the tingling space between her thighs, no matter how much she arched into him. "I love the feel of your skin."

"Then touch me everywhere," she begged.

"Sweetheart, don't fret. I intend to, but I don't want to rush. You taught me how to be the man you always thought I was. Now I want you to savour every moment by showing you the man I've become."

And he did.

Philippe touched, stroked and massaged every inch of her body with his hands. Then he began the whole process again. This time with his lips.

As he shifted his weight on the bed, spreading her legs he slid between them, his lips poised above the little curl-shrouded mound. Watching her reaction, he let a finger slide through the slick moisture laden folds.

Nadia's breathing quickened and her body rocked into his caress. Joining his tactile fingers, his tongue tormented, teased, pushed her into a storm of sensation where the world disintegrated into the background of escalating pleasure. Nadia's desperate cries only encouraged Philippe to continue his ministrations, sending her speeding toward exquisite bliss as blistering waves rolled through her.

Philippe's tongue stroked over the bundle of sensitive nerves, the most incredible pleasure blazed through her. It was unlike any sensation she'd ever known. As he sucked the swollen bud, his tongue lashed against it, throwing her senses into overdrive by the friction he was causing.

"Oh God, you're good at this. Don't stop."

Sweetheart, I have no intention of stopping. Ever! Philippe thought to himself, answering her by increasing his efforts.

Fisting the sheet beneath her, Nadia's whimpers and gasps tumbled from her lips. Shudders began to work through her body. She couldn't bear it, it was too much. The suckling heat of his mouth, the hungry flicks of his tongue and his pleasure filled growls vibrated through her core, sending her careening toward a precipice she had no hope of holding onto. Nadia cried out as her orgasm struck with the force of an atomic bomb, sending her headlong into a cataclysm of rapture.

He waited for the crescendo of sensation to subside and then eased up her body, settling between her thighs. A small whimper of anticipation broke the steamy silence, the folds at her entrance parting once more for the girth of his blunt crest.

His hands pressed into the pillow on either side of her head as he flexed his hips, pushing inside the moist, rippling entrance of her heated sex. Her flesh stretching as he impaled her with his heavy stalk, dragging a desperate cry from her lips.

Like the expert he was quickly becoming, Philippe began moving his hips in rhythmic motion, keeping a slow, sensual pace. He moved inside her, taking his time. Making her hungry for more. And she cursed him for it, even though it came out suspiciously like a moan. She wanted more. Needed more. She couldn't stop herself from begging for it. "Philippe," she cried.

Her wish was his command. As exhausted as he was from the fight with his brother, Philippe gave her every ounce of energy he had left, and then some. Need consumed him as he rocked into her harder, faster, until he came undone.

In one swift move his fangs punctured the soft skin of Nadia's neck. The dominant growls coming from deep within his chest were hotter than Hell, detonating her orgasm like a nuclear bomb. His own hit him just as hard. Pulling his fangs free he threw his head back and roared. His hips locked into the V of her thighs, he pumped his hot seed into the depths of her body as the convulsions of her sheath milked him of every last drop.

Both spent and both breathing hard, Philippe collapsed on top of Nadia, his sated length still buried deep inside her, his weight draped like a limp blanket. Beneath him, she floated on a cloud so light, she doubted she was ever coming down.

"Are you okay?" Nadia finally asked when he found the strength to pull free of her body and roll onto his side next to her.

"Never been better, why?"

"Because you just killed your brother?"

Philippe's eyes locked onto hers for a brief moment. Looking away he subconsciously began playing with a lock of her hair, wrapping it around his fingers. "I'll admit it makes me a little sad, although I think it's the version of him that only existed in my mind that I'll mourn. I always wanted to believe he was a better man than he ever truly was. I can't help wondering if I could've done more to keep him from doing what he did."

"You know, the test of a true hero is to struggle with feelings of loss and hardship and overcome them, not to avoid them. And for the record, there was nothing that you or anyone else could have done for Nicholas. He chose his own path," Nadia told him.

"When and how did you become so wise?"

"I've been listening to you for years," she told him simply.

"I'm no hero though."

"You're my hero," she told him honestly. "And you know I'm always here if you want to talk about it."

"I know, and I promise I won't try to bury my feelings if that's what you're worried about. I'm just not sure how I feel yet, there's such a jumble of emotions inside me and I'm not sure what to do with them all. I had so much rage and hatred toward Nicholas stored up, there were times I couldn't think straight. I felt betrayed by him, abandoned. I know that sounds strange, but for so many years it was just him and me. I really thought I knew him, how wrong I was."

"You're not the only one, he had us all fooled. In hindsight, I'm sure we can all say we saw signs of the monster that lurked behind his pretty face, but he was so good at covering up his true nature that those signs were easily dismissed. After what he did here at the manor, when he got me to read Morganna's book again for that potion, I have to admit I was afraid of him. I also felt really sad for *you* that he'd done what he had. I knew that the rift between the two of you would be irreconcilable after that. Although, I have to admit too, I can't help being grateful that he tried to kill me…twice."

Philippe's brow creased together, puzzled at her statement. "Why would you ever say that. I nearly lost you *twice*."

Nadia cupped his face in her hands and kissed his lips gently. "Because my wonderful *mate*, if it wasn't for him, I wouldn't have become an *Ei'Ambriath*, and you wouldn't have found a way to become an adult vampire, and we wouldn't have had the chance to become *mates* at all. And, if it wasn't for him shooting me between the eyes, right in the centre where my new sight seems to be coming from, my vision wouldn't have improved. It's like it recalibrated my sight somehow."

"What do you mean?"

Nadia chuckled. "Now I can see everything more clearly. I'm still seeing your aura when I look at you, but now I can see you, in the flesh, too. And I can see plastic and nylon and polyester, and all the other man made synthetics."

"Seriously?"

"Yep." Nadia snuggled into Philippe's side, draping her arm across his chest. Lifting her hand, she stared at her mother's engagement ring on her finger and sighed. "Are you happy?" she asked him quietly.

"Deliriously. Why do you ask?"

"Well, because everything has happened so fast. In just a few short weeks both our lives have completely changed."

"Are you worried that once things settle down I won't be so keen to marry you?" Philippe twisted his neck so he could see into Nadia's eyes.

"No," she reassured him with another kiss. "I was just wondering if you felt like you needed to slow things down a bit, wait awhile before we get married."

"Actually, I was hoping we could keep the momentum going."

"What do you mean?"

"Tomorrow's December 1st, right?"

"Right."

"What do you say about having our wedding on New Years Eve?"

Nadia laughed. "Start our married life off with some real fireworks. You don't think we've already had enough of those in the last few weeks, figuratively speaking?"

"You don't like the idea?"

"I love it, but what's the hurry. Are you still afraid my dad's going to try to cut off your *flagpole*, if we don't get married right away?"

This time Philippe laughed. Lifting her hand up, he played with the ring on her finger.

"A little, but in truth, I can't wait to put another two rings on that finger. One's that I've bought for you myself."

"Two? Why two? The tradition is one engagement ring and one wedding ring," she told him.

"True. But there's also a tradition to add an eternity ring to that collection."

"Yes, but you're not supposed to be given that ring until a few years after you're married."

"Nadia, I've already waited an eternity to find you. I don't want to wait another minute to show the world how lucky I am."

"And you want to do that by showering me with jewellery? My sisters are going to be so jealous," she chuckled. Nadia held her hand up a bit higher to imagine what it would look like with a couple of new additions.

"I'm pretty sure your sisters are already a little envious of you, especially after what you did to Nicholas this afternoon. And once word spreads, every supernatural between here and Fey will be in awe of you."

"Don't say that," she chastised in a doubtful tone, giving his bare chest a slap.

"It's true. Think about it. How many people can do what you did today?"

"Paige can. Or, she should be able to."

"When you teach her."

"How am I going to do that, somehow I don't think I'm going to get too many volunteers to use as guinea pigs. If Vanessa and Nicholas' high-pitched screams are anything to go by, I'd say it's a fairly painful experience having your soul separated from your body."

Philippe thought for a moment, a slow smile creasing the corners of his lips. "Ask Alex. He's immortal so it won't affect him. Plus, if you tell him it's for a science experiment he'll be dying to give it a go."

"Also, telling him it's likely to hurt won't be a deterrence either. In fact, he'll probably find the experience quite *arousing*," Nadia added with a chuckle.

"Yeah, I don't quite get that whole BDSM thing he and Abby have going, but each to their own."

"I don't know, you seemed to really get into it when I was holding onto the chains on the wall in the shower. And, I have to confess it did make the sex more enjoyable, a little. The chains made it feel more raunchy and erotic somehow, and boy did it feel good when you were able to go deeper inside me."

Philippe's eyes glittered with unabashed agreement. "True. Maybe we should stay in this suite for a while longer, test out some of the other features Alex and Abby installed."

"Now, let's not go overboard on this, but....I did notice the hooks in the ceiling where they used to hang their sex swing from," Nadia pointed out.

"Do you think they'd mind if we borrowed it, just to test it out?" Philippe suggested.

"Probably not. If you get the swing, I'll borrow one of Abby's leather dominatrix outfits."

"What, do you mean now?" Philippe sat up so fast, Nadia nearly tumbled out of bed.

"Is there a better time? No one's home except us, they're all still at the party," she winked.

The enthusiastic growl rumbling from Philippe's chest sent Nadia's blood pumping. Even if he hadn't agreed she wouldn't have cared. Today was the first day of the rest of a wonderfully happy, and extremely long life with the man of her dreams. In the space of a month, she had gone from being a perpetually single, insecure woman with more hang-ups than Imelda Marcos had pairs of shoes, to being confident and content, and happier than she had ever imagined possible. Plus, in another month she would be married to the man who had made it all possible.

Her future life may have its ups and downs, but one thing she knew for certain, throughout it all there would always be one person by her side. Philippe.

How did she get so lucky.

25

Dray, Saladin, Alaric and Hawke arrived back at the party just in time for the speeches. Not that any of them heard a single word being said. Entertaining stories of Mrs Philpot's life were followed by laughs and cheers. One by one her family spoke and finally Mrs Philpot herself.

Unbeknownst to her, behind the scenes the lycan military remained vigilant in and around the Drunken Duck. With Morganna and Scorpion once again in the wind and a large number of Alliance members at the party, they couldn't afford to take any chances with everyone's safety. They were all sitting ducks if the evil duo decided to attack. Fortunately, it seemed, they either weren't interested in the easy pickings or they had other, more pressing matters to attend to.

Whilst most remained at the pub, Oliver ordered several of the lycans to do what they do best, clean up the evidence of the brothers battle at the old church. As expected, two bodies were found. Nicholas, and the poor stooge he had used to lure Nadia. The latter they removed and staged his death at another location to be found by the authorities, careful to leave no trail back to them. While Nicholas' body was burned to ashes. They weren't leaving any chance that he could come back from the dead to plague them again.

After the events of the afternoon, Dray was not thinking with a logical frame of mind. In fact, it was debatable whether there were any true thoughts firing between the synapses in his brain at all. Instead, the remnants of adrenaline seemed to be driving him to function under the guidance system of heightened emotions.

He wasn't the only one. Alaric hadn't spoken since they left the old churchyard, whatever was inside the chapel had spooked the crap out of him. And, since Philippe and Nadia had returned to the manor it was left to Dray to reassure Gustav that all was well. Regardless of the good news, Dray still got the distinct impression that the lycan leader's own emotional state remained less than optimal, understandably.

One other at the party battled emotional turmoil, specifically a sense of pervading inevitability. Marek stared down at the screen on his phone. He didn't need to read the words again to understand them, but he did anyway.

I crushed your precious binding stone. Tell me, how do you feel? Did you notice when I destroyed it? Think of it as an opportunity for personal growth, Scorpion wrote.

Marek couldn't speak, his body shook too violently with rage. He did feel it, how could he not. Only a moment before the text came through Marek was wracked with a sudden overwhelming pain. He didn't need Scorpion's taunting message to tell him what had happened, he already knew. Every cell in his body vibrated uncontrollably as his soul snapped back to his body. He was mortal again.

Marek vented his anger with a silent barrage of blistering curses. On the inside he seethed, but on the outside, he remained his usual calm self. He had spent so many centuries hiding his emotions it came as second nature to him now.

It wasn't his loss of mortality he was angry about though, not really. From the moment Scorpion had let on he had his binding stone, he knew this moment was inevitable, and he had resigned himself to it. It was Scorpion's really shitty timing that made him angry.

The majority of guests had left the pub, leaving behind only the usual familiar faces. Marek helped collect dirty plates and glasses, stacked away chairs and relocated tables. All the while he watched from the corner of his eye, waiting for the right moment to get Shani alone, but time was running out. He only had one chance to win her over if there was any chance of making his plan work.

Shani walked toward the far corner of the room, cloth in hand to clean down the benches. This was it, if he was ever going to do this, it had to be now.

"Shani, can I have a word with you for a moment?" he asked politely as he came up behind her. Momentarily startled, Shani turned quickly at the sound of his deep voice. "Sorry, I didn't mean to scare you."

"Hey Marek. Don't worry about it, I guess my mind was a million miles away," she smiled, her heart pounding vigorously within the confines of her chest, loud enough to wonder whether the rephaim could hear it too.

For a moment he just stood there staring at her, wondering how to start a conversation that no doubt, to her, would likely be considered inappropriate and probably a little bizarre.

"You wanted to speak with me?" she prompted, putting down her cleaning cloth to focus her attention on Marek.

Clearing his throat, Marek leaned down toward her to keep his voice low. There was no easy way to say this, so why not just come out with it, he figured.

"I've spoken to Abby. I know about your situation and I can help you," he told her simply. His sharp eyes watched her like a hawk, assessing her every twitch and blink at his unnerving announcement. Marek had to admit he was impressed. She was almost as good at covering her feelings as he was. His plan just might have a chance of working after all.

Shani inhaled a small gasp and took a step back from him. In the blink of an eye her expression shifted from surprise to annoyance and finally to reluctant acceptance that her secret had been shared. She wanted to be angry with Abby, but couldn't. Somewhere, deep inside she felt relief that someone else knew. While it didn't change her circumstances, somehow it made the burden she carried seem a little lighter.

"What did she tell you?"

"Everything she knows."

Shani picked up the cleaning cloth again and began wiping the bench, daring not to look at Marek's face. She didn't need his pity.

"Shani, I can help you."

At the sound of Marek's steadfast tone, Shani stopped cleaning and reluctantly looked up. She dared not take a breath, a rush of sudden emotion threatening to fill her eyes with years of unshed tears. It wasn't pity she saw in his face, it was determination and confidence.

"I don't need help. I'm fine. Everything is fine," she answered sadly, her voice barely above a whisper. Her resignation to the contrary nearly broke Marek's heart. He doubted there was anyone aside from her cousin, Abby and now himself, who knew the horrid truth of her life.

"Shani, you can trust me. I only want to help you."

"Why? Why would you want to help me, what could you do? Nothing. There's nothing you or anyone else can do. My life isn't perfect I know, but I've come to terms with it and I'm content."

"I don't believe that for a second." Marek's dark eyes drilled into her soul with the precision of a knife. "You remind me so much of my *mate* Jenifer. Strong and determined, but foolishly pigheaded," he said, one side of his mouth curling up in a reminiscent smile. "Answer this one question, wouldn't you like the chance to be free of your husband and have a chance at real happiness with Dray?" he asked.

Shani stared down at the cleaning cloth in her hand and began picking at the lint collecting along its edges, unable to answer him honestly without also acknowledging the truth to herself.

"I know you don't want Dray to know your secret and I understand why. I promise I will never tell him. But, secrets have a cost Shani, they're not for free. Someone always pays the price. I know that better than anyone," Marek told her.

Marek was right, far more than he realised. Shani's shoulders slumped as the weight of her world crushed down upon her. Once again, she reluctantly looked up to meet his gaze. "A life with Dray? That would be wonderful…In a perfect world," she confessed.

"A perfect world doesn't exist, but we can make the one we live in better if we try."

"I don't understand."

"It's simple, time decides who you meet in your life, your heart decides who you want in your life, and your behaviour decides who stays in your life." Marek told her. Shani dropped her head down and nodded in agreement. "You're not happy with your current life, maybe it's time to make a few changes, don't you think?"

"You don't know what my life is like. It's not that simple. I don't get to choose what I do or who I can be with. I'm trapped."

Marek let out an involuntary squawk of reproval. "Bullshit!" If anyone knew what it was like to be trapped, it was him. He'd literally been trapped for centuries in a cell, tortured over and over by Morganna until she finally got bored with him and let him go. Even then he wasn't free. He was imprisoned inside the Valley of Vardin, a renegade nephilim labelled a traitor, a rephaim. He'd made the mistake many years earlier of blindly following Morganna, and it had cost him everything. First his freedom. Then, he nearly lost his sanity at her hands through years of torture. Finally, it cost him his *mate* and his son.

"You have no idea what my life is like," she told him again, her voice hardening with anger.

"I can take an educated guess." Marek rattled off a list of scenarios she probably found herself living through on a regular basis.

"How could you know all that?" she asked apprehensively.

"I've lived through it too, and much, much more."

She didn't expect to hear him say that. Shani's jaw dropped open and she stared at him with astonishment, as though seeing him for the first time from a whole new perspective.

"You can only let someone throw stones at you so many times before you pick them up and start building a wall so they can't do it again. I can see you've made a pretty thick wall for yourself. The question is, are you ready to throw a few stones back his way?" Marek asked.

"How can you help me?" she asked curiously, her scepticism lessening, although not yet defeated, as a glimmer of hope lightened the weight of dread in her soul.

"I have my own gifts. I'm a skinwalker, which means I'm very talented in the art of deception."

"How so?" she asked.

"I can assume someone else's outward appearance, adopt their mannerisms and even access that person's memories."

"Wow, really? Teagan told me you were a skinwalker, although I didn't know exactly what that was. I thought you could make yourself invisible or something. Can you assume anyone's identity?"

Marek laughed at her assumption. "Yes, but my gift has its limitations. In the process of assimilating someone's DNA, that person dies. Very painfully," he told her matter-of-factly. "Although, I make a point of only assimilating criminals and murderers," he clarified quickly when Shani's face clouded with a wary expression. *Well, mostly*, but he kept that to himself.

"And, how is this supposed to help me?"

"I plan on coming to India with you, if you're agreeable, and...."

"Kill Saadir and assimilate him?" she jumped in with another assumption, her tone hardening.

"No. Abby told me you don't want that piece-of-scum husband of yours, dead. Although, if you change your mind I'd be happy to accommodate that for you," he smirked. "In the meantime, I was hoping you'd nominate someone else I could assimilate. Someone close to Saadir, who knows all his business dealings, who he and the rest of his associates trust. Someone who can come and go easily from your home."

"To what end?" she asked, her curiosity rising.

"To work against Saadir from within his own organisation. Bring his empire crumbling down around him and put him in a position that will force him to grant you a divorce, if that's what you want."

"I do."

Shani turned her back away from Marek and walked toward the nearby fireplace. Her eyes followed the flame as it danced lazily in the hearth while she considered her options. Sadly though, the heat of the fire barely made a dent in thawing her ambivalence. "I agree, it's time to make some changes in my life, but you still haven't told me why you want to help me?"

"Let's just say I don't like tyrants who bully young women."

"That's not a good enough reason. Why would you put yourself at risk for me, someone you barely know? What do you stand to gain from helping me?"

Marek really didn't want to dredge up his past, but he could see that without honest disclosure Shani wasn't likely to trust him. And the truth was, if he was going to be able to help her, she would need to be able to trust him with her life, and he trust her with his. Literally. He was asking her to play a very dangerous game of deception.

Marek let out a long sigh, his eyes locking onto Shani's puzzled gaze. "Peace of mind," he answered simply. "After Morganna tortured and killed my *mate* Jenifer, I vowed never to let the same thing happen to any other woman. I am forced to live every day without my *mate*, and my son without his mother." Marek let out another heavy sigh. "The bottom line is, I couldn't do anything to save Jenifer, but when I see someone such as yourself who I can help, I can't sit idly by and do nothing. I'm offering you a chance to create a better life, if I was you, I'd take it."

Shani nodded. Whether she was nodding in agreement or to fortify her resolve despite the odds of success, she wasn't sure. What she was sure of, was she would be a fool to pass up Marek's offer.

"I'm flying back tonight. When were you planning on coming?" she asked.

Marek's smile broadened. "I made the pre-emptive assumption of buying a ticket for the same flight tonight. We'll have eight hours for you to get me up to speed on everything, and decide which lucky bastard I'll be impersonating for the foreseeable future."

Shani shook his outstretched hand, sealing their new arrangement.

Holy crap! What the hell was she doing? This could only go one of two ways. It was either the best decision she'd ever made or the worst mistake possible. Regardless, she had to take the chance. It wasn't just her anymore. She was going home to a daughter who needed her. It made no difference to Shani that the child's mother was probably a whore her husband had coerced. The result was an innocent child. A female child. That fact on its own tugged at Shani's heart strings. If she didn't love and care for the baby girl, no one would. Her father, Saadir, certainly never would. The girl would be doomed to live a similar life to her own. Resented and rejected by her father and when she was old enough, she'd be married off to the highest bidder. Shani wasn't going to let that happen.

Dray didn't catch much of Shani and Marek's conversation, although he overheard enough to know she was leaving tonight, and Marek would be escorting her. He wasn't sure how he felt about that. Grateful? Jealous?

Stepping out of the shadows, Dray approached Shani as casually as ever.

He should walk away, leave her alone. But he knew he couldn't do that. Not yet. Shani was a fever in his blood he simply couldn't cure, at least not until he had her. Perhaps if he took her to his bed once, he could purge his need for her, as he had every other female. But he couldn't do that. Even as the thought entered his mind, he discarded it just as quickly. He would never do that, not to Shani. If anything, having sex with her, even once, would likely seal his bond to her. And that, he couldn't risk.

Stiffly, Shani stepped back a pace, feeling like she didn't have the courage or the heart for good-byes. *Fake it*, she thought to herself, but she had a sudden urge to run.

As though Dray had heard her thoughts, he caught her by the wrist. His grip gentle but firm, effectively locking her in place.

Swallowing hard, Shani looked down to where their bodies met. The effect on her was more devastating than the conversation she was trying to avoid. Could he feel how her pulse had suddenly quickened from his touch?

Shani tried to pull away but Dray's grip tightened about her wrist, not painfully but quite firmly. She was so close, he could feel her body heat radiating off her.

"I believe you're leaving tonight." His voice was low and the strained undertone stung Shani's heart. Whether he was feeling hurt that she was leaving or his pride had been dented by hearing the news from someone other than her, she couldn't tell. Since she might not see him again anyway, what did it really matter. What if she never saw him again? There was no guarantee that whatever Marek had in mind to free her of Saadir, would work. Another twinge of pain tightened her chest.

"Yes, I am. I've done the job you brought me here to do. Now I have to go home," she told him, her gaze cast downward unable to meet his eyes. If she did, she would probably start to cry. That wasn't an option.

Dray's hand on her wrist loosened, although he refrained from letting go, instead his thumb began to caress small circles on the soft underside. Shani's body began to heat from the inside out and without realising it she began to sway toward him.

"You're wondering what it would be like…You and me. Just once," Dray stated, but it came out sounding more like a wishful plea.

"Truth?" she looked up at him. For a moment she forgot how to breathe. She couldn't answer him, not yet. Her feelings were too raw, too painful. Instead, she turned her head away and remained silent for a moment longer. "Yes."

Dray nodded, inhaling her scent deeply. With her body so close and her confession spoken so softly, he would accept whatever she was willing to offer him.

Dray stepped in closer, but not so close that they were touching. He kept a respectable six inches of clear air between them, but only by sheer will. The need to touch her, hold her and kiss her, was almost too much to bear. In the effort to keep his distance, he was caught off guard when she lifted her free hand to cup his face in her palm.

Dray's whole body shook, all those thick muscles and heavy bones vibrating with need.

"You have no idea how much I want you," Shani told him softly.

Oh, I bet it's not half as much as I want you, he thought, as she slid her hand behind his neck and gently drew him down to her level, Dray bending easily under the subtle tugging pressure. Tilting his head toward her he lay a gentle kiss on her lips.

At first the kiss was hesitant, tentative. Little more than a feather-light caress of lips, but quickly it gave way to a more urgent stroking of open mouths and heated demand.

A purring sound rumbled from Dray's chest as he brought himself hard up against Shani's body, her arms sliding eagerly about his neck.

More! Dray needed so much more.

Shani reached down and lightly stroked her fingers down his abdomen. When he didn't remove her hand, she slid her hand under his shirt, splaying her fingers over his rigid abdomen.

Dray let out a shuddering gasp when she slid her fingers along the inside of his waistband and a jolt of pure delight flushed her cheeks, knowing she could affect him so strongly.

"You're playing with fire," he hissed, half warning, half plea.

Normally Dray's face was unreadable, but today it was a billboard of frustration. Maybe it was wrong or simply a sign of bad character, but a shiver of excitement shot up Shani's spine, knowing that she'd elicited such a strong emotional reaction.

"I'm sorry, I shouldn't have done that," she replied, pulling back from him ever so slightly. They were no longer touching, but the temptation to reach out for him again was overwhelming. With a low hiss she slammed the door on her traitorous thoughts. Instead, she watched in fascination as the muscle in Dray's jaw twitched and his gaze softened.

"If I asked you to stay?" Dray said.

"I can't, I'm sorry. More sorry than you could ever know," she replied, her voice cracking on a stifled sob.

"Because you belong to another man," His voice was quiet, barely above a whisper.

Dray hit the nail on the head with that statement. If he only knew how right he was. In Saadir's eye, Shani was property to be controlled, nothing more. There was no love between them, no desire to share each other's thoughts and dreams. There was nothing but obligation and contempt. And here was Dray, the only man she believed she would ever love standing only inches from her, but he might as well be on the moon.

"Can we just have a few more minutes together?" she asked.

A storm of emotion crackled in his eyes as he stared down at her. Transfixed, she didn't move. She couldn't move.

Everything in her body spontaneously melted and she swayed unsteadily.

Dray pulled her to him, whether to keep her upright or because he needed the excuse to touch her one last time, she didn't know and didn't care. All she could do was revel in the way her soft curves filled the spaces between the hard lines of his body.

For a long time they stood there, her head against his chest, their arms wrapped about each other like a lifeline tethering them together.

She couldn't explain it, nor did she care. She felt like she was a lightning rod in the middle of a thunderstorm, soaking up all the energy pouring from him, and she was completely content to just stay there.

Shani took a slow, deep breath as their eyes locked. His eyes were so dark she could barely distinguish his pupil from his iris, except for the flickers of iridescence that floated in them.

"I have to go," she told him sadly.

Stepping back, he removed his hands, breaking their connection and the loss made her want to cry.

His touch felt like home. She couldn't describe the feeling, let alone understand it, but in his arms she felt like she was where she was supposed to be.

Pulling back from Shani felt like his flesh was being peeled from his bones. It ripped at his soul and pained him in a way he had never thought possible. He couldn't breathe from the effort of restraining himself from touching her.

Dray's gaze roamed Shani's face. He lifted a hand, as though to touch it and then froze, his hand suspended, his gaze ricocheting to her eyes. "Shani," he said, his voice loaded with regret, it was half plea and half lament.

Shani looked away. "This is so much harder than I thought it would be."

She thought he'd argue but instead he nodded and took a step back to give her space.

It was the right thing, she knew. So why did it hurt so much?

She could give in to her lust, to her deepest, darkest desire, and throw herself into his arms. Then return to India and her horrid life, with the best memory she could ever give herself. But that would be selfish. It would only put him in danger too, that she knew for certain. No, it was time for her to be strong. She was tired of being weak. This was her new beginning.

"Dray," she began, looking up into his dark eyes, his jaw clenching tight with conflicting emotions. "Um, I'm not sure what you'll make of this, but I believe that the next artefact you need to find isn't on the Templar's tablet. It's something called a Thunderstone. I don't know what it is or where you'll find it, but the impression I'm getting is it's well hidden."

"The Thunderstone, are you sure?" he asked, his heavy brow slamming down over his eyes.

"Yes, I have a strong feeling that it's very important that you find it, and soon. I believe it's the object that Morganna and Scorpion are looking for. You need to find it before they do. I hope that makes sense to you," she told him.

"It does." Dray reached out a hand toward her again, his mind in turmoil. Somewhere deep inside he knew her touch would help settle the anxiety and unrest bubbling beneath the surface, but he stopped just short of making contact.

Shani's body stiffened as she dragged in a sharp breath. She wanted so much to feel the warmth of his body, the stroke of his hand against her cheek and the strength in his arms as he held her close. Just one more time. "I'm sorry, I have to go," she told him, forcing the words through the stricture in her throat.

Turning, Shani walked away, letting the tears fall freely. She refused to wipe them away. Even though there might not be any happy ending for her, she had no intention of disrupting Dray's life, especially now that her own was about to become so much more complicated.

Dray watched her walk away, his mind and heart at odds with one another.

Without even trying, Shani had captured his attention to the point of distraction, which was both unusual and unnerving. Many females had come and gone through his life, very few of whom he could even recall their name nor appearance. At most, he could say they were all attractive in their own way, and while they had all been attracted to him, he had seen them as nothing but a convenience of the moment. He'd fed from them and had sex with them, but he'd never once shared his thoughts or his heart with any of them.

This preoccupation he'd developed with Shani, his mind fixated on a woman he couldn't have, it wasn't healthy. From the moment he met her he'd felt like he was staring at blue skies, but really it was just the eye of the storm and shit was coming at him full force from the opposite direction.

He'd been such a fool to let himself feel something again. He had to get Shani out of his system. Wipe the slate clean. He had to let her go. Not just from his heart but from his thoughts as well. Cut off any connection to anyone or anything that would remind him of her. Let her slip from his life as though she had never existed. The alternative was to mourn the loss of the only woman who should have been his *mate*, which would destroy him. That wasn't an option.

She mentioned the Thunderstone, what if we need her to help locate it or something else down the track, he thought.

That issue seemed to have already been taken care of. With Marek going with her, the rephaim could act as their go-between.

Why Marek had chosen to go with her to India never crossed Dray's mind. The wall he was building around himself had already blocked out his natural curiosity.

"Marek," Alaric called when he saw the rephaim heading for the door. "Hold up, I want a quick word with you."

"What can I help you with?" he asked Alaric, turning to face him.

"Nothing actually. I just wanted to tell you I agree with your decision to go with Shani back to India."

"You know about that?"

"Of course. Not much escapes my notice," Alaric stated. *Except the existence of Scorpion,* he added to himself silently.

"Do you know why I'm going?"

"Abby filled me in…discretely." *Telepathically.*

Marek chuckled at Abby's tenacity. She had promised Shani she'd never reveal her secret to Dray, however she never said anything about not telling anyone else. At this rate, everyone, *except* Dray, was going to know before she even got on the plane.

"It's probably a good thing to get away from here for a while anyway. Out of sight and out of mind from Morganna would be a good thing for you right now since it seems she and Scorpion have teamed up together."

"That's not a very pleasant scenario. I did consider that fact too. Not that it will make too much difference on my life expectancy. I could be jumping from the frying pan into the fire on this trip," Marek told him sombrely.

"At least you've still got your immortality."

"Ahh yeah, about that…." Marek grabbed a cheese knife from the platter on the table and dragged the tip across his palm. Blood oozed lazily from the shallow wound. It didn't heal. "Scorpion crushed my binding stone a couple of hours ago. I'm mortal again."

"Fuck. Marek, I'm sorry." Alaric told him, his voice full of remorse. "This is all my fault."

"How do you figure that? You're not the one with a psychotic vendetta against the world, who hates me with a passion. And you're not the one who stole and *destroyed* my binding stone."

"No, but I am the one responsible for creating Scorpion."

Marek blinked once, twice and then stared into Alaric's stricken face. "Excuse me? Who exactly, is Scorpion?"

Alaric took a steadying deep breath, his shoulders slumping on the exhale. "I believe he was the very first vampire I ever created. Only, I didn't know I created him. You know the story of how I was created and how my first wife Jessica was killed." Marek nodded. "Well, I was in a rage at what had been done to her and I wasn't thinking straight, all I could think about was getting revenge for her death."

"So, who is Scorpion?" Marek asked again.

"He's Judas Iscariot."

"As in, one of the twelve disciples who followed your first brother-in-law around?"

"Yes. The same one who betrayed my wife and me to the Romans when he betrayed Jesus."

"Holy Mother Fucker!"

"Yeah, exactly."

"But how did he become a vampire? The bible states he hung himself."

"He did. With some help," Alaric told him grimly. "I went after everyone I thought responsible for Jessica's death. Judas was on top of my list, along with the Centurions who actually stoned her. I found Judas hiding in a grotto near Gethsemane. I remember I dropped my spear when I grabbed him, he picked it up and slashed me with it. I didn't think anything of it at the time. He struggled in my grip uselessly, and I hung him in the tree. I stayed there and watched him die. Then I left."

"Do you think he swallowed some of your blood in the struggle?"

"In hindsight he must have. No one else could've turned him. I am the first vampire, and I'd only been a vampire for a few days myself when I found him. Back then I didn't even know I could make others like myself. It took me a couple of years to work that out. If I'd known, there's no way in Hell, I would've given him any chance of coming back to life, I would have ripped him limb from limb instead of hanging him. You can trust me on that."

"I have no doubt. It looks like we have more in common than we once thought. Scorpion, ah...Judas, is responsible for the murder of your first wife, and Morganna murdered mine."

"It seems that way, yes. The question is, what will it take to kill them both?"

"I have a feeling we need to figure that out sooner rather than later."

"Agreed. Shani thinks they're searching for the Thunderstone, and they may be close to finding it. If they do, we're going to have bigger problems to deal with than just them, if, as Alex believes, the Thunderstone has the ability to power the portal device...." Alaric began.

"They can open a portal to the Underworld and release every nasty-arse demon in there..." Marek interjected.

"And the nastiest demon of them all. Mephistopheles," Alaric finished.

Holy Hell!

Turn the page for an exclusive look at
The next title in the Eternal Series

HUNT FOR ETERNITY

Available from your favourite online retailer

1

Dray stepped outside the narrow cave's entrance, his eyes scanning the surrounding region thoroughly. The only living creatures within a mile was a tiny sand rat scurrying beneath the safety of a boulder, away from a hawk circling the skies nearby, and a couple of camels which had wandered from their tethers.

Walking quickly through the valley, he avoided the scattered groups of tourists and guides. Following the sand rat's example, he kept his visibility to a minimum as he climbed the ragged cliff face, making his way across the stony ridge to the plateau, almost one hundred and seventy feet above the hustle and bustle of people below. Not that anyone noticed him. If there was one thing he knew how to do in a land such as this, it was blend in, disappear into the background. Even if someone did notice him, he would likely appear to be nothing more than one of the locals with his white thoub robe and keffiyeh headwear. The only part of him visible was his face, and that too appeared nondescript. His native American skin tone blended well enough with the local's olive complexion, such that no one gave him a second glance.

Would he care if they did? Nope. He had ways of dealing with anyone nosy enough to attempt to talk to him. Not that many did, he gave off a definite vibe of *fuck-off,* which worked well as a curiosity repellent. For those not smart enough to walk the other way, mind compulsion was his first *go-to* response when dealing with unwanted or inconvenient attention. Compelling someone to forget they'd ever seen, talked to, or even heard of him, was a great asset to his arsenal. The alternative usually required body disposal and was best avoided whenever possible, especially in the desert. The ground was too damned hard to dig up. There were always the caves he supposed. He'd found more than one set of bones hidden away over the past couple of days, another couple of bodies would blend in well...after a decade or two of decomposition.

Fortunately, there hadn't been a need to give that option too much consideration.

It had taken two days of searching more than one hundred caves and tombs, but he'd found what he'd come looking for. It would have taken much longer if it hadn't been for sheer luck. Finding the Templar's clue in the mosaic floor in the Byzantine church definitely had been helpful. Although, as they had learned over recent years, the Templar's clues to find the artefacts which they'd so carefully hidden, often led them to dead-ends. Either because time and human habitation had erased the clues, or nature had. In one case the artefact never made it to the designated destination, the ship it was being carried on had sunk, so the pre-designed clue had been worthless. If it hadn't been for Shani and her gift of finding lost objects....

Dray shut down the thought before it took him into an area he didn't want to go, refocussing on his surroundings and finishing his current mission.

The Templars were smart. Petra had been so inaccessible it had become relatively forgotten for centuries. Which made it a perfect hiding place, especially after the earthquake of 363AD, crumbling many of the buildings and all but destroying the city's water management system. The city died almost overnight. In the time of the Templars, the city had become somewhat of a curiosity in the Middle East, but because of its location in the middle of a desert, it remained just that, a curiosity. Only a select few were crazy enough to temp their luck at finding it. Of those, there were many who did find it but never managed to leave. Their food and water rations already low from the trek to find it, ran out long before they could replenish them. Unless of course they happened to arrive during a rare rainfall. Although that too presented its own hazards. With sheer cliffs surrounding the valley and only one narrow passage in and out, flash flooding was likely to catch the weary travellers off guard.

Even today, more than eight hundred years later, this city was almost inaccessible.

Dray sat down on the plateau above Al-Khazneh, laying the sacred artefact carefully beside him and surveyed the land below. The last of the day's tourists were making their way toward the Siq gorge for the trek back to civilisation. A couple stopped to take one last photo, capturing in the dying light, the richly pigmented sandstone structures of the Rose-Red City of Petra.

And then he was alone.

The peaceful solitude and cooling, late afternoon desert breeze had a lulling effect, shifting his thoughts toward quiet reflection.

Shani stepped into his side as his arms wrapped around her.

It was a slow series of movements, but they had a profound effect on him. Her scent filled his nose. Her warm, soft body fit the hard contours of his like a hand in a glove, his senses so in tune with the way her shoulder fit under his arm and her head rested on his chest just under his chin...

Dray shook his head irritably, intent on dislodging the memory of the moment, indelibly burned into his brain. Turning his back on her was like putting his heart into cold storage. It wasn't quite dead, but it wasn't living either.

Despite the passage of three years, thoughts of Shani still dominated every one of his brain's higher functions, along with his body's base needs. Sadly, neither one could ever be appeased.

He consoled his *loss*, if you could call it that since Shani had never been his, by pretending he'd never felt the pull of the mating bond toward her, instead putting her out of his mind as if she had never existed. Obstinately he continued his daily routines as though nothing had changed. As though *he* hadn't changed.

At least, he had tried. He hadn't succeeded.

Dray began to question his own purpose. There had to be more to this life than work and the occasional aimless shag with strangers. What was the point of living for centuries if all it provided was empty embraces and quiet misery? No female could ever alleviate the hollow centre in his soul, but sometimes they were just the gym workout he needed.

When there was actual work to do, he functioned without any problems. His focus never wavered from his job. It was only when there were no immediate matters to deal with that his cognitive abilities began to wane.

He was self-aware enough however, to realise that this current funk in his mood was not likely to subside. The thought that this was his lot in life now, wishing for a woman he could never have, giving his palm calluses from his nightly workout on his ever-ready hard-on, made him want to scream....or kill something.

His frustration was reaching nuclear territory.

Which was how it came to be that *he* was the one in Petra, Jordan, to retrieve the recently located artefact. A change of scenery and routine was supposed to reset his volatile mood back to neutral. It seemed logical at the time. A desert location far away from civilisation and the pressures of his daily life should have been just the thing he needed to accomplish his goal. As it turned out though, too much of his past was tied to places similar to this. By coming here all he managed to accomplish was to dredge up regrets of a love he could never have, and distant memories of a life he'd lost and thought buried long ago.

Glancing at his watch he did a quick mental time zone conversion with England which was only two hours behind, it was still mid-afternoon there. Pulling his phone from his pocket he dialled Alaric.

"I hope you've got good news." Alaric was nothing if not straight to the point. Just the way Dray liked it. None of those annoying pleasantries or meaningless chit chat.

"I've got it. I'll head out to Amman tonight. I'll be on the first flight back tomorrow."

The line was silent for moment, which wasn't necessarily a good sign.

"Alaric, if you have an objection to that I can head across to Israel and charter a plane from there?"

"No, it's too risky. I have something else in mind. Stay put and I'll send someone to collect you."

"What, get one of the nephilim to open a portal? That's not possible, I'm in the middle of a desert. There are no forests for a thousand miles of here."

"Not exactly what I had in mind but, yes. I'll send someone who can open a portal. He'll arrive just after the sun has fully set."

Dray didn't object. He wasn't too happy about it either. "Who?"

"Raif's youngest brother Ky. See you soon."

Again, there was none of the pleasantries to end the conversation. The line just went dead. And again, Dray was good with that. He could bitch and curse as much as he wanted at the blank screen without running the risk of having his unflattering words overhead, which would lead to getting his arse chewed out later, or worse, losing his head, literally, because he'd pissed off the most powerful vampire on the planet.

Dray checked his watch again and looked to the horizon. By his calculations he had just over an hour. Great. What was he going to do to kill the time? He could think about all the things he's been trying too hard to forget about since arriving in Petra, or he could do what he'd seen other people do when they're bored.

He flicked through the apps on his phone, opening one Teagan had downloaded as a joke, which of course he swore he would never use. Candy Crush. What the Hell, it killed the time. Who knew that popping those bottles and saving those bears could make the time fly by so quickly. Before he knew it his concentration was broken by the sound of a sonic boom.

Just one more minute, I only have two more bears to find and three more moves left, Dray thought.

Okay, so he was beginning to understand the addiction to the ridiculous game. Not that he planned on confessing it to anyone though. Ever!

Putting his phone back in his pocket, Dray looked up. Overhead Ky circled the valley. It wasn't quite fully dark yet, he noted. Although it was a risk arriving early, clearly Alaric had decided the risk was minimal and worth taking. It was a remote location, so it probably didn't matter that there was a *mythical* dragon flying about the skies in full view. There wasn't anyone around for miles to see it.

Ky circled the plateau one more time before coming into land. For such a large beast, the dragon barely made a sound when it touched down. Its body shimmered and a moment later a dark headed wyvern man stood in its place.

"Dray, good to see you again," Ky said as he walked casually toward him.

"You too," he replied.

Ky sat down beside Dray and looked about the canyon below, drawing in a few deep breaths of the cool air.

"Wow, I love this place, it reminds me a little of my home. Our citadel in Avengard is carved into a mountain like this, as you know. Although, our granite is more robust and durable than this sandstone," Ky said, picking up a handful of the red dust and small stones, crumbling it between his fingers. "I think I would've liked the people who built this city. Who were they?"

"The Nabataeans."

"Hmmm, right. And what's so special about this blade you recovered?" Ky picked up the seraph blade from the ground beside Dray, turning it in his hand, testing its blade's handle length and weight ratio, and examined the intricate design engraved along the blade's length on either side.

Dray watched him carefully but didn't move to take the blade back. "You talk too much," he growled instead.

"Actually, I'm usually accused of not talking enough. I prefer nature to people."

Dray mumbled something under his breath about leaving his body in one of the caves, which Ky couldn't quite hear, but he caught the gist of the remark in his tone. Regardless, the wyvern wasn't deterred and kept up the conversation.

"Do you know what it says?" Ky asked, running his finger along the engravings.

"I didn't realise it said anything," Dray's brow creased as he reached to take the blade from Ky and re-examine it again himself. He had assumed it was just ornate decoration.

"It's an ancient angelic language. I've seen it written in old wyvern historical records."

"Can you read it?"

"No. I'm not sure there's anyone left who can. This blade must be eons old, but it still looks as good as the day it was made," Ky said in curious wonder.

Dray knew someone who could probably read it, and she just happened to live at the manor where they were headed. Nadia.

"We should get going."

"You don't want to stay a bit longer and soak up the atmosphere of the place?" Ky could never understand why people preferred to be in large cities with their concrete jungle of buildings, all crowded together like cattle. He preferred his jungles to be green and filled with birds and animals and most importantly, peaceful.

"I've already been here too long."

"If you're worried the Guild may be waiting for a chance to sneak up on us and steal the blade, I had a good view of the area before I landed and didn't see sign of anyone for miles. Even if there was, my dragon doesn't mind the occasional meal of evil arseholes," he chuckled, although not surprisingly Dray didn't so much as crack a smile, if anything his scowl deepened. "So, are you going to tell me what's so special about this blade, besides it having been crafted by angels?"

Dray waited a few moments debating whether or not to answer. Chances were the wyvern would shut up if he told him.

"It's a seraph blade."

Ky's eyes dropped to the blade in Dray's hands, widening in unison with his slack jaw dropping open on its hinges.

"Okaaay then, I think it's probably time we get going." Not waiting for a response, Ky was on his feet and headed for the centre of the plateau, Dray only a couple of steps behind. "Ever ridden a dragon before?" Ky asked.

"Can't say that I have," Dray grumbled.

"You're in for a treat then. I'll try not to make the ride too bumpy for you when we cross the dimensional barriers," Ky smiled. "You might want to stand back a bit first though. I don't want to squash you," he advised.

Dray stopped and watched as the air around the wyvern began to shimmer, growing larger and distorting everything within it. A second later an emerald dragon stood where the man had once been, his reptilian slitted eyes viewing him intently below a thick brow of bronze tinged spikes. With a quick flick of his head, Ky urged him to climb up on his back, extending out a foot for him to climb up. Not that Dray needed it.

Being a vampire, the ten-foot leap onto the dragon was barely more than putting a little extra spring in his step.

Ky's large dragon head swung around, waiting for Dray to get settled. The corner of his mouth curved up into a grin and winked. Dray wasn't sure what was more disturbing, the fact that a male dragon winked at him, or that his broad grin exposed a set of razor sharp teeth, each as long as his forearm. Not that he had time to debate the matter, in the next moment Ky spread his wings wide, crouched on his back legs and sprang into the air.

It was exhilarating, all that power he could feel surging through the dragon as it soared higher into the atmosphere. He'd always wondered what it would be like, he'd heard others talk about it, although he'd assumed that because of the accompanying burst of adrenaline they'd exaggerated it somewhat. He could dispel that hypothesis now. It was amazing. The paradox of feeling so big and so small at the same time was incredible. At least it was until Ky punched through the dimensional barrier.

Reaching a height above the thin layer of clouds, Ky twisted his head around and grinned again. It was the only warning Dray got before the dragon surged forward faster, his head lifted and his tail whipped through the air behind him. He felt a moment of disorientation. The night air felt suddenly thicker, colder, like they were passing through water, and he wondered if this was the veil they had to pass through between the dimensions. It wasn't nearly as unpleasant as others had made it out to be.

He was only partly right. They were nudging the veil, pushing through was another experience altogether.

With a loud roar, Ky punched through. Every cell in Dray's body seemed to vibrate from the force of the accompanying sonic boom, and he wondered if it was too late to change his mind and catch a plane home instead.

About the Author:

K.G. Inglis is the author of the Eternal series. When not writing about the sexy vampires and alpha lycans and dragons, she can be found reading about them and spending time with her family. Native to Australia, she lives in a beach town on the Southern Coast which many call a holiday destination. If you like your men hot and the action steamy, mixed with a heavy dose of humour, then the Eternal series will find a space in your 'must read again' collection.

Follow her for updates at:

www.kginglis.com/

facebook.com/kginglis.official/#

instagram.com/KGInglis

twitter.com/KG_Inglis

bookbub.com/authors/k-g-inglis

goodreads.com/author/show/17230080.K_G_Inglis